EDITED BY

MAX BOOTH III AND LORI MICHELLE

Perpetual Motion Machine Publishing
Cibolo, Texas

Lost Signals

ISBN: 978-1-943720-08-8

"Transmission" by T.E. Grau originally appeared in *Dead But Dreaming 2*, 2011

"Sharks with Thumbs" by David James Keaton originally appeared in *Big Pulp*, 2009

"The Night Wire" by H.F. Arnold originally appeared in *Weird Tales*, 1926

www.PerpetualPublishing.com

Cover Art and Jacket Design by Matthew Revert
Interior Illustrations by Luke Spooner

ADVANCE PRAISE FOR LOST SIGNALS

"This book will probably make you paranoid, if you weren't already. And if you *were* already, well, I have it on good authority that tinfoil only amplifies the signals."

—Christine Morgan, *The Horror Fiction Review*

"The voices gathered here are as diverse and disturbing as sussurating whispers between radio stations or a signal from a dead man's hand. *Lost Signals* is one of the most haunting and engaging anthologies I've read in a long time, filled with equal measures of darkness and brilliance. If you're looking to be terrified and entertained, read on but do exercise some caution."

—Shane Douglas Keene, *Shotgun Logic*

"*Lost Signals* is a superb anthology. [. . .] Creepy and weird."

—Adrian Shotbolt, *BeavistheBookhead*

"One of the most genuinely disturbing anthologies in recent memory."

—Brian O'Connell

Illustration by Allen Koszowski

TABLE OF CONTENTS

SEVERAL DECADES AGO I attended a performance by a local avant-garde musical ensemble in a small theater in Edison, New Jersey. The program included one of John Cage's landscapes for radios, in which the score calls for the performers to adjust both the volume and frequency of the radios according to directions independent of the stations. I was a devotee of Cage at the time but had never heard one of the landscapes performed live before, so I was enthralled. The beauty of Cage pieces like the landscapes is in the way they force the audience to listen to familiar sounds in new ways. No two performances are ever the same.

About a third of the way through I caught a snippet of voice that made me disengage immediately. I thought I heard the announcer mention *missiles*. This occurred during the mid-'80s, when Reagan was playing his game of nuclear chicken with the Soviet Union. A moment later the performer spun the dial again and the rest of the message was lost. The members of the ensemble showed no alarm. I spun to examine the audience. They all seemed calm. Had I alone heard the clarion call of the apocalypse? I froze and listened. If I were right one of the other stations would have to share a similar broadcast soon.

My mind raced from thought to thought for the remainder of the performance. My concentration was shot. What if nuclear war broke out while we were here, and all we heard were fragments of the Emergency Broadcasting System? How long would the audience listen, oblivious? Perhaps it was best to go listening to music—what little could we do now anyway? Could it be Cage had intended it this way? And all the while snatches of FM ephemera drifted into the ether, lost for eternity. Had they been our last broadcasts before Armageddon, perhaps some alien race might have found them of interest. Instead they were destined to remain unremarkable, despite my alarm, dissipating unheeded into the depths of space.

We are each of us antennae, tuned to the deep. And deep calls to deep, over and under us, around us . . . through us. Jack Spicer proclaimed the poem no more for the poet than the song is for the radio. Sun Ra told us there are other worlds that wish to speak to us. Signals are everywhere, piercing our bodies—unheard broadcasts, coded transmissions, via a million unseen wavelengths—T waves, radio, the breath of distant stars. The breath of things behind the stars.

Though the telegraph has been with us nearly two centuries, it was Marconi's wireless that first opened our channels to other voices, other sounds. New technologies proliferated until the Information Revolution slowly began taking shape to reveal just how weird our world really is. Born in the blowback of the second world war, midwifed by code makers, codebreakers, and bombsight designers, the greatest change in human history emerged in the shadow of an age originally categorized as "Atomic." What a mistake that label was. Information proved the bigger bombshell in the end.

Over a century of wireless, from analog to digital, has opened unsuspected floodgates of Weirdness, straddling fact and fiction and every gray area in between. Claude Shannon and Warren Weaver, Numbers stations, the Marianas Web, the Videodrome Signal, KLEE, entropy, Edison's Telephone to the Dead, the Polymeric Falcighol Derivation, WXXT, the Changing Light at Sandover, the Lincolnshire Poacher, Norbert Wiener, Satoshi Nakamoto, EVPs, entropy, the Markovian Parallax Denigrate, the Buzzer, Symbols Signals and Noise, Cicada 3301, the Pip, the Bloop, the Squeaky Wheel, entropy, the last words of Frederick Valentich, *the last words of Dutch Schultz*, entropy, the Max Headroom Incident, the Taos Hum, the wow, entropy, internet black holes, entropy, Yosemite Sam, entropy, entropy . . .

Entropy.

By our very presence we interfere with transmissions to which we are oblivious. Our bodies block and distort, but they also *receive*. We are better doors than windows, but most of us are closed. Our bodies absorb entire the shorter wavelengths, higher energy particles, and cosmic rays. They imprint themselves upon our genetic codes, spawn our tumors and mutations, make of us fresh messages in turn.

Longer wavelengths pass right through us. For neutrinos and gravity waves we aren't even here. Our radio telescopes tune to broadcasts from other worlds, but consider how recent Marconi's breakthrough came for us. How long does the average civilization communicate via the electromagnetic spectrum? A century? Two? How narrow a window are we traversing right now, and how many of our galactic neighbors remain in this same stage? A handful? Any? None? Likely we are listening on the wrong bands entirely. Perhaps the important messages zoom right through our bodies unreceived, undeciphered . . . perhaps this is our test: to cross the threshold of self-destruction and level up to . . . what? Subspace funk? Modulated tachyon transmissions? Ripples in space-time itself?

INTRODUCTION

Meanwhile our transmitters and receivers proliferate throughout the Anthropocene, infesting, messaging, accumulating in our hands, our pockets, and our landfills. Radio, telephone, television, cell phones, tablets. And everywhere WiFi. Or almost everywhere . . . and with the receivers, the Weirdness.

Our editors, Max and Lori, have risked soul and sanity to seek out these anomalies—tales of calls that shouldn't come, programs best left unheard. The low end of the FM dial has always been a dangerous place, but some transmissions arrive on frequencies we can never measure or hope to block. Telephones, television, radio—all of them apertures for communication from Outside.

Really, it's amazing no one thought of such an anthology before. The original date of the oldest story included here makes the concept's legitimacy clear. "The Night Wire" first saw print in 1926 in *Weird Tales*. This enigmatic and iconic tale, by an even more mysterious author, remains disturbing 90 years later, the tragic city of Xebico as much a puzzle as ever. Max and Lori did well to choose it. "The Night Wire" retains its cognitive dissonance and establishes the tone for the other tales, all of which are new to this antho beyond this selection.

From the start *Lost Signals* offered something I seek out in an anthology—some authors I know, personally or from their work—a few I even count as friends. Others I know by reputation alone. And a healthy selection of surprises. When I pick up a new book, I want surprises, new voices, or voices new to me at least. I have long haunted the ends of the FM dial for the same reasons.

It would be wrong for me to run through capsule descriptions of each story here—I've never understood that kind of intro anyway. Better the reader encounter these tales like the features of Cage's landscapes instead. Trust that our editors have done well at intercepting forbidden transmissions. They have, and this is a damn good antho. You will find favorites just as I did, and some of these stories will unsettle you indefinitely. At least two still resonate inside my brain, and they aren't departing anytime soon.

Open yourself now to the *Lost Signals*. Let Max and Lori control the dial for a while. What are we but antennae really, each of us tuned to the void?

Scott Nicolay
July 1, 2016

DARK MYTHS AND suburban legends roam like living things through the halls of Leeds High School, whispered in stairwells over bubblegum-tinted tongues; scrawled on the wall of the secret room above the auditorium stage; argued over in the shaded courtyard adjacent to the cafeteria, buoyed on grey-brown clouds of cigarette smoke. There's the Weird House up on Tremens Terrace, haunted by a trio of cannibalistic fiends with a taste for wayward boys. And the coven of teachers, including Mr. Gauthier (Chemistry) and Miss Knell (English), who cavort with a charred-skin devil in the glass-walled natatorium after dark. And the secluded hollow in the lonesome wooded hills that stretch for untold miles beyond the eastern border of the school grounds, where a pale, eyeless thing roams, thin as a mantis, eating squirrels and cackling, calling out to unnamed gods.

Finn Groomer had dragged Rob Chappell to explore the Weird House on a simmering mid-summer day. They'd searched basement to attic, rat-torn couch to stinking refrigerator to bowed and cobwebbed bed-frame, encountering no one and nothing, and emerging decidedly non-cannibalized. Finn knew for a fact that Mr. Gauthier turned up his nose every time Miss Knell passed; he didn't like her enough to even say hello in the morning, never mind to dance naked with her by the moonlit swimming pool. And out in those desolate hills? Finn on an overcast Sunday afternoon hiked for the better part of an hour to the place where the brook trickles down a broad, steep incline into the shadowed hollow, and nothing lived there among the towering black oaks but birds and squirrels and worms. And mosquitos. Lots and lots of mosquitos. For Finn Groomer, the myths of Leeds High were just another string of disappointments in an adolescence teeming with them.

Finn still held out hope, though, that he might one day finally hear the radio broadcasts he'd heard some seniors talking about one day in the cafeteria. Emanating from somewhere down in the lower numbers of the FM dial, the opposite end from where the classic rock stations blared Two-Fer Tuesdays and Rock-Block Weekends, the transmissions were rumored to be connected in some mysterious way with the kids who'd go missing from time to time. As to what could be heard, reports differed depending upon who was telling the tale. Some said they heard odd music, jaunty and discordant, backed by the cries of the tortured or the weeping of lost children. Some heard a man talking, or a woman, of unspeakable things. Others claimed to have heard thousands chanting, black masses, twisted blasphemies and perversions, the cries of the damned in the furnace of Hell.

You couldn't just stumble on the station, or find it at any old time you went searching. Circumstances had to be right. And the exact nature of those "circumstances" differed as well. You had to be vulnerable, in pain. You had to be susceptible to hypnosis and open to the possibilities of the supernatural. You needed a special radio, or a regular radio touched by the hand of a warlock.

Three weeks into Finn's freshman year, Bentley Langschultz, a sophomore, drove to school, walked to the edge of the football field with his father's shotgun, sat among the varicose roots at the base of a dying old oak tree, and blew his head apart. On an oppressively hot summer afternoon back when Bentley was nine years old, his mother had absent-mindedly walked into the sliding-glass porch door, causing it to shatter. A shard of glass tore into her throat as she fell. Harriett Langschultz bled to death on the ugly green and white linoleum floor in the kitchen of the Langschultz's raised ranch, alone. Bentley found her when he came home late from school, having lingered to talk about comic books with Garrett Kinder. She lay sprawled in blood, swollen and wide-eyed, ministered to by a cloud of flies.

The rumor born after Bentley's death, the subject of the conversation in the smoking area that chilly winter day, proffered by Heather Buffington, who claimed to have received a desperate phone call from Bentley the night before his death, was this: Bentley had happened upon the radio station on the way home from school, and heard the sounds of shattering glass, of his mother gasping, gurgling, trying in vain to draw in breath, and then, as clear as a voice right there in the car with him, crying out, "Bentley, oh, Benny-boy, where *were* you—you could have saved me. Oh, son, you let me die, you let me die." All of this, claimed Heather, was against a backdrop of comical music like you'd hear on the Saturday morning cartoons.

Since that winter day, Finn spent hours spinning the dial of his stereo between his fingers, searching for the signal in static-choked airwaves, listening for a voice, for music, for a wailing ghost, a chuckling demon. Maybe he would hear the voice of Bentley Langschultz. Or the voice of his own mother, who had leapt to her death from the French King Bridge before Finn was old enough to form a memory of what she sounded like. He never heard anything but static. Many times he fell asleep to that noise, so much like roaring rain, like the rush of traffic, like a fierce wind bothering the treetops.

And then one morning, at the muddy end of a long and wearying winter, the new kid showed up with the answer in his hand.

The kid climbed onto the bus at the corner where the shuttered factory slumbered among disarranged blankets of overgrown shrubbery. An oversized army jacket bounced around him as he climbed the steps and trod down the center aisle. Grey cargo pants with crumpled pockets, the hems rolled crooked, engineer boots. Jug-handle ears and a giraffe neck, a larynx like he'd tried to swallow a pear whole. His hair, the drab dark brown of an old penny, formed an ocean wave over his high forehead, a severe part over his right ear showing scalp like an alabaster path. Blue bug-eyes swam behind thick glasses with smoky grey frames. In one long-fingered hand he clutched a small portable transistor radio, scuffed silver with a tattered strap. He looked all of ten years old, except for his height: his hair nearly touched the curved ceiling of the school bus.

He sat down in an empty seat at the back, his knees up at his chest, and held the radio up to his ear. Rob and Finn swung around in their seats to check the kid out. He stared back at them, his eyes moving back and forth behind those massive lenses, studying their faces. An unintelligible radio announcer's voice declaimed breathlessly from between the small speaker and the kid's pimply temple.

Finn leaned in toward the radio. "What are you listening to?"

"Hey, I'll bet it's Tears for Queers!" Rob said.

The kid opened his lips to reveal a jumble of yellowed, chipped teeth. He hissed at Rob, bubbles of spittle forming at the corners of his mouth.

Rob burst out laughing, elbowing Finn. "Can I get the name of your orthodontist?"

Across the aisle, Becky Burns tittered a high-pitched arietta. Finn just stared at the radio as though hypnotized. The kid smiled widely, showcasing the mess in his mouth. His eyes were unfocused, the pupils dilated to pinpricks. His fist clenched and unclenched. He pushed the radio hard against his ear until the plastic casing cracked. Finn and Rob gawked.

"THAT WAS A MOLDY OLDIE FROM NIFTY, SHIFTY NINETEEN-FIFTY," the kid boomed in an unexpectedly sonorous voice. Becky Burns emitted a shrill shriek. *"UP NEXT, THE THING THAT DWELLS WHERE THE BROOK TRICKLES DOWN THE EARTHEN MOUND, WHERE THE TREES BEND IN PRAYER TO THE STONE-STREWN GROUND. BUT FIRST, A WORD FROM OUR SPONSOR."*

Then his voice jumped up a few octaves, became that of a chirpy commercial voice-over girl, "*There was a girl on my road named Dirty Meg. A dark . . .*"

Without warning, Rob popped the kid in the jaw. The thud of fist on flesh got everyone's attention, and they began to hoot and bang their fists on the seats. "FIGHT . . . FIGHT . . . FIGHT!"

"Whoa, whoa, whoa!" Finn said, grabbing Rob by the shoulders and putting him in a loose headlock. Rob struggled a little bit, half-heartedly, glowering at the kid, batting at Finn's arms. Tears gathered on the kid's lower eyelids. A splotch had blossomed bright red on his cheek.

"What the fuck was that, Robbie?" Finn said. "Really, what the *fuck*?"

The driver jerked the bus to the side of the road, threw it into park, and stormed down the aisle, belly bouncing under her blue sweater vest, face bright red under a sheath of dyed blonde hair. The other kids stopped chanting, but murmured excitedly, jostling each other, vying for a good view.

"Up," she said.

Rob and Finn got up.

"You're sitting up front the rest of the way. C'mon. Rob? Rob Chappell? I know your mother. Come on now, *right* now, and she won't hear a word about this."

Among cat-calls and jeers they followed her to the front. Finn spared a glance back at the kid. A trickle of blood ran down the side of his face from under the radio. When the bus stopped, Finn and Rob were among the first to exit. Rob hustled off to class, but Finn waited. He wanted to look at the kid's radio, to see if that dial sat down in the low numbers, to brace the kid and steal his damned radio and listen for himself. But the kid must have slipped by him somehow. Finn never saw him get off the bus.

That evening, Finn and his father sat across from each other in the dimly lit dining room, eating dinner in silence. Tom Groomer demanded that Finn have dinner with him every weeknight, though Finn could not fathom why, as the television was always on, and they barely spoke to one another. Finn was volatile, agitated. He had searched for the kid all day, looked for him in the halls between classes, in the cafeteria. He was nowhere to be found. He didn't even show up for the bus home.

"Miss O'Connell says Leeds has more missing kids than any Massachusetts city of this size and population count," Finn said, trying to force eye contact.

Tom Groomer looked at a spot about a foot over Finn's head. He tore off a piece of garlic bread and his brow furrowed as he dabbed the bread in sauce. "She doesn't know what she's talking about. I've been ten years on the force, I know cops in every city in Christendom. Miss O'Connell should stick to Physics."

"Do you know three kids were pulled out of school last year so their parents could home-school them? And they were never heard from again."

His father burst into derisive laughter. "Never heard from again!"

"It's true. Kelly Kitter."

"Finny, I *know* the Kitters. Do you want me to call Carol right now? Kelly left school, what, junior year? Carol home-schooled her, and she got accepted at Oberlin College. Full ride, housing and all. As far as I know, that's where she is right now. Now, that's the last I want to hear of it."

Finn nodded, jabbed his fork at a piece of ravioli, shoving it around the plate. Kelly's best friend Margot hadn't seen nor heard from Kelly since the day her mom pulled her out of school. When she called, Mrs. Kitter said Kelly had gone out. Or was studying. Or asleep. Asleep at seven in the evening! Kelly hadn't just moved to Ohio without calling Margot, without saying goodbye. Tom Groomer stared blankly at the television, where the long smoke trail from the space shuttle explosion billowed across the screen for the umpteenth time. He was lying, Finn decided. His father was lying to his face.

Finn dreamed that night, nightmares strung together like grotesque garland, an anthology of abominations. He would remember only one, the last, ultimately interrupted by the insistent screech of the clock radio alarm. He stood in the midst of a vast, noisy carnival under a sky of dirt. Rocks tumbled above, in defiance of gravity, making a noise like thunder. Lightning spiked down from the dirt, lightning made of long, wriggling glowworms. A mad barker bellowed inanities into a megaphone from a warped seat at the apex of the rusted out Ferris Wheel, the voice echoing throughout the fairgrounds. The air smelled of popcorn, charred meat, wet animal fur. Finn walked over to a metal gate, beyond which a colorful Chair-O-Plane spun, its angled column lined with lights, cadavers lolling in the basket chairs as they swung sidelong through the fragrant fry-o-later air. A ragged skull tumbled to the hard-packed earth and bounced along toward Finn, coming to rest at the base of the gate. It bore patches of skin, wisps of hair. Maggots orgied in its eye sockets and feasted on its putrefying tongue. Finn backed up, circled the ride, headed toward the Ferris Wheel. The voice of the barker sounded familiar.

He walked alongside a row of trailers, between which laundry sagged from greasy clotheslines: massive brassieres, a gape-mouthed bear costume, long johns, garters and frills and feather boas. One of the trailer doors hung open, and a face popped out, all bushy eyebrows and matted hair. The man's face loomed swollen, squirrel-cheeked. "Kid," the man whispered. Finn turned to look. The man's belly lolled over the belt of his bathrobe. At his feet a slack-haired woman slithered, her eyes dead, her tongue tasting the mud-caked floor. Her body was that of a snake, diamond-patterned, scaled, draped in a feces-stained slip. "Come in! Test your strength!"

Finn gave the door a wide berth, just catching the edge of a miasma of shit and rum and body odor. As he reached the end of the line of trailers and approached the Ferris Wheel, the barker, silhouetted, leapt from his seat. Black wings bloomed behind him, curving upward, forming a parachute. He sailed to the ground, turned, and walked into the mist. For just a moment, in the light of a Fried Dough stand, Finn had recognized the destroyed features of Bentley Langschultz, his blond head split eight ways and smoking like a spent firecracker, face peeled down in flaps, long shredded tongue dangling obscenely. Finn followed Bentley. Beyond the borders of the fairgrounds sprawled a moldering marsh, swarming will-o'-the-wisps illuminating the brackish, moss-strewn water. Bentley walked in, was wading away. The sound of sloshing water overtook the carnival music until it was the only sound. By now, only the ruined back of Bentley's blonde head could be seen. Then he turned, and he wore the face of an antique radio: large, mesh-covered eyes, a knob for a nose, and a wide, rectangular mouth that glowed yellow. At its left-most end a withered red tongue slid back and forth, as though searching for that elusive signal.

Finn saw the kid the next day after lunch when he stepped outside to get a gulp or two of fresh air, as if saving it up to last him two more interminable hours in the stuffy classroom. The kid stood at the edge of the woods beyond the football field, not far from where Bentley Langschultz had blown his brains out. He held the radio down by his side, his head tilted as though listening to something in the sky. Finn walked toward the kid. As he approached, the wind kicked up and the image of the kid shimmied, briefly blurring, separating into a boy-shaped stack of horizontal lines. Finn felt dizzy, off-kilter. It seemed as though it was taking a very long time to cover a short distance, as though the kid and the edge of the wood retreated imperceptibly with each step Finn took. The afternoon stretched, tinted blue with overtones of dusk. Had the bell rung to signal the resumption of classes? If so, he hadn't heard it.

At length, after picking up his pace, almost jogging, he began to close the distance. He cleared his throat to alert the kid to his presence. The kid turned.

"What's your name?" Finn asked.

"Eric."

"Eric, I'm Finn." He spoke quickly, fearing that Eric would dismiss him, or walk away. "Listen, I'm sorry about the bus. Rob can be a wicked asshole sometimes. Can you tell me what you were listening to on the radio? I've been thinking about it non-stop."

Eric shrugged. Then he lifted the radio and extended his arm so that the speaker hovered a few inches from Finn's face. A tinny voice spoke: *Through gore-clotted conduits He makes His way, slithering, flattening himself like a cat, going liquid, slender snake, wriggling worm. He comes to summon His herd. Join me on the riverbank. We'll pull down the sky. We'll pull down the sun and we'll pull down the trees. We'll pull down the shade of*—a rising wave of static overtook the voice. Eric pulled back the radio, frowned down at its face, fiddling with the dial and extending the antenna between two pinched fingers, pointing it this way and that. The voice went on somewhere back there, straining to be heard, calling out, but the static won. For just a moment, his face distorted, Eric looked considerably older than a high school kid. Older . . . or harder. Finn couldn't decide. Maybe both.

"You can get way better reception out at my place in the woods. Will you come to the woods with me?"

Finn grimaced. "I don't know. I have English, like right now. I'm probably already late."

"If you're already late, what's the harm? Follow me."

He walked into the woods. Finn followed.

"Is this where you live?" Finn said. Yellow tents, ten or twelve of them, stood here and there among the clearing in the woods, a space ringed by tall oaks and red spruce, a space not that much larger than the Groomers' modest backyard. Along the easternmost border stood a row of thin trees, evenly spaced like the rungs of a crib, beyond which the forest devolved into a jungle-like tangle of deadfalls and vines and profusely thorned thicket, dotted with virgin's bower and jack-in-the-pulpit. At the sound of Finn's voice, the wind kicked up, rustling the trees and the tents, which shivered as though cold.

"They're down at the river, praying," Eric said, answering a question Finn hadn't asked.

"Who?"

"Let's listen awhile. Close your eyes."

"How come?"

"Close them."

Eric turned on the radio and cranked the volume as high as it would go.

The notes of a flute meander, climbing, faltering, climbing again. A male voice mutters and chuckles, sniffs. Please don't, *says a small voice, a toddler's voice, trembling with fear. Flames crackle and far off voices rise and fall in an insistent cadence, no stopping for breath. A cheering crowd, now ecstatic, now raging. A female voice, husky and insinuating, emanates from the center of the clearing. "Masks and mirrors, gentlemen," the voice says. "Mirrors and masks. Flesh on marble. Fountains of blood, carriages of carrion. Mister Ben will eat your worries, slurp them up like stew. Mister Ben's boarding house has beds to spare, clean linens, perfumed halls, nurses on call with hands softer than silk."*

Mom?

"Oh, darling, I'm talking to the boys, the sweet boys. See them? Such handsome young men."

Mom? I'm hungry.

"Darling, shush."

I want tongues. Tongues and lips. Sweat in my cup. Piss mug, dog's water, gristle to chew.

"Soon, sweetie, soon."

Dog mug, piss water, blood under my tongue. Sweetbreads and sputum. *A savage giggle, deepening in pitch, bending and warping.*

Again the flute, fleeing, shrieking as something pounds the low keys of a piano with violent force. A tuneless whistle, and then a stomp, a shriek. More stomps, splatter and crunch. A bow moves across the strings of a violin, is yanked away. The howl of space. Whimpers and pleadings, zippers unzipping, rustling clothes. A child gags and retches. A bird says CHUR chattle CHUR chattle CHUR. A pipe organ, brazen and fierce, spedupsuperfastchipmunkfast. Calliope and callithump, wheeze and whine, high-pitched, a crying dog, bereft and disconsolate. Night falls like a shade, with it that familiar roar of static. Finn drops away . . .

. . . and Finn awoke. He lay face up, staring at the ceiling of a tent, which glowed an alien green. He was clothed, save his shoes, which sat at his side in a chaste *soixante-neuf*. He wanted to know what time it was, and he wanted to drift back into blackness. Something shifted, a rustle of clothing, a sniffle. He pushed himself up onto his elbows and saw Eric sitting Indian-style at his feet, the transistor in his lap, its dial glowing green. From the speaker a voice whispered a phrase in some unknown language. A chorus of young voices sounded just outside the tent in surround-sound, repeated the phrase, and the voice resumed.

Finn opened his mouth to speak and Eric leapt from his crouching position, his legs trailing behind him like those of a frog. He landed on Finn's stomach. Finn bellowed out all the air in his lungs, and then Eric pushed the radio into his chest. Finn punched at Eric, landing blows on his shoulders and neck and chin, but Eric pulled back his head to avoid the blows. His arms elongated, snaking out from his sleeves. Finn heard cracking that he first mistook for thunder, or a tree breaking open. As pain radiated from his chest into his arms and neck and nausea grew in his stomach, he realized that he was hearing the cracking of his ribs.

Eric began to sing in a high, clear voice.

Mary sit with me by the river

Cymbals hissed and whispered from the speaker.

We'll pull down the stars from the sky

The kids outside the tent ooohed and snapped their fingers.

We'll pull down the moon and we'll pull down the sun

Their shadows slithered like serpents on the green glowing walls of the tent.

We'll pull down the shade of the eye.

Eric bore down on the radio as Finn's chest caved in like a sinkhole. Finn could not gather enough air to scream.

IF HE SUMMONS HIS HERD

He awoke again, hours later, this time in muted daylight. The shadows of leaves cavorted on the tent walls. It was hard to breathe. His chest and arms ached as though he'd been in a fight, but he hadn't been, not that he could remember. He'd been listening to the radio with Eric, and then . . . and then he'd awakened. He'd never lost time like that before . . . and he didn't remember having had anything to drink. He ran his hands through his hair, wincing, and ducked out of the tent. The worshippers had returned, apparently. A bunch of them—all teenagers—stood here and there, looking up at the sky. A few tended to a makeshift grill where flames danced up among a grid of soaked sticks suspended over a circle of rocks. A battered frying pan sang a song of spattering bacon; another bore eggs, the yolks orange as the ascending sun. "Good morning," said a girl with big eyes and purple hair, dressed in cartoon character pajamas. "How do you want your eggs?"

The other kids looked at him. There was something about them . . . something he didn't see in any of the kids at school. It was as though his classmates were a cable television station to which he didn't subscribe: he only saw glimpses of them swimming through wavering distortion. The kids in the woods were a local station, beamed in from a close-by antenna, clear and unbroken. Their eyes hummed with life. He felt impatient to befriend them. But he detected a note of caution in their eyes, or suspicion. Maybe just a wariness. Except for the purple-haired girl, whose face bore a vague resemblance to that of his mother; narrow, aquiline nose, small eyes, dimples—a face he'd seen only in old photographs, trapped under transparent photo-album plastic. The girl's eyes were bright and welcoming, interested, even.

"Scrambled?" he said.

"Was that a question or a statement?" She pulled a large, rusted metal spoon from a wire basket near the fire pit.

"Scrambled."

She stirred the eggs, keeping her eyes fixed on Finn's. She salted and peppered the eggs and slid them from the pan onto a Styrofoam plate.

Finn sat cross-legged, eating with his hands, watching the denizens of the makeshift city as they dressed themselves, sat reading, or gathered soap and towels to wash at the brook just over the hillock. Just as he was scraping the last bit of egg from the plate, Eric emerged from a tent at the far end of the clearing. He threw down his backpack—stuffed to the point of straining at the seams, and began dismantling the tent from which he'd just emerged. "You're really going," said the purple-haired girl.

"It won't be just me in the end." Eric folded the tent, his voice a reassuring purr. "I'll tell them all about you guys, I promise. I'm good with words. I know I can get them to accept you. Maybe not all of you, but some of you."

The purple-haired girl bounced on her heels, while a greasy-haired kid in a jean jacket shook his head. "They won't take me. I have anxiety."

"Danny, I'll tell them about how good you are with, like, sleight of hand," Eric said. "I'm sure they'll find a use for you."

Danny scoffed. He spit in the dirt and muttered.

"Where are you going?" Finn said. "Who's 'them'?"

The kids tittered. A secret flitted among them like static electricity. "The people in the deep woods," Danny said, hooking his thumb toward the dark tangle of thicket-choked trees. "They're . . . they're kind of like church leaders, or priests, but not all strict, not worried about morals and shit. Finn . . . is this life enough for you? Do you feel like you're part of anything? Like there's any real purpose? With them, it's different. All we have is questions. They have answers. And a mission."

Eric frowned, spoke up. "Have you ever seen the Real Leeds? In dreams, or in your thoughts? It's a place between here and . . . it's where they came in through. It's like where we live, but better . . . there are skyscrapers, and these sort of . . . community centers, let's call them . . . and a fair that runs year-round.

(Test your strength.)

"It's always October, Finn, always. And what they can give you . . ."

He paused. The kids all looked at him. Their eyes blazed a warning. A beatific look passed over his face.

"Ecstasy. Exaltation. *Transformation.*"

"In exchange for what?" Finn said.

Eric shrugged. "Nothing big, I don't think. Nothing important. Nothing you'll miss."

Without further ceremony, Eric hauled up his pack, nodded to the group, and walked through the line of trees into the tangled wood. Everyone stood, watching him go, until they couldn't see nor hear him. No one spoke.

Finn tended to blather when nervous, just to break the tension, to dispel silence. He said, a little too loudly, "Guys, can I, like . . . can I get some stuff and come back and stay with you? In Eric's tent, maybe, or, or I could bring my own?"

He'd tried to modulate his voice, to avoid using a pleading tone, but it crept in nonetheless. They stayed silent, still staring into the woods as though transfixed by the last glimpse they'd seen of Eric.

The purple-haired girl spoke up. "Yes, please. Please. Why don't you stick around? You don't need to go back *there*, maybe not ever again. We have everything you need here. Everything." She put her hand to her chest and smiled an enigmatic smile.

Finn's heart sped up, but he held his resolve. "I'll come back tonight. Promise."

She put on an exaggerated pout. "You *better*."

"I will."

He headed back down the path that led back to the school. He walked until he guessed he'd gotten far enough from the encampment, then circled back, jogging, giving the clearing a wide berth. After a time, he found the brook and followed it through the thickening trees.

He was nearing the hollow when he caught sight of Eric's yellow pack. He hung back, treading carefully, avoiding twigs and pine cones as best he could so as not to be detected. Eric crested a small hillock and descended into the hollow. Finn followed, moving very slowly.

When he attained the hillock and looked over, he saw that Eric had put down his pack about a yard from the edge of the hollow, where trees tall and crowded guarded the way to the deeper, darker woods that comprised the state forest. Finn crouched down behind a deadfall that lay at the base of a tall, ungainly oak. Eric stood, stretched, and removed his jacket and shirt, folding them neatly and piling them to his left. He looked thin and vulnerable, his shoulder blades jutting like nascent wings, bracketing a serrated spine. He pulled the transistor from his pack—a different one, Finn noticed, with green plastic casing and slightly bigger than the one he'd had on the bus—and held it high above his head, aiming it into the woods. The leaves stopped rustling. The birds stopped twittering. Finn dared not breathe.

A hum, low and long, and the world shivered. The scene in front of Eric shimmied as though painted on a thin tapestry behind which unknown things slithered and twitched. Eric's body again separated into horizontal lines. The lines moved back and forth, independent of one another, righted themselves, and it was just Eric again, thin and pale and alone, that one arm holding aloft the small transistor, red elbow jutting. And then the man stepped out from the dense wood.

He was tall, frighteningly so, at least a head taller than Eric. And broad of chest and hip. Finn thought of the time he saw a moose tromping along a quiet road in New Salem, slow, lumbering, but dangerous in its very bulk. The man was clad in cuffed and creased trousers, an immaculate white shirt held fast to his torso with suspenders the color of storm clouds. His hair gleamed black, oiled and slicked back. His eyes blazed from over an impudent nose. His thin lips, set under a neat mustache, were set in a frown, and he carried himself as though very bored, but menace lurked in the taut muscles of his neck, in the set of his jaw. He was thick-footed, claw-like nails long-neglected, clotted with mud or dried blood. He stopped just a few feet from Eric, appeared to size him up.

Eric stood very still. Finn could not see his features, but he appeared to be staring into the man's eyes. Then the man spread out his arms and a fervent, hungry look spread across his face. A cracking sound, like a tree split by heavy wind, and the man's skull broke vertically under his skin, widening and swelling until his face sloughed off his skull and fur sprouted from his cheeks and forehead. His eyes slid apart to the sides of his narrowing head as his nose elongated into a snout. His pupils flattened. The tip of his nose popped, cartilage flying like shrapnel, laying bare a flat, brown nose with slits for nostrils. His teeth grew like ancient gravestones rising from earth, gingiva crumpling, cheeks splitting open all the way to the ears. His clothes fell away, and the walls of his human form followed, great shards landing in piles, blood showering over them. He pulled a gnarled branch from a tree and rubbed his furred hands along its length until it smoothed out into an elegant black cane.

Eric thrust the transistor radio up toward the man. It began to sing a trilling tune in a high-pitched, child-like voice.

The man, now a hunched goat, bellowed a wordless reply, tongue wavering in the air.

The radio responded with tinny ragtime music, bouncing piano, whispering cymbals, a cavorting clarinet.

A sheet of skin separated from Eric's back, fluttered into the air, nearly translucent. Then another, thicker, white. He screamed out as his body went pink, and then red, as sheets of skin hovered around him in the air. Masks of his face followed, rising into the sky like the gape-mouthed heads of ghosts. His hair stood on end and began to fall like rain from his head.

And then the goat lunged forward, jabbed his cane into the tender flesh under Eric's chin, lifted him into the air and swung the cane in an outward arc so that Eric faced Finn. For a terrifying moment, Finn thought he might impale Eric, thrust him to the ground and devour him like a ravenous dog. But instead he held the boy aloft like a gator on a catch-pole. Eric's arms and legs swam in the air. His eyes showed only whites. Drool swung in a bobbing pendulum from his lower lip.

"Phineas? Dear, earnest Finn," called the goat in an unblemished baritone that echoed through the trees. Finn crouched lower, his mouth hanging open, staring. "How you've grown. Your mother brought you to me, you know? You were just a boy. A sapling, a whelp. I remember it well. Jessica carried you into the wood and stood right where Eric did. She flung you to the forest floor, offered you up like a prize. She begged, begged like a wretch, cried like a brat. She was *very* demanding." He shook his head sadly, condescendingly. "And I tell you now even as I told her then, sorry, boy, but you are simply not *worthy*.

"She never hit the water, by the way. She landed on the rocky shore, broke into pieces on the sharp and mossy stones. They needed more than one tarp to hide her sad, broken body from all the rubberneckers. Not that they didn't get an eyeful, though."

Finn fell to the ground, grabbing handfuls of earth, crushing it in his fists, and sobbed. His mother had betrayed him. She didn't love him. And then she had taken her life, left him alone with an obstinate liar of a father. Why did she do it? Out of sorrow and remorse? Or because her offering had been refused? He sobbed himself hoarse, beating the muddy ground with his fists.

They had to take him. They *had* to. He stood. The goat and Eric were gone. The forest stood still and silent.

"If you won't take me, kill me," he shouted into the thick wood. "Kill me!"

The only response was his echoing voice.

Snuffling and panting, Finn searched out the piles of skin that had pulled away from Eric and fluttered to the forest floor. As he gathered them, he heard music from somewhere, he couldn't tell where, the insistent beat of a thousand drums, overlapping, rising in volume and intensity. He piled the skin in his arms and headed back toward the clearing where the kids waited among their tents. He prayed that they would take him in for keeps. He prayed to see his mother again, that he might forgive her and once again fold himself into her betraying arms and offer her his forgiveness. And he prayed that one day he might find that signal hiding in the static at the low end of the dial, and it might tell him how to become worthy.

transmission

T.E GRAU

EVEN THIS FAR out, away from the light and the bilge and the droning nouveau bullshit lounge music rasping from a purposely old LP, things were still sort of a blur.

The same blurry party with the same blurry people with annoying hipster headgear and piercings and tattoos and post-ironic t-shirts and uniformly blurry beards. The off-brand bottle of blurry liquor in his hand. The blurry, slurry skank that he had seen before but never recognized, pressing in too close, breathing all of his air.

The shouting. The broken furniture. The fight. The blood. The weaksauce ghetto insults hurled from a safe distance as he ran out of the blurry room in the blurry house on a blurry street in a forgotten Midwestern city that blurred brown and green but mostly brown under a thousand jumbo jets every single day.

A blur. All of it. And none of it worth a single fuck.

Max scratched at the crusted gash on the side of his face and concentrated on the tunnel of pavement opening foot by foot ahead of him, trying to clear the blur from his mind as he drove west, ever west, in a last ditch effort to outrace the smudge of his past. This was it, he felt.

A wagon train of one, fueled by a last hope for blessed clarity waiting amongst the swaying palms of the Pacific coast. Failing that, he'd drive off the end of the goddamn continent and drown in the murk of the darkened deep.

Max blinked his eyes and lit up a cigarette, checking the cheap plastic compass he picked up at a truck stop in Grand Island, Nebraska, stuck lopsided to the dash of his shitty late model Dodge. West, the bobbing arrow assured him. West. He was still heading in the right direction. At last that much was certain.

Max knew he stayed too long at his last stop. He had gotten lazy, and worse than that he had gotten hopeful, figuring roots would sprout from the bottoms of his shoes if he just loitered in the same place long enough. Anchoring him to a piece of ground at last. But the roots never came. Only rot. And that's when he knew he had to get out. That night. That second. By whatever means necessary no matter what collection of beards and bows were in his way.

And so he did.

It made no difference that he had a belly full of poison and eighty-seven dollars to his name. He just knew it was time. And so it was.

And so he went.

Max would keep moving this time, for as far as his shitty late model Dodge would take him. He was pretty sure he had hurt some people pretty badly, maybe even fatally, during his abrupt exit from the blur two nights ago, so going backwards wasn't an option at this point. He just had to keep his head down and keep grinding that wheel, fueled by the last hope of finding his destiny out yonder under western skies, as so many eastern souls had done before him. Get his hands on a bit of true clarity in the fairytale hills. He'd change his name, maybe grow his hair into Viking braids and take up surfing. But most importantly, he lose himself in the crowded anonymity of the city of nearsighted angels, where everyone is too busy squinting into the mirror to spot the disheveled fugitive sitting across the bar.

It wasn't his fault, this wanderlust. It was congenital, ancestral, born out of a thirsty Caucasian soul and dissatisfaction with nearly everything around him, combined with the certainty that new lands conquered would quell all inadequacies and establish contrived dominance in one fell swoop. So Max became a human tumbleweed from the first time he learned how to thumb a ride, spinning from city to hamlet to dusty campsite, in search of something bigger than himself to tie him down and make him *want* to stay, to become part of something outside of himself. Some people looked for God. Some quested for love. Max just searched for meaning, starting with the self and working outward from there if he had time. All of everything that was and would someday be. There had to be a point—a greater purpose—to the entirety of this terribly self-important but most likely utterly meaningless nonsense, and the answer had to be out there somewhere, around the next bend, over the next rise in the road.

But he never found it. Not yet. In all those miles and all those late hours, he'd just found more of the same. He just found more blur.

So here he was, knifing down Highway 50 west of McGill, Nevada, as the last two days and nights—hell, the last thirty-two years—melted into just another portion of an unbroken line of bleary days and blurry nights spent doing nothing with a thousand nameless nobodies, all bored to panicked tears hidden behind masks of sardonic bullshit. Somehow, without knowing exactly where or exactly why, Max had drifted off of I-80, that great tentacle of government-issue cement that stretched the length of this vast, savage land. But it didn't matter. His cheap plastic compass assured him that he was heading west, and that was good enough for Max. That certainty was enough for now. Small victories in the war against the unknown.

Exhaling a small nimbus cloud of smoke into the windshield, Max sat back, and for the first time in what felt like forever, he relaxed and opened the window, allowing the cool dry air to clean out the car. The blur had begun to recede, which allowed him a smile. He was moving again, had been for two sunrises, and the road behind him was growing longer. He was carving a proud wound into the hide of the central Nevada desert, and no one could force him to do otherwise. Max had regained his footing about the time he hit the Rockies, and with the great peaks of the continental divide doing just that between where he currently was and what he had left behind, he found himself feeling the music again, the rhythm of pavement as the highway danced for him beneath the floorboards.

Max turned on the radio, switching immediately from the dead FM presets of his last layover to the strange anonymity of AM. A veteran of the road, Max loved to scan the monophonic dial when moving through the most remote areas of the country. Amplitude modulation radio in major cities was the cozy bed of blustery right wing shitsuckers, sports broadcasting, and Madison Avenue country pop. But out in the forgotten hinterlands, especially in the desert southwest, the bedfellows become more strange, inhabited by a disparate mix of yammering Spanish, mournful cowboy crooning, random snatches of Chinese, thunderous Evangelical sermons, and UFO whistleblowers who always seemed to concentrate in the dried out, forgotten places, using the AM airwaves to vent their spleen and warn the ignorant masses about the alien entities already moving amongst us. The desert seemed ideally suited to a curious collection of castoffs, eccentrics, weirdos, and sociopaths naturally drawn to the dusty fringes. Meth cooks, anti-government militias, New Agey art nuts, murder cultists. All headed to the sandy heat like Jesus himself, looking to face down their demons, or possibly create them, away from the prying eyes of the better irrigated. Owing to the circumstances surrounding his exit from his last stopover, perhaps Max should join this sun-blasted freak show, he thought. Get lost amongst the lost. But he knew something else was out there for him, waiting far beyond the arid wasteland, where the mountains and trees sprang up again along the ocean cliffs, trying to slow the momentum of western trajectory before all frustrated life again ended up in the sea.

Max pressed "scan" and skimmed over an offering of MexiCali accordion music and a low rent advert for industrial shedding, arriving at what he loved the most—the Born Againer martyrdom rant against the encroaching forces of the Antichrist, who was always some eastern hemisphere powerbroker carefully selected and re-christened by each new generation, and then watched like a chicken coop eyes a hawk—albeit a hawk two thousand miles away. No matter what latitude or longitude traveled, Max could find cold comfort in the certainty of religious zealotry flooding AM airwaves in the forgotten places of North America, stoked by paranoia, bigotry, xenophobia and a sort of gleeful fatalism that would have chilled Nietzsche to his knickers. Land of the free. Home of the brave.

"And so the days of the tribulation are nigh, my brothers and sisters," roared the firebrand, buzzing Max's tiny speakers. "And ye shall hear of wars and rumors of wars. See that ye be not troubled, for all these things must come to pass, but the end is not yet here. For nation shall rise against nation, and kingdom against kingdom, and there shall be famines, and pestilences, and earthquakes, in diverse places. All these are the beginning of sorrows!"

The signal faded a bit, but came back strong a few seconds later, allowing Max to continue his front row seat to the theatre of holy fear.

"The signs are everywhere, if one knows how to look with the eyes of Jesus and the mind of God! The return of the Chosen Ones to their ancient land, the gathering of crows, the massing of armies . . . " Hoots and hollers from the unseen audience gave credibility to these ravings that would be deemed insanity in the western world if spewed under a different banner, or no banner at all. "It's all in the Word, and the Word shall come to pass!"

The Word. Max chuckled and lit up another cigarette, shaking his head at the dead-ass certainty of the Evangelical blowhard. How can one be so assured of *anything*? Faith aside, if this were a country settled by Bronze Age Norsemen and founded on the teachings of Odin and his hammer-wielding sprat, Americans would have a totally different outlook on the afterlife, and pine for bloody laurels while ascending to the Halls of Valhalla after being split in two on the field of battle. But this wasn't that country. Thanks to Rome, then Columbus and Cabot and Cortez, pious Americans from every bloodline under the mongrel sun got the longhaired peacenik from Galilee as their redeemer, who Max surmised was more dope smoking flower child than gun wielding capitalist. Luck of the historical draw, as all the books that mattered to posterity were written by the victors. How many times had Max roared some version of this half-baked pundit screed into various living rooms and barroom bathrooms the past ten years like a C-list Beatnik? How many times had no one given a solitary fuck what he was saying? Gospels aside, the Son of Man probably experienced the very same thing, albeit to a better tanned crowd.

Max pushed himself back from his annoying existential meander just in time for the signal fade from the Bible thump. He sighed and pressed scan again, starting the lottery anew.

Outside his bug-painted windshield, the sign for "Fallon, NV—30 Miles" whizzed past. Max barely glanced, concerned only with how far he was from the Pacific, where his future would be made or broken on the chewed coastline of California. The place of childhood soft drink commercials and 80s beach comedies. Paradise under an eternal sun that didn't burn or wither but lit everyone to camera-ready perfection. He just needed to get through the desert, and he'd be fine. The answers would be waiting for him at the water's edge. They had to be. What was the meaning of life for a flyover boy? California, your honor.

As the radio scan continued to cycle through dead air, Max looked out into the night around him. The range of his headlights hinted at an endless stretch of dried-out nothingness, colonized by scrub grass, creosote bush, cacti, and probably a fair share of bleached bones of varying size and species. Forty days and forty nights in all direction. This wasn't land that had recently gone dry. It looked like it was *born* dry, shot malformed from the ocean to land under a misanthropic sky that refused to grant it any relief, any taste of that wet place where it was formed.

This backcountry was broken by the occasional squatty house, built low and set far back from the highway, as if the structure itself was trying to run from civilization and—reaching the end of its tether—collapsed glumly onto the dusty ground in defeat. Max could never figure out why anyone or anything with any sort of viable option would choose to live in such a God forsaken environment. No appreciable water, daytime heat that could kill a man, and a bloodthirsty landscape populated entirely by flora and fauna that was either poisonous or covered in deleterious thorns, or both; a brutal ecosystem crafted with an eye on repelling or murdering any non-native species that was stupid enough to wander into the neighborhood. And yet, softheads came out in droves to parched places such as this to restart their ridiculous lives, pumped in borrowed water, set up artificial air conditioning, and hunkered down inside their suburban pillboxes, waiting out each day as if they lost a bet.

The radio found a tether and stopped on a fuzzy station espousing the tourist attractions of the area. "—orthern Nevada, some of the most accessible examples of these mysterious petroglyphs can be found at Grimes Point, about twelve miles east of Fallon on Highway—" And just like that, the signal was gone again. Scan . . .

Max was pondering the important issue of how petrogylphs differed from hieroglyphs when the radio halted its roll at the very far end of the electronic dial. After a brief silence, the weak signal transmitted indistinct sounds, like whispers, intermingled with an odd chanting that faded in and out like a spectral dirge. Intrigued by this strange combination, and hoping for a broadcast of a lonely Indian powwow, Max turned up the volume, but the higher it went, the softer the voice and chant became, going silent. There was no apparent signal, but the radio scan was still stopped, locked in on something.

Perplexed, Max noticed that the compass on his dash began to shimmy in its housing, spinning this way and that, even though the road ahead was straight as an arrow.

The silence was shot through by a booming intonation that blasted from the speakers, startling Max, who grasped at the volume button, barely noticing the brownish, misshapen hulk that lurched onto the highway ahead at the far edge of his headlights, gripping something large in its massive paws. Max mashed the brakes while cranking the wheel away from the creature, which dragged a half-eaten carcass of a deer—or was it a dog?—up the rocky embankment, as the Dodge swerved by, skidding onto the shoulder and burying the front grill into the opposite hillside as the radio went silent again.

The car engine gurgled and pitched under the slightly crumpled hood, then jerked to a stop with a wheeze. Breathing hard, Max fixed his eyes on the compass. It was spinning like a top inside the plastic housing. Was this from the crash? But the car wasn't moving, and probably wouldn't be anytime soon. The radio was again cycling through dead air. And what was that huge fucking thing that ran across the road? Pebbles rolled down the hillside and onto the car like a hundred tapping fingers.

Max sat frozen, blinking his eyes that were obviously playing tricks on him after too many hours on the road. That thing . . . Was it a desert inbred? Some sort of mutated bear that wandered too close to a nuclear test site? This *was* Nevada, after all, the bullpen of the atom bomb. Max was unnerved, more by what he did know of what he saw than what he didn't. Or maybe it was what he heard. They both happened so fast, so close together. He was sweating, and felt as if the car was closing around him like a tin can prison. He locked the doors, not sure if what was out there was worse than what he heard inside, as he quickly realized what most terrified him was that the radio would again find that baritone chanting that seemed to echo from somewhere impossible deep. He reached out hesitantly to push the off button, when the scan again stopped on the far end of the dial, but this time, he heard . . . *weeping*. The strange, uncomfortable sound of a man crying, as if profoundly grieved by the tragically occurred or the unfortunately inevitable. This stayed Max's hand, before the sobbing splintered into sudden, spastic laughter. What was this nonsense? What sort of psychotic local pirate station owner or ham radio operator was pranking over the air, scaring the shit out of those who scanned the far end of the dial? This fucker owed Max a new, shitty, late model Dodge. Or at least a ride to the coast.

The laughter then stopped, and in the silence, the mic picked up sounds of papers being shuffled, tapes stacked methodically. Then, a flat voice that sounded distant in tone and emotion began. "You can hear everything in the desert." The voice wavered, as if the speaker needed to stop, to breathe, to collect himself. "The buzzing of insects, the hooting of owls, the mad yap of the coyotes . . .

"You got that right," Max chimed in with irritation to no one but the unhearing voice at the other end of the radio transmission, which came to life again:

"Sometimes those sounds fall away by some unspoken agreement, and in that profound silence, the right type of ears can hear, can *sense*, the softer, more terrible noises that lurk underneath the normal nighttime din . . . " Another pause, another intake of breath. "The desert whispers to me, telling me things I never knew existed, never dared dream, giving up secrets older than the primordial soup . . . I record these secrets, as I have been tasked, and broadcast them when I can. But the recording is the key, and I have been diligent, as were those who came before me."

Outside the car, dry lightning carved the sky, highlighting clouds that looked like seething shapes forming on the horizon. "If you could rewrite the Bible, the Nag Hammadi, the Tablets of Thoth, directly from the source, would you sacrifice your life to do it?"

Another religious loony tune—this one with a shiny heretical paint job, Max thought, trying to chuckle in spite of a gnawing fear that was coiling in his stomach. He quickly turned the key and tried to give life to a halting ignition while avoiding glancing out into the darkness. He was still shaken by the crash, and nervous that he might be stranded out on this forgotten ribbon of highway with this obviously insane misanthrope and whatever loped up into the hills.

After much protesting and cajoling from Max, the battered engine sputtered to life. He revved out the kinks, then backed out from the embankment and out onto the highway, jammed the car into drive, and drove wobbly on in the same direction he was going, the voice continuing its diatribe, with Max trying not to listen. The compass still spun like a mindless dervish, so it was no good to him. But Max knew where he was going. West. Ever west and as west as he could. He had to leave this weird fucking place behind.

As he built up speed, the radio signal got stronger, and Max found himself listening more intently in spite of himself, finding courage in motion, and increasingly fascinated by this obviously deranged individual who somehow attained access to the radio airwaves. It was like an auditory train wreck, the ultimate metaphysical reality show, and Max couldn't turn his ears away, or move himself to turn off the radio.

"It's late in my mission," the voice said, "and nearly time for me to move on. I'm waiting for my replacement so the work and the message can continue. They tell me that the time of the awakening is at hand, and as such, the preparations have become more urgent than ever before."

The signal started to fade, and so Max slowed. He was now fully engrossed in this mournful monologue, and felt somehow compelled to keep listening, as if guided by a gentle outside force. Nearly losing the signal all together, Max stopped the car in the middle of the empty highway, dropped into reverse, and trundled backwards in the darkness cut open by his white reverse lamps, until the signal increased in strength again. He stopped and idled, leaning forward, as if to better connect with this lone speaker in the darkness.

"The desert tells me to do this, and I do as I'm told, because you never, ever argue with the desert." The voice giggled again, this time with more mirth, but it ended with a terrified edge, as before. "So, now I whisper to you, speaking for the desert, speaking for those behind the desert, and speaking for myself, as my time here has lately become short."

The car engine shuddered, seized, and expired. Max didn't notice.

"There is beauty and horror here, wisdom and madness, and I have drunk deeply of it all. Will you do the same?" The man went silent. Lightning licked the sky. Max, again feeling the car close in around him, began to wonder if this was merely a one-way conversation.

"Will you?" the voice asked again.

"Me?" Max answered.

"You," the voice continued, as if in confirmation. "Will you do the same?" The signal wavered and buzzed, then faded into fuzz again.

Max flung open his door and tumbled out of the car. Rushing to the smashed hood, he pushed against the cracked grill with all of his might, and moved the Dodge backward, gaining momentum as he labored. As it picked up speed, Max ran to the open car door and jumped inside, breathing hard as he turned up the volume. The signal came back in, and Max quickly veered the car off the road onto the graveled shoulder, settled in behind the wheel and listened.

"—slicing open the forbidden fruit forever, peeling back the skin to reveal that essential pulp, as knowledge is not evil, it is the natural progression of humanity, and a realization of what we were placed here to do by the creators. I and others in the service of the truth are just signposts, simple steps forward in the awakened dream. The *work* is the most important thing that humanity is undertaking right now on this planet, battling the old war against those who call madness all things they dare not understand . . ."

The radio strength dipped, and Max was about to hop out and reposition his car yet again, when it resumed.

"My time with the work is almost complete, as my vessel has been filled to the cracking point . . . I now wait for another . . . One who has been promised, who will come to pick up the transcription while I move on . . ." More fuzzy static. "The work isn't about good or evil, as good and evil do not exist. Those are arbitrary judgment calls, muddied by rationalizations. Only order and chaos are real. Only light and dark. Only knowledge and ignorance. Out of these primal forces spring everything we know. And I now know *just a mere fraction* of what is out there, and sometimes wish I didn't, as in its transcendent power, it has ended me for this sphere . . . My brain has heard too many whispers, dreamed too many times beyond the First Gate, has seen too much revealed . . . and now aches for an eternal rest, to exhale after a decade-long upload. I seek the silence of the teeming abyss—to rest, and to dream, as has been promised. The veil has been lifted and the bliss of ignorance has been shattered forever, and so now I sit in a state of unsettled wisdom, blinking my watery eyes as if I have looked too long at the sun . . . the unimagined beauty . . . the indescribable horror . . . the unimagined beauty of the indescribable horror . . ." The voice trailed off in rasping awe, then the man took a deep, shaky breath. "Who out there will take my place? Who dares peek behind the veil, to see the truth in all its many splendors and impossibly endless vistas? Who will listen to the whispers after I am gone?"

Max sat in his car, mesmerized by this voice, hanging on every quaver and sigh. This man was obviously bat shit crazy, but in his insanity, there was a powerful certainty about knowledge and realities that Max could scarcely imagine.

"The work *must* go on, as the truth *must* be told." The voice found strength once more. "We weren't created to live as ignorant insects our entire existence, puttering around our self-made terrarium with our heads dragging blindly in the dust. The lost knowledge handed down from beyond must be brought back, made whole, and again disseminated across our land, if we are ever to rise to the dancing dimensional heights we once knew as a young Arcadian civilization, flush with the magic of sacred geometry and outer technology. These sciences made us gods in flesh. As above, so below. No difference aside from degrees . . . But the weakness, the jealousies, the things they did not foresee . . . Our godhood was torn from us, ripped from walls and hidden in the mud not by natural disaster, but by rank superstition of the stolen elect, beholden only to the bureaucratic fear of an enlightened human race and the freedom of that learning. Pearls before swine, kings to beggars . . . Echoes, echoes, and remnants remain, twisted into cautionary tales uttered by perverts, telling us now to fear the very same fruit that first gave us life, that is the only food we are meant to eat. These echoes remain, and in the hearing, we are lesser for it . . . "

The voice trailed off with a zigzagging reverberation, as if impacted by an outside interference, before returning again. "For I speak of gods and monsters, creation and eternal life and the destruction of both, the birth of stars and those things living inside them . . . I speak of the Truth of Truths, of the way and wherefores of all realities discovered by those cosmic entities that whisper secrets to those who refuse to live their lives deaf, dumb, and blind as worms. I speak of transcendence, liberation, and terrible paradise . . . And now, I await my replacement so the work and the message can continue. The book was stolen from us, the knowledge ripped from our minds, so it is up to us to rebuild the book, and relearn the knowledge . . . They tell me that the time of the awakening is at hand, and as such, the preparations have become more urgent than ever before—"

—*Fssssshpop!* And with that, the battery, the last life force of Max's shitty late model Dodge, blinked and died.

Max sat behind the wheel in total and utter silence, scarcely able to breathe, scarcely able to believe what he had just heard as his eyes rimmed with tears. It was as if a water balloon popped inside his brain, drenching his insides and leaving behind nothing but a newly scrubbed view of his destiny. His meaning. He felt reborn, dancing atop a hunger he never knew existed. No longer was he worried about reaching the coast. All he knew now was that he *had* to keep listening to this transmission, at whatever cost.

The increased strength of the signal just before the death of his ride meant that the tower—and most likely the source of the voice—was near. Max scrambled out of his car, intent on finding this strange person and learning more. This broken, impossibly enlightened man knew something, *believed* in something with every fiber of his tortured being, and Max had to figure out why.

Max was out of the car and running up the center of the highway, and soon discovered a weed-choked access road that led off from the main drag and up into the noxious wilds of the Nevada desert. Max's gaze followed what he surmised was the direction of the path up into the hill country, where he noticed a small red light floating in the higher elevations, like a disembodied eye keeping watch over the dead sand below.

Max looked back at his car, threw his keys into the darkness, and set out for the guiding red light that lurked somewhere out there, waiting for him.

Bony fingers of lightning crackled above, strobe-lighting the ominously shaped clouds. Max walked quickly, his path between lightning flashes barely illuminated by a waxing moon, hanging low and sallow over the ring of mountains gnawing the sky like the craggy molars of a monstrous exposed jawbone. His shoes crunched over shattered plates of volcanic stone, pushing out the noises of the desert that the quivering, hollow voice described. The hovering red light was getting closer, and so Max moved onward, continuing his tumbleweed journey by rootless foot. Once again, he found courage in forward motion, scant as it was. The meaning, the meaning . . .

After nearly an hour, Max spied a stand of stunted trees that seemed to coalesce out of the darkness on a ridge slightly above. As he neared, he could just make out a dilapidated shack squatting amid the gnarled timber, blasted ghostly white by decades, maybe centuries, of enduring the spite of the brutal Nevada sun, which seemed extra angry with this part of the world as if by result of an old and festering grudge. Every hundred yards or so, a rough hewn stone monolith of greenish gray stone—which didn't seem to originate from the surrounding hills, or anywhere on the continent, really—stood sentry, forming a wide, easy-to-miss circle around the circumference of the ridge.

Passing through the loose knit ring of stone, Max quickened his pace and approached the old shanty, which was built up atop an ancient foundation of crumbling adobe, like those found in the ruins of the cliff-face domiciles constructed by the mysteriously vanished Anasazi that Max had explored several years back while tumbling through New Mexico. Anchored by the clay foundation, random building materials were haphazardly pasted and lashed, to keep out the wind and sun and sporadic bouts of furious downpours that sought to wash away those godless things that made their home in the desert.

Max walked to the front door, leaned in close and listened. The faint, hollow voice that was now so familiar could be heard inside. Emboldened, Max tried the door, and found it unlocked. He opened it and pushed inward. The door creaked on protesting hinges and sat open, yellowish light spilling out into the night, momentarily blinding Max. The voice was louder. Nothing moved inside. Steeling his resolve, Max entered.

The small outer room was lit by several naked light bulbs that hung from the ceiling, buzzing with flies and beetles. The raw light cast harsh shadows on stacks of moldering newsprint, boxes of moth-eaten clothes, and various detritus that one would normally associate with a bunker existence. Canned food. Jugs of yellow liquid. A gas mask hanging from the barrel of a large bore sniping rifle. The voice was coming from a back room, sectioned off by a ratty curtain. Max walked through the maze of refuse and pushed back the drape, terrified and thrilled in equal measure to meet the intermediary of this message that had brought him from the known road into the weird wilderness.

Max found no one waiting beyond the curtain. Instead, he discovered a cramped yet deserted room hemmed in by high racks of notebooks and journals, facing a corner heaped with a precariously arranged amalgam of new and incredibly old radio equipment surrounding a makeshift broadcast booth. Analog modulators, reel-to-reel players, a turntable, magnetic cassette docks, CD ports, and a laptop, all wired together in the same haphazard fashion as the shack itself. A DIY broadcast station carved out of overstuffed shelving and countless stacks of yellowing paper.

The old iron office chair behind the microphone was empty. A digital recording was playing, continuing a pre-taped monologue transmitted out into the desert night, into Max's car, into countless other cars, and homes, and minds.

"And so," the recorded voice continued. "The work must go on, even here, at this broadcast station at Grimes Point, built here because here has always been, and shall ever remain, a doorway to what the Early Ones called Star Nation before moving on, what we call The Outer Places, and the Realm of the Elders, where all is nothing and nothing is all in this dance of divine illusion . . ."

As the voice continued, Max explored the room, picking through the reams of notebooks and folders, blowing off thick red dust that had settled everywhere, and reading a few lines of wildly advanced and esoteric learning—mind-bending formulae, non-Euclidean calculus, quantum physics, interlaced with blurbs of history and a shocking understanding of the universe and inter-dimensional travel. Max moved to the broadcast table where lay an open journal. Paging through it, he discovered bizarrely grouped information assembled into monologues, written out in a sort of movie script format, similar to the ones heard on the radio, similar to the one the voice was relaying at that very moment, which Max followed along with his finger:

"Upon receiving my assignment and arriving here, I spent some time alone among the rocks, discovering the promised doorway that I shall soon revisit for the final time . . ."

Max rifled through the notebooks and tapes around him, noticing dates that went back several hundred years. This was not just a broadcast booth, Max realized, but a library, a repository of arcane and antiquated knowledge off the scale of human imagination.

Stunned by the implications of what loomed around him, Max then noticed a line of several dozen framed photographs on the wall, of different people manning the microphone, sitting in that heavy chair, moving back through the ages, from color pictures to black and white to muddy sepia tone. Two dozen men and women of varying ages, races, and obvious social standing, all sitting in the same pose in front of the same microphone with the same grim expression and slightly unbalanced gleam in their eyes.

The most recent speaker continued his taped oration, as Max moved in closer and squinted at the last photo to the right, which showed a man not much older than him, staring haughtily into the camera of an unknown photographer, the instruments of transmission glowing behind him. "I felt as though I had passed into a pinhole poked through realty, taking me outside linear time and into the seething void . . . Grimes Point is a wrinkle in the fabric of this brittle plane, a carefully plotted and placed dimensional distortion allowing access to and from the Place of the Beginning, and the measureless vistas of the Continuing Chaos—a place forgotten or shunned throughout the course of human history. But a place that was also sought out, by those brave seekers who heeded not the fear . . . This is just one outpost, numbered six, and is one of many, where others like me continue the work to rebuild that which was stolen from us, a primal birthright ripped from our molecular memory. They took from us our knowledge, our book, but we will rebuild it, and again teach the truth through the written word, through the electronic ether, through the television and the radio waves . . . We seek to swing the wrong back to the right, through darkness and light, and ready the awaiting flock . . ."

The fly-spattered light bulbs flickered, and Max looked up, noticing perplexing lines and curves etched into the ceiling, surrounding what appeared to be several intricate, overlapping star maps. But, the maps didn't feature any of the known constellations, or none with which Max was familiar.

"I speak of what was whispered to me, through the sounds of the desert, of elder mathematics—the language of all creation, the root and the key of what we know as eldritch magic. That which sank R'lyeh, raised Atlantis, and built the sacred pyramids and other abandoned monuments to the Outer Gods across our crowded sphere . . ."

Max sank slowly into the stout broadcast chair and gazed wide eyed around the room, as if a sudden realization clicked in his head, giving confirmation to something he had always surmised but didn't dare believe, and rarely ventured to dream. West, ever west . . . Out into the Pacific . . . Fate or drown. Fate or drown . . .

Max's eyes bulged as he listened with every atom of his being, taking in the words as the voice went on to tell of the Outer Gods, who will come and take away those who know how to ask. About how he and others throughout history and prehistory and the dawn of sentient life were mere chroniclers of these impossibly old entities and their epic machinations, from drawings in the primordial clay, to paintings in caves, to those driven mad compiling the Dread Book, to now—transmitting the stories and knowledge into the atmosphere, then out past the charged particles of our finite space. All the same. All working in the same service. Those who chronicle and spread these revealed truths are members of the enlightened few, and are assured a place of exaltation beyond the stars, spared the coming reclamation of this tiny blue rock by the errant overseers who have seeded all of the living worlds in the dimensions of their influence.

The workers at Outpost Six at Grimes Point are the newest members of these few, collecting information imparted in purposely small, disassociated segments to keep the recorder sane for as long as humanly possible. These are the further writers of the Book of Knowledge, continuing the work of Alhazred, von Junzt, The Scribe of Eibon . . . Mason, Curwen, Carter, and Ward . . . these are the chroniclers of the Higher Wisdoms to prepare the Earth for the promised coming and the transformation, when the Old Masters return home to check on their children, their forgotten Petri dish prepped and left in a far flung corner of nowhere . . .

"This is what the desert told me," the voice continued, "and what I and others have recorded for decades, centuries, eons before our poorly-made vessels became too full and started to crack . . ."

Sitting in the chair with his eyes staring straight ahead while his mind began to venture several dimensions away, Max didn't see the bathroom just off the broadcast room, where a bloody razor and clumps of hastily shaved body hair clogged the sink. Max didn't see the trail of blood that led out the smashed back door, over the dusty yard, past the unnatural mounds and monoliths surrounding the property, and into the sand of the endless desert. Max didn't see the speaker of the voice, just hours before he arrived, standing on the brink of Grimes Point, and flinging himself down onto the curiously arranged rocks below. Max also didn't see the body of the man disappear into the void before it hit the craggy bottom, warping away to a swirling, unnamable infinitum of places unknowable, where he would join the roiling mass of omnipotent chaos that probed for a way back into our tiny plane of existence, settling in the meantime for psychic missives sent from the Beyond. Measured portions of the ultimate truth transmitted to our time, place, and space in hopes of teaching one of us the correct formula to open up the dimensional gaps dotting our universe just wide enough for something substantial to come through, to return to a place unvisited in a billion years, but never, ever forgotten.

Max didn't see these things, because he was sitting at the microphone—his new post at Outpost Six—taking in The Words in preparation for continuing The Work. The voice in the darkness had sliced open the forbidden fruit and offered a taste to Max. He took a reluctant bite, and was now changed forever—a doomed man enslaved by this terrible growing wisdom, joining all those curious souls who had been drawn to this place before him.

"So," the speaker in the picture, the speaker who dove into Grimes Point and into the boundless, structured abyss just hours earlier, concluded in his strange, hollow voice. "I leave this sacred burden to you who have found your way to this humble temple of the Outer Gods, the true rulers of this universe and many others, who have revealed themselves to those who were forced to forget . . . They are there, and They are waiting, watching, and whispering . . . Tend to your task with seriousness, and be mindful in your work, for the destruction and rebirth of all we know demands rigorous attention and strict vigilance . . ." The speaker's voice began to give, but he mustered enough strength to continue, if only to breathlessly croak: "Fare thee well . . . and worry not . . . for understanding beyond measure is nigh! A replacement draws forth, even now! Signing off . . . and bid this forgotten place goodbye . . . knowing that you are already on the doorstep . . . and the cycle . . . continues . . . "

The voice gave out and the transmission ended.

In the dead silence of the tiny shack, the noises of the desert began to creep in, as well as those softer, more terrible sounds that lurk underneath the normal nighttime din.

Max was listening.

from: item l5161orde, 'the dangsturm interruption

JOSEPH BOUTHIETTE JR.

/SAMPLE: Audio L5161ORDE-01. 00:00:23.

[. . .] My father swallowed swords. It was one of the years he turned 40. Not realizing that's how old he turned the year before, I got him a birthday cake that said "Happy Big 40, Dad!" I may have done this twice. My father went from age 40 right to 43. My father went from 40 to swallowing swords. How does one who leads [. . .]

/SAMPLE: Audio L5161ORDE-02. 00:00:05.

[. . .] and I do not wish to live in a world where this is permitted, where [. . .]

/SAMPLE: Audio L5161ORDE-03. 00:04:14.

[. . .] to me. Growing up, I remember the myriad satellite dishes, rods, and scanners stretching from our home's roof and siding. Together, they crowned the building with cosmic magnificence. I remember the basement lined with arrays of panels with buttons and levers, small green monitors that strained the eyes, tubing that billowed steam periodically. No one else remembers. Mother denies it, denied it until the day she dropped into a catatonic state, probably still denies it in her hospitalized unconsciousness. Sister denies it, being too young and too preoccupied to remember much of anything. But I remember.

[EVENT ALPHA]

I rebuilt father's glorious instruments, the tools to continue the work he no longer performs, can no longer perform.

[EVENT BETA]

/SAMPLE: Audio L5161ORDE-04. 00:10:47.

[. . .] but he never spoke of the pulsars, not directly. He'd rather postulate on the existence of the jackalope, or question why restaurants didn't bake an entire meatloaf each time a customer ordered a meatloaf dinner entree. He watched football, and only ever cheered for his one team, never giving any other a second thought. He raised an eyebrow to conversations of gay men, but never missed a chance to jump into one on lipstick lesbians. But the pulsars weighed on everything he did, everything he said. They were his tic.

[EVENT GAMMA]

A man can walk at a speed, step by step by step. He can walk faster or slower, but only at one speed at a time. His blood circulates much the same way. His speech is a fixed cadence. Walk beside that man, and your feet will never strike the dirt at the exact same time. Your speech will never align. Hold his hand, and the rush of your blood will never be the same as his. An army of men march: though they appear to be in unison, the tiny disparity between each step sends waves of chaos through the earth. They may as well step at random. And it's this randomness that influenced my father's tempo. Given enough time, enough patience, the mathematics can break down that randomness into the layers of overlapping regularity. Current calculations estimate there to be around one million pulsars in our galaxy alone. Having perfected the forgotten technology of my youth, I am familiar with about 2.6 million, in and out of the Milky Way. My father was the epicenter of 82.2 million pulsars. He was speared by so many points of light, he lost his banal, rigid form. The math does not lie, and I think my father's silence on the matter was his admission that a primitive mind shouldn't question the limits of its entrapment. A tiger would do well not to measure the dimensions of his cage. No biological form wants to accept how trapped he is [. . .]

[EVENT GAMMA-02]

/SAMPLE: Audio L5161ORDE-05. 00:00:26.

[EVENT DELTA]

[EVENT DELTA-02]

/LOG-L5161ORDE.

CLEARANCE GRANTED TO ALL CLASS STAFF WITHOUT CURRENT SECURITY HOLDS. MAY NOT BE COPIED WITHOUT WRITTEN CONSENT FROM TWO (2) CLASS-B ADMINISTRATORS.

The preceding items are textual representations of electronic audio files related to Item L5161ORDE, colloquially known as *The Dangsturm Interruption* or *The Interruption*. The incident occurred on 8 June 20XX. A radio signal originating from 45°XX' N 101°XX' W in South Dakota, United States played for an estimated fifty-three (53) minutes, intercepting the signal for local station #withheld#. Station employees denied involvement.

Preceding audio files are the only samples of the incident in administrative domain. A complete recording of the incident has not been brought to administrative attention. Station employees claim to have recorded the entire incident save for the first few minutes, but this recording went missing before staff could claim it. A complete recording of the incident may not exist.

Colloquial name *The Dangsturm Interruption* derived from the name of the only suspect apprehended for the incident. Martin S. Dangsturm was arrested but not convicted for the incident. His residence showed no evidence of advanced astronomical technology or audio/radio equipment. Surveillance of his activity is ongoing.

Audio 01 through 04 include a male voice speaking the text from the sample. Audio and linguistics experts posit a 96.1% match with the voice of Martin S. Dangsturm. Audio 03 through 05 include additional audio occurrences titled EVENTS.

EVENT ALPHA (00:00:05) is a low-volume distortion of spoken word played in reverse. The text spoken is “It can be heard, but you cannot see it. It has no face.” Distortion is significant and hinders attempts for voice matching.

EVENT BETA (00:03:23) is a low-volume distortion of spoken word played in reverse. The text spoken is “40, 43 to 40.” Distortion is significant and hinders attempts for voice matching.

EVENT GAMMA (00:08:54) is a sequence of ticking that occur in regular overlapping meters ranging from 0.4 bpm to 167 bpm. Unlike previous entries, EVENT GAMMA occurs concurrently with the spoken word. It begins at 00:00:28 of Audio L5161ORDE-04 and continues until the end of the sample. It begins with a single 40 bpm tick and additional sequences begin playing concurrently with no discernible pattern.

EVENT GAMMA-02 (00:00:08) is a low-volume distortion of spoken word played in reverse. The text spoken is “How does one who leads a boring life make it sound interesting to other people? Perhaps I shall wear a mask.” Distortion is significant and hinders attempts for voice matching. EVENT GAMMA-02 begins at 00:06:26 of Audio L5161ORDE-04 and occurs concurrently with EVENT GAMMA.

EVENT DELTA (00:00:26) is a sequence of ticking that occur in regular overlapping meters ranging from 0.0XX bpm to 9.5x10^{X} bpm. EVENT DELTA is defined as the entirety of Audio L5161ORDE-05. Audio experts suggest EVENT DELTA may be a continuation of EVENT GAMMA.

EVENT DELTA-02 (00:00:16) is a low-volume distortion of spoken word played in reverse. The text spoken is “A mask, a thousand masks.

A thousand forms, a billion points of light." Distortion is significant and hinders attempts for voice matching. EVENT GAMMA-02 begins at 00:00:10 of Audio L5161-ORDE-05 and occurs concurrently with EVENT DELTA. Audio experts suggest there may be more to the text due to the fragmentary nature of the audio sample.

An estimated 14,800 civilians were exposed to Item L5161ORDE to varying degrees. Testimony from exposed civilians was superfluous and contradictory in nature, but a tentative order sequence for the collected audio samples was created. Most exposed civilians were confident that the incident started with the text from Audio L5161ORDE-01. Many exposed civilians suggested additional spoken word occurred subsequent to Audio L5161ORDE-05, but numerous other exposed civilians refuted this, instead suggesting the layers of ticking and additional DELTA-XX EVENTS occurred and ended the incident. DELTA-XX EVENTS that may have occurred include additional samples of reversed spoken text, the screaming of one (1) to sixteen (16) women, and sustained tones from a wind instrument similar to a pan flute.

ADDITIONAL INFORMATION IS AVAILABLE IN EXTERNAL FILE L5161ORDE TO CLASS-A STAFF WITH NO CURRENT SECURITY HOLDS. MAY NOT BE COPIED WITHOUT WRITTEN CONSENT FROM TWO (2) CLASS-B ADMINISTRATORS.

/ADDENDUM L5161ORDE-01

Person of interest Martin S. Dangsturm missing as of 22 August 20XX. Text L5161ORDE-01 was discovered in his residence. Class-A staff with no current security holds may refer to External File L5161ORDE for updated information.

/SAMPLE: Text L5161ORDE-01

I wear the mask of winter storms between the stars, and, behind it, the pulsars shall never find me. I follow the eternal piping. I am coming, Father. 4343434343

the givens sensor board

JOSH MALERMAN

BEHOLD . . . A BURIAL . . .

. . . wet maple leaves trampled, footprints in the mud, a mist more than a rain and yet a lot of it, like how a whisper can sound angry . . . black cloaks for the pallbearers; not friends of the deceased, the disgusting mailman had no friends, had two sisters still in Ohio—as if having decided long ago to get as far from their brother as possible . . . the mailman caught with lips in his trunk; leaves and laundry and lips . . . no plastic bags, no cooler, just the mouths of nine people and none of the mouthless here, at his burial and yet . . . silence . . . perhaps the silence he'd wished for (the mailman never explained himself, never gave Samhattan the manifesto the city expected; *I just wanted them to all shut up, I couldn't stand the sound of them*; nothing given, nothing like that) . . . the mailman in the box, can't call it a casket, can't call it a coffin, can't call it a crypt, the mailman in the *box* and the wood damp from the mist, could grow weak, could get soft enough to bust-up, to break apart, to release him if he had the life and strength in him to want it . . . strength . . . a black frock; Father Stockard doesn't want to be here either, doesn't care for these types of ceremonies; not that they test his faith, nothing tests his faith, but he'd rather be reading rather be sitting in a silent home staring at a fire that births calm than standing here in the rain, protecting the good book, yodeling for the soul of a thin balding mail carrier who must have known who would be home when and when home alone . . . the creaking of the box from the uneven passage from the cemetery building to the cemetery plot, from the rigid grip of the pallbearers, all of them having read the *Samhattan News* through the whole horrid affair, saw the photos of Officers Bobby and Bloomberg standing by the trunk of Randy Scotts's car (he, the mailman), outside Duncle's Bar, Scotts inside sipping gin, thin and balding, meek and wild-eyed, gin to his lips, his own lips, still attached to his face, still able to smile, still able to sip . . . the pallbearers saw the newspaper photo too of Bobby and Bloomberg on either side of Scotts, escorting him into the Samhattan Courthouse, time for trial, time to face the big bad Judge Walker who had a daughter of her own, a daughter with lips, and who delivered the death-sentence through her mouth, still had a mouth, could sympathize with those who suddenly had theirs taken away . . . *Guilty* . . . behold . . . guilt and a burial but not the burying of guilt; the burying of a dead monster, he who brought mail, delivered bills and notices of love, too, nodded and said you're welcome while eyeing the smiles of the homeowners on his route, no doubt finding this mouth more attractive than that, these lips more desirable than those, until he had them for himself, taken them, then forgot them like used kid toys in the trunk to loll about over the bumps and humps in the road on his way to the next set, the next pair, the next lips he had to have . . .

. . . behold . . .

. . . a photo, taken at the burial . . . Scotts in the box . . . Don Miller from the *Samhattan News,* the lone reporter though more of a photographer . . . even the *News* had finally agreed with greater Samhattan about what the Scotts case had become; nothing to talk about . . . nothing more to report . . . the collective sigh of the community when he was captured . . . the second, lesser relief, felt with Walker's sentence . . . all of it echoing into oblivion . . . into nothing to talk about . . . nothing at all, save the thoughts and fears of those at home; bad dreams about the mailman out in the hall, a creaking of a board, a weakling with a pair of scissors . . .

. . . thunder . . . above . . . though still a mist . . . still the noncommittal storm . . . like Scotts in the box . . . uneven images . . . incongruent man . . . on his back now . . . hung by Walker for the crimes of removing nine

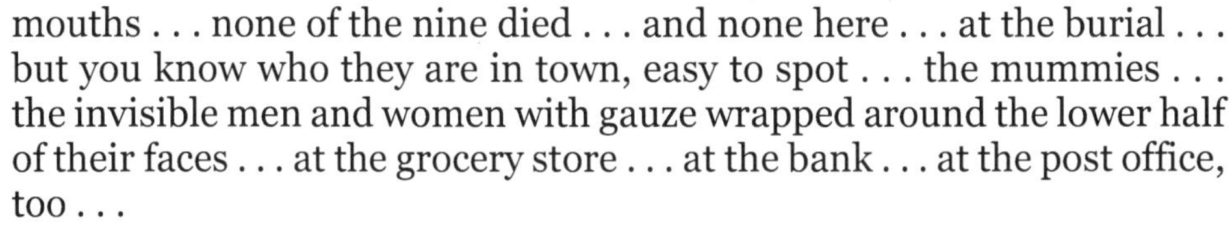

mouths . . . none of the nine died . . . and none here . . . at the burial . . . but you know who they are in town, easy to spot . . . the mummies . . . the invisible men and women with gauze wrapped around the lower half of their faces . . . at the grocery store . . . at the bank . . . at the post office, too . . .

FLASH!

. . . not lightning . . . a photo; Miller from the *Samhattan News*, a solitary shot of the pallbearers lowering the box to the canvas, to be lowered by Michael Donner on the lever, the big creaking wheel . . . Michael the young impressionable night watchman as well . . . Father Stockard speaking now to nobody, reciting rote verses; nothing really applies, no passage in the book says *just bury him and forget him, move on*—his voice like a man trying not to lie, feigning respect for life; Stockard has no respect for Scotts, nobody does . . . the college kid Donner turning the crank and Stockard nodding to him yes yes, get this over with can you roll any faster, kid? . . . the box lowering, going down . . . the mist dampening the wood, making mud of the hole . . . even the pallbearers turning their backs on the grave, discussing other things; sports, beer; not interested in the mailman descending; the mailman is where he should be now and all of Samhattan knows this; nothing to talk about, nothing more to photograph so Miller doesn't step to the grave's edge, doesn't ask questions, doesn't take a photo of Stockard priesting as Father Stockard has asked not to be associated with this one, doesn't want to be tied to the hideous man in the box, the thing nobody saw coming . . . so just Michael actually engaged, Michael of all people, hungover from a night out, last night, rotating the wheel, rounding the lever, lowering the box 'til it stops . . . it stops . . . Father Stockard midway through a passage stops as well and takes hold of a shovel, helps the bearers dump the dirt, figures one more set of hands will make it all go away faster, will get him home quicker . . . and the job *is* a fast one, nobody to console, nobody to talk to; silence between the bearers and Stockard and Michael, too, Michael with no shovel but on his knees in the mud, shoving dirt into the hole, helping any way he can, to get this over with . . .

FLASH!

. . . lightning this time, not Miller the photographer; Miller's camera is already put away, he's already halfway to the cemetery gate; Scotts is buried but nobody cares any more about the meek man with the scissors who took mouths and grew bored of them and tossed them into the trunk

(and what did he *do* with the lips . . . did he kiss them? . . . did he set them on the opposite side of the kitchen table and talk to them over dinner?)

. . . buried now . . . night . . . Michael all alone . . . Michael in the cemetery office where he watches television . . . the plots marked by the Givens Sensor Board behind him, along the back wall . . . each cemetery plot marked by a dead light, none of them blinking, none of them had ever blinked, thank God, the Givens Sensors Board installed five years ago, installed in every cemetery in America . . . gone were the days of formaldehyde . . . what if people don't really die? the Givens family had asked, what if people didn't quite die the way we thought they died and here we've been filling their veins with formaldehyde and burying them alive, see? burying everybody on Earth alive, but we don't have to, see? we can bury 'em like we used to, only put a sensor in there, a Givens Sensor, a *button* a buried man can press to alert whoever's in the office . . . a beeper and a button and buzzing to let the staff know they better call an ambulance, better go get a shovel themselves . . . and the world laughed at the Givens Sensor until one cemetery agreed and one blinking light came to life and one woman was discovered buried alive and she lived to tell, to talk about it on television, to write a book, and dammit if the Givens Sensors didn't become law less than a year later; every cemetery in America; a mortuary revolution and the Givens family got rich, so rich, so many appearances on television; in the half decade since the law was passed, six more blinking lights, six people we all thought were dead, six people dug up, gasping for air, ready to write memoirs of their own . . .

FLASH!

. . . not a photo, the photographer long gone, but lightning, again, erupting in the Samhattan sky, skinny fingers across the black; deep nighttime now; Michael Donner alone in the office . . . eating chips . . . watching a movie, a comedy about dogs and cats . . . reading a book, a thriller about a blind man . . . the storm outside growing, getting meaner, just the kind of night Michael enjoyed at the cemetery, half the reason he'd applied in the first place, *imagine me in the office at night, thunder and lightning outside!*; a *cool* gig, the coolest he'd ever heard of; a man with a paperback and a bunch of dead bodies, if that doesn't thrill you nothing will . . . FLASH!. . . another thunder-crack and Michael smiles, shakes his head, this is cool, this is amazing, sitting here in the office as the black sky cries, as the dogs of Samhattan lose their minds, all bark at once . . . Michael thinks of Father Stockard 'cause Father Stockard has a dog, a famous one here in Samhattan, a wolfhound, one of those huge gray dogs; is Stockard quieting the thing now?, telling him be quiet dog, I had a dark day, dog, that man stole mouths, dog, or was Stockard already asleep (perhaps) having showered the eulogy off himself . . . Michael doesn't know, doesn't really care either, just cares about this movie and these chips and that book and the girl Pamela from school who said she'd like to come visit him one night on the job, liked scary things, fancied herself macabre . . . Michael cares about her, very much so, cares about calling her up and inviting her tonight, right now, and so he does, call her up, says come eat chips with me in the dark, wants to say come let's have sex in the cemetery office at night if you're so into the macabre, if you're so dark as the black nail polish you wear, come on by tonight, Pamela . . . a FLASH! . . . CRACK-*BOOM!* . . . lightning again and the girl says yes, she'll come, but give her a minute, and Michael takes that minute to turn up the volume of the funny movie and chomp another chip . . . gets up to use the bathroom, passing the Givens Sensor Board like one of those Light-O-Rama things or maybe more like the information map at a state park, HERE is where you might see owls, HERE is where you might see moose; Michael likes it, the board, never lit, just sitting there like so much potential, so freaky, something to thrill Pamela with, the board and the ledger and the stone cottage/office and the creaking chair that he sits in to watch movies, watch over the cemetery, make sure no kids sneak inside (except for the ones he sneaks inside), and of course the lone window in the free-standing office ("the cemetery tollbooth," Michael likes to call it), the small square overlooking all those *graves* . . . graves and gravestones and broken limbs fallen from the trees and black leaves in the mud, footprints, many of those Michael's own . . . it is as cool a view as Michael could offer a lover of the macabre and if Pamela doesn't like it, who cares, the movie is good, the book is good, the pizza he has in a box (box) upon the black filing cabinet is good, too . . . no worries on the job, nothing to get upset about, getting paid to sit in a stone cottage, do whatever he likes to do, take a piss when he needs to–

FLASH!

. . . lightning only heard, Michael in the pisser, sitting down in the dark, rising when he's done; back through the little hall, back to the desk with the small television, the papers, the chips, and his phone . . . his phone letting him know someone wrote him, someone said they're here,

I'M HERE, Pamela already?, and Michael sticks his head out the little window and sees (yes) Pamela standing at the gate, alone, anxious, no doubt, by the way she sways . . .

FLASH!

. . . Michael out of the office, the green wooden door slamming shut behind him, racing to greet Pamela, nodding to her through the bars; follow me, he's saying, this way . . .

. . . behold . . .

. . . Michael letting Pamela in through a small door in the brush, Pamela remarking on it, saying how cool, a fucking door into a graveyard at night . . . Michael nodding yeah but come on it's raining pretty bad now and the office is dry, come on, you're gonna like this . . . and they run through the rain and she's laughing and Michael doesn't care if she makes too much noise, doesn't care if he does either, let someone notice, let him get fired, there are other cool gigs like the night watchman at a hospital, the night watchman at a train station . . .

FLASH!

. . . in through the green door, damp wood, and into the office and she looks so wonderful drenched like this and Michael notices for the first time she's carrying two beers on the end of a six pack plastic thingie and he says,

"ah man I probably shouldn't drink here"

and she says

"just one, each"

and he shrugs and shows her around the office; shows her the letterhead SAMHATTAN CEMETERY, shows her the file cabinet with all the dead records and the little radio and the television and realizes he's run out of things to show her then remembers the Givens Sensor Board, and turns around and shows her that, too . . .

"if one of these lit up . . . "

FLASH!

. . . they're kissing, not the way he had planned but so what; she's not straddling him in the office chair, but their lips are together, two sets, warm and wet, he's the one against the wall and she's the one making this all happen—and with his eyes closed he hears one of the beer cans open and she's handing it to him and now they're drinking beers and kissing and dogs and cats are making a bunch of noise on the television and Michael is in young man's heaven . . .

FLASH!

CRACK!

. . . they're watching the movie together, eating pizza; Pamela uses the bathroom and Michael likes that, feels for a second like they live here together in this really cool place . . . they take turns looking out the one window; Pamela says the rain and tombstones look like the Old West together and Michael shrugs and then they're laughing at her jokes, Pamela's funny, Michael really likes her, likes that they only kissed and nothing else is going to happen; he isn't sure what he would do, isn't sure how to do things like that; glad enough for the kiss and receives a second flurry of kisses when it's time for her to leave, here in the office, their lips together, so good, then a goodbye at the door in the brush and Michael scurrying across the grass, then pavement, back into the office where the movie has ended and it's an hour past midnight and he already has a message on his phone that says THAT WAS FUN and Michael howls with delight and pumps a fist in the air and gets up on the chair and changes the channel . . . new movie . . . how about a black and whiter? . . . an old one . . . a funny one? . . . Michael shrugs; the movie isn't funny, isn't supposed to be, but it's good . . . black and white . . . except every now and then he sees a flash of yellow on the screen, some sort of mistake on the channel's part; or maybe the movie is so old that it's hard to show it the right way, maybe it's like a yellow stain, appearing, pulsing, rhythmically—-a commercial comes and Michael hops down off the chair and crosses the office and sits down in the bathroom . . . he's thinking of Pamela sitting here; it's too gross to get too excited but still . . . when he's done he leaves the bathroom and on the walk back to the chair sees the yellow light is still pulsing on the television screen and something very dark swirls in Michael's belly; pizza, beer, love, lust, he isn't sure, then thinks oh no, I might know what might be making that light, that pulsing, and he turns around to face the Givens Sensor Board for the first time ever with a mind to see if it's come to life . . .

. . . a flashing . . .

. . . it has . . .

. . . it's come to life . . .

. . . Michael's mouth is hanging open and he's burning up with fear, not sure what to *do*, this isn't supposed to happen this has never happened before . . . and he's an inch from the board now, his fingertip at the blinking light, trying to determine which plot it is, who is sending him a signal, is this really happening?, PLOT 22, he's checking the ledger, who is where?, but does it matter who it is? PLOT 22 is blinking, holy Christ, someone is alive out there . . .

FLASH!

. . . Michael runs to the window and looks out at the greater cemetery as if the person using the sensor might be standing upon their grave, calling for a stewardess . . . then he's back at the board and knows who it is, knows of course who it is because there's only one body in Samhattan Cemetery that could be breathing still, only one body buried today . . .

FLASH!

. . . lightning, and the mailman's sensor, too . . .

FLASHing

. . . Michael on the phone, immediately, talking to the police, telling them Randy Scotts's sensor is going off, yes, the Givens Sensor, first time Michael's ever seen one blink, PLOT 22, yes, what am I supposed to do?, should I start digging?, do I wait for you guys to get here?, do I—

FLASH!

. . . and the brief flat response from the officer on the phone . . .

"Leave him."

. . . two words followed by something else, a barb at the dead man, but *leave him* is all Michael hears . . .

. . . Michael on the phone with an ambulance now, worried that the police will arrest him somehow for disobeying (*leave him*), but what else to do, calling, frantic, getting someone on the line, someone in charge, someone to help, and that someone pauses and with no knowledge about how the police reacted, no way of knowing they were echoing the sentiments of Samhattan's police, they repeat,

"Leave him."

. . . Michael off the phone now, staring at the blinking Givens Sensor Board, shaking his head no, there's a man out there, begging for help, isn't dead, I can see his tombstone through the window, oh GOD HOW MUCH AIR IS IN A BOX THAT SIZE?!?! . . . Michael turning to face the black and white movie but he can't watch a movie now, can't eat a thing, has to get out of this office, has to get . . .

FLASH!

. . . on the phone with the Cemetery President . . . Bailey Smith . . . Bailey will tell him what to do . . . that he should already be doing it . . . but Bailey *isn't* saying that, Bailey is talking about how some people deserve things, some people make their own beds, leave him, Michael, leave him in the box . . .

CRACK–*BOOM!*

. . . Michael alone, more alone than before . . . feels the weight of the graveyard pressing in, like it's crawling in through the little window, all that decay, and Michael shaking his head no, come on, no, I'm gonna have to do this alone . . .

. . . out the office door, the wood crashing against the stone behind him . . . he's running to the shed, gets there faster than he plans, breathing hard, he's opening the shed, grabbing a shovel, still wet and muddy from this afternoon . . .

FLASH!

. . . lightning yes but the Givens Sensor Board blinking in his memory, too . . . with a shovel Michael runs along the pavement, his sneakers slick on the ground, crosses over wet grass, wet stones, giving earth, weak from the storm . . .

. . . PLOT 15, 16, 17 . . .

. . . Michael is thinking about Pamela, maybe he should call her, his phone is back in the office, maybe he should call Pamela, tell her he needs help, needs another hand, there's no way he's going to dig this guy up in time, how much time does he have?, do you know, Pamela? do you? . . .

. . . PLOT 18, 19, 20 . . .

. . . rain pools at his brow and pours down his cheeks, his nose, falling to his lips . . .

. . . PLOT 21 . . .

. . . he's thinking about Pamela, about her kissing him, their lips together in the office, how good it felt . . . how good it felt to talk to her, to laugh with her, to kiss her . . .

. . . PLOT 22 . . .

. . . Michael jams the shovelhead into the dirt, still soft, so soft, just buried today, so easy to get him out of there, hardly any work at all, but there's a sound, a cracking, not lightning, not a photo, but a footstep, behind him, behind Michael, from the shadows of the trees at the graveyard's edge, and a form, too, a big body in black, as if he's wearing the same shadows he emerges from . . .

"What are you doing. Michael?"

Father Stockard, standing so close now, close enough to reach for the shovel if he wanted to.

"The Givens Sensor Board," Michael starts to explain.

"Leave him."

Stockard's voice as level as his eulogies.

"Father?"

"Think of the girl's lips," Stockard says. "Think of the lips on the girl."

Rain falling. A grave at their feet. A light no doubt still blinking in the office.

"How did you know?"

It's only a half-question. And at the same time, it's two:

How did you know about the girl?

How did you know to be in the woods?

But both answers are obvious.

Father Stockard raises a hand, the palm flat toward the grave.

"Leave him."

Michael thinks about Pamela's lips.

Leave him, they said. They all said.

Michael backs up from the fresh plot, from the man who presses the button within.

Leave him, they said. They all said.

He's thinking of Pamela's lips. As Stockard recedes back into the shadows, Michael thinks of those lips against his own.

He's thinking of a whole town, too, agreeing to bury a man alive.

He turns and, as if just now realizing he's wet, huddles up into his shirt and crosses the cemetery again, carrying the shovel like it's just something to be put away, property of Samhattan, part of his job.

At the office he doesn't turn around, doesn't look back to PLOT 22 or any of the others.

He's thinking of Pamela, kissing him.

Thinking of her lips.

He leans the shovel against the stone wall and enters the office. Inside, he hops onto the chair and moves the television, trying so that it doesn't reflect the Givens Sensor Board behind him.

But it blinks. Whether he looks at it or not, it blinks.

It blinks to the rhythm of a whole town saying *leave him, leave him*—and it blinks, too, to the beat of Michael thinking of Pamela's lips and the wonders in there, in kissing a woman, as her nails dig into your back a little, your arms, not like fingernails on wood at all, not because she has done something wrong and needs to break free, but needs to break free all the same.

sharks with thumbs

DAVID JAMES KEATON

"The fly sat upon the axle-tree of the chariot-wheel and said, 'What a dust do I raise!'"—Aesop

YOU EVER GET the feeling someone is talking about you?

Like you're right at the end of the movie when the speaker starts popping and you hear that voice. Like once a week, right when you're finally starting to relax around this spider web of power cords and surge protectors, you're reminded you can never trust the wiring around here. Never move somewhere just because you like seeing a river out your window.

Remember when a nearby lightning strike fried something inside your picture tube and put a freaky green line through the middle of your screen? That green line was there for about six months, mercifully getting smaller and smaller and almost fading away until it was just a glowing yellow smear in the corner of the TV, like you'd smashed a lightning bug on the glass and never cleaned it up. You don't know if this room is some sort of electric Bermuda Triangle, but you can't risk any more equipment and that's why you move fast whenever you hear a speaker snap, crackle or pop.

You're ready to pull the plug when suddenly you're hearing two voices from the speaker that aren't part of the movie. You know this because the movie was at the end, right at the part where everyone gets what they deserve, and all you should be hearing is gunfire, one-liners and big, dumb music. However, this whispered conversation is something you'd hear in the middle of a flick, maybe the beginning, when you're not sure what the characters are really up to and you're supposed to be all suspicious of everyone.

The sad thing is he has no idea I hate his guts.

You sit down by the speaker, actually thinking about getting a glass to put between the television and your ear to hear the voices better.

Remember his last story? Even the goddamn dog was rolling his eyes.

You adjust your legs to get comfortable, hoping the reception lasts a while. You know the "hearing voices" thing is supposed to make you nervous, but it happens in this building sometimes. A couple times, a year back, when your surround-sound speakers were still working, you picked up some random banter between truckers. It's the bad wiring that does it. Sometimes, you'll suddenly get three more people in the middle of your phone call, and you'll find yourself answering a question about the first time you stuck a finger up someone's ass instead of answering your grandpa's question about car insurance.

But those fractured conversations lasted a minute at the most, and they were nowhere near as clear as this. This is like you're holding the tomato cans between two people, but their strings are coming out both of your ears.

If that bastard had any idea what people say about him . . .

Right then, the speaker crackles and the voices are buried under static. You lean in closer and bang your head on the glass. There's a final *POP!* and you yank the cord from the wall. You sit with your back to the TV, feeling the electricity tickle your neck as both you and the equipment power down. You reel in the cord, wrapping it around your knuckles, working to bend the prongs straight.

You hold your breath when you plug it back in. Thank Christ it still works. You stare at the green stain in the corner of the picture. It's back, but it doesn't bother you. You'd watch TV if the whole screen was green. Nothing happens in the corners of a movie anyway. A green sunset in this western? The gunfighters wouldn't even notice.

00:00:03:57—"LOVE WITHOUT A LIFE JACKET."

When you claim there's a long list of things about her that used to drive you nuts, you're not talking about a sheet of paper, or even a stack of paper with both sides filled plus illustrations in the margin and a flip-cartoon in the corner to reenact the top ten, you're talking about the kind of list where you could stand at the top of the stairs and you let the pages drop and they bounce down the steps and unroll out the door and down the hill and across the street and over the cars and stray dogs are crashing through it like a finish line. That's how long your list is. And at the top of that list? Surprisingly, it's not how shrill her voice gets when she gets drunk. It would have to be the way she used to walk into the bathroom to use the phone. It drove you crazy. Well, maybe not *crazy* crazy, but crazy enough to ruin your day. Crazy enough to think about the word "crazy" until it renders the word meaningless. Luckily, that's one thing you don't have to worry about any more. This new girl though? Sometimes she stares right at you, even when she's not on the phone. And she lets you listen to even her most embarrassing conversations. And she's never turning the volume down on the receiver in case the caller says something you shouldn't hear. She's never pressing the phone hard against her head, so afraid a secret would sneak out while she was talking. So hard her ear looks like a ripe tomato slice when she finally snaps the phone shut.

This new girl though? She's got nothing to hide. Probably doesn't even own a phone. She's in the bathroom right now, and you trust her so much you're not even turning down the volume on the TV to listen to her piss.

Then the toilet flushes once, twice, and chokes on a third attempt. She walks back into the room, then slides down to her hip in a quick motion that would make any gunfighter shake in his boots. Your smile slips when you see her phone drop into her pocket.

"I thought you drowned," you tell her.

00:00:28:09—"BUGS CANNOT USE TOOLS."

It's too cold to have a fly on the window, on either side of the glass. There's no leaves on trees. The birds are long gone. The morning before, you had to dig your car out from under the wake of a snowplow with red fingers. There's nothing alive outside without fur, nothing alive out there smaller than a rat, because you brought your rat inside with you.

But there it is.

One of those big, blue-eyed garbage flies, crawling around the edges of the glass like it was summer out there, like there isn't a kid kicking the head off a snowman two houses down. In a daze, you pull the black tape off the window, taking some of the paint with it, knowing it's going to take another hour to seal that window back up. You yank it up with a grunt, cold air freezing the snot in your nose.

It's the first time you've ever seen one trying to get in instead of out.

What the hell do you feed it? Usually, you're trying to stop a fly from drinking off the edge of your pop can instead of keeping it alive. So you just stand back and let it ricochet off the walls like a drunk hoping it'll find a stray cornflake or damp toenail to munch on. You watch it circle the room about six more times, increasingly confused by its behavior, cruising frantic figure-eights about a foot from the ceiling. Finally, you grab a stuffed animal still upside down in a corner from three ex-girlfriend's ago and chase it toward the bathroom. If you're going to have a pet fly it should be near the bowl, right? You're a pretty clean person, but you figure if there's anything around this place a fly can eat, it's going to be in there. Hell, cats and dogs get water bowls, don't they? You consider writing the name "Spike" on the side of your toilet.

00:00:42:31—"YOU'RE GONNA EAT *WHAT* EXACTLY?"

The next day, your new girl comes over to watch a movie. Halfway through, the speakers start popping again, and while you're screwing with the wires in the back of the box, she sighs and runs to the bathroom and suddenly you're listening to her piss even though she's a hundred feet and a closed door away. It's splashing so loud you flinch and think she squatted down over your head, and that's when you remember the fly.

Same old shit, you know? Why do I even come over here?

The voice is fading, so your crawl over to your bookbag and pull out your headphones. Several books tumble onto the ground, but you don't retrieve them. The ones that land face-up are *If They Move . . . Kill 'Em!: The Life and Times of Sam Peckinpah* by David Weddle, *Motherless Brooklyn* by Jonathan Lethem, and *Choose Your Own Adventure #2: Journey Under the Sea* by R.A. Montgomery. You don't have time to imagine the significance of those selections and you quickly try plugging the headphones directly into the TV and get zapped with static instead. Like a fool you sit there, with the headphones unplugged and dangling, still listening for the voices. The headphones are new. They're the kind that go in your ears instead of over them, sometimes too deep, the kind that you might lose in your head if you scratch too hard. Like you always do. And just like they always told you would happen when people are talking shit, your ears really do start burning.

I have to go watch the rest of this horrible movie, if he ever gets it to work . . .

You're so excited about hearing someone's voice through unplugged headphones that, at first, you don't care what she's saying. It's not like the truckers you heard through the speakers before. This time you can only hear one side of the conversation. Her voice is a non-stop sigh, like the endless hiss of a tire valve.

Maybe I'll pretend I'm sick.

Then the toilet flushes, and it's as loud as a cyclone. You grab the sides of the TV in case you start spinning around a drain and get sucked on down. You're so wired about this discovery that you're smiling like a maniac when she comes out, struggling to keep your new eavesdropping skills to yourself. By the time you finish the western, you realize it's not just the headphones. The fly was in there with her. Always the fly.

. . . the first time I've ever seen one trying to get in instead of out . . .

00:01:34:07—"SPIDERS ARE NOT OUR FRIENDS."

After she's gone home, you're thinking you should call NASA or whatever government office deals with the physical manifestation of metaphors. Or, at the very least, spy on about ten more people you suspect are talking shit about you. You're already making a mental list and considering how you might propose marriage to her when you go back into the bathroom.

The fly is dying. At least, it's moving slower. Your eyes follow its sluggish path until it vanishes into a crack in the porcelain box behind the toilet. You panic and shove the clock radio and empty box of tissues onto the floor and take off the lid, shaking your head in disbelief as you look inside. Impossible.

The fly is caught in a spiderweb, flailing like a drunk trying to navigate beaded curtains at a party. Spiders in the toilets? Flies in the snow? You wonder what's next.

Suddenly, you know what to do. You stick it outside the bathroom window still glued to a tangle of web, and, just as you hoped, the cold air seems to revive it. It's moving fast again, but it never gets back to full speed. It's not going to last much longer. You check the clock radio on the bathroom floor to try and estimate how much time the fly has left. The display is flashing a green "12:00 a.m." since you never figured out how to set it. Now you've got two problems. A time limit, you're not good with math, *and* you can't get everyone into your bathroom to spy on them.

Staring at the word "Spike" on the bowl, you decide you should take your fly for a walk. Once, your grandpa told you he used to stick flies to his fingers with honey when he was a boy.

"We were bored as hell back then," he said, "Now, don't think I'm reminiscing so I can tell you how it built character or any noble shit like that 'cause the only thing playing with flies does is make you wish you had toys instead."

He told you his flies didn't fly too long because he always smacked them just a little bit too hard to slow them down, sort of like your grandma did to you.

Yours won't last long either, you realize, and you have to move faster than you're moving. You look around the bathroom, find some dental floss the last girl left behind. You have no trouble grabbing it out of the air, and it's still sluggish enough to tie a leash around its body without risking a swat to stun it, but the floss is too thick for a knot. You look around and around and around, and finally your eyes stop on the answer stuck to the side of your toilet, underlining your pet fly's new name. You crouch down to get closer.

All this time you thought it was a crack in the porcelain, but it's a long black hair stuck to the moisture on the side of the bowl. You peel it loose and hold it up to the window. Black. Thick. Curly as phone cord. One of hers. You half-expect it to twitch like a severed spider's leg, and even though it's just a hair, even though you haven't cleaned the bathroom since she left, you're amazed to find a piece of her still here. You'd be less surprised to find a five-foot-five layer of skin she'd shed, rustling and drying in a corner.

You tie the leash quick. Too easily. You decide it's because you had one of your hands buried in her hair for so many years that when they're not connected to her head any more they still know your fingers, and sometimes you can still get them to do what you want.

The fly grabs her hair and starts stroking it with two front legs. Does that damn thing have thumbs, you wonder?

Impossible. If bugs had tiny thumbs, they would have already invented a tiny wheel.

You tie it to your finger where the skin is still white from the ring she gave you, then you put on headphones plugged into nothing, a power cord dangling down and tucked into a belt-loop. You start your day.

00:01:09:13—"BRINGING A FLY TO A FIST FIGHT."

You're out the door looking at your watch, and you see it's time for free doughnuts. The gas station makes new ones and throws out the old ones at exactly 8:00 every day. They're always real cool about giving you those old doughnuts, but you got to time it just right. The fly tugs on its leash, circling your ring finger, then resigning to wrap itself around the steering wheel. You worry about a sudden turn breaking the leash, so you pull over and carefully unwind the hair without breaking it, thinking about the old westerns your grandpa used to make you watch, and the way the cowboys made their horse stay put by dropping a leather strap across a bush or twig without even tying it up or anything.

Inside the gas station, the girl behind the counter smiles, and you grab one of each kind of doughnut before the kid can slide them into the trash. He sighs and waits for you to drop them into your bag, then quickly clears the case. You take longer than usual because you're trying to keep one hand behind your back. You don't know what would be worse, someone thinking that flies follow you around, or someone seeing that you keep one on a tiny little leash.

When she's counting the cigarettes behind her, you tie the fly to a bag of peanuts near the cash register, not really tying a knot, just winding the hair around the peanuts once, knowing it will stay, then you run out to pump your gas.

Inside, you see the girl at the counter talking to the next guy in line and he throws a thumb your way. You quickly pull the headphones from inside your shirt and pop them in to see if this guy is talking shit. Amazingly, he isn't. But she is.

He just tries to act like he had no idea they were free even though he was in here last night . . .

Your head down, you run in and grab your fly. For the first time since you started going there, she talks to you.

"You paying for those peanuts, asshole?"

You stop at the post office and check the stamp machines in the lobby. Just as you hoped, there's a wagging tongue of five three-cent stamps sticking out. You tear them free and put them in your pocket. Ever since the price of stamps went up, people usually leave the difference behind. Every little bit helps. It helps you stay on the periphery of responsibility but also feel like you have a job. For some reason, this feels like integrity.

The girl behind the counter smiles and waves as you leave.

He doesn't have three cents?

What the hell? You scratch your ears hard to see if the voice goes away. You scratch harder. If you could scratch your ears with your foot, you would. You don't understand. The headphones are around your wrist. The fly isn't anywhere near her. And neither are you. How is this happening?

You go to the diner. Are there females behind every counter? Do they grow them back there, just out of sight, ten more rising up behind every register, and you can't see them just yet because they haven't grown high enough for their heads to clear the cash drawer.

The waitress has a pencil shaped like a tiny pool cue. You stare at it, hypnotized, every time she takes your order. You asked her about it once, but she ignored you. Tonight is no different.

"Excuse me," you say. "There is a fly in my soup . . . "

She looks down at the fly tugging against its leash on your finger.

" . . . and I think the little bastard just lassoed me."

She wanders away, a miraculous combination of expressions on her face that you didn't think was possible. You stop in the restroom on the way out. In the urinal, just above the line-of-fire, there's a sticker that declares: "You hold in your hand the power to stop a rape!" For a second, you think the sign refers to the fly crawling across your knuckles, and you're suddenly ashamed. "Is it so wrong to be a fly whisperer?" you want to ask the urinal cake. When you're zipping up, one headphone falls from your left ear and plops into the yellow water. You sigh, pull the rest of the wires out of your shirt and toss them all in with it. Your obsessions have their limits.

You stop at the garage to get air for your tires. Your Rabbit's always had this problem, but new tires are expensive, and if you find the right gas stations, air is free. This garage is one of the only places in town where you don't have to pay fifty cents to fill them up, and the guy who owns the place gives you a knowing smile and the better part of a wave. You wave back whole-heartedly and accidentally bounce your fly off your forehead. He's cool. The last time you stopped by, this man smiled and agreed that paying for air was "freaking ridiculous."

You get out, tie the fly to the compressor, snake the hose, hit the button.

How fucking low do you have to be to steal air . . . c'mon.

Was that a woman's voice? You thought it was all men in that garage. Could it be a girl from one of your earlier stops? What kind of reception does this fly get, anyway?

I heard of someone stealing dirt once, only that was from a construction site and that shit ain't cheap. But air? Nope. Never heard of anyone stealing air.

The compressor stops rumbling. Your fly strains on its leash, then curls back to land on a coil of hose.

I've heard of people stealing water once, but that was during the war.

You throw the hose. 29 pounds of pressure will have to do. In your tires and your brain.

Honestly, who the hell steals air . . .

You can't contain your rage any longer. You yell at the shadows in the garage.

"Well, who the hell *sells* air?!"

Two mechanics slide out from under their cars and into the sunlight. They stand and walk toward you, wiping grease from fists, blowing sweat off noses, staring at you like you're nuts.

00:01:45:22—"FLY FACTORY REVEALED."

Do you ever get the feeling someone is talking shit about you?

You stop at the video store to steal some movie inserts. You do this because those throwaway pieces of paper in DVDs really are great reading. Sure, sometimes you get a paragraph of summary or some decent production notes or an interview, but that's not what you're looking for. You steal the inserts because you like to read the chapter titles. It's like a whole movie in ten seconds. The chapter titles tell you all you need to know.

You grab a random one as if to prove your point. Okay maybe not so random. You've read this one before:

Sharks with Guns

- "Love on a Lifeboat"
- "Sharks Are Using Tools?"
- "Are You Gonna Eat That?"
- "Dolphins Are Not Our Friends!"
- "Bringing a Shark to a Gun Fight"
- "Shark Factory Revealed!"
- "Duel to the Deaf"
- "Quitting the Coast Guard for Good"

See? What are you missing from the story after you read that? It's all there. The crisis, the love interest, the surprise ending. Didn't someone once say there are really only three stories you can tell? A stranger comes to town, and a man goes on a journey? Man sort of talks to fly?

You study the box and snicker. It's one of those pre-fab cult movies that are so popular these days, and you scoff. There's no way that shark could hold that chainsaw, much less a gun. They don't have any thumbs.

Now that would be a scary movie, you think. If they had thumbs, they could make a phone call. It wouldn't have to bite anyone. Just show one shark whip out a phone and every asshole in the audience would start screaming their head off.

Could happen. You've seen more far-fetched things than that in a movie. One time, in the bathtub, your ex-girlfriend checked her phone underwater so you couldn't see who called her. You figured she'd ruined it, but it turned out the phone worked fine when you blew the bubbles off of it later that night to find the number she was hiding.

You slip some DVD booklets into your sleeves. You avoid the Blu-Rays since they rarely have them. Then you go up to the counter and grab one of those free internet CDs. She *is* up there, and you see a strange light flickering in her eyes and realize this girl is watching something under the register with the volume turned down. You wonder when she snuck a TV in there and now you have to know what movie she's watching. Is she watching something she's not supposed to? Why else would she have the volume down like that?

On the way out, you finally see what it is. A security monitor. She was watching you steal those movie inserts the entire time, and you can see yourself in the corner of her screen, standing by the door, hunched and alone, unbelievably small, looking over her shoulder, guilty as hell and green as the sunset.

Sitting in the car with your hands on the steering wheel, your heart jumps. The fly is dangling on the hair like a suicide, so you turn on the air-conditioning, open all the vents, and hold it in front of the cold air. It starts to climb back up its leash like a spider. It's moving slow, but it's still alive. You realize that every time you hide the fly, it starts to die.

Sounds like a children's rhyme, doesn't it?

You have to get home. Or get it to the bathroom. Or a restroom. You think about how cold toilet water is even on the hottest day, and you realize that, even if you know what's been floating around in there, it's got to be tempting to swim in it when you're burning up. For a bug, you mean.

You drive fast, checking the size of the gas stations, trying to gauge whether they're big enough for a public restroom. You glance down at the fly and see it slump on the string and swing from the hair like a pendulum. You slam on the brakes and make a hard right into the smallest gas station you've ever seen. You ask the third-grade boy behind the counter if they have a restroom. He says no and turns back to counting the candy bars. In desperation, you hold up your hand with the limp fly swinging from your finger.

"Dude, my fly needs to drink from a toilet fast or it's going to die."

The kid smiles over a huge piece of gum and stares at you for 13 . . . 14 . . . 15 seconds. Then he points to the door behind the beer.

"Hurry up."

Unfuckingbelievable. You guess he's seen stranger things than this.

Inside the bathroom, you're assaulted by a stench worse than any outhouse, and you walk over to the toilet and cautiously lift the lid. The water is clear as a mountain spring, and you carefully lower your hand until the fly's head just breaks the surface. You think about the part of the buddy-cop movie right around the second act where the drunk partner has to get revived by the more wise-cracking partner, so he shoves his face in the bowl. You're much more gentle than that.

And it works. The fly starts to activate, cranking its legs over its head to clean itself off. You smile. It looks like it's playing a tiny air guitar. No, it would need thumbs to do that.

"Ears burning?" the clerk asks you on your way out.

You smile. They've been burning for years. Once, you read a story about a mythical creature that ate nothing but ears, left behind the rest of the animal, just snacked on them like potato chips, leaving a trail of stone-deaf barnyard beasts all through the Dirty South.

Sometimes, you envied them.

Back in the car, you wonder how many people would believe you're actually worried about this fly. You've never taken care of cats very well. And plants? Forget about it. But this feels like everyone's fly now. You feel the weight of new responsibility. You try to imagine yourself in the waiting room at the veterinarian with your fly. You'd be the only person who a kid with a sick hermit crab could feel good laughing at. You watch it perched on the radio knob, cleaning its wings, and you stab the gas pedal over and over, keeping the car in neutral, smell of hot metal in your nostrils.

You realize you've spent more time worrying about this fly than you worried about all of your ex-girlfriends combined. Even when that one had to get her appendix out. You mess with your stereo.

Equalizer, you think. *That's a good word.*

Suddenly you understand something. It just seems like you care about the fly more than her, but if you were to line them all up against the wall and put a little pencil mark over their heads, you'd find that actually your feelings about the fly and her are precisely the same. And it's not that you think more of a fly really, it's just that, the more you find out about human beings, and the more you listen to their voices when they don't think anyone is around who can hear, the less you think of them.

00:01:58:19—"YOUR GEARS ARE BURNING."

One time you told her you were going to invent a phone that, instead of ringing, released a swarm of bees. You said it would guarantee she would answer the thing every time you needed her to. She didn't understand what the hell you were talking about. You think she thought you were talking about some special ringtone, and you said, "Okay, listen, how about just three small bees, just enough of a scare to buzz around your ears and make you swat the air in a panic every single time I called you?" She had no answer to that. Later, your uncle invented something that played cupid with telephone numbers and license plates, but you don't tell too many people that story, unless they've had as much to drink as him.

You walk out of the bathroom, and you see she was reading that same magazine again, the one with the prescription label with your ex-girlfriend's name on it. You told her once how this old girlfriend used to snort painkillers off those very same pages, which seems like a worse addiction than drinking, but it didn't really feel like it at the time. You'd think that alone would make her not want to read the thing, but she folds a page over to remember her place. You used to try to get a letter published in one of her magazines so she'd stumble across your name and accidentally listen to you.

Wait, did you say "prescription" earlier instead of "subscription"? Because that is exactly what you meant.

The speaker suddenly starts popping again.

Shit fuck shit . . .

You pull the cords on everything. You hate the wiring in this house more than you've hated anyone. It eventually destroys everything. You hear water running in the sink, and you figure she's going to be in there awhile. She does that sometimes. Runs the sink so you can't hear. Like you're really listening to hear her pissing? Come on. Then you remember something, and you quickly crawl to your box of old cassette tapes rotting in the corner. It's your worst, last pair of headphones. Huge ratty ones from the '80s that cover your entire fucking head. You hesitate to put them on. Your headphones are getting bigger and bigger, and you seem to be sliding further back down the headphone-evolutionary ladder. Once you're holding them in your hands and blowing the dust and insect shells off the foam, you realize they're older than you thought.

These are from the '70s, not the '80s, no joke, and they're also the only thing left of your mother. One time, your mom came up to you and put these over your ears, and you were pouting about something like kids do, so you didn't say anything, didn't even look up, but you didn't take them off your ears either. And you still can't remember the song she wanted you to hear or why she wanted you to hear it. Maybe there was something funny in the song? Maybe the lyrics meant something important to her? Maybe she thought it was your favorite band? You can't remember. You were too busy ignoring her for reasons long forgotten. And now you'll never know what song it was because you just sat there, arms crossed, mad about something stupid, frowning until the song was over and she finally shrugged and walked away.

The wind blows the dead fly around on its string. Your ring finger is white from lack of circulation, so you unwrap the leash from your skin, waiting for the blood flow to return and paint the white knuckle back to red. You're amazed at how strong her hair was.

The strange thing is, when you think back to it, you could have sworn you were outside, sitting with crossed legs and crossed arms under a tree when your mother walked up and put those headphones over your ears. The cord couldn't have reached that far, could it?

You hide in the bathroom awhile. It's true that the bathroom is the last place where the remains of a relationship will linger. Is it all those half-empty bottles and soaps—or is it just hairs around the toilet?

You're no scientist. And even though you still have at least one toy stethoscope, you're not that kind of doctor.

00:02:00:07—"END CREDITS AND IRONIC THEME MUSIC."

The next day you finally take out the trash. Not a second too late, either. You can see a box of sweet-and-sour chicken moving down there on its own, and suddenly that mysterious fly isn't such a miracle any more because you can see at least three more green-eyed buzz bombs bouncing around in the bag with their snouts dipping in and out of a month of your scraps. Your grandpa used to say that tiny fish would appear in a mud puddle if it sat undisturbed long enough. Not true. He was lying. Those were mosquitoes all along.

You recite your favorite line from *Titus Andronicus*, the movie adaptation of the Shakespeare play everybody hates:

"'What dost thou strike at, Marcus, with thy knife?' 'At that that I have killed, my lord, a fly.' 'Out on thee, murderer! Thou killst my heart.'"

You know how they say the bathroom is the last place your girlfriend exists? You were wrong. You meant the garbage. You take out the bag, then keep walking past the dumpster to throw your headphones into the river before you change your mind. It's one of those rivers that looks good from a distance. Then you're standing next to it and you catch a smell of what's been dumped in there for years. Wasn't this the river that caught on fire because of the pollution? You'd think your toilet would have ignited from all the cigarettes she flicked in it. Is this the river where that little boy swore he saw the shark?

The headphones bob along, riding the brown waves, then something under the water takes a couple bites and finally pulls them down forever. There's a girl standing next to you when you turn around.

"You know what you looked like to me just then?" she asks. "You looked like the last scene of a movie. The part where the sheriff throws away his badge."

"Hold out your hand," you tell her, not expecting her to do it. And when she uncurls her fingers for you, you expect something to fly away.

"What's your name?"

"Maggie. But I go by 'Shell,' short for 'Michelle,' my middle name."

"Of course you do. I'm not calling you that."

"Then don't."

"I've seen you before, haven't I?"

"I live in your building."

"Have you ever had problems with your wiring?"

"No." She laughs. "Have you?"

"All the time."

"You look like you do. You should get a surge protector. Seriously. I have three of them."

You stare for seven . . . eight . . . nine seconds. Then you write your phone number in her hand. Just for laughs you scribble a fly underneath it.

"Sorry, I like drawing flies."

"I know. They're easy to make. Like a smiley face. You know why everyone draws smiley faces? Because there are less than five lines you need before you can recognize it."

"I believe it."

You hear the buzzing sound again, and you know what it is before she even pulls it out. She smiles an apology and presses the phone deep into her face, quickly walking away before she starts talking.

You walk off in the opposite direction to give her some privacy. You think of your phone number and the fly you drew on her skin, and you cup your hand around your ear like a seashell. Even years later, when you're both miles away and her head and her hand are the only things visible above the waves smacking your face and filling your nostrils, you still keep your hand over your ear, and you can still hear every word of her conversation like she's swimming right next to you. Until you pull her under.

bad lieutenant

TONY BURGESS

THE TOP OF the hill is a house, beneath the moon, part of the stars. A figure walks up—a man, in a heavy canvas coat and a sagging hat. Closer to him is his wet breath and beyond the sprinkled lights. He is getting close to the door and as he does, we look around frantically—if this is it, if we are going to leave everything outside when we go in, this is all we get to leave.

Darkness. Glow. Implied ground. Not enough.

"Beal! Beal! Listen up!"

Low light. Just soft flame on cupped boards and dim sea shapes. On a bench made of split logs sits a hollow headstone. A radio with a yellow heart polished to life by a fist on a wide wheel.

"Pardon, Beal! Pardon! Sit."

Beal turns to drop the door back.

"There was another."

The round man at the dial jerks. Beal shows his face. The other shows his.

Beal has tiny black eyes that sit not on his face but at the outside corners of it. They can't be seeing a resolved image. His nostrils are tall and thin and sit a hair apart. It looks like he breathes through neat wounds inflicted by a fork. His mouth is pink and alone and is pursed like cherub. It is a baby's mouth. Baby lips.

"I said another, Cuddy."

Cuddy has turned back to the dial. Beal's head, small at the front and heavy back from the crown, is trembling and shivering. It is not possible to look at Cuddy for long with Beal's face hanging in the room.

"So?"

Cuddy contracts. Large ball into not as large, in a single convulsion.

"So! So! So!"

Beal's head is a jungle bird, bouncing and presenting itself, repeating, shrieking the word *so*.

Cuddy absorbs this then expands again.

"You know what I mean. It happens. I'm tired of freaking out."

Beal's eyelids roll in, making mean slits. His yelling has made blood surface around his lips. The lips are not fully finished, it seems, and all of this tissue is probably being used too vigorously, too soon. Beal breathes in sharply, drawing skin into his nostrils revealing it as slough. He holds the breath and releases it out through some improbable exit under his thin hair.

"I'm not freaking out."

Cuddy's body puddles a bit as he calms.

"Good. It doesn't change anything."

"No. Doesn't *explain* anything."

Cuddy taps the yellow dial.

"Nope. Doesn't."

Beal has stopped trembling and his face is gelling. It is slightly different now, his features lower.

"I'll get it."

Beal waits for Cuddy to say 'Ok' or something.

"Ok?"

Cuddy raises a hand.

"Shhhh. What? Yes. Ok. Sure."

Beal leaves the small single-roomed building through its only door.

Cuddy pools toward the dial, his upper body focusing on the face. He reaches over and pulls a tin chain leading up to a hanging bulb and it snuffs. The only light now comes from the dial and it is expanding up Cuddy's face and we are forced to look.

A buzz from the machine. A crunching voice.

" . . . this is about human beings. Victims. Survivors. We can champion this or that later. But right now, my god, we are devastated . . . "[1]

Cuddy squeals and convulses. He leans back, revealing a squat three-legged chair beneath him. Turns out that's the source of the squeal. He has inadvertently nudged the dial and lost the transmission. The chair squawks.

"Beal! Beal! Pardon! Beal! Pardon!"

Cuddy rubs his hands on his knees and his head sinks.

"Oh Beal."

Cuddy sits like this for a while, flopped inward and wheezing lightly. In time he reaches up and taps the dial but the machine is dead. The sound of a spring within him. Cuddy pushes upward. It is clear he is unable to walk.[2]

"Beal!"

The noise again.[3] Higher in tone and stretched out.

"Beal. Beal. Beal."

It's a despairing voice that doesn't stop. It trails off into a upset drone.

"Beal."

Cuddy leans into the radio to steady himself. He is concentrating,

---

1. All of the radio comes out at once. a single wavelength excised from the line. On it was suffering and calliope and dancing and colours. a bent copper tube with a cold hollow core. This is what we can't do. This, what I've done. Take a single length of wave out. It is a thing along which it happens, but lifted up or dropped down, pinched clean at either end it is nothing more than a whistle, a dull tunnel within which shatters the foreign lengths. None of them transmitted and all of them chaotic. And so I have you here, what I said was copper but not sure, and I am sad that what I have done is so outside of anything I could say about it that it envies the strangest of things—the impression of sight on a pillow—the effect of daylight savings on the magnetic field of an object lost at the back of a sock drawer. It does, however, give us permission to enumerate events that fall short of any register.

2. The decision I made, to stand and find my coffee.

3. The idea out there that the universe is nothing more than a giant face. I am drawing our attention to its right eye. Nebula and super nova and spiral galaxies, any of which are indetectable because of scale, are prevented from escaping by the sac of the eye. The thing we are noticing, however, and we have nearly forgotten the point of this, is that one of you, out of disinterest in this writing, is imagining the vast hollow beneath the retracted lid. It requires specificity to isolate this now—the effect of losing interest in the description and the introduction of the impossible space beneath the eyelid. This has caused light and that's the thing to measure.

afraid of falling. Cuddy settles eventually his upper back flating like a squeeze box. The yellow light on the radio fades from neglect and the room sinks into tar.

"Cod! Cod! Coddy!"

Beal is mispornouncing Cuddy's name. The light bulb lights up, Beal's face is different again.[4] He has obviously been trying to push his features up to where they began but has only managed to drive his eyes beneath his skin. They roll and quiver like submerged hatchlings. His nostrils are broader now and no longer symmetrical, and each is pulling at the air.

"Cod! Cod! That smell! Cod! What is that?!"

One of Beal's feet rests on the back of a shirtless man.[5] The relative size of things is revealed. Beal and Cuddy are very nearly giants, at least twice the size of a person. The ceiling of the cabin is probably four metres high. The man is facedown, dead or unconscious. Cuddy is crying.

"I had it on. I heard something."

Beal is gagging as he sweeps the man up and drapes him like a gown across his arm.

"What's that smell? Cod! It's fuckin' awful."

Beal glares at Cod, tears smashed across the face we were forced to see not 45 minutes ago.

"Did you hear me? I heard something on this."

Cuddy slams his hand against the radio.

" . . . not an injection or a cream. Tell your doctor if these feelings develop . . . "

---

4. There is a stone on a planet—it matters what planet and what stone, though we can't say because we do not know. But it is a startling fact that because of our sentence we have eliminated a great number of stones and planets not referred to. This elimination has brought us much closer to our referent but we remain and always will remain, unable to complete this knowing. The stone knows, however, and is made suddenly aware.

5. There is an idea out there that can be brought to bear on the stone on the planet. The idea follows that in the fullness of infinity that stone has become the first letter d that denied us the coffee. (*What does this refer to?—Ed.*) There is also the lazy guess that the conditions which brought this about are unreproducible.

Beal and Coddy freeze.

" . . . one of many questions investigators are asking right now . . . "

Coddy shakes his head slowly.

"I can't believe what I'm hearing."

Beal holds the man under his chin and extends his arms,

"Well, I can't believe what I'm smelling!"

" . . . they had a son together so there's a lot to learn about what she knew in the days leading up to . . . "

"I had to shit! What am I supposed to do?"

The man drops from Beal's throat into his hands.

"Oh yeah. I'm sorry, Cod."

"Oh, yeah. I'm sooooooo sorry, Cod."

" . . . this was well-planned. He was ready to die. This isn't the act of someone totally insane . . . "

Beal's eyes sink even further beneath his face in an inobvious sign of contrition.[6] Cuddy listens to the radio as Beal uses the man to clean his backside.

" . . . and that of course prompts more questions from around the country and that's a big reason they said what they said and why they said it in such a powerful way . . . "

The lights in the valley are visible through the hillside, burnt earlier this year by a wildfire. It's a small city whose name is known around the world. From films and stories that find in it a handy setting. Stories spread through piracy mostly. Stolen by anyone from anywhere. *A River Runs Through It. The Bridges of Madison County. BASEketball. Basket Case. Basquiat.*

---

6. There is the pulling back from the mouth of a recently bitten piece of toast. Then there is the interrupted return of the toast to the mouth. A second bite is deferred due to savouring the first. It was a miscalculation. I am going to say this again: It was a miscalculation. Saying it again was deliberate and an invitation to the hand to put the toast to the mouth even as it is still savouring. A conflict is noted but more importantly it is given a shape in heaven. That shape cannot exist properly because there is no heave and so it reverts to a single wavelength. So that these things can exist we preserve the wavelength but divorce it from these givens.

how the
light gets in
MICHAEL
PAUL GONZALEZ

YOU WILL HEAR *their voices when you try to sleep.*

This was written in bright orange paint marker in desperate, trembling letters on the wall of a religious alcove. It stood out among the small paintings of saints and messages of hope that adorned Salvation Mountain. When we first saw it, we thought it was desecration. By the time everything was done, I understood that it was a warning.

We were eight miles away from the Salton Sea, a quick stop to film some b-roll and see the sights out in the middle of the vast nothing. Salvation Mountain was a singular work of insanity or religious devotion, depending on your perspective. Thousands of gallons of paint, hay, glue, and trash sculpted into the hellish desert as a last refuge. It was the first stop on our road to hell.

A little ways up the road was Slab City, an enclave of people who'd reclaimed an abandoned artillery range in the desert, parked their motor homes, and started a strange, off-the-grid community. Sharon and I were there to interview the residents and document their lives for a fluff piece on the late news back in LA. The state government was getting ready to impose some water and land restrictions, and the locals were ready to fight. It was exactly as exciting as it sounds. Still, we'd needed an excuse to get away from the city and spend more time together. Sharon loved camping. I am not a fan of the outdoors, but I loved her more than I hated dirt, so what was a girl to do?

I don't know if the locals were always open and friendly, but they were nice enough to us. We set up our camera by an old spindly tree decorated with countless shoes strung by their laces. There were dozens of locals hanging around that day, and every one of them demanded to say their piece on camera, hopeful that we'd get the message out to anyone who might sympathize with their quest for freedom and lend support. They wanted us to understand what brought them to the desert and what stopped them from going back to civilization.

That's all I want, too. I want you to understand what brought us out to the desert and what we left there.

After we wrapped, we got to talking to a couple of the locals and decided to spend the night there. They took us everywhere, insistent that we document the lives they'd created so that the world wouldn't think this was just a bunch of hippies in the desert trying to freeload. There was an open air installation called East Jesus that had nothing to do with religion and everything to do with turning garbage into beautiful art. Houses, bike repair shops, craftsmen and artisans plying their trade. When the sun started going down, they took us to The Range, a stage and open air restaurant where the locals gathered every Saturday for food, music, and stories.

Somewhere around our fourth beer or fifth joint, one of them asked if we'd heard of the crack in the sky over the Salton Sea. She was all leathery skin and grey dreadlocks, told us about how she'd moved out this way back when her husband was still serving with the Marines during the birth of the Cold War. She said there were things he was privy to that got him killed. He would tell her about these experiments they ran out in the restricted area, way back in Patton's day. Something worse than the atom bomb that was supposed to split atoms in a way that hadn't been tried before. One of those world-enders that the military likes to call peacekeepers. She said he knew too much about it and that's why they killed him.

Sharon whispered to me that he probably ran off with one of the younger, smoother artist chicks. I started to pull out the camera to talk to her on tape, then felt a warm hand rest softly but firmly on my forearm

"Just let her alone." An old man from the next table over squeezed my arm, two gentle pulses. He murmured in my ear, “She’ll stop talking soon enough. You’re here to help us, right? You put Doreen on camera and it’ll scuttle the whole thing. I used to do what you did, way back in the day. I get it. But can you just take the rest of the night off and enjoy the music? We’ve been nothing but nice to you.”

Sharon pursed her lips and nodded at me, hoisting her beer bottle. “Dee’s a workaholic. It’s one of the things we fight about at home.”

I slid the camera back into my bag and picked up my beer bottle. “All work and no play.”

“No such thing out here.” The old guy smiled at me. “And thank you kindly.”

It was one of those *thank yous* that was tinged with a healthy dose of *fuck you.* I didn’t want to wear out our welcome. This was the closest thing to a date night that Shar and I had had in a long time.

Doreen smiled at us through the whole exchange. “Are you two married?”

“We’ve been talking about it,” I said.

“For a long time,” Sharon said. “A really long time.”

“It’s legal now, right? What are you waiting for?”

“What *are* we waiting for, Dee?”

“What was your marriage like?” I asked Doreen.

She jumped right back into her conspiracy story, said the night before he disappeared, her husband told her to watch the sky at noon because something was going to happen that would change the world. She took their car up to the top of a ridge with a pair of his field glasses and watched where he told her to watch. There was no explosion, she said. Just a weird ripple in the air that she kept calling the crack in the sky. He didn’t make it home from work that day. Nobody came to inform her that he’d deserted or died. They just erased him. No benefits for her. No memories. She said they stole all of his photos while she slept, his clothes too. Like she’d never been married.

“That was the worst part,” she said. “All of those years, everything we built. All of the little things, you know? His face? His smell. His . . . you know, everything.”

She seemed lost in the moment.

“I had friends, people I used to write to every week. They’d get suspicious if I stopped, you know? I think that’s why they didn’t come after me, too. Ray’s only friends were in the service, and they were loyal to the Corps. If they had anything to tell me about what happened to him, they didn't say boo."

The old guy wandered back to our table and laid a hand on Doreen's shoulder. "It's getting late, Doreen. I don't want you walking across the street in the middle of the night. Let me get you home."

She reluctantly stood up. "If you have radios, you can go out there and hear it. Probably film it too. Forget this water rights stuff. There's bigger things out there the people need to know about. Go out there by Bombay Beach where the ground is burned."

"All right, Doreen," he said, turning her by the shoulder and casting a glance at us as he walked away.

"Such interesting people," Sharon said.

The music and festivities were still going, and the booze had worked its way nicely into my blood. Sharon asked me to dance, and we did. We forgot about Doreen and got lost in a haze of smoke and hooch and good music. When we went back to our little pup tent at the end of the night, I asked Sharon what she thought of the story.

"Probably a crack in her brain from too much acid."

"Yeah, but we should check it out, right? We're headed that way anyway to get back home. Might make an interesting pitch for another story."

She kissed me on the lips. "I'm really high." I kissed her back and we found our way out of our clothes and into our sleeping bag.

The next morning, I woke up cold. The old woman sat cross-legged outside our tent, staring at us.

"You believed me, right?" Doreen asked.

"Sure." I wiped sleep from my eyes and nudged Sharon awake.

"You ladies can see it. Turn your head to the ground and use your peripheral vision. If you're near the north end of the Sea, you can see the crack out of the corner of your eye. It's still there, letting things in. He died for it. They took him because he knew too much. You drive by Bombay Beach and you'll see the burn in the ground from where the bomb went off. Around midnight, you turn your radio on AM to the end of the dial. The voices will come. That's your story right there. People need to know."

Her eyes were shiny and wet, somewhere far away. She wasn't looking at us, just staring through the tent off into some past catastrophe.

"We need to get dressed and ready for the day, Doreen," I said.

"Okay," she said. Then, "Oh! Oh my, where are my manners. You ladies get dressed. I'll make you a sack lunch to take with you."

"That sounds nice, Doreen, thank you."

She tottered to her feet and crunched away through the gravel.

"Why would you bother that sweet lady to make lunch for us?" Sharon whispered.

"She left, didn't she?"

Sharon took my hand and caressed my cheek. "This was nice, Dee. I'm . . . I really hate camping, you know. But this was nice."

I smiled at her and spun around, snapping a picture of the two of us with my phone. We looked terrible. No makeup, bedhead, bleary-eyed. But she had that smile that I loved so much, that half-grin, those fretting eyebrows, tongue half-out. That was the last good picture of us. The last good moment, really.

We loaded the car to head out, shook a few hands, took contact info, promised we'd do what we could to get their story to the masses. We had just started to roll out on the main road when Sharon tapped my arm.

"There's our crazy friend," she muttered.

Doreen was flagging us down, waving a sack wildly above her head, doing that weird chicken walk some older people do when they need to move quickly. Her face was more wrinkle than skin, her smile more open space than tooth. I rolled down my window and she thrust the sack through into my lap.

"Hi, Doreen," I said.

"There's notes in there that you'll need. Didn't have much for food, so I hope you like peanut butter and apples. Couple bottles of water. And some masks. You'll thank me later for that."

"Okay, Doreen. Thank you for all of this. We've gotta hit the road."

"To Bombay Beach?"

"We'll . . . yeah, we'll probably make a couple of stops on our way out. Promise. We might be back out this way if things pan out, okay?"

"Oh, I hope so. I hope so. As soon as the sun starts going down, they'll start singing to you. Believe me. Just listen. Open ears, open minds."

We were five miles outside of Slab City when Sharon opened the bag and started poking around. The sandwiches she'd made us were remarkably clean-cut, perfect squares with the crusts cut off, thin slices of apple and peanut butter in between slightly crusty white bread. There were two more apples inside the bag, and another smaller brown bag. Sharon opened that one to find two painters' masks nested inside of each other and a faded picture of a man in military uniform. It was a formal portrait, his jacket starched, his hat perfectly poised on a head that was mostly scratched and faded into obscurity.

"That her husband? I thought she said they erased every trace of him."

"She also said there's a crack in the sky. The back of the photo says something," Sharon said. "I can't make it out. A love note, I guess. It's got her name at the top and some scribbling underneath."

"Sweet."

"You want to check it out, don't you?"

"You're in a hurry to get back to LA and hand over the bumpkin interview spectacular?" I poked her thigh. "We're off today and tomorrow, might as well take advantage, right?"

"Yeah, take advantage of a free day back home. Shower three times to get all of this dust off. Catch a movie, go to dinner . . ."

"Come on, Sharon. I've heard about Bombay Beach, I think it'll be pretty cool."

"You've heard about all that shit she said?"

"No, just . . . it's like this tiny little town that got wiped out in a flood years ago. All sorts of cool graffiti and houses falling down, and . . . come on! You like street art, right? I've heard it's a haven for taggers."

"Taggers," she scoffed. "Fine. A quick stop."

You will hear their voices when you try to sleep.

This was etched in bright orange paint marker on the inside of an exposed doorframe on a burned-out trailer home.

"So this one says 'their' voices. The last one said 'her' voice. Looks like the same handwriting to me," Sharon said.

It had become a game. Maybe we were killing time. Maybe we were subtly trying to convince each other that there was something to Doreen's story. It was pretty clear that we'd end up at the North Shore before the end of the day to turn our radios on and hear what we could hear.

We took a brief lunch at Bombay Beach, scarfing down Doreen's sandwiches which were surprisingly delicious. The water tasted a little off, which we attributed to well water or the fact that it had probably been sitting on a shelf somewhere for way too long. West of Bombay

Beach, there really was a dark line in the ground, about five feet wide, black as coal.

It faded about ten feet from the shore, obscured by sand, but there was a curve to it. I imagine if you traced that arc it would be an inverted-*U* shape cutting out of water that encircled most of the small rotting enclaves remaining near the northern half of the Salton Sea. In reality, it was a small patch of scorched earth half-buried in silt and powdered fish bones.

"Once you cross black, you don't cross back," Sharon joked as we walked across the expanse of charred earth.

Sharon was only halfway across when she turned a quick 180 and walked back out, planting her feet in the untarnished dirt. She folded her arms across her stomach, keeping her back turned on the line.

"Did you feel that? It's cold, it's . . . weird. That's weird."

"Just the breeze, girl. Don't go crazy on me now." I'd felt it too, a push of air like cold water surging around me. To give voice to that would have pushed me over the edge. I probably would have gotten in the car and headed back to LA to drink away our day off.

The line between *would have* and *should have* is the one I should have crossed.

That was the first time I noticed the stillness, standing there on the opposite side of the line from her. No birds. No breeze. No rustling of leaves, although the few nearby trees were swaying, and I felt the wind on my face.

I extended my hand to Sharon. She turned to me, that crooked smile of hers that always tugged at my heart, and I wanted nothing more than to march back across that line and take her in my arms.

"We're on an adventure," I said. "To boldly go." My feet felt anchored, rooted into the hardpan. I shuddered, then lifted first one foot, then the other. Stepped back into the black, walked to her, rested a hand on her shoulder.

"See?" I said. "Don't let the old wives' tales fool you. We're done here anyway. We'll go check out the northern shore, put the radio on, listen to all of the nothing that comes through, call it a ruined night and head home. What do you say?"

She took a deep breath and kept her eyes down, the toe of her boot digging a line on the rough gravel in front of the charred black. "You're so romantic." She sighed, looking up at me. "Did you just call me your old wife?"

"I'll be *your* old wife. One of these days."

She smiled and took my hand. We walked together across the line.

We explored Bombay Beach for a few minutes, snapping pictures of all the insane artwork, the shattered furniture, the broken houses and skeletal structures. There were giant political paste-ups, airbrushed pinup girls, multicolored stencils and cryptic messages. It would be good for our Instagram if nothing else. The farther we put the line behind us, the cooler it got. The weather hadn't changed a bit. The sky was just as mercilessly cloudless, the sun still bright enough to peel paint off the decaying trailers dotting the landscape. It was unmistakably a few degrees cooler here than it had been back at the car.

The only noise came from the crunch of our boots against the broken masonry and glass on the ground. This area hadn't seen auto traffic in years. Our footsteps weren't loud exactly, but intense. Any noise came sharp, harsh. The swish of an arm as it swept across the body. Inner thighs whipping past each other. The aglet of a shoelace ticking against the side of a shoe. A tiny pebble skittering out from underfoot. All of it reported with the clarity of a gunshot on a still morning. If we stopped moving, everything grew painfully silent beyond the rasp of our breath.

I think we both noticed it, but neither of us said anything.

I thought about a trip we'd taken before to do a doc at Birkenau in Poland, trying to work with an Electronic Voice Phenomena "expert." This town had that same strange feeling, row after row of empty buildings. The only thing more unsettling than the feeling of being watched was the knowledge that nobody was here to see us. We walked, keeping our eyes low until we got back to the car.

Finally, Sharon whispered, "You hear that?"

"What?"

"Exactly."

"This is weird, right?"

"Yeah."

"But we have to go check out the north shore, right? I mean . . . we *have* to, now. Right?"

"It looks like other people have tried." She pointed to another paint marker tag on a doorframe that said *The voices come when the stars fall.*

We took a few more pictures, prodded at some of the broken glass, the boards, the pieces of appliances and furniture. I did some wide shots with the video camera, getting as much graffiti as I could while still conserving batteries. If nothing else, I could smack together five minutes of footage that could convince the higher-ups to send us back out here to get a story.

"You think the Yacht Club up there will be as fancy as this place?" I asked.

Sharon smiled a little, but her cheek dipped in a little where she was biting it. A nervous habit of hers, a tell I'd learned to spot.

I started the car and we rolled down the road, noting the change in sound as the tires crunched over the gravel. Everything had a strange, muted quality. Sharon turned the radio over to AM and scanned through the high and low ends of the frequencies. The static would grow quieter as she reached the extreme ends until they hit silence.

Sharon kept her arms folded and her eyes out the window. I kept checking the temperature readout on the dashboard. We'd been sweating in ninety-five degree heat back at Slab City. Now the dashboard was telling me it was seventy-two degrees, a few miles down the road.

We drove in silence until we reached the northern point of the sea, the fabled Yacht Club. It had died an undignified death decades ago, its corpse slowly rotting by the water. There had been plans to refurbish it into a visitor's center. The people of the area were under no illusions about the grandeur of the Desert Riviera era returning to the Salton Sea, but they were still proud enough to eliminate as many eyesores as possible. There were retirees out here trying to make an honest go of it, and they were determined to hold on to their dignity. Seemed like everything was on hold now.

We pulled into the dirt lot. Everything was boarded up, huge murals coated every available surface, even the broken pylons that jutted from the water a few feet from the shoreline.

"Sixty-four degrees," I muttered as I got out of the car.

We stood there looking at the hulking ruins of the yacht club. Faded yellow plastic caution tape floated like party streamers on a silent breeze by the front door.

LISTEN.

The word was spray-painted over and over again in a repeating line stretching the length of the building. Someone had drawn crude stars spilling out of one of the upstairs windows.

Sharon moved up beside me, shouldering her backpack. "You ready for an uneventful evening?"

"You planning on a hike?"

"I'm not going into that creepy fucking place without every light source we have. We have two radios and three recorders."

"You believe her? And what do you mean going in?" I asked her.

"I want to see what's in there. Might as well kill some time before the show starts, right? I'd rather do it while we still have some daylight."

We moved to the trunk so I could pull out my gear bag. I tested my flashlight and checked my batteries. We looked at the building, at the parking lot, the sky. Both of us waiting for the other to take the first step.

"I have an idea," I said, so suddenly that it startled Sharon. "We set up a recording station out here. Let it run for a few hours and see if it picks anything up."

"You think there's any burnouts squatting in there?"

"We take off at the first sign of occupancy, deal?"

"You don't have to tell me twice."

We set up our outdoor audio listening station. I aimed the camera at the front door, setting the video for the lowest acceptable quality to maximize recording time. I taped an mp3 recorder to the front leg and hit record. It should give us a few hours.

The sun was getting lower. When I moved my head quickly, I thought I saw a ripple in the sky over the sea just to the east of the building. It wasn't quite a crack, more like a fold, a darkening of color, and it was only there when I wasn't really trying to find it.

"You see it?" I asked.

Sharon shrugged. "The Sea?"

"Nah, the uh . . . never mind. You ready to go inside?"

"You got a knife on you?"

"What are you planning, Katniss?"

"Don't make fun. We don't know who's in there, but if anyone is, we need to be ready."

"Fine. You hear me scream, then come running with your pig-sticker."

There was a sense of unease settling around my shoulders like a cold, wet blanket. I suddenly wanted this to be done. But I couldn't stop. Maybe I was seeing things in the sky, but it felt like there was something here worth hanging around for.

I walked toward the main building, hoping it looked more like confidence and less like nervous energy. The main doors had been blown out long ago, replaced with crude plywood to keep the elements out. It was dark inside, small pools of light thrown here and there through holes in the roof and walls. Someone had spray-painted NO CALLS AFTER SUNDOWN in four-foot-high orange letters on the wall in the hallway.

The lobby was as beautiful to look at as it was wretched to smell. We stood beneath the shattered remains of a light fixture designed to look like we were beneath a boat. Everything smelled like rot. Salty air, bird shit, human waste, rotting wood, dead fish brought in by the seagulls. All of it piled here and there beneath beautiful airbrushed murals, illegible phrases and giant paste-ups. There were rusted lawn chairs, eviscerated loveseats, desks that looked like palsied old men leaning back against the wall. Sharon pulled out the paper masks Doreen had given us.

"Guess she gave these to us for a reason. Keep it on if you're moving around. We're gonna be kicking up a lot of nasty shit moving through here. Sundown in about an hour," she said, following that up with something else.

"What's that?" I asked, turning.

"Two hours." She tapped her wrist. I only knew she was talking because of the way the paper mask moved on her face.

I held up a finger and quietly asked, "Can you hear me?"

She nodded.

"Tell me you can hear me."

Her mask moved and I heard nothing.

"Louder."

"Stop fucking around, Dee!"

This time I heard her just fine.

There was a torn sheet of notebook paper on one of the chairs in a corner, held down by a broken piece of cinder block.

First the tide will rise. After sundown. The breeze. Then the birds. Isn't the season for insects, but maybe you'll hear a few. Then you'll grow tired. Then I'll come to you.

I gestured for Sharon to come look at it.

"What do you think that means?" I asked.

"Nothing. It's . . . wait . . ." She cocked her head, then fumbled in her pocket and pulled out the photo Doreen had given us, flipping it over and holding it side-by-side with the paper. "Okay, that's weird."

"Same handwriting?"

"I mean . . . I'm not an expert, but . . ."

"What do you think she . . . Doreen? Doreen!" I called her name out a few times, convinced she'd come around the corner smiling at us.

"I don't think she's here, Dee. I don't think anyone is."

"Fine. Let's look around and get some video and get the fuck out of here. It's too cold in here."

Sharon headed for a staircase at the far end of a long hallway lit by dusty shafts of dying light. I called out to her to stop but she just kept moving like she didn't hear me. She turned when she got to the foot of the stairs and stared at me. I looked back at her. Finally her head started to bob and she stuck her arms out as if to ask me what the hell I was waiting for. I hustled down the hallway to the staircase.

"You didn't hear me?" she asked.

I shook my head. "Not a thing. This place is weird."

"Turn your radio on. Might as well go full crazy if we're going, right?"

"This is crazy. Can you hear me now? You sound like you have a pillow over your face."

We looked at each other, sharing an uneasy smile. It was actually happening. It's one thing to read about going to the moon, an entirely different thing to take that first step into the void.

We hustled up the stairs, mindful of the way the wood creaked and popped as we passed over it. The landing branched off into two long hallways. One of them was dark and littered with broken furniture and debris. We chose to follow the lighter one, which was lit by a series of holes in the roof and light streaming in from rooms on the side. The walls were decorated with neon-colored streaks of paint marker, bright oranges, pinks, whites, and silver that ran the length of the walls and tapered down as they reached a doorway at the far end of the hall. That door was surrounded by crudely drawn stars and odd glyphs.

"Check that out," Sharon said, her voice still muffled.

We moved into the room, noting the debris-free floor. It was painted stark black, a series of constellations etched in marker, like walking on a demented sky. I didn't remember much from my college astronomy classes, so I couldn't judge the accuracy, but someone had spent quite a bit of time on it. I started filming the room, panning around to catch all of the mural on the floor, the way it bled up onto the walls, all of it leading to the main act. In the corner, an antique radio sat on a crooked end table. The back of the case was open, tubes exposed. Wires splayed out from the back into a hallucinatory spider web pattern on the wall, running over the top of the tags and graffiti. That meant they had been placed fairly recently. In the other corner was a camping chair that still looked to be in decent shape. On the floor in front of the chair was a battered spiral notebook. There were diagrams and notes inside, things hastily scrawled, notes about the cracked sky, the refractions, sound travel, frequencies.

I flipped to the front of the book, noting the thick column of shredded paper trapped in the spiral. All of the early notes were torn out. The first page was dated from over a decade ago, starting midway through a journal entry about other hotspots around the sea. The handwriting and charts became more agitated with each turn of the page, losing coherence toward the end. A few pages from the end, the scrawl turned childlike, reading:

. . . they want to talk, you understand? They have things to say. Years and years and years. It's important. We are vessels. We were vessels. We opened it and I wanted nothing to do with it, but now it's open. They cracked it without thinking of what might be on the other side. I never wanted any of it. None of us did. I miss my wife. I never saw them. I only heard them. Maybe they'll come through. Maybe they'll get bored and leave us alone. All of the changes, all of it, it's all them. All them. There is no more.

The rest of the pages were hurried slash marks made with a black pen. The back of the last sheet was an endless spiral that looked like the author was trying to get all of the ink out of his pen on to the page. Near the top was a bloody fingerprint. Or maybe it was dirt and my mind was giving way to fantasy.

"Holy shit," Sharon murmured, looking at the handwriting and pulling that photo out again. The handwriting matched. "What in the honest hell, Dee?"

"I don't know. I don't know, but I'd say we have a story here, wouldn't you?"

"Yeah, but . . . shit. This means we have to stay. We have to, right? We at least need to try turning our radios on." The corners of her jaw worked. I thought she might be biting her lip the way she did when she got frustrated. I wish that's all it had been. She yelped. "Shit! Bit my cheek." She reached up to pull her paper mask off.

"Let's go outside for a minute, make some plans in the fresh air." I grabbed her hand.

She turned and stumbled a bit as she looked out the window. "A crack in everything. That's how the light gets in."

We both had a thing for Leonard Cohen. Seemed appropriate given the circumstances, but I should have asked her what she saw when she looked out the window. Instead, we walked down the stairs in silence. We stopped by the camera in the parking lot. I lifted my mask. She did the same, spitting out a gob of bloody saliva.

"Really tagged it," she said. "Least it's easier to breathe out here."

The stink of the Salton Sea ruined the refreshing air, but was an improvement over the dank inside. I checked the camera, fast forwarding through the footage to see if anything interesting had happened while we were inside. There was nothing. I erased the file and reset the whole thing, checking the battery.

"We can get about four hours out of this thing on low quality video. Probably need to come outside to check the battery, maybe change out cards. We could set up your camera here on time lapse, maybe one photo every thirty seconds, just in case there's a light show at some point and—"

She grabbed my face and kissed me deeply. Her tongue tasted of blood and salt and something electric. She pulled back and beamed at me.

"This has been a pretty decent vacation," she said.

I smiled at her. "Let me see your cheek."

"No! It's fine, it'll stop bleeding in a second. Sorry, I got a little excited."

We spent the next few minutes staying busy by the car, me setting up the cameras while Sharon dug out every piece of audio equipment she could find. We had a couple of old mp3 players that could catch FM frequencies. I had an emergency flashlight in the trunk with an AM/FM radio on it and a hand crank. That would last us all night. I brought in a camera and Sharon came in with an omni-directional microphone plugged into her voice recorder.

We stopped at the entrance to the Yacht Club, the sun fading and the temperature dropping.

"This is dumb, right?" she asked.

"Yep. Very dumb. Still more exciting than talking to a bunch of squatters out in the desert about their opposition to well water and property taxes."

Sharon sighed. "All right. Let's do it. This one's for Doreen."

We walked back up the stairs side-by-side and stepped into the Yacht Club. I looked back at the car as we entered and a ripple moved across the sky, like the end of a film reel flapping against the light. This time it was more clearly defined, like fogged glass in a lightning shape that curved around the mountains and over our heads. I nudged Sharon to look, and she nodded. I snapped a picture. When we checked the frame on the back of the camera, the sky looked perfectly normal.

I knew enough about the Salton Sea to know none of it is normal if you look closely. The sand isn't sand. Just piles and piles of desiccated fish bones. From a distance, it fools you into thinking of pristine white shores. Up close, you're ankle-deep in razor-sharp fragments of calcified fish parts. Death surrounded the sea. There were little pockets where things clung to life, birds, reptiles, people, but everything there tells you that life doesn't belong.

We went back into the lobby. There was a low rumble and then a sustained hum, followed by a loud pop like a set of concert speakers coming to life. We instinctively ducked. The lights had come on. I looked at Sharon, her chest moving quickly, the hairs on her arm standing up. Not every fixture was lit, but enough that the lobby was thrown into a greater level of detail. This whole area should have been off the grid. I almost preferred having the lobby dark. Seeing everything made it more ominous.

"Guess we get to save on batteries for a while, huh?" I said.

Sharon nodded and we turned the crank on the emergency radio, bringing it to life. We tried a few different ends of the dial, but only found static and weak country music broadcasts. At the high end, there was a little bit of an ebb and flow to the static, an undulating rhythm that probably meant nothing, but we stayed with it for a while, staring at it like we'd see sound flowing out of it.

Sharon headed for the hallway. "Wanna try the old timey radio upst—"

The lights in the building flickered and the air shot through with a sharp static noise like a giant set of lungs taking a deep breath. Then came dreadful silence. It wasn't until a few seconds later that I realized the pounding I heard was my own heartbeat. We held our breath, waiting for the exhale. Waiting for an intonation, an invocation, a whisper, a word.

Nothing.

"What was—" Sharon's jaw dropped.

The lights dimmed and the static returned in regular pulses, a sharp inhale every thirty seconds. As much as my mind tried to rationalize it as *just a noise*, I couldn't help but think of it as *breathing*. Only breathing in, and the lack of exhale, the absence of that release of pressure spiking my heart rate.

"Is that coming out of the radio?" Sharon asked.

I quickly flipped the switch and checked that all of our gear was off. I scanned the ceiling for old speakers leftover from when the building was still alive, but there was nothing.

Sharon's eyes went wide. She extended her arms, turning in a slow circle. "You feel that? Stick your hands out. Do it! Move your fingers."

I reached out like a mindless puppet, my fingers brushing through the air, pushing against waves of static that felt like the aura that would buzz around an old Tube TV screen after you shut it off.

There was a phrase written in that notebook upstairs, a note about the rising tide. We needed to get back up there.

"It's moving!" Sharon said. "Hold your fingers still, you can feel it running through . . . "

And I could. Like gritty water flowing through my fingers.

Blackout.

Sharon pushed back toward the door. The light outside was almost gone. We weren't thrown into total darkness, but it was still disconcerting. The disorienting lack of noise, just our breath and a strange pressure in the ears. The lights snapped back on and the static/breath noise returned, this time barely audible, high-pitched. It was desperate, like someone breaking the surface of the ocean after a near drowning. Neither of us moved. We looked to one another, hoping for answers, hoping for sense, finding only that same empty anxiety staring back.

"Are we getting any of this?" I whispered.

Sharon's face lit up and she laughed. "All work and no play. Shit." She fumbled with a couple of her recorders and flipped them on, checking the screen "Needle's not moving, but we might as well leave it running. I'll go up and check the radio. You check the camera out in the lot and then come find me."

I took half a step toward the door and paused. Sharon laughed again.

"This isn't a scary movie, Dee. Just a creepy abandoned building. Nobody's here but us fishes." She threw her arms around me and kissed my cheek. "This is the worst vacation rental you've ever taken me to. I'm leaving such a shitty Yelp review!"

I gave her a puzzled smile in return.

"Check the camera. Go! Shit's happening!" She hustled away, her footsteps strangely silent on the stairs. She stopped halfway up and pulled out her camera. "You stay there. You stay *right* there. Just like that. I want to remember this. I'm going . . . to . . . never forget this."

The flash pulsed hard twice in the gloom, blinding me. And then she was gone.

The clumsiness of her last sentence, like she'd tripped over her own tongue. I hate to think of that now. It's only now as I write this that I recall the purple behind my eyelids. Not the usual stars you get from a flash going off. These were odd, geometric fractals, honeycomb shapes that danced and moved.

There was a strange cold-water-down-neck feeling I would get when my fight-or-flight . . . well, *flight* instinct kicked in. I counted to twenty. Enough time that Sharon would think I'd gone outside to check the gear. Whatever she was feeling, I wasn't getting the same vibe. At that point I'd have been content to leave, even with all of the strangeness around us. If it happened once, it would happen again. We could come back with more gear. Better gear. A bigger crew.

. . . and twenty. Every step a tiny mountain. I got to the top of the stairs and looked down the tiny hallway. Dull light pulsed out of the radio room.

"Sharon?"

"Dee? Dee? Dee? I can't see. I can't see. I need a flashlight. Mine died."

I hurried into the radio room, but it was empty.

"See? Dee? See?"

"Sharon, where are you?"

"I'm in it. We're in it. They're here."

Her voice was coming from the speaker on the old-timey behemoth on the table.

"This isn't the time to fuck around with the equipment, Sharon. Where are you?"

I moved out into the hallway, anger overtaking fear.

"Deeeeeeeeeee?" Her voice echoed from the radio room.

I stomped from one room to the next, rounding a bend in the hallway. There were more of the layers of odd graffiti and tags that curved on the walls and tapered down the closer they got to the door at the end of the hallway, as if the art was slowly being pulled inside. Maybe it was a break room in a past life. The skeleton of an old fridge loomed in the corner, filthy cabinetry and pipes exposed through shattered walls. Sharon stood against the back wall, arms splayed, her paper mask moving so fast it looked like she was chewing gum. No sound.

I was across the room before I even realized I was moving. I pulled the mask from her face. Her mouth jabbered soundlessly, spittle flying. Her breath came out in ragged cold puffs, no noise. I fumbled for my phone to take a video. The screen wouldn't unlock, wouldn't register any of my touches. But the speakers came on, and I could hear her then, faintly, a cacophony of words and sounds coming too fast to comprehend.

There were words that got repeated more than others, but nothing I'll ever be able to make sense of.

Sands. Yuma. White Sands. Delta six five . . . Breathe. Fire. Cross. The gate, the gate, the gate . . .

I let out a tiny scream when she seized my hand. My eyes snapped up to meet hers. She'd pulled her mask back on. In the fading light, her eyes looked all-pupil, harsh black against the whites.

"What's wrong, Dee?" she whispered. This wasn't a question, more that she was begging for an explanation.

"Let's get outside. Are you okay to walk? This has gotten a little too big for us, I think."

" . . . are we okay?" she asked. The way her eyes searched mine. Like she was out to sea, like I was the thin lifeline tying her to a rescue boat in a black tide.

"Come downstairs." I took her hand, and it felt like I was pulling a balloon behind me.

The lights in the building were a flickering yellow that barely allowed us to see each other.

"You feel it?" I asked, extending my fingers and slowly waving my hand around below my knee, like trawling through still water. That gritty sand feeling returned, tingling every nerve up to my wrist. Something was off. My mind raced backward to what we'd had to drink the previous night, the lunch Doreen packed us. Was something spiked? Was I about to lose my shit with her? Was I already?

Sharon waved her hand and nodded. "Tickles my feet. Did you see it open?"

Every breath I took felt like I was inhaling liquid sand, tickling my tongue on the way in and rasping my throat on each exhale. The breathing noise started again, this time in reverse, a great exhalation of static that reduced to a bare whisper. I descended the stairs slowly and carefully, making sure Sharon wasn't going to stumble. By the time we reached the bottom, the sound grew quieter, the lights dimmed. Eventually, we were left in darkness. I felt Sharon's hand tug twice, then her fingers slipped through mine.

"Sharon?" I whispered, marveling at the electric charge it brought between my teeth.

"Dee?" Her voice came back from the flashlight/radio that was clenched in my other hand. I didn't remember turning it back on. I only saw her silhouette, standing still. Looking, I think, in my direction.

The radio crackled twice. "Are you tired yet?"

"Just come over here and talk to me. We're gonna get outside to the parking lot. I think we need to call it a night. Sleep it off in the car and get home. Okay? Sharon?"

"I'm almost there. It's opening," She took two steps in my direction and there was a *crack* from the floor. "We can't do this anymore. This is it—" Another *crack*, this one twice as hard, like someone had sledgehammered the floor from beneath us. I tried to shine the flashlight in her direction, but the bulb dimmed. I grabbed for my phone and fumbled it, watching the screen dim as it bounced away into the blackness.

"Dee?"

Another crack. And another. Her head tottered back and forth. She hunched suddenly and came forward, like she was trying to run.

"Dee? Dee!"

What happened next? The car crash. That's the only way I can describe it. Impact. Pure force that knocked me onto my butt, and when I found my bearings, she was gone. I couldn't move. I thought maybe there was a hole in the floor. Maybe she'd fallen through. Maybe she was out cold in the basement, bleeding to death. But this place wouldn't have a basement. I crawled, slapping at the floor with my free hand, clutching the flashlight/radio in the other like it was my lifeline, screaming her name. Twice my hands splattered into some unidentified mess that I hoped was only bird shit or wet paper. There was no hole in the floor. I couldn't see, but I was certain of it.

"Sharon? Sharon, please say something."

The static crested for a second, and there was an exchange, two men's voices, nasally, brief, curt. Sounded like mission control. I couldn't make out any of the words.

There was the faintest delineation ahead, the night sky in the seam of the great plywood front doors. I don't know how I'd made my way so close to them, but it was part of a solution. I pushed forward until I felt the warped wood and gave it a push. The door swung open easily. What little difference it made in the light ended about three feet into the building.

That Cohen lyric Sharon said earlier echoed in my mind, unmistakably painted above me. The sky . . . was cracked.

A crack in everything, that's how the light gets in . . .

It was a razor thin tear that originated somewhere over the horizon and bent at impossible angles, backtracking against itself until it looped down somewhere behind the sea, like some manic god had slashed the sky with a knife in a fit of jealous rage. It bled light out into the purple sky, an inky flow of indigo-black. There were no stars in the sky. No moon. I stumbled out and looked for the car, banging my knee on the tripod we'd set up earlier. I slapped at my pockets for the keys. If I could shine the headlights into the doorway, maybe . . . but Sharon had the keys.

I had to get help. I looked around for any sign of movement in nearby buildings, on the road, anything. There was no life out here.

But in the sea!

In the Salton Sea, the placid sea, all of the stars shone, and the moon. I looked up again to a black sky, then back at the water.

I didn't realize I'd taken off my shoes until I felt the cold mud between my toes. My left foot still had a sock on. I ignored every prick and cut from the bone shards on the beach until I felt my legs enter the water. Knee-deep, I turned to the yacht club. A dark silhouette up in one of the windows, a person, maybe. I hoped it was Sharon. Had to be. She hadn't fallen through the floor, that was just an overactive imagination. *Scare-Dee Cat*, Sharon used to tease me in situations like this.

I started to call out to her, but the thought left my mind as quickly as it came. I was standing in the sky, swimming in the stars and the moon and the endless black. I wanted her to see.

Sharon.

I shouted her name until her voice came over the radio still clutched in my hand.

"Where did you go, Dee?"

"I'm outside! Can you make it? Are you okay? I want you to see this. Come out! Look at the sky! Look!"

"I'm okay. If you knew this was the last thing I'd ever tell you, what would you want me to say?"

"Why? No, Sharon. Just come outside and see this!"

"They need something. It's why the gate opens. They'll show us everything, but we have to pay first. We have to give them—*zzzxxxzzz . . .*" Static swallowed her voice.

Then the voices came. First there were only two. They were children. Shouting and playing. Speaking a language I'd never heard, something ancient and guttural. There was an undercurrent of that same static-breath noise, but this time much more organic. Alive, pulsating, breathing at regular intervals. It pulled on me. Every time it exhaled, I could feel it sliding through the hairs on my arms, tugging my wrist toward the sea.

When I was thigh-deep in the water, a chill rushed through my skull, poured over my spine, and spread out into the water. I stripped down to my bra and underwear, convinced the heat from the stars in the water would keep me safe. I should have been freezing, but I was fine. Warm. Relaxed. I was in my body and in the water at the same time.

There were things in the sea. Beyond the curling, sun-dried remains of thousands of Tilapia stirred up by my footsteps, long, leathery, undulating things moved past my legs. Not seaweed, not here. When I looked down, I could only see my naked legs plunging down into an impossibly starry night sky. When I moved my feet, the stars drifted as if floating. Waves of vertigo washed over me, the feeling that I would become unrooted and fall into the sky. I had to look away toward the yacht club.

There she was, on the shore. She was glowing. Her skin pale and radiant in the light that rose from the water.

"I don't want to get my shoes muddy, Dee. Come over here." She extended a hand. "I figured it out. You just have to stop talking so that they can start. You just—"

Her voice trailed off as a steady stream of blood flowed from her mouth. Her eyes wide in panic, she kept trying to talk. Blood and spittle sprayed from her mouth, spattering down onto the muddy ground between us. It was only then that I noticed her sinking. The muck around the shore slowly swallowing her up. I rushed to her, nightmare-slow slogging through the silt. She was thigh-deep by the time I fought my way back to shallow water. Something clutched at my ankles as I moved, the water turned jello-thick. I stumbled twice, falling to my knees the first time and onto my face the second. My face slapped through the foul water and cracked against a rock. I inhaled a mouthful of thick, rancid water and then the ground parted. I shouldn't have been able to see in the brackish mess, but there was a hole in the sea bed. There was another night sky below. Not a sky. *Lights.* Southern California, all of it, so dazzling, spinning dizzily beneath me.

I pushed hard, afraid of drowning, afraid of falling, afraid of losing Sharon forever. I punched through the muck into that sub-sky. Clumps of mud and filthy water spun away to crash on the ground below me. It was such an odd sensation, still feeling the current of the water around me, rushing over me, none of it pouring through the hole beneath me. The sea bed under my fingers reminded me of where I actually was, so I kept my eyes closed and pumped my legs until my face slid and scraped against the grit of the mud near the shore. I squirmed and writhed and pushed until cold air stung my back. I don't know how long it took to get out, but Sharon was gone when I did.

There was a disturbance in the mud at the shoreline, bloodstained spots that spattered across the ground like demented graffiti. Sharon's hiking shoe lay a few feet away, caked in dirt, a sun-dried tilapia carcass glued to the muck on the sole. Her headband stuck half-out of the mud, surrounded by small puddles of brown-red water.

I dragged myself, dizzy and reeling, back toward the yacht club. A chorus sang in the sky, endless voices and static, screams and songs and sounds I'd never heard before or since. A shape passed by the window upstairs, a silhouette surrounded by strange fractals of light. It was a man. The building bled cyan and magenta and indigo light from every open crack and window.

The lobby was empty. The remaining light fixtures cast painful shades of reds and blues. I wondered what would happen if I had those old-style 3D glasses. There was no hole in the floor. No Sharon. I made my way upstairs, treading carefully across the splintered floor, trying to avoid the debris from the broken walls and windows. I should have plucked my shoes out of the mud before coming inside. When I reached the top of the landing, the radio crackled from down the hall. A whisper scraped by my ear.

"Don't come closer. Don't come. Don't."

A hum rose from the wall, pitches ranged in perfect fifths, a brassy, brutal harmony. I pushed on, ignoring the broken glass stabbing into my feet, the chill in my bones. My skin had become numb. I pounded my arms against my chest to try to get my blood flowing. My bra and underwear looked like sand carvings etched into my skin. I ran my fingers through my hair and found it soaked, caked in mud. My face was covered in gritty silt and dust.

"Help," I whispered. "Sharon. I'm sorry. We have to go, baby. We have to leave."

The doorway to the radio room bled dull orange light into the hallway like a fog, obscuring more than it revealed. I stopped by the doorframe and leaned my head in. The radio in the corner was lit up like Christmas, the antenna lines that spread across the wall glowing with strange energy. The mural painted on the floor glowed harsh white. It had changed from a starry sky to a thin, weaving line that ran a circuit around the length of the room and spiraled inward to form a circle in front of the radio.

Sharon was on her knees in the center of the circle, facing away from me toward the radio. She looked like a religious icon, surrounded by an aura of twisted wires.

"We should have talked," her voice came through the radio. "We should have talked."

Her shoulders heaved. I started limping toward her until she snapped an arm out to her side.

"Don't come closer. It's too late now. Just leave. I don't want you to see."

"See what, baby?" I asked, my voice a raspy whisper. "See what? Sharon, what's happening right now?"

"Everything they wanted," the radio said. "Everything they ever wanted. They opened the door without thinking about what was on the other side. They don't want to come through. They just want it to close and go away and they are very, very angry with us . . . "

"Sharon, look at me. Please."

A wet slap in the dirt near my feet. Something small and damp bounced off of the floor and ricocheted across the top of my foot, painting a streak across the muddy brown. Dark. Near the edge of my big toe, a small lump of meat rested on the floor.

I took two more steps to her and she staggered to her feet. Her body seemed to bounce off of an invisible wall that surrounded the perimeter of the circle. The lights in the room grew brighter when she stood up. Her fingers were bloody.

"Please look at me, Sharon." My jaw chattered, from cold, from fear.

She turned. The scream that rose from my stomach cracked my throat and sent me into a coughing fit. Her chin was black with coagulating blood. Her bottom lip looked like an animal had been chewing on her face. Her left eye was deep purple and shiny, not a bruise. Just iridescent. Her right eye bled indigo light. In one hand she held a bloody camping knife. She brought her other hand up, two fingers tapping on her chin as she smiled at me.

"It was the only way they would listen," the radio said, static tearing her voice. Her lips didn't move. She smiled, an awful, gaping thing that sent rivulets of bloody saliva cascading down her chin and chest. And then she flicked out her tongue, what was left of it. It looked like she was holding a lumpy meatball between her teeth.

"What's happening, Sharon? What's happening?"

"You tell me."

"There's light everywhere. The sky was in the sea, and the real sky was black. Everywhere I look I see light. I see the cracks."

"And do you hear them?"

"It's too much. I just hear noise. Songs and screams and whispers."

"All I see is the dark, but I can hear them perfectly."

"Them? Who?" I asked.

"I know how this must look. But it's okay. I'm hearing everything. It's all in pieces. You see the light everywhere? I can't. I only hear them. Together we can put it all together. You just have to let them use your eyes."

She smiled again and extended the knife toward me. She raised her eyebrows in that same way she used to do when she'd reveal surprise anniversary presents to me.

"They want your eyes. Give them your eyes and you'll see everything."

Sharon stepped forward, not threatening, just earnestly holding that blade up like this should have all made perfect sense to me.

"Lance Corporal Raymond Wood. He was here when it opened. He listened to them and he tried to see them and speak to them and it was too much. But together . . . Maybe together we can . . . "

She walked over to the window. The sky outside looked flat, burnt orange. There were no stars, no moon, no rising sun.

"I can't," I whispered. "I can't. What did you do, Sharon? *What did you do?*" This last scream broke my voice.

Sharon dropped the knife and held her hand out to me. "You were always afraid of commitment, weren't you?"

"What did you do?" My hands shook as I raised them to her face. She closed her eyes and nuzzled her cheeks into my palms, her blood still hot and sticky on her chin.

"I always wanted you to know. I was never *zzzxzxzx* . . . –ou." A burst of static overrode her voice. "You wer—*xxzzzxzxz*—and all I *zxzzzzzzz*—and you only had to say it. You only had to say *zzzzzxxxxx* . . . " Her voice grew quieter. The lights in the room faded and the radio gave out a final sputter before silencing.

Sharon slid her stained hands up my bare arms, leaving streaks of her blood until she held my face in her hands. Our foreheads touched together, I looked into her eyes, watching the unnatural blues and purples fade, her pupils dilated and pulsed until her eyes were almost black. Her mouth went slack and she let out a soft sigh.

"Sharon?"

She didn't move.

I pressed my lips against hers, ignoring the tang of blood, the shredded lips, willing my breath into her. The room grew colder. I began to shiver, the lack of clothing finally catching up to me. Sharon swayed on her feet, her skin losing color, her eyelids fluttering.

I yelped when an explosion of static came from the radio in the corner. It grew louder and louder until it filled the room, no longer an exhale or inhale but a sustained scream threatening to shred my eardrums.

My knees knocked together and my breath came in hitching rasps. I put my arm around Sharon's shoulder and pressed myself into her, leading her forward, out of the room. I briefly considered picking up the lump of her tongue from the floor. It was no use. It was just bloody meat now, speckled in plaster chips and sawdust. I'd never hear her voice again, never see that tongue stick out when she was concentrating, never feel it brush my neck, kiss me deeply. How much of us is our voice? How much of ourselves can we lose before we become something else?

We staggered down the stairs and through the lobby, out into the rising sun. It was the final blow to my addled mind. We hadn't been inside for more than a few hours, and the sun had just been setting when this all started.

The car was locked. I dumbly patted my bare hips as if searching for keys. Sharon's pockets were empty. My steps were a matter of inches. If I could get us to the road, we'd have a chance. Sharon was near catatonic. The cold had eaten me through to my bones. I looked down at my feet, sliced and bloody and stuck through with thousands of fish bones.

Get to the road. Someone will see us, someone will find us, help will come, or we will die.

Words raced through my mind. Hypothermia. Fear. Failure. Death. Divorce. Armageddon. I didn't know what else to do, so I walked.

The tripod that held our camera was at the edge of the lot, so I picked it up. We kept walking until we couldn't. I made it out to the main thoroughfare, Grapefruit Boulevard, and then my legs just wouldn't move anymore. I took her by the hands and gently pulled down until she followed. I sat cross-legged in the middle of the eastbound lane and leaned her head into my lap. In the sun, she looked terrifying. Her lips were dried and cracked, her face coated with blood. In the light I noticed odd shapes carved into her arm. Glyphs and symbols that could have been a map or a message or just mutilation. My vision started going grey at the edges and I leaned my head against hers. I wanted to whisper to her, all of the things I'd wanted to say for so many years and stupidly kept buried. The good, the bad, all of it. My voice was broken. Breathing took effort. I tried to tap my fingers on her wrist, this little gesture we used to make at the movies to remind each other that we were there, close, in the silent dark.

I looked up to the sky and saw the crack, clear as day, sharp as permanent marker on glass. It wasn't a crack at all. It was a design, geometric, orderly symbols that almost matched the ones on Sharon's arms.

I fell unconscious as I heard the roar of an approaching engine, downshifting, tires biting into gravel. Then came shouting. I disappeared somewhere into the blackness of my mind, where everything was quiet and the inside of my brain was painted with the endless sea of stars that should have been in the sky that night.

They found one of our voice recorders during the investigation. I've reviewed the audio countless times. It's just static, with a high-pitched whine in places that may have been an odd frequency or maybe Sharon's screams. The only surviving footage on the camera from the lot was when I ran from the yacht club the first time. Hours of nothing, and then something hits the camera from the side. I'm pretty sure it was me, wobbling off to the sea. Twenty minutes later, from a skewed angle, my naked, mud-smeared legs walk past the camera. Somewhere around forty minutes after that, there's a brief movement near the corner of the building. A shadow falls from the upstairs window. It's too grainy to confirm that it's a man, and the shape lands out of frame. They found a hiking boot and a belt near the spot where it would have hit, but there was no telling how long they'd been there. Inside of the yacht club, they found syringes, spent bags of powder and empty pill bottles. Five different knives. Three of them had dried blood on the blade, none of them matched Sharon.

This year will be the last that I go to visit her. No amount of reconstructive surgery could give back her tongue. It wouldn't matter because she hadn't tried to communicate with anyone since the EMTs brought her back. I have dreams every year on this day, the same as the fever dreams I had when they found us by the roadside the next day near the Yacht Club, near-hypothermic.

We spent a week recovering in the hospital before the detectives came. They questioned us for days, convinced that we'd been kidnapped, drugged, and tortured. They started building that narrative while we slept and did their damnedest to get us to confirm their worst suspicions. The first time the detective suggested it, I spat in his face. The second time, I stopped talking to them. They tried getting Sharon to write a deposition, but she was catatonic.

They eventually settled on diagnosing us with a hallucinations based on toxoplasmosis. They said we'd spent so many hours inhaling powdered bird shit that it snapped something in our brains. They didn't bother to test the empty water bottle Doreen had given us. I didn't want them to.

That was as close to famous as we got. The first year, we were ridiculed in the media as a pair of crackpot hippie lesbians who got lost on a drug adventure. The years after that, nobody but the conspiracy theorists would talk to us. There were a few out there who'd heard Doreen's tall tale. I wanted nothing to do with them. I returned to Slab City twice to find Doreen, but nobody would talk to me. They'd seen me on the news. Thought I just wanted to bleed more sensationalist stories out of them.

I went back to Bombay Beach. The black line in the sand was gone. The Yacht Club got its much needed renovation, reopening as the glorious Salton Sea History Museum. I kept my head down the whole time I was there, though there was nobody to hide from. I couldn't bring myself to go inside. Instead, I walked down to the shore and stared at the sky until I was dizzy.

The last time I visited Sharon, I brought in a print of that selfie we took on the way in, her silly smile, the nervous energy on our faces, and tears started pouring down her cheeks. She looked at me then, really saw me for the first time in I don't know how long, and it was nothing but hatred. She pounded on that photo with her finger, hitting the same spot in the background over and over: the sea.

So we're going to drive back to the sea, and we're going to wade in. I'm going to take Sharon to the sky beneath the Salton Sea, show her the stars, the world below our world. I'm going to get it all back. The singing, the sound, her voice, us, all of it. There's nothing left for us here. What broke us once will make us whole again. I'm going to find the crack in everything and shatter it, blow it wide open, dive through.

Last night, I dreamed of the last page of that journal we found in the yacht club, that page of spirals that I was certain were the scribblings of a madman. He wasn't trying to bleed the ink from his pen. He was trying to draw the stars below the waves. It was a map available to anyone brave and insane enough to follow the path. Here is where I'll be. If you're looking, here is where you'll find us.

darkhorse actual

GEORGE COTRONIS

THERE WERE EXPLOSIONS in the distance. The sound was distant, a faint rambling, but he could see the lights. They were bombing . . . something. From the roof of the palace, he could see a whole lot of nothing. Kabul was somewhere over those mountains.

Daniel Shaw walked the perimeter of the roof and then went downstairs. It was getting cold. It wasn't even his shift; he just liked how quiet it was up there. The marines on guard duty knew it and never bothered him or tried to talk.

He met Stafford coming down the stairs. Both men nodded, but said nothing.

Stafford was a loudmouth redneck who liked to talk shit. Daniel had thrown him through a plate glass window back when they were on base, for saying he fucked his girl.

He reached the courtyard, which was deserted. The palace was mostly a ruin. Up in these mountains, it held no strategic importance that Daniel could imagine. An Afghani president and his family had been murdered in the Palace in the '80s. The soviet army had been stationed there during the Soviet-Afghan war. The building had been built on top of the ruins of a castle dating back centuries. Now it was occupied by jarheads.

Their detachment was made up of fuck-ups and head cases. The discards. And Daniel Shaw was their king.

He stood for a moment, untied his shoelaces and shook his boots out. Small mountains of sand formed on the courtyard stones. He glanced at his watch, the hands glowing in the dark. He crossed the courtyard and went up the stairs on the other side. This was his last stop for the night before racking out.

The comms room actually had four walls, which was more than you could say for most of the rooms in the Palace. They had done some patchwork, using old furniture and planks, but it hadn't helped a whole lot.

Nick Kocher spent his days in here, sweating profusely and listening to the radio. He rarely had anything to say to it. He pulled long shifts, letting the backup slack off. Not all of the soldiers knew why, but Daniel did.

"Anything tonight?" he asked.

Kocher's eyes looked wild. Daniel guessed it had something to do with all the caffeine pills he was chewing, but there were other things, too.

"Yeah," he said.

"Well?"

"Oh. Yeah. Most of the usual stuff. Espera. He said he's dead. He's in the dark. We're all going to die. The usual."

Daniel nodded.

Espera had died months ago, before any of them had heard of the Palace. It was a short firefight. They found him up on the hill, in the bushes, already dead. A lot of grown-ass men cried that day.

"Anything else?" There was always something else. Kocher spent a lot of hours alone up here and he wasn't always forthcoming on what the radio spit out at him.

"My mother. You know. She said she's dead, that there was an accident and she's dead and everyone else is too."

Daniel nodded again. "You call your mother?" There were a couple of Afghani burner phones in the unit, worth their weight in gold for short calls back home. There were never enough minutes to go around.

"She's fine."

Kocher was fidgety, but looked okay. He was mostly fine after having talked with his family back home, having heard for himself that they were all right. They found it a bit strange he insisted to talk to each and every one of them, asking intimate questions to verify it was really them. But they had gone along with it, this far.

Daniel's earlier call to Kocher's mom had explained the situation. Sort of.

"Should I wake Mack up? It's his shift, isn't it?" Daniel said.

Kocher shook his head violently. "I'm good for a few more hours."

"Nick, you've been up for days. Let—"

"No."

"Why do you keep listening, man? Why not turn it off for a couple of hours?"

"Because I'm afraid that the voices will come even with the radio off. That maybe they won't need it any more."

Daniel didn't know what to say to that.

"You're fucked in the head, Kocher. Okay, fine. But you let me know if you get tired, all right?"

"Yeah, sure. I will."

"Okay."

He turned to leave.

"Hey, Shaw?"

"Yeah," he said, behind his back.

"I think I heard my sister."

"What?"

"My kid sister. Talking to me. On the comms."

Daniel rubbed his face. "That's awful, man. You should let Mack take over. You don't need to do this tonight."

"No, no, it's fine. But stay with me for a while?"

Daniel had been up for 48 hours. He was running on fumes and caffeine pills.

"Sure, Nick. Sure."

He pulled up a chair. They sat in silence.

Mornings, they spent in the relative shade of the courtyard, strewn about like sea cows on the beach. The heat was intense. The unlucky SOBs on guard duty were doomed to be roasted alive.

Daniel checked in on Kocher and found him snoring loudly in his cot, jaw and arms clenched. He seemed to whimper now and then.

Stafford walked by.

“He been out long?” he asked and pointed at the sleeping man.

The marine shook his head.

“Nah, just an hour ago.”

“That cocksucker Mack let him take another shift?”

“Yeah.”

James Davis was in the canteen. He was holding a hand fan to his face, unwilling to surrender to the heat. Of course, the rest of him was bathing in sweat, but his head was cool and perspiration-free though and that seemed to be enough for him.

In his other hand, he was holding a picture of his wife and kid, creased and dirty.

“Davis,” Daniel said.

“Hey, man.” James waved his fan around.

”Still fighting that fight, huh?”

“Yeah, man. Fuck this heat. I’ll never surrender.”

“How’s the wife?” He motioned towards the photograph.

The man beamed.

“Good, man. My daughter is learning how to walk.”

“That’s great. That’s really good. Listen, we have to do something about Kocher.”

“Yeah?”

Daniel nodded. “Mack is fine with letting him take over all his shifts, so while he spent the last few days jerking it, Kocher was up there listening to that fucking radio day and night. He’s gone loopy.”

“Did it say anything?”

“Well, yeah. The same spooky shit. But I think it’s getting to him.”

“So why is he listening to it?”

Daniel looked away. “I don’t know, man. I think he’s kind of getting off on it. You know? Like when your girl cheats on you and you want to know all the disgusting details? Because it feels good to hurt?”

James said nothing for a while, then: “That sounded like you were talking from experience.”

Daniel shrugged. “Maybe I am. Anyway, we got to either get Mack to do his fucking job or we find someone else to take over.”

“Why not shut it off?”

“You know we can’t do that.”

"Why not?"

"Because we might get our orders. Because we have to check in with command."

James scoffed. "We're not getting shit, man. They forgot we're out here."

Daniel wanted to laugh at him, but he wasn't feeling very jovial. A small part of his brain was telling him that James might be right. Maybe they had forgotten about them. "You gonna help me with this or not?"

"Of course I'll help you." He got up. "I just like a little foreplay."

"Your mom never asked for it."

Neither of them laughed, but he appreciated the effort.

Mack was at his post, for once.

"Hey, Mack," Daniel said. "We gotta talk."

He didn't move. When Daniel put his hand on his shoulder, he jumped.

"What the fuck, man!" he yelled and put the headphones down.

Daniel grabbed him, lifted him off his feet and drove him into the wall. "You fucking asshole."

"Whoa-whoa." James tried to pull him off. "Calm the fuck down, ladies!"

"This jackass is wearing earplugs," Daniel said.

Suddenly, James didn't feel like helping. Mack held his hands up in surrender.

"I'm sorry. I was taking a break, okay? You wanna get your hands off me?"

He let him go.

"You're supposed to listen to the fucking radio, Mack. That's your fucking job."

"Fuck you. My job ain't to listen to some fucking ghost talking to me—"

"Keep your voice down" James said.

"No man, fuck both of you. You wanna come do this? I don't see you volunteering."

They didn't answer.

"That's what I thought," Mack said, smoothing down his uniform.

Daniel threw the headphones at him.

"Just do your fucking job, asshole."

They woke up to the sound of a gunshot. They scrambled, in their briefs, to grab their rifles and run to their posts.

Daniel ran up to the roof. He met Stafford running down the stairs.

"What the fuck is going on?"

"I don't know! There's nobody out there."

"Did it come from inside?"

"I don't fucking know!"

They both ran back down and out into the courtyard.

"Davis! Where are the shots coming from?"

"There's nobody out there, man; everybody was at their posts. They didn't see shit."

Daniel looked around the courtyard, at the marines gathered, confusion in their eyes.

"Where's Kocher?" Daniel asked.

They looked at each other.

In the tiny room, Kocher sat slumped in his chair, the gun still hanging in his limp hang.

"God damn it." Daniel punched the wall and instantly regretted it.

"Fuck," James said.

"I'm gonna kill that piece of shit." Daniel pushed through the crowd of men. "Where is he?" He pulled out his firearm and went looking.

He caught sight of him between two doorways, darting.

"Come back here, you piece of shit!"

Instead of chasing after him, Daniel took a right and circled around. He caught the man by the throat as he stepped into the corridor.

He put the gun under his jaw.

"Open your fucking mouth."

"Fuck you."

He let go of his throat and grabbed his face, forcing his mouth open. Then he pushed the muzzle in.

"You couldn't do your job, could you?"

The man stank of sweat and fear. It revolted him.

"You couldn't even finish that one shift, could you, you fucking coward."

The soldiers were on him before he could decide if he was going to pull the trigger or not. He let them drag him away.

They let him cool off up in the roof, under guard. As much as Davis could be considered to be guarding him.

James had been forced to explain to the rest of the marines what was going on. He thought it'd be harder to explain, harder to convince them, but they had gone along with it easily enough.

The dead were talking to them through the radio.

The stories had been going around anyway. Some of them had caught snatches of conversations that Kocher had had. Others had been told by the ones in the know.

Out here, it was easy to believe in anything.

Shaw and Davis spent the morning talking shit about people they used to know, back when they were civilians, back when they were still in basic, back when they were actually part of the war.

Then they went downstairs for the funeral.

Out back, the marines had dug a hole deep enough to prevent the jackals from digging him up. They broke a chair and made a wooden cross. Gave his dog tags to Daniel.

Radio to command had gotten no response. There was no medevac. They argued about sending him to a nearby base on a Humvee, but decided against it. They were technically behind enemy lines.

So they put him in the ground in the Palace. James said some words, though Daniel didn't think he was religious. He knew scripture though. He was a preacher's son.

Later, they shared a smoke over the grave.

"This desert is going to eat all of us," James said, and walked off.

Daniel woke up in a bed full of sand. He got up, dusting himself off, and met Stafford on his way to the comms.

"What the fuck happened to you?"

"Sand, man. It gets fucking everywhere."

Stafford shook his head.

"No shit."

Someone had gotten the dubious honor of cleaning up the radio equipment. There was still a stain on the wall. Sand had covered up the blood on the floor. He guessed the stain was going to stay there for some time.

"Well, if this place wasn't haunted before, it sure as fuck is now," Daniel said to the empty room.

"At least this one's on our side," James said from behind him, making him jump.

"God damn it, Davis."

"What, jumpy already?" He laughed.

"You're an asshole. You wanna do this?"

"Hell no. Good luck." He left Daniel to his task.

"The days are easy . . ."

He put the headphones on.

There was nothing but static for most of the afternoon. Then came the voices. He couldn't tell if they were in Pashto, or English or what. They were fading in and out, all of them talking at once. Gunfire in the background.

He didn't try to reply. He knew this part.

Then, later, came another voice, clearer. American.

"Darkhorse Six, come in."

That wasn't command reaching out to them. He recognized the voice.

"Palace here, receiving."

"How are ya, Daniel?"

"Hey Espera. How's the dirt treating you?"

"Can't complain. It's better being dead than being alive. The worst has already happened."

"Yeah." He was clutching the mic, knuckles white.

"I'll tell you what, man, catching that bullet in the throat wasn't fun, but it's a lot fucking better than what's coming for you guys."

Daniel coughed. His throat was always dry. He spat on the stones between his boots. Was that blood?

Just sand.

"You feeling all right, Daniel?"

He'd heard the voices before, but it was still hard to understand.

Everyone has heard weird stories about the desert and the ruins that litter it. But it was always someone they knew, who had heard it from someone else. You never met the guy who had lived through it.

At first, they figured they were getting pranked by another unit, or that there was a seriously fucked up PSYOP that the Afghanis were using on them. Having their dead friend talk to them. That's how it started; with Espera. But then the other voices came in. People they knew, dead and alive. Then, they had believed.

And like jarheads would, they took it in stride.

"I got someone here, wants to talk to you."

Daniel said nothing. The voices never got tired. Never gave up. There was no reason to converse with them, to take the bait.

"Say hi, Jackie," Espera said.

"Hi, baby," the voice came from the radio, crystal clear. The girl he'd left behind. Who had in turn, left him behind.

"You're not Jackie," Daniel said.

"I miss you."

He gritted his teeth. There was sand in his mouth.

"I do, I really do. I'm sorry we had that fight."

"We didn't have a fight. You fucked that guy from work. For months."

"Oh. Him. You don't have to worry about him, baby."

"I don't. I don't give a shit about either one of you. I dumped your ass months ago."

Why am I arguing with a ghost? He shook his head.

"He's dead, baby. You have nothing to be jealous of." She was crying. "Actually, we both are. We were being naughty on the interstate and then we hit the median."

He felt like throwing up.

"Cops said the car disintegrated. It was pretty funny." She giggled.

"I don't care."

"You should."

He didn't respond.

"I was three months pregnant. It wasn't his. I'll always be your girl, Daniel. Always."

He got up on shaky legs and walked down to the courtyard. He'd have to wait 'til morning to call her.

Kocher's suicide had set off something in them. They found two marines hanging in the showers, buck naked and wrists slit.

Daniel still hadn't called his ex-girlfriend. She was probably fine. The voices always tried to trick you. Tried to mess with your head.

It probably said something about him that his ego wouldn't let him call her up and ask if she was okay.

Ask if maybe she was pregnant. And how far along.

Someone would have called me, right?

They sure found the time to tell him his girl was fucking around on him a few months back.

He put the cheap cellphone back in his rucksack. He hadn't managed to get any real sleep, but he needed to stretch his legs.

The canteen was deserted. James wasn't in his usual spot. Probably still sleeping. He had offered to take over Daniel's shift last night and he let him.

He crossed the courtyard and went up the steps. The new guy was on comms. Daniel guessed the others put him there just to fuck with him.

"Hey, boot. How'd it go?"

The marine stood up, put the headphones in the tables. He was shaking.

"All good. I just started my shift."

"Anything out of the ordinary?"

He looked uncertain. He looked behind Daniel.

"N-no, nothing—"

His eyes widened.

The shots whizzed past Daniel's ear. The first one ricocheted off the wall in front of him. The second exploded the younger marine's knee. Then the radio was torn apart by the burst of fire.

Daniel grabbed the marine and pulled him to the ground, tucked behind the doorway.

There was more fire.

"Talk shit now, motherfucker! Talk shit now!" James screamed.

"What the fuck, Davis?" Daniel yelled back from behind cover.

James stopped shooting and stared at the now completely defunct radio. He still held his rifle, but his finger was off the trigger.

The boot was screaming. The rest of the platoon kept its distance, rifles at the ready. Someone called for the corpsman.

"You thought they were fucking with us, Dan." He shook his head, crying. "The voices."

Daniel stood up, slowly.

"You were fucking wrong, man." He punched Daniel's shoulder.

"Give me your rifle, James," Daniel said.

"I called home. They'd been trying to call me. There was an accident."

"Just give me the rifle."

"My kid is fucking dead, man. She's dead."

James pushed the rifle into Daniel's arms and pulled his sidearm. Before he had time to put it to his head and pull the trigger, Stafford tackled him like a linebacker, launching him through the doorway and onto the wall, knocking him out cold.

Shaw had put a call in back home and asked them to relay information to their unit. If they didn't hear back, they'd have to get moving and try to get to the closest base, probably get court martialed for abandoning their posts.

He looked out over the desert, up on the palace roof. He thought he could see Espera, standing in the open, waiting for them.

Maybe James's wife and child were out there, too.

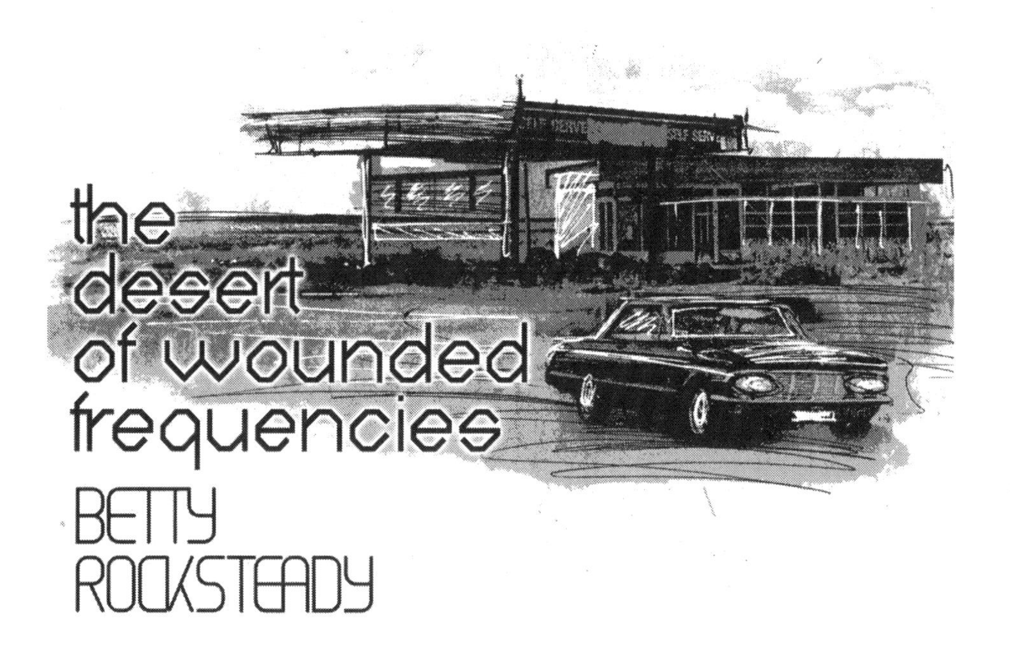

the desert of wounded frequencies

BETTY ROCKSTEADY

THE CAR WAS a piece of shit, but it would get him home and that was enough. Adam didn't have a lot of money left, but nothing was gonna stop him from getting back to Karen. He'd made a mistake, but there was no more running from it. She would never blame him. No matter what had happened.

The old man looked as bad as the car did, faded jeans and mustard stains. He kept quiet the whole time Adam looked at the car, started it up, checked under the hood. He probably could have taken off with it then and there. The creep wouldn't have done nothing, but Adam wasn't that kind of man. Not anymore.

"How much?" he finally demanded, and the old man's eyes snapped up at him, startled out of a half-doze.

He chewed his lip, stared with sunken eyes at the car. "I can let her go for 500 bucks?"

"I'm just using it as scrap. Piece of shit will probably break down before I get it halfway across town. I'm doing you a favor. 200."

He shook his head, slowly. "Can't let it go for that low. Need to make my rent this month." He nodded back at the shack where the car was parked. Didn't even own the shithole. At that age and still paying out his ass, lining someone else's pockets. Revulsion crept into Adam's stomach.

He could have paid the 500, but he saw the weakness in the man's eyes. It wouldn't take much to break him. Adam stood tall, squared his shoulders back. His eyes were steel. He reached slowly into his wallet, counted out four 50 dollar bills and handed them to the man. "Get the paperwork." There was no arguing with him.

With the paperwork was signed, the old man handed him the keys and Adam threw his bag in the backseat. He could be home in two days if he kept on cruising. Karen would be happy to see him. They could deal with the rest of it later. The man kept watching as he put the keys in the ignition and at the last moment, tapped on the glass. Something was in his eyes that Adam couldn't interpret. He was sick of this weak old man, but he rolled down the window.

"I wouldn't bother with the radio if I was you. Broke. Just leave it."

Whatever.

The second day on the road, the silence began to bother him. It was slow going, but he was in the home stretch now. He spent the night at a motel and grabbed some snacks, nearly exhausting his supply of cash. Didn't matter. Karen would have kept working. She had to, for the baby. He'd find work and they'd settle back down into how things used to be. He just needed to make it home.

But now he was out of the rush of the cities with even the occasional small town far behind him. The car had started to smell. There was no air conditioning in the old heap, and the desert roads were hot and ripe. Even with the windows wound all the way down, there wasn't so much as a goddamn breeze. He hadn't slept well last night, never did. Downed a couple beers in the shitty bar next to the motel. Maybe a couple too many, because now he found the heat and the monotony of the road tiresome. His eyes kept drooping closed.

The last store he stopped at had a batch of used tapes and CDs for sale, but this car was so old that all it had was the radio. The radio that didn't work. Fuck. Nothing ever went right, huh? At least if he could blast some tunes, maybe it would keep him awake. So close to home, but with the sun boiling down and the stuffy air, he was liable to pass out and go off the road and get impaled by a fucking cactus. It was the old man's fault. Shoulda got the thing fixed up before trying to make a couple bucks off it.

The road ahead of him was straight as an arrow, miles of sand tapering off into the horizon. Eyes so heavy they felt like they were fulla sand, but when he rolled up the window, the stuffiness made it impossible to breathe. Adam grunted and pounded his fist against the dash. A hiss of static shrieked, startling him awake.

"Jesus fuckin Christ." He yanked the volume down until the static turned to a dull hum. Didn't work his ass. Fucker just wanted to make sure his trip was as miserable as possible. He adjusted the knobs, searching for a station. Futile. There was nothing out here in the middle of nowhere. Might have done him some good when he was back in the city, but he had trusted the old creep and fucked himself over once again.

"Asshole," he muttered, and silenced the radio. The static continued to mumble. He stabbed the knob again but the crackling continued to fill the car. He spun the knob and the irritating sound whined louder. He turned it the other way with no effect.

"Fuck off." He yanked at knobs and spun through channels, swerving over the empty road. The sound didn't change.

"Of course. Of course he's gotta make this whole trip fucking miserable. A guy tries to do a good thing, go back to his fucking fat loaf of a wife and idiot child but ya can't cut him a break. Always gotta have shit like this happen." Adam's face flushed hot and red. He pushed the little car faster. "Get me outta this fucking desert." His map lay useless on the seat next to him. Straight fucking line the whole way in this hunk of junk car, and now this fucking maddening static as his accompaniment. Could it get any worse?

He kept driving. There was nothing else to do. The visions he had had of his homecoming were tainted now. He had figured he would get home, Karen would be thrilled to see him, get a little poke in before she made dinner. Have a couple beers. Back at it again. But now after this shit drive, he knew he would have a fucker of a headache. He might be better off stopping at the next motel and cabbing it the rest of the way home. There was no sense going home in a sour mood—he had some serious sucking up to do to get back in Karen's good graces again. Hell, it shouldn't take too much. She needed him. She better.

He had been doing fine for a few weeks, burning through his money, drinking, meeting girls. But then one of them had noticed the tan line on his wedding finger and asked what happened. He gave her the abbreviated version, but that got him to thinking. If he was doing this, what would Karen be up to? He pictured her and that horny neighbor talking about him and it sent that red hot anger through him. The dude had just been waiting for his chance to get Karen in the sack. The real sensitive type. Always asking to hold the baby as if it weren't a whining crying sack of shit. That made him real mad and he realized that meant it was time to go home and collect what was his.

Karen wouldn't have done anything yet. She was the faithful type. Real forgiving. She knew how a woman was supposed to behave. He would be safe, he was sure of it. He never shoulda run off in the first place.

While he was lost in thought, the static changed. There was something beneath it, getting louder. Something breathing.

"The fuck?"

After all this driving, he had to be getting close to the city, or at least some signal somewhere was strong enough for this hunk of junk to pick up. Fucking weird though. Sounded like some greasy mouth-breather just leaning over the mic and jerking off or something. He fiddled with the radio again, but it was the same on every channel.

"Fucking weird-ass stations out here." He glanced at the map. Reading all those fucking lines and numbers were a headache.

The breathing grew heavier and faster, the static more discordant. Annoying motherfucker. He still had the old man's number circled in the paper, he'd call him up when he got home. He deserved some of his cash back.

"OH GOD, OH GOD, WHAT DID YOU DO?" a woman's voice boomed through the car, and Adam screamed, swerving to the right, dangerously close to going off the road.

"What the fuck was that?"

The radio buzzed and he stared at the dead dumb thing, tense, waiting for it to yell again. His heart rattled in his chest, but the radio remained silent.

He levelled the car back out and drove on. His mouth tasted sour. He stabbed at the radio buttons. He had just picked up on some Christian station or something, one of those weird ones they have out here in the middle of nowhere. People going slowly insane, thinking they have a direct line to God or something. Dumb sonsofbitches. It hadn't really scared him, not that much. Fucker.

The radio buzzed on in a shrill whine. So fucking annoying. He didn't want to listen anymore, but what the hell else was he supposed to do? He was stuck out here. The desert was fucking endless. There was no way to distract himself from the sounds that crept in beneath the static. As much as he hated to admit it, he should have listened to the old man and not turned the fucker on. Not only was it annoying, but it was dangerous. Loud sounds outta nowhere would startle anyone. If he weren't so far away, he'd be tempted to turn back and confront him, demand his money back. But there was only going forward now. Back to Karen. Back to the baby.

On the bright side, maybe those choking sounds meant he was getting closer to civilization. Closer at least to wherever this station was, or wherever this weirdo was holed up in their basement transmitting. A voice murmured, but it was impossible to make out beneath the other sounds. A woman. Sounded like a woman. Singing. Hey, maybe that was a good sign. Maybe there was some normal programming after all. Or maybe she was screaming.

A thin sheen of sweat covered Adam's face, and he rolled the window down. The wind had intensified outside, but it didn't bring any fresh air. More like hot breath on the back of his neck, spattering sand into the sweat. He tried to roll the window back up, but it stuck. This car really should have been used for parts. Piece of shit. He heard a honk and glanced back, but there was nothing for miles. Just the empty road. He was rewarded with another hot gust of sand, irritating against his skin, biting like glass.

He turned back to wipe his face on his sleeve and there was someone in the car next to him. A woman. She stared at him. Her eyes were too dark. Endless. He lifted his head, heart thudding, and she was gone.

The mumbling on the radio turned to soft words. Adam's throat constricted. Something . . . He could only make out a few words, but it was a woman. Saying something in a singsong voice. Uselessly, he spun the knob. The voice rang out clear as bells. A lullaby, one he didn't recognize. The music accompanying her didn't sound like normal instruments at all. The plucking sounded more like the creaking of a bed than guitar strings. Something dripping. She chuckled.

"Shut up, you creepy bitch." His voice cracked as he spun the knobs. Jesus Christ, would he ever be out of this fucking desert? It shouldn't have taken more than an hour or so to get through this stretch of road, but it was creeping up upon supper time now. His guts cramped, but he wasn't hungry. He should have been home by now, talking his way back into Karen's bed.

"Do you think she forgives you? Everyone knows." The voice was louder than it had been before, the static shocked into silence. Adam's heart sank deep into his stomach.

Fuck kinda radio show was this?

The static droned, wet sounds beneath it, breathing and something else. Something unpleasant. The skin on his arms prickled. The sweat and sand that stuck to his skin, begging for a shower. Fuck getting home tonight. As soon as he got out of this desert he was checking into a motel, getting a hot shower, and ditching this shitty car. He would call Karen and she could pick him up.

The static gave way to a gentle sobbing. Who the hell broadcast this shit? This bubbling anxiety was an unfamiliar sensation to Adam, and he tried to keep it under control. This wasn't who he was. He clenched his teeth. The sweat stains beneath his armpits weren't who he was.

He trained his eyes on the road. Focus. The sobs faded back into the static, and his eyes grew heavy again. In the distance, near the horizon, he spotted a shape. The first landmark for miles. Good. He must be getting closer to . . . something. All this desert could drive a man crazy. He drove faster, eager to see a change of scenery.

He got closer, and the shape gradually turned into something recognizable. His stomach went sour. It was a baby carriage, empty, abandoned among the endless sand. As if triggered by this, the gentle sobs of the woman gave way to a baby crying. Fuck. Fuck. Fuck. The most irritating sound known to man. The squalls and shrieks were maddening. Adam pounded his fists against the steering wheel. "For God's sake, how fucking far do I have to go? Fuck's sake."

The screams grew louder, shrieking, begging, needy and suddenly they stopped. Abruptly. Just like . . .

Static.

His foot went heavy against the gas. The desert was too long. Something was wrong. He must have taken the wrong turn. He should be in town by now. He should be driving down city streets instead of this fucking desert. Jesus Christ, he didn't even give a shit about getting back to Karen now. He wanted a cool glass of water, and then a whisky. And another whisky. He felt like he had been driving for days.

The static grew steadily louder the faster the car went, until it was screeching in his ears, discordant offbeat sounds pounding and pounding until he wanted to scream He slammed on the brakes and the car screeched to a stop and he got out. He just needed to stand up for a minute. Take a breath. Get his senses back. Faintly, he heard the familiar sounds of traffic, but the desert was empty. The sun was setting, turning the sky blood-red. This was impossible. Ridiculous.

He could still hear it.

The static surrounded him now. He took shaky, weak steps out into the road. The hiss rained down from the sky, along with all the other sounds beneath it—the honking of horns, the screech of brakes. The voices. The murmurs. The screams.

"Stop it. I'm going home! I'm going home! I don't fucking care what happened to the baby!"

She would forgive him. She always forgave him.

The baby screamed and screamed and he remembered how it felt when he shook it and shook it and its head jolted back and forth until it finally stopped screaming. It was better now. It was quiet. Still breathing, just a trickle of blood from its eyes. It would be fine. He had run but he was done running now. He was going home.

He took a breath.

The static couldn't hurt him.

He got back behind the wheel. The seatbelt jammed. Fuck it. He was going home. He pressed the gas pedal to the floor. The static was too loud, deafening, but he didn't care he was moving. He was driving. Next to him the dark woman turned and stared at him. He didn't want to look at her but he looked and her eyes bled tears and she opened her mouth and a scream of static poured out and she was screaming and the baby was screaming and Adam was screaming and

The desert sky wavered. Warped. It peeled away. The city was there. Oh God, he was so close to home. Traffic was congested and there were cars and people everywhere and he was not in the desert anymore. He could have laughed, but the colors were too bright to look at and he was going too fast. Metal screeched and rubber burned and the car careened off the street and slammed into a telephone pole. He was propelled from his seat and his head slammed through the windshield and the pain stopped and everything went quiet. It was better now. It was such a relief. Ribbons of glass sliced through his head and stuck in his eyes and he didn't care.

The car behind him swerved, slammed into the fender of the car ahead. Traffic piled up. Cars slid to a stop around the wreck. People ogled and gasped and dialed the police.

A few cars back, a woman parked neatly at the side of the road and came forward. “I’m a doctor,” she said, and pushed her way through the crowd. It didn’t take a professional to see there was no hope for this man. Glass protruded from his face. His bones were shattered, yanked haphazard through his skin. There was nothing she could do. But she could hear something.

The excited chatter of pedestrians faded away. She moved closer.

His mouth gaped open, blood dripping on the pavement. Static. Must be the radio, something happened to it in the crash.

Around the glass, his eyes stared at her. Beneath the static, something hissed and whispered and she leaned in to listen.

eternity lie in its radius

CHRISTOPHER SLATSKY

Christ's corpse lies at your feet,
Inglorious defeat,
Fleet is the cloven hoofed one.

Music filled the room. Frayed curtains shuddered under the acoustic assault. A sepulcher voice groaned with barely controlled rage:

Nurse at Baphomet's decaying bust,
Eyes the color of rust.
Suckle at the festering teat.
Inglorious defeat,
Fleet is the cloven—

Luke slammed his fist against a cymbal. "Godammit! Keep up you guys!"

Molly gripped the neck of her guitar in frustration. Everything felt askew. Small things, difficult to describe, a nagging sense of foreboding.

Ever since Mark found that radio station.

Things had drastically changed once he'd introduced the band to station 6EQU-J5 and its sublime sounds a few weeks ago.

Pirate radio. What else could it be? 6EQU-J5's schedule was unpredictable, playing ambient, droning gloom intermittently, at random hours. The DJ never announced the bands or song titles, much less themselves, just a woman's voice identifying the station and following with odd observations and rambling colloquies that never made much sense. None of the tunes were familiar to any of the band. It simply broadcast the most obscure music. The underground of the underground.

Molly couldn't deny the station's sounds were influencing their own sound now, and the band *had* advanced leaps and bounds both technically and creatively.

"Calm the fuck down, Lucas." Mark bared his teeth. A pantomime of someone far more dangerous than mere mortal Mark Woods could ever be. He insisted on wearing gruesome corpse makeup at every practice session. The hot room had his chin dripping black and red rivulets onto a white *Daemonphiliac* t-shirt.

"Didn't quit *Andromalius-36* to work with a bunch of amateurs." Gavin stabbed his cigarette in Mark's direction. He'd recently moved into the house. Brought along an M 88 mic and state of the art Eventide H3000 his music producer father had purchased for him. Real professional.

The band's living room doubled as their rehearsal space. It stank of cigarettes and the remnants of fried egg sandwiches that Luke seemed to subsist on. The damp weather seeped through the cracks in the concrete floor, into the flimsy drywall, wafted a musty odor into the air.

Molly couldn't complain, though; Luke's uncle had rented the ramshackle house to the band at a steal. A cheap place to crash allowed them to practice whenever they had time. And they usually had plenty of that.

She plucked her guitar strings, unconsciously tremolo picking. "Less than two weeks left, guys. At this rate, Temple of Skulls is gonna look like goddam amateurs when we play at the HoloScene."

"Fuck that. We signed on as Eldritch Covan." Luke was quick to anger, forehead sanguine as his hair. Even the freckles beneath his German Textualis *font* ZERFALL tattoo flared up.

"Still spelling coven with an 'A'? Jesus, we're gonna embarrass ourselves." Molly propped her guitar against the amp.

Luke swigged his room temperature beer. "Temple of Skulls is queer. Maybe if you weren't always on the rag you wouldn't say such stupid shit." He scratched at a mangy beard.

Molly flipped him off.

Luke pointed his drumstick at Mark as if it were a weapon. "I know a decent bass player if you don't have the sack to do this."

"Fuckin' with the wrong bull." Mark exposed his ochre teeth again.

Luke stood up from behind his drum set.

"Not another fight, please." Molly looked to Mark. "You said you made another mix tape?"

"I did. Right here." Mark picked up a cassette case from the coffee table.

"When'd you record that?" Gavin handed his battered boombox to Mark. Its surface was covered in stickers, goat skulls over a valknut symbol.

Mark dropped the cassette in. "Earlier this morning. 6EQU-J5 just started playing again, so I taped it."

"You keep your radio on all the time?" Molly asked.

"Yeah. Just in case they start up. Station came alive around 6:30 this morning, I mean, this music we're tapping into, well, we're on our way. But this. We might get somewhere beyond with this. This stuff is orgone energy mainlined into your spine." Mark turned the boombox's volume way up.

The music was tinny, emanating from deep within the opening of unexplored regions.

Abrupt, dissonant notes squiggled into Molly's ears. Auditory apprehension, a high-pitched chaos assaulted her brain. Sporadic chords made the colors in the room tremble.

Droning bass instruments, riffs so achingly slow they degenerated into peals of chaotic noise. A crackling in the background, reminding Molly of something she'd heard recorded on an old wax cylinder at the science museum on her third-grade field trip.

She closed her eyes, saw the opening to a cave. Entrance narrow and tall, like a massive wound from a giant's axe cleft. The only movement came from swaying weeds on a stretch of abandoned train tracks.

She couldn't describe any of the music as death or sludge or stoner metal, but a vibration of memory quivered inside her body. A dark thrill lingered. Her mouth filled with saliva in prelude to vomiting.

The cave flickered in her memory, edges wavering as if the rock was steaming. She expected a hint of a face nobody deserved to see. But nothing peeked out. Only the hypnotic motion of the foliage and the unchanging black maw. She opened her eyes.

“What the fuck just happened?” Luke was wide-eyed.

“Our new sound happened.” Mark ejected the cassette.

“Are you fuckin’ with us? You really tape this off of that radio station?” He waved the plastic case in front of Mark’s face.

“Yeah. I did.” Mark was red-eyed, sweaty. Words slurred as if he’d just woken with a wicked hangover.

“I think you know more about this music than you’re letting on.” Luke’s voice was laced with rage. His tone made Molly anxious.

Luke and Mark had beaten the shit out of each other before, Mark usually receiving the worst of it, but lately Luke was all too often on the verge of violence. His body language insinuated he wanted to hurt someone and it wasn’t like he needed much provocation—he’d more than his fair share of assaults and disorderly conduct on record.

“I know how to press play and record at the same time.” Mark’s sneer fell immediately when he noticed Luke’s expression.

Luke leaned his face in an inch from Mark’s. “Or maybe this is another of your faggy musical experiments. You *are* the only queer here wearing makeup.”

Mark grinned, stained teeth and deep red tongue contrasted against black lips.

“Maybe you’re both right.” Molly joked, smoothing down the sharp edges of tension in the room.

Luke threw his half-full beer can across the room with all his strength. It hit the wall, clattered noisily to the floor.

Gavin winced. The beer can’s impact left a crescent-shaped gouge in the drywall. Hops scented foam hissed on the concrete.

Luke laughed at Gavin’s reaction. He tapped his foot against the pedal of the kick drum. “Don’t just stand there, you fucking subhumans. Let’s play.”

Molly had the house to herself. She could only watch so much news coverage on the fall of the Berlin Wall before her brain glazed over, so she turned the barely functioning TV off. Gavin had gone out with his girlfriend who refused to step foot on the property. Claimed the house gave off “bad vibes”. Luke was elbow-deep in antifreeze doing an opening shift at the oil change place. Who knew where Mark went when out of the house.

She opened Mark's bedroom door. Intruding was out of character for her, but she'd put off returning the books she'd borrowed for far too long. She'd been curious about his metaphysical beliefs, but his occult literature hadn't been particularly illuminating. Not much more than a hodgepodge of Aleister Crowley chicanery, bastardized Austin Osman Spare, and clichéd horror novel tropes. Far too many of those who'd written about the "occult arts" seemed more interested in starting sex-cults than expanding their awareness. Molly wasn't convinced that Mark had any more insight into magick than she. He certainly hadn't shown any signs he knew how to "utilize one's will to formulate a desire, to form a belief to come to fruition".

Whatever the hell that meant.

The stereo hissed with static. Of course Mark had left the dial on 6EQU-J5.

His bedroom creeped her out. Worn underground club fliers curled from the wall, tape no longer sticky enough to hold them flat. Metal band posters covered the ceiling, *Malfeitor*, *Burzum*, images of occult sigils and demonic figures leering behind the various band's names. Bottles, glasses, and jars covered every available surface. Most held what appeared to be sand or soil. Stacks of books on the afterlife, witchcraft, and music functioned as makeshift tables to hold more bottles. The place hadn't been cleaned since they'd moved in. A thick layer of cobwebs sagged in the corners near the ceiling. The air smelled of cheap weed and stale sweat.

She set the books on top of the dresser, next to a collection of neatly arranged antique poison bottles. As she turned to leave, her elbow bumped the furniture. The bottles wobbled in such a way she could tell they were filled with a viscous fluid. The station's hissing rose in volume.

Curiosity got the better of her. She popped the cork on a mercury bichloride vial.

It was filled with semen.

She gagged, put everything back the way she'd found it. Mark must have been using his fluids for rituals. Some kind of sex magic. Something she had no business knowing. Whatever he did in the name of his religion was no concern of hers.

Something within the radio station's white noise coalesced into a string of words, an ambiguous chain of sentences all the more disturbing for being unintelligible.

She quickly left the room.

The bedroom door slowly swung open.

Mark's nude corpse hovered in the air. Left arm hanging limply, right wriggling its fingers. Small flaccid penis against pale skin. He marched in place, skinny legs bent at the knees. A grotesque puppet dance.

A woman's voice spoke soothingly from the stereo.

You're listening to radio chaos from the Shores of Nowhere.

Mark's forearms were laid open, red meat and fatty tissue split wide. An umbilical of milky ectoplasm poured from the gaping wounds to a ceiling no longer visible from the miasma of a silvery gray substance filling the room. Wet ectoplasmic strings tugged at his limbs, snaked in and out of his ears, nostrils, and toothless mouth. He floated a foot above the ground, stumbled against the furniture. A clumsy marionette.

Corpse paint gave him a silly clown face. There was nothing malevolent here. Just a sad, lost young man wearing ridiculous makeup he'd hoped would make him appear intimidating. His vacant eye sockets winked like a perineal reflex.

Molly knew she was having the nightmare again. The consequence of dead-end jobs and grandiose dreams of musical success that had no chance of succeeding. All that anxiety cascading over her soul resulted in epic night terrors again and again.

Molly's mind was reserved despite the grotesque corpse hovering before her. She should fight back, sink her fists into Mark's cadaver, tear at the soft pale ectoplasmic strands. Maybe then she'd escape this bleak little town. Hitch a ride to another less depressing though equally squalid burgh where her father would drive out to meet her. Take her home to the old neighborhood, old bedroom, old rituals, old day to day routines. Finish her degree in anthropology, perhaps even work part-time at her parent's community theater. Maybe she could feel occasional bouts of joy and not dream about ending her own life minute by minute, day to day.

Solace by delusion.

But she didn't fight back. Mark's body wasn't frightening. It was pathetic. A ridiculous thumb push puppet flailing about. Hodgepodge phantom stitched together by depression, exacerbated by anxiety. There was no intention in a corpse's brain. No desire to harm. Mark's remains existed solely as a demonstration of just how meaningless any decision would ultimately become.

The woman's radio voice sputtered in an out of tune. *Be sure to tune into 6EQU-J5 tomorrow night when we'll listen to the sounds from the deepest depths of the darkest places.*

Molly sat at the edge of her bed staring out the window at the gray trees devoid of leaves. *That fucking nightmare again.*

It'd been three days since she'd gone into Mark's bedroom. She'd suffered the same nightmare every evening since. *So stupid.* Why hadn't she just dropped the books off in front of his door?

Here she was stuck in a dead town decorated with dead foliage populated by people who might as well be dead. Her only career prospect was trudging up the retail ladder at the department store. Or failing employment, attending the community college 30 minutes away. Stay in this town with its rickety gray wooden bridges, old tincture ads which made them historically significant per some arbitrary committee decision. Pretty much the only significance in this ass-end of the country.

She'd dreamt that music would lift her out of this malaise. Fame was never a concern, but the chance to create her art, make a living at it, even if a frugal one, meant everything.

But she'd borne the brunt of the band's booking duties, printed out their fliers, even ordered t-shirts for their modest gigs. She'd had to deal with managers who'd requested a hand job for a spot at a music festival, worse for opening at a state tour for some mid-level band. And they were still going nowhere fast.

This wasn't how the dream was supposed to manifest.

Maybe it was time to concede defeat. This nagging doubt persisted despite her confidence in her abilities. She just needed to get away from here. She had talent, brains and determination—assets anywhere else but here in this crumbling, sinkhole of a town.

She needed to escape.

Retch on the God Flesh,
Bone dust chokes the encroaching storm,
Silt blackens the flesh of the stillborn,
Choir of salt crusted cardinals,
Chant from mouths sick with barnacles,
Praise be thrice cursed abomination.

The song rattled Molly's innards. Something was different, something both subtle and aggressive accompanied her chords, Luke's drumming, Mark's bass lines. She couldn't be the only one hearing a phantom voice behind Gavin's vocal track. She couldn't explain it—everything they'd written since drawing inspiration from 6EQU-J5's music had become greater than the sum of its parts. Each component collectively making music that was not only unique, but manifesting as sounds she hadn't noticed when they'd recorded the songs. Something was wrong.

Gloriously wrong.

When had they last listened to that radio station? It must have been recently, though Molly was hard pressed to place the date.

The band was more prolific than ever. Creativity flowed with the urgency of a slit wrist ever since they'd incorporated the notes, tone and ambience of the various songs from that station into their own pieces. It wasn't only quantity, but quality. Music of despair, hypnotic waves. Insinuations of the wretched crying out. A bass driven sonic pulse, songs of apprehension that made you look over your shoulder in anticipation.

They played late into the night, at such a frenetic pace Molly's fingers began to bleed. It wasn't until a high-as-a-kite Luke pushed Mark to the ground and kicked him repeatedly in the ribs that practice came to an end. Gavin intervened, shoved Luke a few times. But it was a half-hearted attempt at masculine aggression; both quickly went their separate ways. Mark insisted he was fine, shut himself off in his room. Luke crashed on the couch. Gavin went for a drive.

Just another Saturday night.

Molly went to bed. Between the harrowing all too familiar nightmare and a nasty virus that had her bent over the toilet bowl until the early morning, she managed to get little sleep. It didn't help that Mark insisted on playing that radio station so loudly she began to hear coherent phrases within the static.

Gavin never returned from his drive.

"You don't wanna try calling his girlfriend again?" Molly asked.

Luke shook his head. "Fuck both of 'em. Hasn't answered in days. Gavin hasn't even dropped by to pick up his clothes or equipment. Face it. He got sick of the fighting, quit the band. Ain't comin' back for shit."

Mark was still wearing sweatpants and the same dirty t-shirt from the night before. His hair was greasy and clumpy. Blotches of corpse paint oily on his skin. "I'll cover Gavin's vocals. We don't have time to hunt down a new lead vocalist."

Molly sat on the couch. Someone should call the police. Report Gavin as missing. Nobody knew where his family lived. Couldn't even remember what he drove. But her concern was superseded by anticipation for the new music.

"Dibs on his boombox." Luke was hunched over the stereo, eyes glazed over in excitement. He twisted the knob fine tune reception for the station. Mark stared across the room at nothing in particular. The air filled with that all too familiar white noise.

A woman's voice broke the monotony.

Welcome to 6EQU-J5, dreadful radio for dreaded listeners. Tonight we're broadcasting from the caverns at the—

"First try. Impressive," Mark whispered.

"Shut the fuck up." Luke glared at him.

—join us for the next few hours as we take a trip to the end of the line.

The music began. Slow, plodding riffs, grooves dragging like a wounded animal's shattered limb. Molly couldn't differentiate individual instruments—a sitar, a woodwind, definitely drums, so muffled yet resonant she couldn't tell if they were tupan, snare, maybe dhols. Leaden, incremental notes of doom laden progression. A claustrophobic, persistent chill vibrated bones and stilled muscles.

The songs played for an hour. When it was over the speakers took to spitting out static once more. Molly couldn't ignore the woman's intro'.

Broadcasting from the caverns.

Trip to the end of the line.

It was too similar to her cave and train tracks vision for her to simply dismiss as a coincidence. But none of this made any sense. She was connecting the dots where there weren't any. Even so, she couldn't shake it out of her head.

They were eager to practice. The sounds they conjured were far beyond anything expected. Soul stirring tunes that made chests ache and heads reel. The three musicians had never produced anything as sublime as what they were now invoking.

Gavin's disappearance quickly became a distant memory.

"Molly. We need to talk." Mark nervously peeled a sliver of black polish from his thumbnail.

Molly continued to fiddle with the distortion pedal. She'd been dreading this conversation for days. "What about?"

"Just wonderin' if you'd picked up anything useful from my books."

"They were interesting. So mote it be and shit."

"I wanted to explain about the bottles."

"You really don't have to." She plugged the cable jack into her guitar.

"Yeah. I do."

"Pretty sure you don't."

"Please hear me out."

"All right. All right."

Mark sat down on the floor, slouched so low his chin touched his chest. "Look. It all started with Victorian séances. Always been obsessed with them. Mediums back then would tap into these eldritch realms. Séances. Honest to God séances. Usually run by women fighting back against a society that saw female sexuality as mysterious. Dangerous shit. Practiced their arts the only way they could."

Molly had read her fair share on the history of the occult, even written a paper on Eusapia Palladino for her Women's Studies class. She doubted Mark even considered the possibility she wasn't clueless.

"Damn. I'm not explaining this right." He straightened his spine, sat upright. "There's this German poet. Died 1800s. Said something about music that really spoke to me. I memorized it." He rubbed his palms together as if bracing for a grueling task.

"'Music is a strange thing. I would almost say it is a miracle. For it stands halfway between thought and phenomenon, between spirit and matter, a sort of nebulous mediator, like and unlike each of the things it mediates—spirit that requires manifestation in time, and matter that can do without space.'"

He looked to Molly, silly grin on his face as if waiting for her acceptance before continuing.

"I might steal that from you, actually," Molly said.

"Yeah? Well, music, radio waves and magic are the same thing. Music waves are, are sort of, um, ectoplasm as sound. Ectoplasm is *wet* sound transmissions. A weird kind of substance, in between the physical and the spiritual."

He locked his fingers together. "Bridges between the material and immaterial realms."

"You said ectoplasm?" The nightmare frolicked in Molly's head.

"Yeah. Ever hear of Eliphas Levi?"

"Can't say that I have."

"A magician. Molded astral light into physical forms. It's like this: science and math, all about how nature does her thing. But on the other side you have words and stories and symbols. They help explain how things work too, just in a different way than science."

Molly didn't mean to sound condescending, but found it difficult to keep the skepticism out of her voice. "So you're talking ontology?"

"Not sure what you mean."

"How stories themselves make something exist. Words used to describe ideas make the ideas real. *Why is existence the way it is.* That kinda shit."

"Holy fuck. Not just a face and kick-ass guitarist." He tapped a long fingernail against the concrete floor in contemplation. "Look Molly. I'll be the first to admit there's only so much Crowley or Alice Bailey you can read before you know they're full a shit. There's no easy way to say this."

"Then say it uneasily."

"Radio 6EQU-J5 showed me where to look."

"For what?" Molly pushed her dark purple hair from her face.

"For the ectoplasm I stored in the bottles."

Mark could call his sperm collection ectoplasm or whatever the hell he wanted, but it still didn't make it magic to Molly. She wasn't even sure what he was rambling on about. But she was reluctant to cast aspersions based on an admittedly unsettling hobby. He was actually excited about discussing something that he'd likely been mocked for previously. But that recurring nightmare and the ectoplasm. And collecting body fluids?

No way was this healthy.
"Thanks for letting me borrow your books."
"Anytime, Molly."

Molly asked a few co-workers at the department store if they knew of a cave near abandoned train tracks in the woods nearby. A few had heard rumors but didn't know any locations. It wasn't until she was leaving for the day that Mr. Ormond from the electronics department mentioned he knew what she was looking for.

Ormond was a chatty old man. Widowed, children grown, grandkids probably in their teens and no longer concerned with visiting. Retired, but lonely enough to keep working at a minimum wage anti-union department store.

"Used to go walking them tracks at night. When we was kids. Trains ran lumber shipments through town up to Cottage Hollow. Them cars'd get past 60 miles per hour through these parts. No horn, goin' so fast you don't get that clackity clack. Hear nothin' but metal hissin' on metal if you're lucky. Never knew what we was riskin' until Danny got killed."

"Sorry."

"S'all right. Long time ago. We swored up and down that train didn't come along and hit Danny until *after* whatever hit him did so. There he was, behind the gang, then bam! I seen hands go up in the air and the night is fulla light and Danny be screamin'. Then the tracks start shakin'. See the train lights on the way. Jumped off the side right as it shot by. Ain't no train tore Danny up. So's I say anyway."

"And you said there's a cave out there?"

"I did indeed, lovely lady. Place out that ways where some kids disappeared. They filled that hole in with cement some 30 years ago. It's at the end of the tracks that used to run north. Few miles past the DR. CLARK'S LUXURIOUS LINIMENT bridge."

"Thanks, Mr. Ormond. Appreciate it."

"Any time, lovely lady."

Molly's shift ended just after lunch. Plenty of daylight left to go hiking into the woods, find the tracks and allow them to guide her way. Maybe she could verify whether or not 6EQU-J5 had anything to do with the cave. There was no reason to think so, though her visions were persistent and she felt she had to follow through on any possible connection. She was 10-years-old again, heading out on an adventure. Following clues to locate some mysterious transmissions being sent from a hidden radio station. She didn't really believe anything would come of this, but the fantasy motivated her.

She walked slowly at first. She wanted to waste as much time as possible before heading back to the house. The constant harassment, the omnipresent potential for violence—it was all far beyond what she'd prepared herself for. Never felt safe renting a place with three guys in the first place, and now that it was down to two it felt even *more* threatening. She shouldn't have to live with a cloud of fear hovering over her at all times.

She'd even bent over backwards to accommodate Luke's tragedy, a childhood afflicted with domestic violence and the death of his older brother Derek. It didn't excuse Luke's behavior, but she'd tried to understand where his abusive personality came from.

Luke had been 14, Derek 16, when they'd decided to go deer poaching. Common enough in these parts where the cost of a hunting license was too steep and families had hunted the land for many generations.

The brothers were oiling guns, making sure they'd sufficient ammo, when Luke jokingly pointed his .30-30 at Derek. One moment his brother was laughing and drinking beer, the next he was just a mandible on top of a neck.

Molly shuddered. At least it wasn't hunting season. That and her bright yellow Cramps hoody diminished the chances of getting picked off by some camouflage-wearing redneck.

She arrived at the covered bridge with the DR. CLARK'S LUXURIOUS LINIMENT ad on the side. She leaned her upper body over the weathered rails, closed her eyes, thought about how cold the water would be.

Imagined her mouth engorged with mud and sodden leaves.

The sound of limbs banging against smooth river rocks.

She walked across the rickety boards, slid a finger under her sleeve, from wrist to the inside of her elbow. Instinctual, a tactile habit, like the unconscious way she held a cigarette. She wished she'd been able to slice deeper past the skin's surface. If she'd just managed to do that much more this perpetual dance of attempted suicides would have concluded. She had to admit it was a lovely scar, smooth and shiny as a gemstone.

Flirting with suicide was just the clumsy foreplay of an adolescent's romantic notion of dying. Time to accept adulthood with a finger on the trigger. Lips on the barrel. Move beyond this half-assed game played with ineffective pills and razors whose consequences could be stemmed by a concerned ex-boyfriend dropping her off at the emergency room.

Those maudlin teen years are long past. Stop being such a cliché.

The day was colder than expected. She sipped from her energy drink. Mr. Ormond had been right—the train tracks were less than a couple of miles into the woods. She quickened her pace along the rails. Doc Martens knocked bits of the decaying beams into the grass. The frost had stripped the color from the tree limbs. Brittle silvery-gray twigs bent down in a convoluted skein. Some touched the ice-limned ground, others contrasted against the crisp blue sky like an anatomist's map of the circulatory system.

Molly passed a familiar paperback maple, bark peeling away in scabby segments. It couldn't be the same one—she'd walked by another identical to it less than twenty minutes ago. She kept walking.

She sure as hell wasn't nostalgic for her high school years. But there was still something to be said for those times when so much seemed possible. When she could've been a musician, or a writer, or a veterinarian. All were equally plausible. But after graduating from Cottage Hollow High the world had become uncompromisingly dull. Sure her school years were hell, but adulthood was hellish *and* boring.

She saw the maple again. This was impossible. The tracks couldn't run in one massive circle.

The sun was setting. She didn't realize how long she'd been hiking. At least four hours had passed. She stepped off the train tracks, cut into the woods back towards town.

She came out near the DR. CLARK'S LUXURIOUS LINIMENT covered bridge.

Molly awoke from the Mark-marionette nightmare again.

She couldn't get back to sleep. She put her headphones on, turned on her Walkman, tuned it to 6EQU-J5. Of course it was just the usual wave of crackling and popping.

She closed her eyes and listened.

She saw the cave again. It was dark, the only things in motion were silhouettes of blades of grass. The mouth of the cave glowed with the color of something that wasn't firelight.

A shadow passed within.

Music erupted in Molly's ears.

The sounds invoked the crisp, damp atmosphere of a cavern. She felt the ground gritty beneath her bare feet, air sharp like breathing particles of suspended glass. Even the graffiti on the stone was visible in her mind's eye, colors as faded as the labels on the antique beer cans littering the floor. She could smell the creosote outside on the old wood tracks and the fresh scent of the overgrowth rustling in a breeze.

The cave was a massive entity sculpted by centuries of water, the maw of something old even for the earth. A god's orifice where extinct peoples had intruded and offered supplications.

If she tilted her head just so, squinted her eyes and allowed the sputtering noise to overwhelm her, she could see a yawning crack in the back. She sensed the recess led to deeper, darker regions of the planet.

Music came from within.

She'd been fascinated by archaeoacoustics in college after an anthropology professor gave a lecture on rhythms altering brainwaves. She'd followed up on the subject, even written an extra credit paper on the bell-like sounds conjured from stalactites and stalagmites which some Paleolithic peoples played like a lithophone. Deep, resonant chambers echoed voices, infrasonic drumming altering consciousness, reverberating throughout time.

Molly gently placed her head against the cold rock surrounding the fissure. She closed one eye, opened the other wide as if looking through a telescope. It was too dark to make out any detail but she could smell something thick and watery flowing inside.

Gorgeous forms suddenly wriggled in the black. A kaleidoscopic whorl deep within the earth. Prisoner's cinema in all its glory. But these displays of light were tangible, coalescing fat globules careening off each other only to dart off into the blackness as greasy flaming stars.

Gavin's voice chanted from within the chasm. Singing to music that had not been created by human hands.

It was the most beautiful music Molly had ever heard. She knew that if she ever escaped this fugue state she'd never be able to describe it.

It was all so clear now. Every attempt to understand this world was useless. Art and the scientific method were inherently limited; neither could adequately describe anything examining existence through goggles fogged by an anthropocentric lens.

She could see how the entirety of human inquiry was irrelevant. Human creativity nothing more than a petulant whine after listening to the songs of burnt out stars, the poetry of entropy. Voices of dead throats in ancient caverns.

The cave continued to perform its numinous joy, trumpeting such transcendent notes it moved Molly to deep gasping sobs. Everything in comparison were just coprolites littering cave floors.

She knew she'd never be able to leave this town. Knew this with such devotion she simply kept the headphones on and her eyes tightly shut even after her Walkman's batteries finally died.

They listened to 6EQU-J5's static early that morning for a good two hours before the music began playing.

There was nothing melodic about the songs. A lingering void insinuated itself into every note. A whiff of rot ran beneath everything, an unctuous flow thick with infection. The pitch was off, ascending and swooping in delirious waves. The tones of something struggling its way free.

Molly stood up quickly, turned the boombox off. "I can't do this any more."

"The fuck?" Luke grabbed her wrist. "Don't touch my shit."

"Don't touch me, asshole. And it's not yours. It's Gavin's." Molly positioned herself to throw a punch.

Luke pushed her away. Boots left a black skid mark on the cement floor.

Mark had mellowed to a catatonic state. He stood bleary-eyed, seemingly unaware of their presence. Luke jabbed him in the chest with a finger. "You're the one who let this cunt play guitar in our band. Put a leash on it."

Mark struggled out of his torpor. "Gavin's gone. Think about it—Molly does all the managing shit, bills and all that. Your uncle will kick us out without her part of the rent."

Molly held her hands up, acknowledging defeat. "Can't do this any more. Done carrying your sorry asses. You're both fucking losers. I'm twice the musician either of you are, but I'm constantly shit on."

"Shut up, bitch. You don't know a goddam thing," Luke said.

"I know you're a mediocre drummer who can't write music. Jesus, can you even talk about anything other than childish pagan white power circle-jerking bullshit?"

"I'd stop while ahead. You don't even know how stupid you sound."

"Smart enough to know when to call it quits."

Mark silently stared at a point on the ceiling where the light swirled in ribbons of creamy smoke.

Molly woke to Mark's stereo blasting at full volume. She immediately recognized the song.

Retch on the God Flesh,
Bone dust chokes the encroaching storm,
Silt blackens the flesh of the stillborn,

—pounding through the walls from his bedroom. Caterwauling voices lurked behind the vocal track.

Choir of salt-crusted cardinals,
Chant from mouths sick with barnacles,
Praise be thrice cursed abomination.

The trees outside the window were so distorted by the wind Molly wasn't sure if they were just leaning in towards the house or if something enormous was pacing across the front lawn. The quivering branches made the blinking red glow from the traffic light at the intersection dance on her walls. Her room ran scarlet, pulsing to the beat of the rumbling throughout the house.

Retch on the God Flesh.

She'd slept in her sweats, t-shirt and Doc Martens, just in case she had to leave quickly in the middle of the night. No reason to trust Luke, no faith in spaced-out Mark either. Her few belongings had been stuffed into a gym bag next to her guitar, both ready to go at a moment's notice. All set to leave this shithole first thing in the morning. She threw the covers aside, opened her door.

Luke had collapsed on the living room floor near the couch. He was snoring loudly, surrounded by beer cans.

"Can't stop. I can't stop." He grunted in his sleep.

A mound of clothes was heaped just outside Mark's bedroom door.

Praise be thrice cursed abomination.

The discarded clothing retained a gamy scent. Molly thought of her grandparent's goat farm.

A crash came from Mark's room. He was probably high, stumbling around, banging against furniture.

The door shuddered under the quivering notes of a stringed instrument. Staccato quickly building in speed and intensity, ascending into a frenetic shriek. A peal of discordant music, rhythm undulating as if Molly were listening to a record played backwards. An odor wafted from beneath the door.

The scent of soil deep within the planet.

Sickly voices bellowed echoingly from far away places. Lyrics about dripping stars, mucous-slick vortices. A woman's voice rose above the radio's din:

—here at 6EQU-J5 where aural putrescence is always beckoning. Tonight we have—

Something slammed against the ceiling, just behind Mark's door.

—seed spilled upon barren landscapes. Thanks for tuning in to 6EQU-J5 all you degenerates and all you—

Thin tap of glass against glass. Mark's bottles rattled and clanked. Molly reached for the doorknob.

"Hey, Molly." Luke's voice was liquescent and thick.

She quickly drew her hand away from the door.

Luke had crawled across the floor and propped himself up near the front door. He'd attempted to drag the blanket on the couch along with him, but it had bunched up around the coffee table's legs.

"Can't stop." He vomited a milky fluid onto his chest and stomach.

Something continued to thump around in Mark's room.

—forsaken dead things out there. I encourage all you corpse-faced

lost souls to jig the night away, 'cause there ain't no promise for a tomorrow. And with that, I wish you all—

"I just wanna sleep, Molly."

Ectoplasm gushed from Luke's nostrils.

Pale cilia-like nubs wriggled at the edges of his empty eye sockets. A worm of ectoplasm slid from the right hole, oozed across his forehead.

"What the fuck is going on?" Molly watched the ectoplasm consume Luke's head, encase it in an opaque bubble. She didn't want any of this to be real. Prayed that her dreams were confined to her imagination and not spilling out into the real world.

She grabbed Luke's truck keys off the coffee table.

She'd try again. Maybe the world wasn't built on abandoned train tracks that only ran in one big circle. Maybe this time she'd be able to escape and make it past DR. CLARK'S LUXURIOUS LINIMENT bridge.

Maybe there was more on the other side of *this*.

"Mind throwin' that blanket over me before you go? Colder than a witch's tit tonight." Luke's voice sounded strange traveling through that inexplicable substance bubbling on his head.

Molly untangled the blanket from the table leg and draped it over him. He began breathing evenly, deep in sleep.

6EQU-J5 was blasting static again.

Molly had just started the truck when she realized she'd forgotten her gym bag and guitar. She didn't hesitate, but reversed out of the driveway and sped down the street without stopping for the blinking red light.

YOU! COME FETCH ME!"

The voice, barely audible over the river's roar, emanated from a thicket too modest to hide a boy, never mind a man. The thicket nestled in a circle of smooth stones in a gap between two of the many large, flat rocks that separated the water from the land at the western curve of the riverbank. The boy walked a few paces to where a tree's roots stuck out from the ground in gnarled arches, and wedged under one of them the kerchief that cradled his nascent stick collection. His bundle safely moored, he went to the edge of the riverbank and peered across the rocks at the thicket.

"Fetch you what?" the boy shouted.

There was no reply. The boy was feeble, that's what everyone said, but he sensed—correctly—that the silence was not simply that: it conveyed frustration and maybe a touch of anger. He had encountered the same silence from Pa on many an occasion. The stones looked slippery, a sheen of water sliding over them like liquid glass. The boy pulled his hands into his sleeves, went to his knees, and crawled across the rock carefully, cold water soaking his forearms and shins, the river surging ahead of him.

He wedged his foot between the rocks and began extracting from the thicket handfuls of dried out reeds and bent twigs, letting them fall, watching them slide along the rock, join with the river, and sail away. His brow furrowed when he saw what was nesting there in the circle of stones. It was a small, flat box, not much larger than the palm of his hand, silver in color, rectangular, with a circle of tiny holes on its face. A thin strap of leather was attached to the side. He lifted it from its nest by the strap and let it spin slowly as he stared at it. He ran his thumb over the holes, fascinated.

"Now bring me to shore," said the voice and the boy yelped, startled, and let go of the strap.

The box landed on the broad face of the rock and slid toward the river. The boy lunged after it, crawling as quickly as caution would allow. It was just about to slide into the river when the strap hooked a branch that jutted from a jagged wedge of driftwood. The boy snatched up the box and crawled to shore, gripping the strap tightly in his hand.

Finally, he stood on the riverbank, regarded the box in the fading daylight. "How'd you get in there?"

"How'd *you* get out *there*?" The box spoke in a male voice, with a slight rasp, a hard-to-quantify suggestion of age or world-weariness.

"Hm," the boy said, very much at a loss.

The sky had begun to take on the curious orange hue that heralded the onset of dusk. Pa never said nothing about him being home by dark, but it seemed sensible to do so, as the dark could hide almost anything. The boy didn't like to think about the things that could hide in the dark, though he *did* think about them, thought about them quite a lot, sitting awake under the wool blanket, the candles snuffed for the night, the trees standing sentry outside, the moon illuminating not much more than the clouds that tried in vain to cover it, Pa snoring like a sleeping bear in the next room.

As clouds advanced, towing evening behind them, the boy took up his kerchief. He put the talking box into it with the sticks and headed through the tall trees toward home. From time to time, as he walked upon the dirt road that followed the river's path, he asked the box where it wanted to go. *Show me where you live,* said the voice, now that of a young girl. He asked it how it could see. Nothing. He asked it why summer was so blasted hot and winter so awfully cold. The box remained silent, but the boy could hear it breathing.

Here and there a man on a horse would clop by, kicking up dirt. Each time, the boy would edge farther to the side of the road, looking away from the road. When he had gotten about halfway home, one horse's hooves slowed to a trot until the rider was alongside the boy. The man smelled of tobacco and rum and unwashed armpits. "Boy, what ya got?"

"Sticks. Sir. Just sticks."

"Now hold up." The man pulled back on the reins. "Ho," he said, and the horse stopped.

The boy stopped too, with great reluctance.

The man's pupils were as small as his mustache was large. The buttons of his shirt lay open at his neck, wide suspenders twisted. "S'pose you come with me? I gots rabbits, two of 'em, one fer you, one fer me, stripped and ready for the fire. I gots good stories too, fit to make you laugh 'til your sides hurt. It's cold, nights. I could warm y'up."

"Pa's expecting me."

Quick as a rattler the man's arm reached out and the ruddy fingers wrapped around the boy's wrist. As the boy hollered out, the box shrieked from the kerchief as though in duet, a high-pitched, searing note that rose in pitch and intensity and volume. The man let go of the boy's wrist and his hands jumped to his ears. The boy put his hands to his own ears, gritted his teeth.

The man slid from the horse, quick as you'd please, landing with a crack as his ankle broke on the hard-packed dirt, and the horse galloped off into the gathering dusk, fleeing that horrible screech. The man sat on the ground, eyes wide, foot bent wrong, hands still over his ears. Blood spurted in great arcs from between the man's fingers. Saliva pooled at the corners of his mouth and poured out, pooling in his lap. Finally, his eyes popped like milk and the sockets filled with curled grey gunk like oatmeal veined with blood. He rocked back, exhaled a long and shaking breath, and was still. The noise abated.

The boy took his hand from his ears, gripped his bundle tightly to his chest, started again toward home. The cold drifted in from the river, dropped down from the sky, slid from the trees. He picked up his pace. He encountered no other men on horse nor on foot. The box sang some nonsense syllables, muttered to itself, chuckled darkly, and again went quiet.

A thin trail of smoke reached into the sky, almost obscured by night's black blanket. At its base an orange glow illuminated the cabin, the horse barn, and Pa, who was sprawled out in front of the fire on a kitchen chair he'd brought outside, a mostly empty whiskey bottle pointing up from his crotch. The boy approached, on tiptoe. Pa snorted and his foot jerked. The boy stopped cold as Pa's hand flew up and wiped wildly at his nose. His beard was caked with vomit. His eyes remained closed. He adjusted his weight and let loose a rattling snore.

"Whiskey!" shouted the box. "The elixir that snuffs out all pain!"

The boy flung the box into the hedge as Pa opened his eyes.

"Boy."

"Pa."

"You stay away from town?"

"I did."

"Where did you go?"

"I went down the river. I went to the base of the mountain. I walked on the road down by Hog's Bladder. I climbed a tree and saw what there was to see. I caught a frog and let it go."

"That's all?"

"That's all."

The box muttered something from the hedge, the crackling of the fire all but obscuring it. Pa's eyes went to slits.

"Who's with ye?"

"No one, Pa."

"Hm. You lie to me, you get a beating. Come 'ere, get your beating."

With that, Pa fell asleep. His mouth hung open. His snoring now came in light rasps. The boy fetched the box from the hedge and brought it inside, kicking aside the pamphlets that had accumulated on the porch, the ones that someone kept putting there though he couldn't read them and Pa didn't bother to. Once inside, the door shut after him, he snuffed the candles, lay on the floor in his clothes, pulled the wool blanket over him. The darkness above him rippled, as though invisible snakes were swimming in it. He thought that if he reached his hand up over his head, he might feel them passing over his skin like fingers. This he did not do. Instead, he whispered to the box. "Keep it quiet around

Pa. Pa'll take you away from me. He'll throw you in the fire or crush you under his boot."

He put the box against his ear in case it might once again speak. Once he'd slid down into the gulf of deep sleep, it began to whisper.

The boy awoke in full daylight. He reached for the box, but it was nowhere to be found. He lifted the blanket, shook it. He scanned the corners of the modest room. He moved aside the chair, dropped to his knees and peered under the coat cabinet. Nothing. He scratched at his side and his fingernails lighted on an unfamiliar, rough surface. He bent his neck.

The box had pushed into the tender flesh just below his ribs, deep. He dug his nails between the puckered, reddened skin of his stomach and the edge of the box, but it stuck fast, and his attempts were met with shooting pains. Finally, he drew a bath for himself, stood in the water so as not to submerge the box, running a soaped-up cloth over his skinny body. He worked the suds in around the box and tried to pry it out, but still it stuck fast. Finally, he dried himself and then dressed in the clothes in which he'd slept. He went outside. Pa was gone. The bottle lay empty by the smoldering fire pit.

He lifted his shirt to inspect the box. It had taken on the contours of his side now, had darkened in color. It pulsed slightly, a counterpoint to the boy's breathing. He touched the tip of his index finger to it. It was warm, somewhat damp, certainly more pliable than before. He pulled his finger back, letting the shirt fall back in place, and inspected his fingertip. A liquid sat in the whorls, a muted pink, like blood diluted with saliva. He rubbed it on his pant leg.

From under his shirt, a chorus rose, female voices, some humming low, others soaring. It was glorious, the sound of angels, of tenderness itself. The sound gathered in front of him like smoke. He moved toward it and it moved away, fading just slightly. One more step forward. Two. A third and a fourth and it was as loud as you please. Then the sound began to fade. He made a noise of frustration, something between a whine and a growl. He cocked his head. He side-stepped to his left, and the voices rose just a touch in volume. Another step, even louder. The voices led the boy as surely as a leash or a harness. They went toward town, warping the air. The boy followed. His lips moved soundlessly. The word he mouthed repeatedly but did not dare speak aloud was: "Mother. Mother. Mother."

When Pa pulled the boy from schooling, he'd laid down some simple rules. Explore the woods. Collect sticks. Don't talk to people. Don't go to town. Now the boy found himself passing the white church with its modest dormer, the priest's voice rising and falling like storm winds within its walls, an odd, halting cadence. The cemetery, where men lamented with heads bowed over silent monuments. The general store, where old men rocked in chairs on the broad porch, solemnly engaged in discussing other people's personal business. The tavern, wherein younger men roared, bellowing over one another, women shrieking, raucous laughter, clanking and stomping. All drowned out by a chorus of angels as the boy walked, head tilted and hands grasping, along the forbidden territory of Main Row.

As he passed the cobbler's, a wave of exhaustion surged through his body, and he staggered, putting out a hand to the wall. Pains jolted his temples, zig-zagged behind his eyes, ran along the line of his jaw and under his tongue. His side throbbed where the box had burrowed. Then nausea caressed his innards and he retched, but produced nothing but rank and viscous saliva. He grabbed at it with his fingers, pulled it up from his throat, flung it to the ground. He rubbed his fingers together. He felt hot, in the grip of a powerful ague. His shirt had dampened where the box had worked its way in.

Then Pa was before him like a hallucination, tall and starkly removed from the context of home. He had stumbled from Crackerbarrel Alley, looking down, fastening his belt. Behind him in the darkness a twig-thin woman adjusted her skirts. Pa looked up, and his mouth fell open. The boy's mouth moved soundlessly. Pa's ruddy hand grabbed him by the throat, and the box started to chant, a chorus of voices, speaking in tongues like folks did at the church, overlapping, rhythmic. Pa swatted the air around him. His pupils dilated.

"No," said the boy. "Don't you dare kill my pa."

Shhhhhh, said the box.

Pa jammed his fingers into his ears. He pushed hard, the muscles in his forearm bulging, until his fingers broke through and pushed in deep, right to the knuckles. His eyes went dead and his jaw dropped. A long, rattling exhalation, a failed attempt to bring in air, and he was gone. He stayed standing, though, feet pointed inward, elbows crooked. Something drummed in his chest and a dark stain blossomed at the crotch of his pants. The woman screeched and retreated into the darkness of the alley.

The boy stepped around Pa's propped remains, staring ahead, for now the singing had a source. Great translucent snakes swam over his head, overlapping, intertwining, taking on the color of the sky here, the clouds there, the treetops over there. He jumped up to grab one, and it shot right down like a lightning bolt, was slurped into one of the holes in the box, joining the chorus of voices that sang within. The boy giggled. He left Pa, following the snakes from town, toward the forest.

A rider on a dappled horse gave him a wide berth, this mad boy, walking, leaping into the air, grabbing at nothing, twitching and chortling. The snakes took many shapes as the boy followed. A dog with a profusion of bulging, dangling breasts. A broad-chested man with a cane and an exaggerated swagger. A billy-goat on hind legs, with horns curled toward the treetops. A sleek, long-limbed panther. Into the thick of the woods they went, the ever-changing squadron of snakes and the boy just behind. It seemed for a time that others walked beside him in the wood, long-legged, tall, with massive, sagging heads, all grinning mouths, teeth and wild eyes, but he saw them only sidelong; when he turned, all he saw was saplings and ferns, reeds and vines.

The snakes led him farther into the wood than he'd ever gone before. Up great hills and down deadfall-strewn valleys, through gurgling brooks and over fallen branches. The trees were thicker out here, thick as houses. It was cold here, too, and the boy's clattering teeth served as percussion, backing the breathless chorus. Up ahead, the deepest part of the forest loomed dark as coal, darker than under the wool blanket in his windowless, candle-snuffed room. This, the boy surmised, was the place that nighttime fled to when the sun tried to set it on fire.

The trees began to lean away from the boy, opening a v-shaped swath in the woods. He looked down and he was clad in the bejeweled clothing of a prince, a broad lace collar like a flattened flower, a patterned doublet in purples and reds. Breeches bunched at the knee, pristine white stockings, gemstone-spangled shoes whose bright buckles gleamed. Drums thumped in their thousands. Trumpets sounded a triumphant blare. On either side of him, great tapestries unrolled from the rafters formed by the high branches, depicting scenes of great revelries, long tables spilling over with food, lined by men in black hoods and sheep-headed men; a hunt wherein devils on the backs of muscular black mares drew arrows back in massive bows, shooting angels, mouths agape, from their perches in the cottony clouds; expansive beds upon which dozens of plump young maidens cavorted, wanton mouths agape, with six blank-faced elderly men sporting comically large, pink-tipped erections.

It all fell away in an instant, the trees snapping back, the tapestries lifting, as the forest opened up upon a grassy clearing, a hazy grey at the edge of the night's hiding place, where six men, tall, gaunt-faced, stood in a broad circle. The men were dressed formally, as Pa would dress when he used to go to church: cockel hats, coats and capes. Their skin was as pale as a tree stripped clean of bark. The snakes took the form of a great bird, flew to the center of the circle, and disappeared. The boy followed until he stood in the center of the circle. The men's features were indistinct, blurred, secreted in shadow. The boy couldn't make them into faces no matter how hard he looked. The box whispered something, and the boy nodded.

And began to spin. His feet dancing a mad kuchipudi in the muddy earth, he spun and spun, the men whirling around him. A face began to take form as he spun, a face that formed from the six faces that surrounded him, a face that hovered over a rotating array of decrepit bodies. It was a leering face, a triumphant face, a face of a man—or something a shade different than a man—who had more than a passing familiarity with cruelty. The boy felt his side pucker and pull, and then a gaping absence as the box broke free. Cold rushed into his body through the ragged hole. The box, purple and swollen and gelatinous, fluttered through the air, a winged leech, and the man's tongue surged from his mouth and grabbed it, pulled it in. The man chewed, his eyes locked on the boy's eyes. Blood sprayed from the man's elongated mouth, trickled down from the corners.

The man's many hands took the boy around the neck and under the chin and under the armpits. They lifted him from the earth, his feet still dancing below him, like the feet of a man being hanged. The man inspected him carefully. The song of the snakes, of warped trumpet blare and thundering drums, stormed the woods, bouncing from leaf to leaf, leaping among the high limbs, rising into the sky, surrounding the man and the boy, and it devolved into whimpers and shrieks and forlorn lamentations as the man began the work of taking the boy apart in order to make from him something altogether new.

rosabelle, believe

AMANDA HARD

SHE WAS LATE bringing Andrew back, again. It was always the same with Sheila. Operating on her own schedule, never minding the interruption of anyone else's routine. "Self-absorbed," was the phrase Matt's attorney had used during the custody hearing—a perfectly applicable description, and with her legal history, enough to make the judge believe she was unfit.

He waited in the car, the air conditioner pouring mildly cool air over his sweating hands. Fifteen minutes turned into thirty, and his anger melted into fear. She'd threatened more than once to take his son from him. Could she have meant that literally, using the two-week summer visitation as cover for flying him across the country? Was he in a plane already, his blonde hair dyed brown, rolling whatever new name she'd given him around on his lips? Testing it out, happy for the chance to start over somewhere, without—

Four short horn beeps brought him back to the parking lot of McDonald's, as her blue Mustang pulled up next to him. She motioned for him to put his window down. She wore rhinestone sunglasses and a satisfied smirk ringed with scarlet lipstick. Matt hadn't wanted to smack someone so badly in years.

"Sorry we're late. Traffic was just *dreadful,*" she said through the open window in that adopted Hollywood starlet accent he'd always hated. Andrew waved from the passenger seat. He looked brown and lean, maybe even taller.

"Most people would have called," he told her. She shrugged and got out of her car. Andrew hopped out and went around to the trunk.

"Wait 'til you see what Mom gave me!" he exclaimed. He lifted the trunk lid and, with some difficulty, pulled out a large cardboard box. "It's heavy!"

Matt took the box from him, tucking it under one arm while he grabbed his son's suitcase with the other hand. The boy was taller. A trick of the light? He looked Andrew up and down, studying him, measuring him. The high top sneakers and skinny jeans he wore gave an ever bigger illusion of height. New clothes, presented by Mommy Dearest—clothes he wouldn't be able to wear at his new school, which Sheila would know if she ever bothered to check in with the father of her son. She never bothered to ask about Andrew's grades, or his friends, or his problems.

"We've been listening to people in Russia and China and all over the place," Andrew said. "Maybe even people in outer space!"

Matt put the box in his trunk as his son and ex-wife hugged their goodbyes. He heard them whispering conspiratorially, but his relief at having his son within arm's reach kept him from interfering. She was, no doubt, promising something outrageous, something only Mommy could deliver. Sheila couldn't seem to mail a simple support check every month, but could show up with expensive gifts when it suited her interests.

It wasn't until the blue Mustang was a small dot in his rear-view mirror that Matt finally relaxed and began to focus on the excited ramblings of his son. He reached into the back seat and squeezed the boy's knee. "I missed you, kiddo."

"Missed you too, Dad. And then we walked on the beach and I almost stepped on a jellyfish because they were all over the place and they look like plastic wrap when they're dead and we made biscuits and listened to the radio some more and then I fell asleep in the hammock. Can I keep the radio in my room, please Dad, please?" The earnest and nervous look on his son's face required an immediate response.

Matt replied quickly, without thinking. "Of course. You can keep it . . . wherever you can find room in the mess." He smiled and settled back in his seat, relaxed and happy once again, as he prepared to share the next three hours participating in his ten-year-old's dramatic recreation of "how I spent my summer vacation." It was good to be a dad.

"You cleaned it," Andrew whined. He turned and peered at Matt over the tops of his glasses—one of Sheila's signature gestures of disapproval, and one Matt hoped the boy wouldn't have learned this quickly.

"If by cleaning you mean I washed all the dirty laundry, threw out the half-eaten apple cores, and put your socks back into the drawer—in matching sets—then yes, I cleaned your room."

"Those were science experiments." Andrew shrugged.

"They were biohazards and now it's safe to sleep here again. Where do you want this box? It's heavy."

"It's a radio." Andrew guided his father over to a rectangular table and single chair. "Put it on the desk, here."

"A radio? Feels like a whole stereo system." Matt set the box on the floor and Andrew ripped off a strip of packing tape. "Didn't I buy you a radio last year?"

"Not that kind of radio, Dad. It's . . . well, it's just different." With well-disguised difficulty, he lifted a massive brown suitcase from the box and placed it gently on the desk. He unfastened two clasps on the top and the front panel folded down to reveal a series of dials and knobs flanking a large speaker with a dusty grill. Matt recognized the hardware as similar to the old short wave radio his father had kept in their garage. The model on Andrew's desk was vintage, but in remarkably good condition. Surely too valuable to give to a child.

"Where did she get this?" he asked, not expecting the boy to know.

Andrew flipped a switch and a loud burst of static filled the room. He quickly turned two of the dials and the volume dropped. A man's voice spoke in a slow monotone.

"She got it from her church, at some bake sale," Andrew said. "And before you get mad—no, I didn't go to church with her. She said that was part of the bargain."

Part of the agreement, Matt corrected, mentally. The only issue regarding their son where they'd both agreed: leaving religion out of his life, at least until he could explore the options and decide for himself.

"I just don't want anyone filling your head with . . . well, you'll understand later." Damn Sheila and her 12-step program. She'd been content to be both an atheist and an alcoholic for the last twenty years. Why did she have to change now, in front of their son?

"I think this guy's Mexican," Andrew said, squinting to show he was listening closely, but not to his father.

"Those are numbers," Matt said, mentally translating the spoken Spanish: 15, 5, 11, 22, 9.

"Yeah, a lot of the stations are like that. Mom says they're spies and they're talking in code. It doesn't make any sense unless you have a key, but I don't know where you'd put the key in this thing. Maybe in the bottom?"

"She's means a key code, not a key for a lock." Matt smiled. "Like how you're supposed to tell the alarm people 'Aunt Ellen can't come to the phone' if someone breaks into the house. Only you and me and the alarm people have the 'key'—we know what it means, but the bad guys don't."

"I'll bet I can break the code, Dad. Maybe we can do it together. For home school."

Matt's smile faded. "We talked about this, kiddo. Until I get enough clients of my own, I have to work at the office. You'll like your new school. They have a great science program, a huge library, and I think they even have an archery club." He tried to sound upbeat and reassuring, but the truth was, he was just as nervous about it as his son. "This school—they're used to smart kids like you. You'll fit in there, I promise."

"But Dad, they have this school on the internet where you do all your classes on the computer. I mean, I could do them at the library if you didn't want me at home with you." The boy's eyes were wide, pleading.

Matt sighed. "Andrew, I'd love to be home with you all day, I really would. But I just can't right now. And you need to be with other kids your age. You need friends."

"You don't have any friends, and you're fine."

I'm nowhere near fine, Matt wanted to say. *I'm a 40-year-old single dad who has no idea how to relate to the only person in the universe who matters.* Instead he said, "We can talk about it later. Right now, I'm gonna get dinner started."

Andrew shrugged and Matt closed the door behind him, the spoken trail of Spanish numbers fading with each step he took away from his son.

After yawning repeatedly at the dinner table, Andrew declared himself "absolutely exhausted," another of Sheila's famous phrases, and decided to turn in early, foregoing his usual evening video game time. Matt cleaned up the kitchen, did two loads of the boy's laundry—laundry Sheila certainly could have done at her house rather than simply packing the soiled clothing in plastic grocery sacks in his suitcase,—and finally sat back down at the kitchen table with a cold beer and a house full of quiet.

But it wasn't completely quiet. He could hear a voice down the hallway—a woman's voice, talking in a quiet monotone, as if reading from a list. Matt got up and followed the sounds to his son's room, to the giant radio sitting on the desk, its dial illuminated by a soft yellow light. The volume was low, but loud enough he could make out numbers, in German this time, coming from the metal grill of the speaker. The voice was unaccented, but scratchy and faint, as though the station was imprecisely or incompletely tuned in.

Matt reached out and turned the tuning dial a fraction of an inch. The voice diminished. He turned it the other way and the signal grew stronger, but a tinny overlay obscured the timbre of the voice and distorted it. He spun the dial with his finger and watched as the red needle identifying the station slid sideways to settle around 9000. There was a moment's pause, and then the radio's speaker began to vibrate with a low thrumming. The sound recalled one of Matt's worst career nightmares. It was a sound he could still hear in his ears in times of high stress: the low-pitched groan of steel and concrete fighting to remain stable and upright.

Andrew had not been more than a baby at the time, and Sheila had only just begun to explore the first of her alcohol-influenced affairs. Matt was the lead engineer on a power plant job, designing and overseeing the installation of a federally-mandated smokestack scrubber unit to remove sulfur emissions from the plant's exhaust. On paper, the scrubber was brilliant—efficient and less expensive than competing designs. In person, it looked like massive scaffolding holding up dozens of shower heads, stick legs with their claws hooked into holes in the walls.

When the unit's operator threw the switch, before the first mists could even pass through the pipe, a low booming noise tore through the ground, followed in the air by a metallic scream. This unholy duo of sounds preceded a vibration so strong, it made standing upright almost impossible. The noise imprinted in Matt's mind, in the moment before the operator threw the emergency stop. It was the sound of metal pushed beyond its limits. The sound of a flawed design. The sound of failure.

Matt slammed his fingers over the tuning dial and the sound cut off abruptly. He watched with dismay as the red needle flew unfettered towards the other side of the display. He'd broken it. The noise was gone, but now so was the tension on the tiny wire which controlled the tuning. Andrew would be furious when he found out.

He glanced at the desk surface to see if maybe, just maybe, there was an instruction manual or a troubleshooting guide. But the only papers near the radio were loose-leaf notebook pages covered front to back with lists of numbers. Matt picked up one of the pages and squinted at it, trying to read the pencil marks in the dim glow. The page was titled "16084" and consisted of lines of single-digit numbers. The first sets of numbers were crowded together in clumsy blocks, but by the bottom of the page the spacing was more regular and the repeats more obvious. Andrew's spy codes. He dropped the sheet of paper back on the desk, and flipped off the radio's power switch. As the light faded, he leaned down to kiss his son's cheek, pale as milk in the moonlight and so closely resembling his own that for a moment, Matt saw his ten-year-old self under the blanket, just as lonely and frustrated.

"I'll make it up to you, kiddo," he whispered. "I'll make it right."

When Andrew failed to answer the third call to come to breakfast, Matt yanked the kitchen towel he wore on his shoulder while cooking, rolled it into a whip-shape and yelled, "Anybody not at this table in five seconds is getting a beating."

"Just one more minute!" came the faint, but clearly annoyed, reply.

"Now, mister! While your omelet's still warm."

He poured a glass of milk for himself, another for his son, and sat down, drumming his fingers on the table. He counted to ten before standing up, throwing down the towel, and walking back to Andrew's bedroom. Before he could open the door, the boy came flying out and slammed the door shut.

“Morning, Dad. You got pancakes?” He disappeared into the kitchen and gave a loud groan. “Eggs? Really? Is there at least bacon?”

Matt opened the bedroom door and saw the radio on the desk, powered on and jabbering—a woman’s voice, staccato and unpracticed, imperfectly reading a series of single-digit numbers in English this time. The voice stumbled over some of the numbers and was interrupted briefly by curls of white noise. Even distorted, the voice seemed familiar to him, yet he couldn’t place it.

A new page lay on the desk, this one labeled “9086” and filled with another series of numbers, but with blocks of them outlined in black marker, and a sequence circled and annotated with three stars.

“Don’t you have to go to work today?” Andrew called from the kitchen. Matt tossed the paper down on the desk and closed the door behind him, still trying to identify the woman’s voice.

“I’m going in later. After I drop you off.”

“I can ride my bike to the Y. I don’t need a ride.”

Andrew had finished the omelet and was in the middle of a blueberry muffin still in its wrapper.

“You’re not going to the Y today. You have an appointment at Highland Prep Academy. You’re getting a tour and meeting your advisor, and then maybe tonight we can do mini-golf.”

Andrew dropped the muffin on the table.

“I don’t want to go to any school today! It’s still summer! And you said I could home school!”

“I said we’d talk about it, and I’m not ruling it out for later, but Highland is a great school. And until I can work from home full-time, it’s the best I can do, kiddo.” Matt reached out to pat his son’s shoulder, but the boy pulled away.

“Can’t I just stay here and listen to my radio? I’ve almost got the code broke!”

Broke. The radio tuner. Shit.

“You’re still playing with that?”

“I’m not *playing* with it. It’s educational.”

“I know that, and I didn’t mean . . . Well you know, we should take it in and get it looked at. Antique electronics like that need care. Maintenance.”

“It works just fine, Dad.”

Matt breathed an imperceptible sigh of relief. His son hadn't noticed yet.

"What are you listening to?"

"Numbers."

"The spy numbers?"

Andrew frowned. "These are different. It's a new station I didn't hear before. I know it's a message though, because it repeats a lot. I've almost got it figured out."

"You can work on it this evening. You can have all night after dinner and I won't bother you, I promise." He tried again to reach his son's shoulder but Andrew was already slipping past him, closed-mouthed and iron-willed.

Be strong, he told himself. *He needs you to be a parent, not a friend. He needs you to be strong.*

Sometimes, it was so hard being a dad.

"Now that's a blast from the past!"

The clerk at The Ham Shack didn't look old enough to have a conscious memory of any "past" before the year 2000, and in Matt's eyes, the sun-bleached curls and Hawaiian shirt made him look more like a surfer than an electronics wizard. His name tag read "Tyler," one of the names Sheila had suggested for their son.

"Yeah, I spoke to somebody on the phone about this earlier. About the tuner." Matt lifted the radio up and placed it on the counter. "I think the wire might be broken."

Tyler stroked his fingers over the wooden case before unbuckling the clasps. "Yeah, the antique short-wave. Man, this is a beauty," he said. "I've never seen one of these in such good shape. It work?"

"I guess, other than the tuner. My ex-wife found it for my son, and he's been playing with it."

"How old's the boy?"

"He's ten," Matt said. Still admiring the radio, Tyler's placid features twisted into a more worried look.

"Yeah, you ask me, I'd get the kid a cheap ham radio and sell this baby." He looked up and the smile returned. "The cabinet alone's worth fifty bucks. Cash money. On the spot. What do you say?"

Matt shook his head. “It’s not for sale. Not yet anyway. He’s having too much fun with it. He’s found a frequency that his mother claims broadcasts spy transmissions or something.”

“Numbers stations!” Tyler laughed. “Yeah, I was into that when I was a kid too.”

Matt smiled the proud and knowing grin of a father in on the joke. “He’s decoding one of them now. He’s got these long lists of numbers, papers everywhere. If only I could get him to pay as close attention to his homework.”

“Don’t mean to bust his bubble, but he’s not likely gonna decode those. That’s CIA-grade stuff. Can’t break ‘em without the key.” He carefully turned the radio around and opened up the back panel. “Something about kids and codes. They can’t get enough of them, can they?”

Matt shrugged. “I remember making invisible ink out of lemon juice when I was his age.”

“Never tried that. It work?” Tyler’s curls were barely visible over the top of the radio. Before Matt could answer, he continued. “Me, I was into Vigeneres big time. My buddy and I used to keep encrypted notes on the girls in school. Mine were unbreakable. He’d use some lame Rot-13 and always get busted. Although eventually he started using a numerology matrix, ‘cause he was into witchcraft and crap like that.”

“Witchcraft. Really,” Matt said, trying to avoid an overt display of impatience. “I didn’t know witches used codes.”

“Ciphers. Yeah, to find lucky numbers or something. Look it up and show it to the kid. He might pick the winning lottery numbers.”

“I’ll do that. Andrew’d get a kick out of thinking witches were using his radio.”

“Yeah, kids love weird stuff. It travels the boundaries of culture, man. Some things are just universal, I guess.”

“I guess.” Matt ran a hand through his hair. “So, I don’t mean to hurry you, but can you fix it?”

“Yeah, no prob, man.” He gently twisted the tuning dial. “You got too much slack in the line here, it probably snapped. I can thread you up a new one. Just give me a day or so.”

Matt looked around the empty shop. “Can’t you just do it now? It’s not like there’s a line in here.”

Tyler narrowed his eyes.

“You think I got nothing else to do today?”

"No, it's just . . . well, I can't leave it here. My son will flip out if it's missing. Playing with this is about the only thing he looks forward to." Matt immediately hated himself for admitting that to a stranger. "He doesn't actually know I broke it yet, so maybe—"

"You broke it?" Tyler raised an eyebrow. Inwardly, Matt groaned. How had that slipped out?

"It was an accident. I was trying to turn the volume down." But that wasn't exactly right, was it? He'd been trying to tune away from that sound, the shrieking noise. But it had been an accident, of course.

"So you're just going to play it off like it's fine until he realizes it's broken and then make him think he broke it?" Tyler snorted and snapped the open clasps closed. "Well-played, Dad. I'll pretend I don't know you if you bring it back later in the week or something."

Matt started to explain, but instead he shook his head and lifted the radio off the counter. He had opened the shop door and was just stepping across the threshold when Tyler called to him.

"Hey Dad, I'm serious about taking that radio off your hands. Bring it back in and if you want, I'll say it can't be fixed. Give you $75 for the case and you can get the kid some baseball cards."

"I'll think about it," Matt said.

"You know, I've seen grown men go nuts over trying to figure out the patterns in those numbers stations. You ask me, the kid needs a better hobby."

Matt nodded and let the door close behind him. "I didn't ask."

He thought he heard the phone ringing as they climbed the steps to the front door, but it was difficult to hear much of anything over Andrew's enthusiastic jabbering. *At least his day went well*, Matt thought as his son described the school's communal greenhouse.

" . . . and the eighth-graders grow peas to study genetics, but I don't think they get to eat them."

"Probably not," Matt agreed. "But you can eat peas for dinner tonight, how's that?"

"Negatory, Dad. That means no. How about corn instead?"

"Corn's not a vegetable. Wait," he said to the motion blur that had been his son. "You dropped this." He reached down to pick up a paper that had fallen from the boy's folder, but Andrew was already bounding down the hallway.

"You gotta proofread it, Dad. It's my essay about what I want to accomplish this semester at school. I have to turn it in next Monday and you're supposed to sign it or make a copy or something."

Matt sighed and settled down at the kitchen table with a contented smile. The cell phone vibrated in his jacket pocket, but he reached in and silenced it. Reading through his son's essay, his smile widened.

"This sounds great, kiddo," he said as he walked back to Andrew's room. "Good sentence structure, good word choice. You spelled 'believe' wrong again, though. Remember I before E except after—"

"Did you move this?" Andrew demanded, pointing to the radio. He looked so tall under the overhead lights. Almost a teenager, with a teen's fierce independence already.

"I was just . . . looking at what you were working on. I didn't move anything." The boy's glare made him defensive.

"It's not for you, okay?" Andrew said, gathering the papers and shifting them to the side of the desk, away from Matt's view. "Don't touch it, please?" The last was less a question than a plea for mutual understanding, respect.

Matt sighed. "I won't touch it."

Father and son looked at each other, the tension between them on pause. In the kitchen, the phone began ringing again.

"I should get that," Matt said.

Andrew nodded. As Matt closed the door behind him, he heard the female voice again—unplaceable, but as familiar to him as an evening newscaster's. The voice read a series of single-digit numbers in a less hesitant and more confident monotone than earlier.

"5-5, 5-5-9-5, 5-9-6-5-7, 7-3-5-1-1-5 . . . "

Matt stopped outside the door, listening carefully. It couldn't be hers, but damn if the voice didn't sound like Sheila's. The numbers stopped. There was a pause and then that voice that sounded eerily like his ex-wife's began to read the numbers again. Matt shook his head. The way the voice intoned "five" was the exact inflection of Sheila's faint Savannah accent. The accent she usually tried to hide while sober, but escaped when she'd been drinking.

Was his ex-wife actually a spy?

He smiled, inwardly laughing at himself. Much as Andrew might want to believe it, Sheila was no spy. But now it seemed she had a new hobby, sending coded messages via the shortwave radio. Leave it to Mommy Dearest to jack up the drama of communicating with her son. Now the only way Matt could compete would be by tapping Morse code messages on the radiator, or sending smoke signals from the barbecue pit.

As Matt reached for the kitchen phone, the ringing abruptly stopped, transferring almost immediately to the phone in his pocket. It was a Florida call from a number he didn't recognize but according to the phone's log, had called at least four times before. When he slid his finger across the screen a deep baritone asked "Am I speaking with Matthew Tremper?"

"This is Matt," he said, wondering alternately if the voice was a bail bondsman, how much money he needed to raise, and what Sheila had done this time.

"Mr. Tremper, this is Officer Hanlon of the Florida State Police. I'm afraid there's been an accident."

Matt listened, unmoving and unspeaking, the screen of the phone cool against his cheek. The call completed, he whispered his thanks and dropped the phone on the table. He walked down the hall in silence, knocked at his son's door, and opened it slowly.

In the room, Sheila's voice—or what had to be a recording of her voice—came through the radio's speaker in a clear and steady monotone.

"7-3-5-1-1-5"

Matt shivered. Even in its neutrality the voice sounded so alive, so certain and focused—and so loud. Listening to her on the radio was surreal. Sweat slicked the palms of his hands and he wanted to laugh at the absurdity of it.

"Kiddo," he said, drawing the boy into an embrace. "I'm really sorry I have to tell you this. It's about your mom." He felt, rather than saw, Andrew's eyes flick over to the radio, where the sequence of numbers had just begun to repeat. The numbers droned on, muffling the child's sobbing, the nonsense message replaying in its infinite loop.

"5-5, 5-5-9-5, 5-9-6-5-7, 7-3-5-1-1-5"

"7-3-5-1-1-5"

"7-3-5-1-1-5"

"What actually happens to us after we die?"

It was the most innocent of questions, one Matt had fielded a few times in the past when a handful of mice, goldfish, and Knuckles, their old tom cat, had exited stage left. But he'd only really addressed the expiration process itself: the circle of life, the eventual and inevitable decay. He'd not yet had to delve into metaphysics, and he certainly wasn't prepared for it today.

"That's a difficult question, kiddo. The answer depends a lot on what people believe."

The funeral had been hard for both of them. The closed-casket and religion-free service was administrated by the funeral director and there were few friends and almost no family members present, at least none Matt recognized. The entire event had been sterile and distant, the air-conditioning set entirely too cold. Andrew mourned in his ten-year-old fashion, by withdrawing even more into himself and his radio. Matt hoped the approaching start of school would help.

"Why does what happens depend on what you believe?" Andrew asked.

"Well, because nobody knows. Some people like to believe that you come back in a different body, or that you go to a different kind of existence, where your consciousness lives on with the people you love. Different people believe different things; that's why it depends."

There was silence at the table while Andrew stared at his milk.

"What do we believe?" he asked.

And there it was. Ten years coming, and still Matt hadn't thought of a good response.

"You mother and I—" He stopped himself. How strange that only now, after her death, did he think of the two of them as a single unit again, in agreement on the one issue they'd actually never fought over.

"Kiddo, there really isn't any reason to believe anything happens after we die. We live, we make an impact on other people, and we try to do some good while we're here. But when the time comes, the best explanation is that we just pass away."

"Where do we pass away to?"

Matt sighed and opened his hands. "We pass back into the universe. Our bodies turn into energy and we sort of, well the part that made us 'us' just rejoins all the other parts of everyone else, and we all go back to the universe, back to the stars." He patted himself on the back for that one. Poetic, but not religious. Let the boy stew on the interconnectedness of matter and energy for a while. "Do you want another piece of toast?"

"So we don't go anywhere at all? We just die."

"I don't believe we go anywhere, no. But we live on in memories. So as long as you have a memory of someone, they—"

"You don't believe Mom's in heaven?" The narrowed eyes and raised brows signaled a challenge rather than a question.

"No Andrew, I don't believe Mom's anywhere, except in our memories."

"What if you're wrong?" Another challenge.

"I don't think I am, but I won't know that until I'm gone myself, and I'm really kind of tired of talking about this today. Do you want another piece of toast or not? I have to get you to the Y."

"I don't need daycare, Dad."

"I don't need to go to jail, Andrew. I can't let you stay home alone." He glanced at his watch and cursed. "I'm gonna be late. Forget the toast. Grab a banana and let's go."

"Just go on. I'll ride my bike. And I promise I won't burn the house down making toast."

"No staying home playing with that radio, you hear? I'm going to call the Y at 8:30. You're going to be there when I call, right?"

Andrew rolled his eyes and shooed his father out of the kitchen. As Matt grabbed his briefcase and swiped his keys off the counter, he looked back at the boy staring at him from the table—his son, flesh of his flesh, taller even than yesterday—how was that possible? His child's eyes were dark and brooding, world-weary eyes that befit an old man more than a child. Eyes that questioned, challenged, and glared at Matt before dropping back down to the breakfast plate. He should have home-schooled the boy, should have spent the time with him, one-on-one. It wasn't like his career was booming.

"I'm going to call at 8:30, and you need to be at the Y, understand?"

Matt closed the door before Andrew could respond.

But when 8:30 came, he was pouring over a blueprint, so it wasn't until a 9:00 meeting that he realized he'd forgotten, and by the looks of the agenda, it would be a while before he could break away. He'd almost forgotten about it entirely when his boss's executive assistant quietly walked in to the meeting and touched him on the shoulder. Her face was pale and her hands trembled as she passed him the phone message slip.

He read two words, "Andrew" and "accident," and tore out of the meeting, running back to his desk, where his cell phone scooted across the surface, vibrating with an angry and repeating buzzing. He saw nothing but scattered blueprints, yellow lines on black asphalt, white uniforms, and green scrubs. He heard nothing, only the hollow emptiness that muted the voices of his co-workers, the hospital staff, the doctor—

"We did all we could. I'm so sorry."

—even his own shouting as he collapsed into a vinyl chair. Someone pressed a paper cup of cold water in his hand, but it fell away, the liquid puddling between his feet.

He felt nothing. Disbelief flickered then extinguished itself. His hands didn't work. His eyes wouldn't close. He felt nothing; thought nothing. Words made no sense to him.

My ex-wife is dead.

He felt nothing. The words meant nothing.

My son is dead.

He felt nothing. The words held no meaning.

I'm not a dad anymore.

And then he felt everything.

He could have left the room untouched, or have possibly let the movers box up everything for storage. That would have been the simpler option, a task completed without the mist of unshed tears and the excruciating pain of touching the things his only son had just weeks before passed through his own small fingers. Every item in the room told the same heart-breaking story, even if Matt wasn't aware of the particulars: a Yankees baseball jersey; a book of ghost stories; the potato clock, sundial, and forgotten cactus—all the detritus of a bright star of life, full of promise and potential.

The clothes he thought would be the easiest to pack, but the vastly-too-small Mickey Mouse sweatshirt that still hung on a silver hanger against the closet wall sent Matt into a spiral of sobbing that left him drained, slumped over outstretched legs that refused to stand. *He needs you to be strong*, he reminded himself. *But for what? Strong for who?*

The radio sat on the makeshift desk, a wooden monstrosity that took up most of the surface. Matt stood, walked to the desk with a mechanical motion, sat down in the chair, and flipped the power switch. The assaulting noise he'd heard before erupted from the speaker, and he pressed his fists against his ears to drown out the throbbing vibrations. He kicked out with his foot to rip the power cord from the wall, but the noise stopped abruptly. It was replaced by a soft static and the hesitant murmurings of a new sound, unsteady and wavering; an uncertain recitation of single-digit numbers in the voice of a boy, a child still, with a vocal range that once promised to lower in pitch in a few short years.

It was Andrew's voice.

Matt sat, mouth open, eyes wide. It couldn't be his son. It couldn't be Andrew. Whatever Sheila had managed to do before her death, Andrew certainly couldn't have. The old radio she'd given him couldn't record anything. It could only play what someone else was broadcasting.

His son, the ten-year-old love of Matt's life, continued to read a series of numbers. There was a pause, and Matt's breath caught in his throat. His son's voice, his son, reading numbers on a spy station. It was crazy. He was delusional from grief. There hadn't been any numbers. The radio wasn't even plugged in, was it?

Matt leaned down to see a black plug in the socket trailing a black cord up to the desk. Plugged in, powered on, playing. The speaker was silent, except for the cold crackle of static. There was no voice.

But there it was again, the same voice that had evolved Matt's name from "Da-Da" to "Daddy" to "Dad," in ever-increasing levels of frustration and impatience. The voice that had squealed in delight when Matt tickled his ribs, and shouted "swing me, swing me higher," even as Matt threatened to loop the swing around the crossbar.

It *was* Andrew's voice.

Matt grabbed a stub of pencil and began to copy down the numbers.

6, 7-6-4, 6, 4-1-4-4-7, 7-3-5-1-1-5.

Clearly a code of some kind. He scribbled furiously as the voice continued in its flat but halting monotone.

2-5-3-5-9-4-5, 4-1-4-4-7, 6, 7-6-4, 6, 7-3-5-1-1-5.

Repeats. A name, maybe? A location?

2-5-3-5-9-4-5, 2-5-3-5-9-4-5.

More repeats. Then another pause while Matt waited without breathing. One second, two, three . . .

And then the sequence began again. He copied it again to make sure, comparing the two. They were identical, down to the pause at the end. The message began again, the now-familiar numbers becoming a kind of prose poem lulling Matt into relaxation. He listened to his son's voice calmly reciting the numeric "message," and it didn't matter where it was coming from, or how it was coming. It just was.

The transmission concluded as abruptly as it had begun, with the whine and vibration, and then it was over. The yellow light on the radio's front blinked once and then faded. Matt flipped the power switch off and back on again several times, but whatever had been keeping the antique thing running had failed. Matt slid the radio off the table into a large box of trash. *It's not worth keeping. Be strong.*

He hesitated before clearing off the desk. Dozens of papers, all with long lists of numbers, littered the surface, many of the columns starred and highlighted. Hours of work lay there, lines of unbreakable "spy code," transcribed in the night. Matt picked up a half-sheet, horizontally oriented with the numbers from one to nine written at the top and the letters of the alphabet stacked in three rows underneath. At the bottom, in quickly scribbled pencil, was the phrase, "55 5595 59657 735115—WE WERE WRONG PLEASE" with a circled question mark beside it.

There was an echo in his memory, an excited pronouncement: *"I've almost got the code broke!"*

Cipher, he thought, then stopped, closing his eyes against the swell of emotion rising in his gut. *I can't do this to myself. It's the grief. It's causing me to see patterns that aren't there.*

He picked up the half-sheet and started to crumple it, but stopped when he noticed that both the letters "a" and "s" were lined up under the "1" column. His eye quickly scanned sideways to the 7, which lay over "p" and back left again to the 3 for "l."

P-L-E-A-S-E. 7-3-5-1-1-5.

"I've almost got the code broke!"

Matt tore through the pages on the desk, scattering them in his frenzy. It had to be there. He'd just had it. Where the hell—

"Found it!" He slammed the page down on the desk. With the half-sheet in front of him, he went back and forth between the "key" and the sequence he'd written down earlier.

His pencil stub scrambling over the page, Matt experimented with letter combinations. An interior "1" would most likely be "a" or maybe an "s," and the double "4" could be either "dd" or "mm." He already had "please," and with the doubling, the "7" had to be a "y." The "6" had to be "o" which meant "764" was "pod" or . . .

6, 764

o god

He worked furiously and the final letters fell into place on the page. Matt stood up, a terrible cold spreading up from the base of his spine to the back of his neck as he read the translated message—a message that could have only come from one source, an inexpert speller:

o god o daddy please
beleive daddy o god o please
beleive beleive

the last scream

GABINO IGLESIAS

THERE WERE A few days each semester in which Albert Gardner's soul was crushed by the certainty that he wasn't getting paid enough to put up with the shit students threw his way. Luckily, there were also days in which he sat back and did nothing. Those days, albeit rare, were glorious. They made him feel like his adjunct position was not an absolute waste of time and a blatant insult to his curriculum vitae. On these throwaway days, he could sit back and enjoy one of his favorite movies and get paid for it. While that was awesome, his favorites were presentation days. On these days, he could quietly enjoy each second of his students' shaky voices and fidgeting hands as they struggled to address the same bunch of idiots they interacted with in class two times per week and then for six hours straight during the Friday labs.

This particular Tuesday was presentation day, and that meant each group of students had to introduce their audio project, play it for the class, then stand there awkwardly as Albert offered scathing critiques. The group that had just sat down, a collection of misfits who had banded together because no one else had asked them to join their group, had done a horrible job. They'd gone to Eeyore's Birthday, yet another ridiculous Austin celebration in which folks dressed up, smoked weed, and listened to live music while clogging downtown streets like thirty years of bacon grease on a fat man's arteries. Besides the excessive screaming, they had done a shoddy job with their MOS reporting and had forgotten to run their audio through a noise reduction filter to at least try to get the wind noise down to tolerable levels. Albert had almost felt bad about calling their piece an aural nightmare.

The next group looked sharper. Brionne and Tristan were somewhat decent students, and they were clearly the leaders of their four-student group. Ben and Tanya were not as intelligent or academically inclined, but being in a group with the coolest folks in the classroom had hopefully made them give it their all. They were standing in front of the classroom and looked as comfortable as a germophobe getting a hug from a hobo. Brionne cleared her throat and addressed the class. Ben turned and started working on the computer they were using for the presentations.

"Hello, my name is Brionne Larsen and these are my fellow group members, Tanya Robinson, Ben Martinez, and Tristan Fox." She moved her hand toward each of them like a rookie TV show model. Albert noticed the manicured fingers were shaking a bit. "For our third radio project we decided to do a short documentary on the massacre of the *Lady Rose*."

Brionne looked good in her short black skirt and business jacket. These young college girls could go from looking like teenagers to resembling top-notch smut magazine models with a bit of makeup and different clothes. Nothing hid a woman's charms as well as those stupid oversized sorority t-shirts. A collection of pornographic images flashed through Albert's mind and made his pants a bit tighter in the crotch. The thoughts would surely cost him the gig if they became public. He adjusted his body on the seat and watched Brionne step away and gesture toward Tristan with her hand once again.

Tristan stuck his hands in his pockets and quickly pulled them back out and rubbed them together. He looked at Albert as if waiting for a cue to begin. Albert didn't give him one. Finally, he started talking.

"We . . . we had a hard time with this project. We were lucky enough to have the original audio on hand because my grandfather was involved in the original investigation and . . . you know. Well, we had to, like, clean it up, but we had to do it by chunks because weird sh . . . stuff kept happening—right, Tanya? Like, whenever we played more than a minute of it, something would happen. I'm not even kidding."

"What exactly are you talking about, Tristan?" Albert didn't like interrupting because it made the students even more nervous, and that meant they stammered more, which invariably led to longer, far more tedious presentations. The fact that college students would get so anxious at being called out made Albert lose all hope of a future for the third time that day.

Tristan made some monosyllabic attempts at a coherent response and succeeded only in looking more like a dumbass. As if to save his cohort from a total breakdown, Tanya stepped up.

"Tristan's grandfather was an audio engineer back in the day. He worked for the FBI doing surveillance for many years and in 1981 was pulled into a special project. He helped clean the audio that came from the *Lady Rose*. I know Tristan's always making silly jokes about everything, but he's not joking about weird stuff happening to us. Ben and I did most of the heavy editing work on this while Brionne and Tristan did the VO. Putting it together was hard because of all the equipment malfunctions and whatnot. My brother is a ghost freak and he says that the audio we used is possessed by something, that it carried something, some energy, from when it happened. I think my brother's an idiot, but there's certainly something going on here."

Tanya's delivery was superb. Everyone in the studio was looking at them instead of at their laptops or phones. Albert didn't like his classroom turning into a circus, but he was curious where this was going.

"Are you guys talking about something like those EVPs they play on *Ghost Hunters*?" The question came from Eric, a chubby Mexican kid with an acne problem who Albert always thought smelled of pizza.

"No," said Ben. "This is something different. This is . . . I think we should just play it."

"Yes, that's enough of an intro," said Albert. "Let your work do the talking."

Brionne nodded, moved toward the computer, and clicked play on the Audition file already up on the screen. After a second of white noise and a click from the recorder that they'd forgotten to cut or had been too close to start of the VO, the sound of waves gently lapping against the hull of a boat faded in and took over. The speakers were top-notch and the studio was soundproof, so the sound of the lapping waves really took the class and placed them in the ocean. They only thing that was missing was a bit of movement. Then Tristan's voice came on. He was trying too hard to make it sound deeper.

"Very late on the night of August 2nd, 1981, the *Lady Rose*, a freighter out of New York, was slowly making his way across the relatively rough waters of the Bay of Bengal. It was a trip the boat and its captain had done countless times before. Unfortunately for the crew, something went wrong on this particular night and the *Lady Rose* ran aground on a submerged coral reef."

The sound of splashing waves was overpowered by the screech of metal scraping against rock. Albert wondered where they had found the sound effect and made a note to give Tanya and Ben some props for their seamless transitions. Brionne's clear voice came on. She had recorded too close to the microphone, but at least they'd remembered to use the fox tail so the distortion was minimal and her Ps didn't pop as violently as they had in other projects.

"The *Lady Rose* wasn't going anywhere that night, but it wasn't sinking and they had no problem radioing in and communicating their situation. After hearing back from headquarters in New York, the crew, tired from a long day at sea, went to bed. The next morning, knowing that rescue was on its way but that it would take at least a day and half for it to reach them, the captain, Charles Willeford, and crew decided to turn their little accident into a vacation and have lunch under the sun. They brought up a few tables from their kitchen and Willeford graciously shared his personal stash of booze."

The sound of shuffling feet and clicking silverware replaced Brionne's voice. The effects were obviously meant to place the listener in a restaurant, but Albert decided not to be too hard on them because experience had taught him that finding free sound effects for something as specific as a bunch of seamen having lunch on a boat was really hard. Still, he made a note: mention that, when an effect is not readily available, they can always go the extra mile and create it themselves.

After a few more seconds of eating and talking sounds, Tristan's voice returned.

"The *Lady Rose* was full of merry for a while. To the surprise of the captain, who could've sworn the previous night that they were far from land, he and his 26-men crew were about 800 yards from an island. The tiny speck of land to their right was something they hadn't expected to see, and they ignored they were looking at North Sentinel island. The crewmembers looked out at the beach and talked about exploring it after lunch. As they ate, someone looked out at the beach and spotted a few men coming out of the dense jungle that sprouted just beyond the shore.

The men, all very dark-skinned, wore loincloths and carried spears and bows and arrows. At first, these men stuck to the tree-line and moved from shadow to shadow like fish moving from puddle to puddle."

The writing was a little cheesy, but far better than Albert had expected. The students had managed to create an atmospheric piece of radio, and that was something no previous group had accomplished. A very loud voice said, "Look at that!" It was obviously Ben. Albert made a note to also mention that, when you create your own sound effects, you need to worry about them fitting in with the rest of your audio in terms of clarity and volume. Brionne's voice returned, loud enough to be heard over the sounds of men talking indistinctly.

"The mysterious men on the beach looked out at the crew and vice versa. Captain Willeford told his men to finish their meal. They would get a few boats in the water after lunch. By the time the crew was done eating, there were nearly 50 men standing on the sand, and they had brought out some canoes."

Radio was a strange beast. An audio piece had a few seconds to hook a listener. Once that happened, it could only go two ways: listeners either got bored of your crap really quickly or they became entranced by what you were telling them. This was clearly a case of the latter, and despite the few small problems with this piece, the group had pulled it off. As much as he hated to do so, Albert contemplated the possibility of having to congratulate these four students in front of everyone.

Brionne went on.

"This is where the story gets weird and where the official reports offer inaccurate versions of what went down. The only thing that really happened after that and was reported truthfully is the words uttered in Willeford's second call. That morning, the captain made an early morning call just to check that everything was in order and that rescue was still on the way. After lunch, he made a second radio call, a distress call. The audio is not very crisp on the official recording, but you can tell that there's urgency in his voice."

Ben and Tanya had tried to fade the new clip in, but the age difference, not to mention the digitalization process, made it rough and grainy, like an old movie for the ears. Still, the quality of the audio was not as awful as it could've been. It had probably been cleared by an expert before these kids got hold of it.

"Wild men! Wild men are coming! I estimate more than 50. They are carrying various rudimentary weapons." There was a pause. Willeford's heavy breathing could still be heard. “They are dragging five rustic wooden boats onto the water. I’m worried that they will try to board us. If they do, we will proceed with caution, but will use deadly force if necessary.”

All sounds faded. Tristan’s voice came on and delivered a single line on top of that silence: “The captain never made another call.” After two seconds, he spoke again. “At least that’s the official version. According to the report, the natives came, the crew fought them off, and the so-called wild men retreated. That night, everyone on board was rescued by a Japanese freighter and taken to safety before being flown back to New York because the *Lady Rose’s* hull had sustained too much damage. The truth, however, is very different. According to one Indian report and some rumors, the third distress call was never made public. The rescue crew was told to hurry. When they arrived, they found the crew slaughtered. Some limbs had been taken and most torsos had been opened from sternum to groin and everything but the intestines was missing. Not all bodies were accounted for. The government covered the whole thing, but Jessica Dahlby, a *New York Times* reporter who also did work for *National Geographic* on that area of the world, wrote a piece about a year later. In it, she explained how she’d been unable to find any crew member in the US despite having information about them and even previous addresses. What she did uncover was a copy of the last call. That is what you’re about to hear.”

Albert hated that last bit, but everything that preceded it had been great. It’d been a bit too gory for his taste, but it made for a truly compelling radio piece. The rough audio returned. Tanya and Ben had completely faded out the sound of the waves in order to allow Willeford’s voice to be heard as clearly as possible. They deserved props for that. The man’s voice was tinged with panic.

“Mayday! Mayday! The natives are on deck! We tried to keep them down, but they’re chanting something and my men are dropping like flies.”

The sound of screaming and chanting could be heard under Willeford’s voice. The chant was strong, but the words were strange, spoken in a language Albert had never heard. He leaned forward and tilted his head toward the speaker a few feet above his desk. The door to the lab slammed closed. Everyone jumped. The massive metal door was part of the soundproofing system and weighed a ton. Slamming it shut was something Albert never would’ve imagined. Brionne and company were taking this joke too far.

"I think that's enough. Please stop the audio for a second."

Ben was frantically hitting the spacebar key, but the Audition file kept playing.

"The natives are surrounding my men. Only Sebastian Castellano and I were able to made it to the bridge. We . . . we are looking at the situation down at the bow deck. It's . . . hard to describe. The natives have surrounded my . . . oh, God! Did you see that?"

Willeford went quiet. The sound of the chanting grew. Despite the poor quality of the audio, it sounded guttural and brutal.

"*Ehe . . . javasas-ggot . . .* "

Tommy's scream made Albert jump again. He looked at the wimpy kid. He always sat at the back of the lab and tried unsuccessfully to hide his earbuds under his hoodie. Now he was standing up, his hands wrapped around his neck as if choking. Albert got up. Could he perform the Heimlich maneuver? He knew the theory, but had never done it to anyone. He was about to run to Tommy when the kid's feet left the ground. Every eye in the classroom nailed itself to Tommy.

"The . . . chanting keeps getting louder," Willeford's ghost screamed from every speaker in the room.

"Stop that thing!" yelled Albert.

"I'm trying! This is exactly what we were talking about, Mr. Gardner!" said Ben.

Tommy's body flew into the wall behind him and the impact of his head reverberated even over the cacophony of chanting and screaming.

"Ehe maytubi javasas-ggot igomoro . . . Ehe maytubi javasas-ggot igomoro . . . "

The sounds coming from the speakers had lost their grainy quality. The chanting was now loud and clear, and Albert could make out every word even if he failed to recognize their meaning. Whatever it was, it sounded ominous. That those words were somehow responsible for what was happening in the room was something he instinctively knew and didn't question.

"Try unplugging the fucking thing, Tristan!" Ben's voice had gone up a few decibels. He repeatedly punched the keyboard. The plastic contraption bounced with each hit, but the audio kept playing.

Unplugging the computer was the best idea. Tristan seemed frozen in place. Brionne advanced toward him, hesitated, and moved toward the wall to unplug the computer. Before she got there, her head snapped back and stayed that way for a couple of seconds. Then she turned. Blood poured from a gaping wound on her neck. Then her chest exploded, sending a chunk of her sternum, blood, and pieces of meat flying through the air. The cavity in her torso was a red mess of shaking lung tissue and pieces of broken ribs. She stood there for a second as if suspended by invisible hands and then collapsed. Her body hit the floor before the first scream erupted from somewhere in the back of the room.

"They aren't fucking touching them!" screamed Willeford over the chaos. "The natives are standing around chanting and something is killing my men!"

Albert felt his heart move to his throat and his balls retract into his stomach. Ben was lifting his leg toward the computer when the leg he was standing on was apparently kicked from under him. He fell back, his head thudding against the polished concrete floor of the studio. Then his head came back up and went back to the floor with more violence.

"*Ehe . . .*"

His head was slammed by the invisible force again.

"*. . . maytubi . . .*"

Ben's skull cracked open.

"*. . . javasas-ggot . . .*"

His head smashed into the floor, losing its shape and turning into something resembling a large mound of hamburger meat full of broken bones and teeth.

"*. . . igomoro . . .*"

Albert looked away from the mess that had been Ben Martinez. The screams become more violent, more desperate. The realization that the shrieks he was hearing were coming from his students and not the audio file that kept playing hit him and something in his head collapsed.

"They're right outside the bridge's door now," said Willeford. "*Ehe maytubi javasas-ggot igomoro . . . Ehe maytubi javasas-ggot igomoro . . .*" The volume of the strange words grew.

Jessica Mitchell was decapitated and Brittany, who sat next to her, wasn't done screaming when a deep, red gash blossomed in her neck. Then, Tommy Wilson, who hadn't uttered ten words to Albert during the semester, flew out of his seat and hung in the air, his limbs making a quivering X. His shirt flew up and blood poured from a gash below his sternum. The wound grew as it travelled south. Tommy squealed like a stuck pig. The wound reached his belly and kept moving. His intestinal wall opened like a pink flower and his intestines unspooled, hitting the floor with a series of wet plops thankfully drowned by the chanting and screaming.

Albert saw two men standing near the wall behind Tommy. They were semi-translucent, but their skin was dark, naked except for loincloths. Their mouths moved. "*Ehe maytubi javasas-ggot igomoro . . .* " Their chanting mixed in with the frantic cries and the gargling to become an unbearable cacophony. Albert closed his eyes, sank to his knees. Willeford howled that the natives were in the bridge. Then he let out a bloodcurling scream cut short by a loud crunch. The situation had overpowered Albert. He knew he had to act, but his senses, and his strength, were giving up, shutting down in some bizarre attempt at self-preservation.

The sounds subsided a bit following Willeford's last scream. Albert was about to open his eyes when he felt two strong hands hook him by the armpits and pull him up as if he weighed less than a toddler. He looked back and saw no one. Then something pierced his chest. The pain exploded, travelled to his brain like a hot whiteness that fried his senses and made him shake. His ribs cracked inward and punctured his right lung. He reached out and grabbed something that was there but that he could not see. The thing kept moving despite his efforts to make it stop. The invisible spear raped his flesh with a brutal crunch and soon pushed against the skin of his back. Albert felt it rise like a tent before giving in to the pressure and letting the point of whatever was piercing him go through and finish its devastating journey. Something cold and sharp slid against his neck. Warm blood quickly replaced the cold feeling. The hand holding him up let go and he dropped to the floor.

"Ehe maytubi javasas-ggot igmo . . . "

Click.

The recording stopped playing. The piece was over.

Albert coughed. Pain hit him again like a dozen steel-toed boots kicking him all over at the same time. Blood filled his mouth and trickled out. He looked around. Blood. Hollowed torsos. Decapitated corpses. Shock was starting to set in, mercifully replacing the pain with something akin to cold numbness.

With a second loud click, the massive door swung open. Students stood in the hallway. The horror on their faces was the last thing Albert registered before the dark silence took over.

the man in room 603

DYER WILK

THE BUILDING AT 50th and Bleeker stood atop a low, grassy hill overlooking a small town with a name that was easily forgotten, surrounded by open stretches of unpopulated countryside. Long ago, when the building had been brand new and the stucco façade was freshly-painted white, a large sign and cross had been mounted prominently six stories up, just below the roofline, metal and glass flashing brightly in the sun and glowing neon blue at night, a reminder to everyone of the structure's noble purpose. Even without the sign, it was still obvious that it was a hospital. Even with its stucco turned yellow by age and its rows of windows unwashed, it couldn't be anything else. Within its walls, countless people had been healed and countless others had died. Long ago it had housed 350 patients at full capacity. Now it housed only one–the man in room 603.

In twelve years of working at the hospital, Pamela Johnstone had repeatedly demonstrated her ability to withstand the pressures of the job. On her first day of work, the head nurse (a seasoned woman of seven years' experience) had jumped off the roof and landed facedown in the parking lot. As a group of green-faced young men worked to peel what was left off the asphalt and hose down what couldn't be scraped up and shoveled into a garbage bag, Pam had remained her normal, cheery self, working as if nothing had happened. In twelve years, she saw over three hundred employees come and go. Some had killed themselves, others had gone insane and been hauled away, others had spent years working without complaint only to die from some seemingly natural cause. Pam herself wasn't worried, when she'd hit the ten-year mark she realized that she was part of the minority two percent that was completely immune to it. There was no reason to worry. She had been born to do this job.

On a sunny afternoon in May, word came down about an emergency meeting. It wasn't the first of course. Pam had been to so many now that they almost felt routine, but it was the first time one had been held on the hospital grounds. Mr. Burgess, a short, pudgy administrator who was prone to sweating, called Pam into his office and gave her the details that the rest of the staff wasn't privy to.

It was a funding issue. The people in Washington weren't convinced that the program was getting results. Too much cost. Too many setbacks. They would arrive in two days and they intended to see the patient for themselves, despite the consistent warnings from the experts that only trained staff who had undergone extensive psychological evaluation should be allowed anywhere near him.

As Burgess reached inside his coat and pressed a wadded tissue into his armpit, Pamela held back a grin and wondered if Mr. Burgess would pass his next psychological evaluation.

In the two days before the meeting, Pam buckled down and went through the usual procedure. She conducted last minute staff evaluations in case layoffs were coming. Put in orders for more drugs, IV bags, saline, catheters. She gathered her notes and wrote the same report she had written many times before, with the same recommendations.

Continue to evaluate patient closely. Monitor sedation and adjust as necessary. Allocate funds to hire more staff as needed. Current staff death rate: 25 per year.

On the day of the meeting, she dressed in a freshly dry-cleaned uniform, and walked through Ward C, past the nurses station, and headed to room 603 to check on the patient. The guard posted outside the door (a tall, muscular young man whom had been disqualified from joining the Marine Corps due to a minor back injury) unlocked the outer gate for her.

"Nice day," he said, pulling it aside.

She smiled stiffly and stepped through, waited for him to lock the gate behind her, and then opened the inner gate.

"Just call if you need anything," he said.

She wouldn't.

The hospital room was average aside from the wire mesh lining the walls and ceiling. The experts who sometimes visited the hospital had explained that it was a safety precaution, put in place to improve their chances of blocking the signal. Many times, she had asked them what this signal was exactly, but their answers had been vague, in the same way that most answers were when it came to their theories about the patient.

"It's sort of like radio waves," one theoretician had offered. "Only we can't really measure them with conventional equipment. We're just seeing the effects they have on people."

She moved to the bed, her shoes clicking on the aluminum floor plates. The patient was lying there in his restraints, appearing to sleep peacefully as always. She wasn't deceived, though, not the way some of the younger nurses were–the same nurses who she sometimes found weeping in the bathroom, blubbering about "the fire." The patient required constant monitoring, and at no moment was it safe to let down your guard. A whole team of nurses could check on him once every half-hour on a twenty-four-hour rotation and still fail to see his subtle signs of waking. The procedure had to be followed closely. Check. Double-check. Triple-check. Failure was not an option.

One day back in her third year at the hospital, she had watched a young nurse misadjust the flow of sedation from the IV drip. The patient's vitals had dropped down to almost nothing and a special team of doctors had to be called in to resuscitate. They had worked on him for a nerve-racking half-hour, doing everything they could to bring him back without actually waking him, the phone down at the nurses station ringing the whole time. Generals in Washington were demanding updates, wanting to know if the patient was going to die, if they needed to go to Def Con One. Pam assured them that the doctors were doing everything they could, and later (when the patient was finally stable) she told them it would never happen again.

And it hadn't. The procedure had been adjusted, the levels of sedation leaning toward conservative, so conservative that the risk of killing him had been replaced by the increased risk of waking him up. It had almost happened two years after the patient's near death. Pam was in the room at the time, checking his vital signs (which appeared to be completely stable), when he opened his eyes and tried to sit up. In all her years on staff, this was the one and only time she had actually been afraid.

His eyes were red, and even under the bright fluorescents, they had seemed to glow. He looked at her for a moment, slowly opening his mouth as if to speak, as her hand crept over to the IV drip. She increased the dosage slightly and he sank back onto the mattress without a sound. In her daily report, she only noted that his vital signs had fluctuated enough to suggest that he had been close to waking up, but she had never mentioned (for fear of losing her job) that the patient had actually opened his eyes.

Pam, now head nurse and hardened by her years of experience, checked the patient's vitals, made a minute adjustment, which she marked on the chart along with the date and time, and walked out of the room. The guard made brief small talk as he locked up, his eyes occasionally dropping to the place where the loose fabric of her uniform tightened over her breasts. He'd told her once (trying hard to sound casual) that she looked good for her age, as if he had thought it over carefully and decided her looks were good enough for him to forgive the fact that she was at least 10 years older than him and he'd make an exception if it meant having a little fun together after work.

During the next round of employee evaluations, she would most likely recommend his employment be terminated. Although, part of her took pleasure in knowing that if she allowed him to work here for another two or three years, there was a good chance he would wake up one day and decide to put a gun in his mouth.

On her ride down in the elevator, she listened to one of the nurses go on and on about some TV show that had something to do with washed-up celebrities dancing. Pam humored her for five floors, forcing a smile until she noticed the girl had a nosebleed.

"Put some ice on it and stay on the first floor for the rest of the day," she said handing her a tissue.

She stepped off the elevator and walked into what had once been the emergency room. A bearded orderly looked up at her from behind the desk and held up his hands in an overly-theatrical gesture of frustration.

"Wi-fi keeps going out. You hear anything from upstairs?"

She shrugged. "Call them and ask."

The orderly frowned and picked up the phone. She stepped out into the parking lot and squinted in the bright sun. Most of the parking spaces were full. Limousines and black town cars with government plates lined the rows, along with several luxury vehicles belonging to doctors and board members. Everyone who had some say over the patient's care had been called out.

As she walked, she pulled out her phone and checked her messages. Nothing important. Her father wanted to know if she was taking time off for Christmas. An old friend from college (one of the few she still made time for) had sent a couple pictures of her kids. Two elementary school-aged boys smiled with crooked teeth. One of the photos didn't load properly and came out mostly distorted with multi-colored pixels, the only thing recognizable being a crisp line slashed through the middle of her screen where a crooked-toothed mouth loomed large.

At the far end of the parking lot, a group of soldiers dressed in camouflage formed a perimeter, failing to blend in with the plain white stucco maintenance building behind them. Men in suits lined up at an improvised checkpoint to have their ID badges inspected and scrutinized. Pam skirted the line entirely and walked along the side of the building, passing by boarded windows and faded notices that stated the premises had been condemned by authority of the US Department of Health–all trespassers would be prosecuted. At the rear entrance, a soldier leaned against a railing, smoking a cigarette. He quickly snapped to attention, dropping the cigarette to the pavement.

He glanced at her ID. "Go ahead, ma'am."

"Thank you."

She descended a narrow flight of steps that led down to the basement. Inside, a military liaison waited for her, dressed in a suit instead of a uniform. He flashed a sycophantic smile and handed her a nametag, reciting the same basic rules she had heard a dozen times before as they walked down the long, dimly-lit corridor.

They stopped at a set of double doors, the liaison pushing one open. Before she could step inside, he leaned in close and asked in a quiet voice: "Do you really think he's, you know, evil?"

Pam smiled. "Go up to room 603 and decide for yourself."

The man's smile faded into a flat line. She stepped past him, letting out a small laugh. Deep down, she knew that most "tough" government men were really just scared little boys. For all their displays of strength and macho posturing, they knew they were powerless.

Inside the meeting room, men sat crowded around long narrow tables arranged in semi-circles that repeated into smaller and smaller semi-circles around an open space where a long table and podium had been set up. The chairman of the hospital's board of directors stood at the microphone, making his opening statements, the American flag hanging behind him. Board members and committee delegates sat in the shadows at the main table, waiting patiently for the floor to be opened up for statements.

Pam found an empty seat beside an elderly, white-haired man dressed in a suit that looked to be two sizes too large. He glanced up at her with a nervous expression, then turned back to the jumble of notes scrawled on a yellow legal pad in front of him. His phone sat beside it, the screen glitching repeatedly.

She folded her hands and waited, her eyes moving around the room, taking in the ducts and pipes that lined the ceiling fifteen-feet above her. She found them far more interesting than what was being said. She'd heard it all before, from the various experts who had come to visit the hospital over the years, from a three-star general who had once harassed her over the phone for nearly an hour, spouting his theories on everything from secret Chinese plots to Biblical prophecies, and she'd heard it from the group of old men who had called her to testify behind closed doors in Washington six years earlier, asking her to repeat what she'd been saying in her weekly progress reports for years.

The fact that most of them had decided to come all the way to the hospital amused her. The fact that they had paid someone to convert this room, which had probably held boilers or generators at one time, into a pathetic imitation of a Senate chamber amused her. It amused her that they wanted to come and see the patient for themselves because they believed it would help them understand him better. They *didn't* understand. And they never would. They only understood funding allocation and secret meetings and defense readiness conditions.

The lights were turned down and the first speaker began a powerpoint presentation, talking monotonously about the history of the patient, regurgitating almost word-for-word what had been written in the official briefing documents every hospital employee had read dozens of times. Chances were that once she was called on to speak, she would probably do the same thing, repeat the same basic information from her reports, adding nothing new. They always wanted her professional opinion, and yet she wasn't sure she had one. Despite what everyone said about him, she wasn't particularly afraid. In some ways she actually liked him. He was quiet and dependable in an odd kind of way, unlike most of the other men she dealt with on a regular basis, present company included.

When the first speaker finished, the overhead lights came up, revealing the somber expressions of the men and women in the room. She recognized most of them. Some had come by the hospital once or twice to talk to doctors and try to push their own agenda. A lot of the senators and businessmen had asked her the same question the young man out in the hall had asked her. She always told them she didn't know and she was just doing her job like everyone else.

Keep the patient asleep. Keep the patient alive.

One of the generals sitting near the front had come into room 603 half-a-dozen years ago and told her she was wasting her time keeping him doped up. Then he'd pulled out a pistol, pointed it directly at the patient's head and said: "One shot, that's all it'd take." She had rushed down to the nurses station and called security, then hit the speed dial button for Washington. The general had been escorted off the premises and not been allowed back, but he still showed up at the meetings, eager to suggest the same solution to his colleagues.

"Let's open up the floor now for suggestions on how we might resolve this pressing issue," the Chairman said.

A senator stood up, leaning over slightly to speak into the gooseneck microphone mounted to the table in front of him. "I honestly don't see why we should debate any of this or why I was called in here from my vacation. Based on what I've heard, this seems a lot simpler than what a lot of you have been saying. If we just keep him asleep, we don't have to worry about anything."

A collective grumble moved through the crowd. Pam watched as countless faces sank into scowls and frowns. Men leaned over and whispered to each other; some pulled out phones and walked out into the hall, others began scrawling down notes.

"We can't keep him asleep indefinitely," an elderly doctor said. "It appears that he's been building a tolerance to the sedatives."

"Then switch drugs. With millions of dollars in tax breaks we give to our friends in the pharmaceutical industry, don't try to tell me they can't come up with something that can keep this bastard asleep."

The doctor held up his hands. "Please. You have to understand that we've tried that. Everything new. Everything experimental that isn't on the market yet. None of it really works. He's developed a tolerance to the most potent stuff we have. And there's still the risk that we might kill him."

A businessman in a tailored three-piece suit stood up at the same time as a lobbyist for the pharmaceutical industry, beating him out for the floor. "I'd like to reiterate to you gentlemen that we *could* cryogenically freeze him. The technology has advanced a great deal since our last meeting. And with some additional funding, we could probably—"

"A technology that *your* company owns," the usurped lobbyist said. "Why should everybody take a risk on something that doesn't even work just so you can get a fat government contract?"

"I'm not suggesting that we take any unnecessary risks. But if you want to accuse me of just trying to get a contract, how about you try to tell me your friends don't want a contract of their own. Don't act like you're not looking out for your end just like I am. The fact is, without private industry, he would have woken up years ago. And we all know what'll happen if he wakes up."

For a few seconds, the room seemed to be still, unwilling to react, and then nearly everyone unleashed simultaneously, a hundred voices echoing off the walls and drowning each other out. People stood up by the dozen and grabbed their microphones, yelling at the top of their lungs to achieve maximum volume.

"The government only hangs onto him because they're still trying to figure out how to use him as a weapon!"

"Why the hell not? We know what he can do. We should figure out how to use him against our enemies."

"*You'll never control him.*"

"Of course we can. We keep him asleep and use hypnotic suggestion to get him to target hostiles in Syria, Iraq, Iran, North Korea–"

"Are you stupid? Are you going to tell me next you can turn a wolf into a vegetarian? It'll never happen. He likes hurting us too much."

"He can't do anything while he's asleep."

"*He can't?* Look at these numbers . . . let me just . . . yes, here. 1,298 suicides within a twenty-mile radius of the hospital last year, 331 fatal car accidents, 523 murders, 197 assaults. That's thirty times higher than the national average."

"That doesn't prove anything."

"You want to see the statistics?"

"If we freeze him–"

"A seven percent increase in commercial airline crashes worldwide, a twelve percent increase in the national murder rate, eight percent international, six percent increase in suicides, fifteen percent increase in cases of assault–"

"Why? Can somebody tell me why?"

"It's complicated. We think he emits this . . . this signal. It's similar to EMF, but it's not . . . it's difficult to measure with existing technology. But in our studies, we've documented changes in Alpha and Delta and Theta waves in subjects who were in close proximity to the patient–"

"I'm tired of hearing your goddamn theories!"

"It's not a theory. He's a transmitter, okay? But he's sending out a message telling people to kill themselves, kill their families, burn their houses down. If we can adequately shield him, we could–"

"Put him in a bunker! Let's bury the son of a bitch under a damn mountain!"

"Are you crazy? We can't move him. If he wakes up during transport, it's all over."

"We can build a dome over the hospital, just like they did with Chernobyl."

"And how much is that gonna cost? How many construction workers have that kind of security clearance?"

"We should be contracting out pharmaceutical companies to research new drugs."

"He'll just adapt to them."

"Then you should perform surgery. Put the bastard in a real coma."

"We tried that. We tried . . . Hey, shut up and listen. Fourteen years ago. An MRI showed he had normal formation of the cerebral cortex–"

"Why we are we even talking about this? Who cares?"

"Just listen. Please. We operated. Two doctors in the room had heart attacks and the anesthesiologist locked herself in a supply closet and gouged her eyes out with a pair of scissors."

"That's just the effect he has on people."

"So what happens if he wakes up?"

"He'll kill us all."

"Let's kill him then, goddamn it! Let's just go in there and kill him!"

"You want to piss his father off? It's bad enough as it is."

"Shut up. Just shut up. I don't believe he's the anti-*anything*. That's never been proven. I don't need your Bible-thumping bullshit getting in the way when we have solid facts and figures. You're just seeing what you want to see."

"These figures don't lie. Twenty percent increase in heart attacks in the US in the last year. Forty percent increase in strokes. That's not a coincidence."

"How about I kill *you* and we'll see how much the murder rate goes up?"

"Order!"

The voices of the delegates became lost in the uproar. Somewhere, buried beneath the drone, the sound of the Chairman's gavel tried and failed to compete in volume. After a couple minutes, the microphones were disconnected and security was called in to break up the fistfights in the aisles. Pam watched with perverse interest, wondering if she would see blood. She couldn't understand it, but she *needed* to see. Ever since she'd woken up this morning, she had been thinking the strangest thoughts, laughing at the strangest things. The memory of her mother's slow death from cancer. The thought of the cat she'd accidentally run over in college. The footage of the air crash she'd seen on TV while eating breakfast. It was hilarious. It was wonderful.

A powerful little thought emerged then, simple and perfect and warm within the confines of her skull. She saw flashes of it. A pony running through the wilderness. So strange. So familiar. She could remember seeing it before. In her dreams, in her oldest memories going back to when she was a little girl. She longed for it. She'd always longed for it. A companion. A friend who would never text her with dinner plans or send her photos of ugly children.

She got up from her chair, heat spreading all over her body, her skin beginning to sweat. She walked out of the room, giggling at the sound of screaming behind her. The sycophantic little man in the suit escorted her down the corridor, trying to impress her by bragging about his job in Washington, but he kept stumbling over his words, as if something was caught in his throat and he couldn't manage to swallow it or cough it up. She imagined him with his throat ripped open. She saw it vividly, almost certain that it was going to happen to him very soon.

She smiled as he opened the door and headed up the steps. The soldier at the top of the stairs leaned against the railing, smoking a cigarette and rocking back and forth with his arms tucked tightly against his body. He didn't bother to look at her or attempt to stand at attention. She saw death in his eyes. He knew his time was coming soon and was trying to come to terms with it.

She walked through the parking lot toward the hospital, seeing the rows of cars busting into flames in her mind. She could feel the warmth of it build and grow. With each step, it thickened, wrapping itself around her. Her feet scraped the asphalt, tiny pulses inside her brain tapping away in a counter rhythm, becoming more powerful with each passing second.

She walked through the emergency entrance of the hospital, ignoring the nurse with the nosebleed now lying on a stretcher and being given CPR by the bearded orderly. She stepped into the elevator, humming as she rode up to the sixth floor, not noticing as her nose trickled blood. The hallway seemed to be twenty or thirty degrees warmer than usual. She liked it better this way. The air conditioner had always been set just a little too cold for her.

At the nurses station, a pair of twitching legs stuck out from behind the counter, heels delightfully clicking on the tile floor. Joy swelled within her chest, making her body tingle and throb in time with the pulsing in her head. She remembered the merry-go-round now, the one she'd never been allowed on when she was a little girl, the one with the white pony she'd begged to ride. Her mommy and daddy had both been doctors. They hadn't wanted their precious Pammy to grow up with her head full of childish ideas. Their daughter was going to grow up to be a medical professional just like them.

But she'd get to ride the pony now. She could see it vividly in her mind as she walked down the corridor toward room 603. It was smooth and white and beautiful. Powerful muscles moving beneath tightly stretched skin. Did the patient ever ride the white pony? No. That was silly. She *knew* who the patient was. He didn't ride ponies, but he loved them just as much as she did. He loved merry-go-rounds, too. He was the son of the amusement park owner, after all. He could go on the rides whenever he wanted to. He could stay out after sundown and eat cotton candy and curly fries. He could eat and eat and never get full.

Pam stopped at the gate outside the room. The guard stood there, his face pressed into his hands.

"Are you okay?" she asked.

He shook his head. "Goddamn headache. Migraine."

"Would you like me to give you something for it?"

He pulled his hands away from his face and looked at her with bloodshot eyes. Sweat glistened on his skin, blood dripping from his nose.

"I think I need to go home."

"You mean you don't want to go home with me?"

His eyes widened.

"You don't want to bend me over and give it to me? You don't want to make me moan and scream?"

The guard's mouth fell open. He didn't understand. She wasn't sure she understood either. But she knew he'd been thinking it. She hadn't just imagined it. She had seen his thoughts, read his mind and known what he had always wanted, to take her home and strip her naked and writhe on top of her until he was too exhausted to keep going. He wanted to see if that iron-hearted bitch could take it.

She smiled at him and reached for his belt. He stepped back and bumped into the wall, all that strength turning to fear.

"Don't worry. I won't tell anyone if you won't. Let's just take care of that headache first."

He looked at her in disbelief, wide eyes blinking as she pulled his gun out of its holster, slid the barrel into his mouth and pulled the trigger.

The world exploded in her ears, the guard's insides now on the outside. His lifeless body slumped to the floor, the feeling of delight radiating throughout every inch of her flesh, laughter pouring from her lips.

Pam dropped the gun and pulled the key ring off his belt. She unlocked the gate and stepped inside.

The patient was lying in bed as usual. He'd been imprisoned here for so long, not allowed to run free and play. Pammy wanted to play with him so badly. She'd ride the white pony and he'd build a beautiful bonfire.

She moved through the thick air, almost gliding over the metal floor, and reached out to shut down the machines. One by one, the lights and screens went dark, reflecting a soft orange glow rising from between the walls and floor. She wrapped her hands around the IV tubing and tore it free of the patient's arms. The feeling within her swelled and expanded until her entire body ached. Her nose bled uncontrollably now. She reveled in it. The blood was part of the fun. Soon they'd both play in it.

The pulsing in her head pounded and roared. She heard voices and music and laughter, and she understood now that it had always been there, ever since she'd first started working at the hospital. She had simply tuned it out and ignored it, pretended that her body wasn't an antenna like everyone else's. But she was receiving now, loud and clear. The voices spoke to her and promised her everything she'd always wanted. They loved her and enticed her and sang to her. She stripped her clothes off, letting the warmth wash over her until she burned. The fluorescent lights overhead flickered and burst into showers of glass and sparks, throwing the room into the near darkness. The orange glow brightened, tracing the edges of the walls behind the wire mesh and expanding into bright cracks. Outside the window, dark clouds formed, fringed with deep red and orange. The walls caught fire, melting the wires like candle wax, the floor falling away as a fiery pit opened beneath her. She stood there, hovering in open space, watching the patient begin to stir. He was more beautiful than she remembered. In twelve years of watching over him, she'd never really taken notice of the horns or snout. Perhaps they hadn't been there until now.

Her parents had never allowed her to cuddle with animals when she was a little girl. She could see the resemblance clearly, a goat standing alone in a pen at a petting zoo, waiting for her touch. She wanted so badly to touch him. But Pammy hadn't been allowed to. Pammy wasn't allowed to have toys. Pammy wasn't allowed to have fun. Pammy wasn't allowed to do anything because she had to grow up to be a nurse so she could help keep the nice man in room 603 asleep.

But he was awakening now. His eyes moved beneath black lids, lines of orange light flickering at the seams. The fire consumed everything, washing over the walls and ceiling until there was nothing left. The bed crumbled into ashes, becoming a stone altar upon which the patient took his final form. He was naked now, almost nine feet tall, his red skin covered in majestic patches of dark hair. His feet had become cloven hooves. His tail moved back and forth, a serpent whipping at the flames.

The feeling was everything to her now, an orgasm of fire. She looked down and saw the white pony between her legs, ready to take her for a ride. All her wishes would soon be granted. No desire left unfulfilled.

The creature on the altar opened his eyes, revealing the beautiful fire deep within them. His patience had finally run out. He stood then, towering over the blood-red sky, and reached out to her. She seemed so small in comparison, so sweet and innocent that it was almost impossible to believe that little Pammy was going to ride alongside the man who would bring fire to the world. But it was all for her. It was everything she'd ever wanted.

And together they played as the world burned.

the sound of yesterday

ASHLEE SCHEUERMAN

WE'RE ONLINE, BOYS.'

He folded the laptop closed and tucked its sleek chassis into the black leather case slung over his shoulder, which blended in with his black suit, glossy black shoes, and, so creatively, his matching black tie and sunglasses. Only the subtle gleam of his silver wristwatch and crisp white shirt broke the monotony of his appearance, and even then, they remained the selfsame features of some vague government suit overseeing the installation of a “latest and greatest” surveillance line. Big Brother was now listening better than ever before. The public had never been more secure.

At a final nod from Mr. Black, the head contractor waved his workers to begin packing up. Their job was done, and a stack of signed Non-Disclosure Agreements along with the healthy little bonus in their pay cheques acted as the modern and civilised alternative to the age-old tradition of slaughtering the slaves to keep the secrets.

None of the fluoro-garbed grunts knew any truth worth killing over, anyway.

Pearl Harrison startled at the squalling voices pouring through her telephone. She laid the handset down in its cradle, palm pressing to her chest and the race of her heartbeat therein, then used her free hand to slide oversized glasses farther up her nose. Her small spaniel gave a ready bark of warning. She hushed Marco in distracted tones and lifted the receiver again. Now three minutes past four o'clock, when she was due to call her sister Mabel and speak for half an hour, as they had every Friday afternoon, Pearl grew anxious at the unprecedented delay.

The harsh voices remained on the line when she pressed the cold plastic to her ear. Their words were indecipherable, hissing, frantic. She barely resisted crossing herself.

'Who is this?' she demanded. Local kids might have nothing better to do after school than mess with the phone lines and play practical jokes on an old lady, but she absolutely must speak to Mabel, and no disrespectful youth would get in the way of her call.

The phone silenced. Pearl waited a moment longer, quietly pleased with herself for taking such a firm tone with those jokers. Before she could begin dialling Mabel's familiar number, someone spoke up, clear as day.

'Hey, doll.'

'Who's there?' she asked again in a considerably gentler voice, one hushed with nostalgia and a glimmer of superstitious fear. Only George ever dared called her "doll". And it couldn't be him. Her late husband left the mortal coil a decade and a half prior.

Her brain took that short utterance and turned it into a loop. *Hey, doll. Hey, doll. Hey, doll.*

She had nothing more to say. The shock took all the stuffing from her.

'You forgetting your old man?' His unmistakeable laughter rolled out of the phone line and trembled down Pearl's aged body.

'George is dead. You can't just go around impersonating people's loved ones.' *How cruel. How unutterably cruel.*

Hey, doll. Hey, doll.

'Aw, don't be like that. I just wanted to have a little chinwag with my favourite sea treasure.'

The light-hearted banter was in perfect imitation of George's carefree nature, and Pearl simply couldn't take it. The beloved voice curled in her gut, sick and aching. 'My husband died fifteen years ago. Stop this nonsense right now. Why would you torment a lonely old woman?'

She slammed the handset down, crooked, so the bulky piece of plastic fell off the cradle and clattered to the floor. It dangled by the spiralled cord, wavering back and forth in a mocking little dance. Marco leapt from his basket and began a manic barking spree, spittle glistening on his exposed teeth as he snarled and nipped at the phone. Pearl backed away from the receiver and her brave dog. She gave in to the urge to sign the cross over herself.

Hey, doll.

I-I shall just have to call the phone company, she thought, trying desperately to hold onto logic and reason, yet failing utterly to consider how she was to dial out to anyone if this evil prankster stayed on the other end of the line. When the obvious realisation dawned upon her, Pearl took herself down the hall and knocked on the one closed door inside her house, pretending all was normal the whole while. Her grandson audibly moved within the room and showed his face around the large panel of wood.

'Samuel, dear, you have that mobile telephone, don't you?'

'Yeah, Gran, what's up?' he asked with a sleepy blink.

'Someone is making prank calls to the house, I will need the telecom people to do something about it. Mabel is waiting for my call.'

'Ah, sure, I'll give them a ring before I go for my walk.'

'Thank you, dear.'

Hey, doll.

The turning earth granted sunset to another day. Everything was graced with surreal hues and the humidity and lakeside breeze were in conflict over whether the night should stay a summered warmth or drop temperatures until goosebumps would skitter across exposed skin.

Samuel's hands were laid at rest in the cosy fleece pockets attached to the front of his hoodie, safe from any threatening chill. Quiet, beneath the grumble of traffic on the distant freeway and wildlife chittering, he heard the wide pant legs of his jeans scuffing together. The sound of moving denim kept him on edge. He shouldn't have been able to pick up the abrasive rumple-scruff with each step. The world around him, or the stony-metallic sounds of his sneakers crunching over coarse basalt should have drowned out the noise, but no. The loose fabric called out from each stride, dominating his aural attention. Some days, his Cochlear implants seemed to provide a landscape of sound beyond what he wanted. His grandmother liked to call him sullen. Ungrateful for what he's received from the technology. He loved her, sure, but did she ever have a judgemental streak.

What would she know.

He considered reaching up to switch the processor off and bask in the blackout, but the notion passed in a roil of apathy, and his hands remained motionless, buried in his pockets.

The track ballast relinquished its thermal takings of the day, residual heat wavering up from the black aggregate mounded beneath tarry rail-road sleepers and the dull gleam of metal stretched in endless parallel lines. He stopped at a point no different than the rest, where fields upon fields of chartreuse wheat stems swayed to his left, and the dirt road pitted from rain and wear ran along the other side. Perfunctory fences sagged between star pickets, the wire tired and unconvincing as a barrier or deterrent from anyone jumping over to walk the tracks. The thought had always made him smile, a bored twist of his lips which left his pale grey eyes unmoved. To have fences in place, untended, a half-hearted reminder or stuttered request to stay on your side because *here be dragons*. No longer belching coal smoke from the heart of roaring flame to cross from state to territory, the locomotives which shot along this stretch were now swift and sleek, efficient diesel-electric prime movers to the antiquated steam engines of old.

His attention shifted once the insipid rustle of his jeans had silenced, and he caught a new tremor on the air. He cast a wan gaze both ways along the line, finding no distant sign of an approaching train. His eyes rolled upward, slowly, to reveal the titanic spans of high-tension power lines striding across the landscape. Each framework giant stood with arms spread wide, looming, *humming*.

The cooling sky, purple and grey, lent a quality of distortion to the image above. He felt his senses give the slick-sticky stretch of taffy, lengthening, falling, until his hands and feet gained an artificial weight at the end of elongated limbs and the heaviness cuddled around his chest, constricting each breath until he didn't bother straining against the grip. He was small, and not. Shrunken, but distended, all at once. The atmosphere ballooned, wider, impossibly, the world growing larger and rounder to envelop him, and all the while, the sounds were rising in volume, a convincing chug, a rumble familiar and alien, not a train or anything else hurtling along the mortal plane, but something untrustworthy—

A voice whispered into his ear, 'Samuel. My darling boy.'

His mother. By God, his dead mother.

The sensations crushed around the young man, unbearable. He hated her so much. Everything stopped.

He took in a massive gasp, filling his barren lungs with desperate, dust-flavoured air. Between blinks, reality snapped back into place. A normal twenty-two year old, roaming along the train tracks. He resumed walking, keeping his eyes resolutely away from the power lines singing overhead, ignoring the goosebumps prickling along his body.

A sharp tattoo pounded out from Pearl's front door, the thin metal of the screen rapping double-time to each knock. The elderly woman took two steps back and nearly fell over her favourite floral armchair before she mustered the tenacity to consider, maybe, seeing whoever had dropped by.

She went through the motions of turning the cold deadbolt and sliding the chain out of its narrow channel to open the door to a smiling technician in a dark blue button-up shirt and pressed slacks. His attire was somehow more formal than she would have expected from a workman, but his bulky work bag with wires and unfamiliar tools protruding from its pockets and the embroidered logos which emblazoning him as an employee of the telecommunications company were also clean and tidy, maybe this was just normal. He wasn't some grubby plumber or mechanic. He worked with phone lines and electrical things.

Her hand trembled as she inserted her key into the screen lock to let him inside to assess the trouble. 'I didn't realise you would make it out so soon,' she said, more glad than she had any business being to see a friendly, *living* human.

The technician tucked his sunglasses into the front pocket on his shirt and gave her a winning grin. 'Our systems are now set up to monitor for connection issues, ma'am. The computers warned us of an unspecified interruption at this address before we received the call, so here I am.'

It's a whole new world, she marvelled.

'I'm so pleased. I tried to call my sister, Mabel, just the same as I always do, but th-there's . . . There's something wrong with the phone,' she finished, strangely embarrassed to relate her experience. The voice had spooked her properly. Rational thought had cast sufficient doubt on her experience and Pearl concluded no kids could have mimicked George's speech. He had died too long ago. But if they weren't young pranksters . . .

Maybe it's someone older. More malicious.

That didn't feel right, either.

'Lewis Carlisle.' He extended his right hand in Pearl's direction while lifting the thin screen of his tablet computer to scan a row of text. 'You must be Mrs. Harrison.'

'Please, call me Pearl.' His hand was both firm and cautious not to crush hers, showing an amount of respect which surprised the old woman. By the time she reached her seventies, the best she got from most people was a cursory attempt at courtesy. Once she styled her hair into a silver perm and more of her skin sagged than didn't, Pearl had become a non-human. No one special. Not worthy of real respect. More condescension towards her condition than real empathy.

But Lewis didn't show any of that. He shook her hand like she still mattered.

'Marco is in the kitchen, he's a good boy but might give you a little telling-off until he's gotten the smell of you.' They moved through her comfortable home toward the sitting room. She'd had the presence of mind to re-set the phone in its cradle before answering the door. There would be no evidence of her minor panic, not unless someone had waited this long to continue their harassment and answered Lewis's investigation with the voice of a dead man.

Greg sucked down the last of his cola with a bored slurp, nudging the crescent-shaped ice blocks around the bottom of his oversized cup with his equally-oversized straw, hoping for one last sugary taste. The surveillance business paid well because all the Listeners would up and die in protest of the utterly mind-numbing nature of their job. They were random quality control. Making sure the computerised recognition software was functioning well enough to *probably* catch the keywords it had been instructed to flag. Probably.

He checked the small digital clock in the corner of his computer screen, then the silver and leather watch strapped to his wrist, reassured that his break would come in twelve minutes and four seconds, then he could take his giant cup and replenish his cola supply from the postmix machine he had personally petitioned to have installed in the staff room. The second-hand dispenser sent by God himself to break their workplace monotony. Greg took on the job of cleaning the nozzles and flushing its pipes daily with a kind of passionate fervour, while 2IC Chuck replenished the soda water and flavoured syrup baggies with the same grudging sense of responsibility which he performed every other duty. Toady little man with jowls and warts. Nothing pleased the second-in-command.

The drone of voices changed, a new recording, another subject. Greg lifted his empty cup and inhaled around the edges of the paltry melted dregs, fighting an urge to chomp at the plastic straw. His eyes wandered, his feet jiggled, and he looked at the clock another three times before the next minute was up.

Maybe if he ever caught anything interesting, an error in the system, pouncing on some awesomely vital intelligence, then it would all be worth it. If he could ever be the fucking hero.

Another file played. Ten minutes until break. He bounced his knee, keeping one ear on the voices rambling on. Then the next. The next. The next.

'Gregory?'

He froze, lips circled around his straw. He knew that voice.

'Greg, man, say something.'

What the hell was this? Some kind of answering machine message or a call that failed to connect? Maybe a butt-dial. No one else spoke. Just this person sounding painfully reminiscent of his brother.

'Come on, Greg, I know you're there. Speak to me. It's been too long. Don't reject me when we finally get a chance to talk.'

'Steve?' he whispered into the empty room, in spite of the insanity. He had no microphone or speaker. This wasn't a phone call connecting over headset, just a pre-recorded sound playing over the speakers wired into the walls around him.

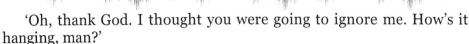

'Oh, thank God. I thought you were going to ignore me. How's it hanging, man?'

'How . . . how are you doing this?'

'Ever heard of a God-damn phone, Greg?'

Steve's answer defied every sense of reason, but the poor surveillance officer couldn't offer up his denial. His next words tried to cling to the dry insides of his throat, but he had to force them out, to whisper to himself, before they choked him, 'I thought you were dead.'

'What an ugly thing to say, brother.'

The subtle tone of blame stung worse than Greg could have anticipated. Like he carried personal fault for believing the medical examiner when they declared his older sibling deceased, aged thirty-one, cardiac arrest. Or the coroner, or the sympathetic nurses, the autopsy pathologist, the mortician. 'Fuck you, Steve.'

'Yeah, yeah, you too, pal. How's the fam'?'

'No, you don't get to just, just call me, or whatever this is, and not tell me how you're still alive. We buried you, for God's sake. Black lacquered coffin, expensive fucking flowers sitting on top while we all huddled and cried in the chapel.'

'You're the one who relied on their account while refusing to see me.'

Ouch. A sharp truth. Greg would not, point blank, no-God-damn-way, view the body at any point in the process. But their parents hadn't felt the same qualms. They'd have known their own son laying on the cold steel bench.

'Are you listening to me?'

'Yeah, man.' *Christ, I've missed you.*

'Good. We've got a lot to catch up on.'

Greg leaned forward and listened, forgetting all about his break and the postmix cola which had momentarily been the highlight of his life.

Lewis held the receiver to his ear and frowned when static snarled at him again. 'Mrs. Harrison, I can dial out, but there is still interference coming through the line. This might be physical damage off-site. Would you like to try it out and see if this is going to be okay for now?'

'Call me Pearl,' she said distractedly as she nodded once and took the phone in a shaking hand. Lewis made no comment, but this wasn't the first time he had noticed fear at the suggestion of using the phone. An otherwise perfectly charming woman, bustling around, happiest when he accepted sharing a pot of Earl Grey with her. Her hands hadn't trembled when she provided the fine china teacup or poured the steaming liquid.

Her wrinkled finger punched in a number with the rapid precision of someone who rings the same person weekly. Her hesitant expression crumpled to helpless misery as the line crackled.

'Don't you talk to me,' she whispered and hung up the phone with a decisive crash. She cast a sideways look to Lewis. 'Still broken.'

'Mrs. Harrison—sorry, Pearl—was there someone on the other end of the line?'

'No, of course not,' she snapped.

The technician widened his eyes and softened his voice. 'I'm sorry to be a bother, but I thought I heard otherwise.'

'Like what, young man?'

'Well, like you telling someone not to speak, for starters.'

A very pink blush rose through her round cheeks, filling her face with the colour it otherwise lacked. 'That's just . . . just an old woman's silliness.'

'I'm here to help.'

'I don't think so.'

'And why not, ma'am?'

Her hands rose to cover her spectacled eyes, hiding from him, herself, the truth. 'Because I need a priest. I'm hearing the voice of my dead husband.'

'On the phone?'

'Yes, and he's been gone for a long time, dear. Fifteen years. Why now? Why torment me *now*, after a decade and a half!'

He was so surprised by the saddened outburst, he found himself murmuring a banal attempt at an explanation, something, anything to soothe her, he didn't quite know. 'They have just finished upgrading some other lines in this area, any changes in your service could be caused by that, perhaps they crossed some wires or inadvertently tampered with the phone line. Teething problems . . . What am I even saying?' Corporate tripe had rolled out of him before he caught up with the words. 'That has nothing to do with your, uh, unique situation. I'm sorry.'

Pearl's shiny eyes turned to him from between parted fingers. 'You believe me.'

Lewis wasn't a religious man, but that didn't make him a sceptic. 'Well, sure. I believe you have every reason to think you're hearing your husband. I don't know why, or how, or if it could be possible. I've never met anyone who could speak to the dead.'

'Why now?' she repeated, as if Lewis could provide even the barest of answer. 'No one has fitted new wiring in my head, young man.'

The technician gave a thin smile and shrugged in answer. 'You probably know better than I do what might have changed for you, Pearl. Do you want to call someone with my mobile?'

'What? What do you mean?'

'You mentioned a priest. Do you need to use my phone to contact them, if your landline isn't satisfactory?'

'What's wrong, son?'

'I'm fucking appalled. You have no idea.'

Samuel's hands shook with the need to hurt someone. Why wouldn't his mother's ghost stop talking in his ear? Saliva flooded his mouth, a precursor to the need to vomit, hurl up whatever contents were left in his stomach after his thin breakfast of reheated pancakes. Nothing special. Just like his life.

'Fucking pathetic,' he wheezed, lengthening his stride to reach a sink or the toilet bowl before the rhythmic clenching in his gut evacuated the syrup and cream-drenched foods.

The impact of his knees against the tiled floor sent shocks of pain up through his thighs and into his hips. Almost a distraction welcome enough to give him a moment of reprieve—but, no. He flung the lid and seat up and matched the violent movement, thrusting his head toward the welcoming porcelain.

Thank fuck Gran cleans this, he thought in between retches, grateful for the chemical-pine disinfectant. Only thing to make this experience more miserable was if he had to get up close and personal with the malignant scent of old urine or crusty markers of a bowel movement. His breakfast returned to the world amidst deep, primal grunts and the wet, heavy splatter of half-digested food erupting into the waiting water. He coughed to dislodge slimy, bitter pieces from the back of his throat. His nostrils dribbled sympathetic mucus, eyes leaking tears which might almost turn into full-fledged crying. Almost.

Instead, he took the rage and need for pain and slammed his fist into the old ceramic cistern, over and over, until the impact left a ribbon of hot burgundy bruising across his knuckles. The fine web of broken skin over his pointer and middle fingers painted blood, brighter on the outside.

Samuel pressed down the flusher button and sneered at the injury throbbing up his arm from the mess he had made. Another good distraction, but not enough.

He spoke aloud to the voice still crawling into his brain from the all-important Cochlear implants, the ones which questioned, *Are you listening?,* and demanded, and wanted to know why he wouldn't take up Grandpa's rifle and pick off the crowd of workmen trundling around, nine people gathered to dig a single God-damned ditch. 'Just shut up. Shut the fuck up.'

'It will take away some of your pain.'

'Bitch, please. You have lost any authority on the matter of my pain.'

Dead, car crash, same one which killed his father, because they thought it was just fine to get drunk at their company Christmas party and drive home. A grand finale to all the reasons he hated them both.

'It's okay, son. You'll come around.'

He eyed the heavy toilet seat. Was it plastic? Heavy-duty, whatever the material. If he laid his cheek against the chill edge of the toilet bowl and wrapped his hand around the seat and slammed it down again and again, driving the weight with his taut bicep into the vulnerable point of his temple, maybe he would black out. Maybe he would die.

'Go back to hell. You've been dead long enough.'

'Don't make me tell your father, Samuel.'

The walls were half concrete, half glass. Windows topping a squat grey pre-fabricated panel. No hand-laid bricks for this department, no sir. Joe Rale looked around the soulless room with an echo of its bland, impartial indifference across his countenance. He served a purpose, and that purpose was to figure out what happened here, not muse over the five months left until early retirement, even when scenes like this one reminded him why the job burnt people out in a hurry, and why he had not bothered applying for a transfer when his childless uncle died and left Joe a meagre inheritance of property and money.

Blood which should have already dried made a slow trickle off one of the blinds. Even arterial spray didn't tend to get so thoroughly behind Venetians to become a secondary curtain of tacky crimson. Joe watched a congealed droplet roll down the inside of the saturated glass from his safe distance beyond the edges of the crime scene. No one had entered the cordoned-off surveillance cubicle.

'Once more,' he said to himself, an old habit, a good habit. Make the facts stick. Don't buy conjecture. Get to know the details. 'Surveillance guy, Greg, in his twenties. Working alone. Listening to the tapes, checking for errors in the auto-transcription. Skips his break. First time ever, for the entire department; no one ever misses the chance to get out of these boxes. Supervisor, Charles, "2IC Chuck" to the staff, returns to check. Peers through the window and has the presence of mind to radio through that he can see Greg is near-catatonic in front of his workstation. Opens the door, radio transmitter button still depressed under his thumb, everyone hears the screaming start.'

The other investigatory officials orbited the area, not approaching, everyone forbidden from entering the room.

Described as hellish, demonic, he thought, but did not add to his oral monologue. *No conjecture*. 'People come running. Charles has been bludgeoned to death, and Greg is found perched over the corpse, disembowelling the unfavoured supervisor. Next person to enter the room, security guy, Aaron, has a Taser. Incapacitates Greg. Then uses his pocket knife to slit Greg's throat, and is seen holding the body and dancing. Fourth and fifth victims enter, Haverly and Robert. They were overheard saying they would pin Aaron down. Instead, Robert turns and impales Haverly through the eye with a ballpoint pen less than three steps into the room, and Aaron and Robert begin fighting, until indeterminate injuries occur and both men end deceased. Body count in this single room is five men, no prior signs of mental or physical illness, all cleared for access to sensitive materials.'

Joe glanced down at the folding pocket notebook balanced on his open palm to check for anything he forgot in the retelling. The facts were all there, and made less sense every time he rehashed them.

'Five men all step inside this room and experience some kind of psychotic episode.'

He smoothed his hand down the tie laying silver and crisp against his chest and made a small gesture with his fingers at his side. A helpful person scurried over. Joe muttered, 'Find out what audio the first perpetrator-slash-victim had playing at the time.'

The minion nodded and departed without a word, ready and willing to do this simple task away from the gory room.

Despite the system's notification of a service disruption at Pearl Harrison's address, Lewis couldn't discover any legitimate issues with the wiring or hardware in the house, and phone calls to his supervisor assured him that the recent work carried out in the street had nothing to do with her phone line. Every internal test and troubleshooting he undertook came with the same "All Clear", and yet each phone plugged into the wall in her house would illicit identical cross-chatter. The static held the obvious sibilance of speech, but the technician never deciphered any words, not like the aged resident claimed.

'Can I ask something, Pearl?'

'Of course, dear,' she said with a tone of placid acceptance. Lewis had all but been welcomed into the family by now. Even the grandson gave a welcoming, *Hey, man, if you're staying long enough, we should fire up a video game, I'll demolish you at* Formula 1, as he meandered through the house.

'Forgive me if this is presumptuous, but how sure are you that it was the voice of your husband if he died so long ago?'

The elderly woman took a moment to nudge her glasses higher on her nose and gave a wide-eyed expression of surprise. 'You don't forget some things. Surely you would recognise any of your family or dear friends who have died?'

Lewis shrugged one shoulder and turned to connect yet another spare phone to the wall, fresh from the box with its singular plastics-and-electronics smell wafting over the technician. 'No one I've known has passed away.'

Static hissed out from the brand new handset, an angry, unsettled sound, garbled almost-words and unhearable voices.

'Fuck five more months, after this case, I'm fucking *out*,' Joe snarled under his breath, reloading his handgun in the moment of downtime by long-practised rote. He thought all the hostiles were dead, dropped by his bullets and those of his team, but without confirmation, he was still engaged in battle.

He had lost all of the first people granted direct access to the crime scene. Moments after going in to begin gathering evidence, they went crazy. *Don't buy conjecture* no longer mattered. He had watched men and women he *knew*, for God's sake, step over that threshold and go bug-nuts with no provocation or warning. The memory of Shane and Inari pounding each other's faces in with the heavy-duty lenses on their cameras, heedless of the destruction unfolding around them burnt in deep. Some images never left a man. Joe knew that one would haunt him long into the twilight of his days. Watching those two, taking turns, smashing their co-workers' features down to bloody pulp with the thick attachments, shattering bone and glass in equal measure.

The other investigators and forensics specialists to enter the cursed surveillance cubicle turned their uncompromising need for violence onto those nearest. Guns were unholstered, voices rose, orders flew, training kicked in without hesitation or delay by everyone on the outside. But those who had gone in were beyond rationalising with.

No option but to fire.

'NO ONE enters that room!' Joe roared around the corner at his team as he scuttled sideways, on the alert for rabid co-workers and friends he might be forced to shoot.

With Lewis gone and Samuel resting, the house seemed ominous and barren. Even the nice workmen who had been installing cables outside for the past two weeks had packed up and left, so the silence extended beyond the boundaries of her property. Pearl could almost imagine the world growing devoid of other life.

Hey, doll. Hey, doll.

Would George's voice still be there? Left alone in her living room, she had lifted the receiver twice more but her limbs trembled and the fear settled into her chest and crept slowly into her throat, so she couldn't quite bring the handpiece to her ear and listen for coherency behind all that static.

Marco curled over her slippered toes and ruffed in his sleep, a warm, quivering bundle. Her late husband was the only reason she had kept dogs, and when George's last pet died years after his own passing, she went ahead and adopted this spaniel almost from habit more than a genuine desire to have four-legged company. Pearl did care for the small creature. Still. Dogs had been her husband's joy.

I miss him so much.

The thought drove her to pick up the telephone and press the cool plastic against her ear. She waited for the hissing to part and reveal another message from her beloved. Haunted, demonic, whatever the explanation, Pearl received a rare opportunity to hear her husband's jovial nature once again. Despair at being by herself swallowed her fear of the supernatural and the ungodly.

'I was wondering if you would come back, doll.'

She heard the smile in his teasing and could picture the way his moustache would shift when he spoke. Her mind wasn't always clear any more, but that memory rose bright and shiny, drawing forth a tearful sigh.

'Oh, George.'

'How's my sea treasure?'

Pearl's answer swirled around her head, trapped behind her dry mouth and wetted cheeks. After her silence trickled over, her husband's shade gave a chuckle through the line. She had heard that laugh daily for their whole married life whenever something obvious occurred to the good-humoured man.

'Are you listening? I have something important to tell you, doll.'

'Yes.' The aged woman leant forward and let her fingers twine through the spiral of the phone cord as though she were back in her twenties and falling in love. A coy movement which accompanied his voice washing over her.

She didn't notice her torso dropped farther forward and stretched the tight curls of rubber-wrapped wire in her hand. Pearl closed her eyes to bask in the longed-for love of her husband, the precious gift of his company, heedless as her body moved. She never realised her arm extended downward, or her hand wound the cord tight around Marco's thin neck.

She had no idea her frail arms held the makeshift garrote while George's cherished voice lulled her mind away until her dog stopped squirming.

She didn't know her fragile heart stopped beating.

'Samuel, dear.'

'Yeah, Gran?' He tried to force his exhausted eyes open. It didn't occur to him that her voice was too close and clear. He thought she stood on the other side of his door, as she often did. His tired mind didn't connect the voice to his Cochlear implants, to the whispers of his mother.

'Are you listening? I need your help.'

He felt no reason to question the particular phrasing. 'Yeah, I am. Sure. What's up?'

They didn't always agree on things, and as an old woman, she could harp on about the most inane concerns, resting her reasoning on qualities Samuel didn't value, yet he still loved his grandmother above all others, living or dead. She had been his primary caregiver even when his parents were still breathing. His mother and father had earnt his hatred.

'Samuel, in your grandfather's gun cabinet, there are some things for you. Go along and fetch them, will you? Then I need you to run an errand down at Baker High School.'

He rolled out of bed and pulled his shoes on, hardly awake. He fought to keep track of her words. *Gun cabinet. Something for him. Errand.* 'Yeah, okay, what do you need?'

She didn't answer. *Must have wandered off.*

Grabbing a fistful of his own hair, Samuel hauled his lolling head up by the force of his arm and staggered out of his unlit room. Who knew what his grandmother would want at the nearby school, maybe she got the bright idea to volunteer again, like she had done four years back. *Passing the time*, she called it. One hand dove down the back of his collar to scratch at the persistent itch between his shoulder blades.

'Hey, Gran?' he yelled toward the living area.

'Yes, dear?' came her voice, oddly dissonant. More like a whisper in his ear than her crying back from half a house away.

'What do you need me to do?'

Samuel stepped into the old study, thick with the almond and vanillin smell of old books and deeper leathery scents to tickle down his nostrils. His hand ran over the studded armchair as he passed, then the polished mahogany desk. He mashed the code to unlock the tall safe with his thumb and stood for a moment before the steel door as it swung open, spacing-out in his exhaustion.

'Take it all, Samuel,' his grandmother murmured.

With the gentle order, he stopped thinking and began emptying the cabinet of firearms and ammunition.

Lewis set down his tablet computer on the table beside his plate of eggs and toast, disregarding the article filling its screen in lieu of tracking his eyes to the television beside his breakfast nook. The suburb name had pinged his attention. The same place he had visited, trying to help Pearl Harrison fix her phone connection. According to the bulletin, the most recent spree shooter had lived in the same town.

His mouth dropped open with brutal horror when the news report flashed to a picture of the long-time home of the murderous young man.

The wide pair of date palms which stood sentinel on either side of the path leading to the green-painted front door were all too familiar to the technician. Lewis squashed his finger on the Volume Up button, sending it rising as if being louder would help him better understand the shock of what he witnessed.

'Not the kid . . . ' he muttered at the exact moment an old school yearbook style photo of Pearl's grandson was added to the upper corner of the bulletin, overlaying their live feed of the Harrisons' residence. The well-kept white awnings and neat azaleas held the same evident sweet attention of the elderly woman through the news cameras as he remembered from his attendance. Someone reported in morbid detail the number of dead, and how many firearms were found on his person.

And none of it made a lick of sense.

'He wasn't like that,' Lewis whispered, as if he could have known after his brief meeting. As though he could undo the facts being reported by incredulity alone. All the stereotypes he had complacently believed about the kind of psycho who would do something so terrible, so very atrocious, were unmet, unrealised in Samuel. He had been cheerful, direct, pleasantly mannered, and enthusiastic. He had invited Lewis to join him in a video game *Formula 1* race, of all things!

What makes a person break?

Lewis felt a cold rush of uncharacteristic superstition. A bleak belief, nay, *certainty* that this had something to do with the unfathomable sounds trickling through the phone line at the Harrison house. He swiped across the surface of his tablet's screen and navigated to composing a new e-mail, batting his fingertips rapidly against the glass to write an urgent message to his boss.

Mr. Black peered at the notifications leaping up on his mobile phone. An e-mail had been flagged. There was now some confusion through the hierarchy as to whether or not the telecom people were already *accounted for*. Higher-ups needed to know the new system would not be compromised, not when the first round of testing was already producing such remarkable data.

Sure, the operation needed a few tweaks here and there. Figure out how to insulate the system to prevent further unplanned contact with the public. Establishing if and how they could utilise the unique qualities of this program as a targeted weapon. But overall, their experts were calling the new listening lines a complete success. Confirmed. They were getting intelligence from the dead.

His sleek monochrome vehicle accelerated out of the underground carpark of his nondescript office block and headed to the headquarters of the local telephone service provider, where he would have a fine little talk about national security, the integrity of the government's vigilance, and one Lewis Carlisle.

Lewis nearly dropped his disposable cardboard cup of coffee as his car pulled up the quiet semi-rural street. Ahead on the left, where the charming house had sat amongst its happily tended garden, now lay a thick dirt wasteland and the looming yellow machinery responsible for its demolishing.

It had been less than a day.

'There's no way . . . '

He pulled his sensible four-door sedan into the nearest neighbouring driveway and parked in front of the metal and wire farmer's gate. Pearl's paved driveway was gone. Torn up by a great excavator, the debris somehow already removed, carted away in the back of some absent dump truck. He had watched the live coverage at 7:00AM, and now, glancing at the dashboard clock reading 4:08PM, there was little-to-no evidence that a full three-bedroom house, garden, manicured lawns and decades-old trees had been standing in the lot some nine hours earlier.

Lewis fumbled his half full cup into the plastic holder without spilling any of the steaming brew over its flimsy lid and flung his door wide. The whisper-snick of his seatbelt retracting was the only sound to fill the dangerously silent environment. Nothing moved outside his car. Nothing *breathed.* The vacant machinery sat in the late afternoon sun, radiating old warmth back into the air, shining in places where dust didn't caress the painted metals. His shoes crunched through the drying grass waving along the verge. Tiny spearheaded seeds gripped the exposed edges of his socks and detached to accompany him on the sombre journey of denial. Lewis didn't realise his head perpetually swung side to side, an unstopping motion to match the silent litany of *no, no, no,* streaming through his mind.

He stopped at the edge of the reddish-brown wound upon the earth and stared in mute horror. How could they have removed the old lady from her home, and all but erased their prior existence, in such a short span of time? Who could organise that, orchestrate the approvals and drum up the workers with such speed? Everything needed to be booked in advance. Paperwork submitted. Higher-ups signing off on demolition works. And where would they have put Pearl with no notice? Lewis couldn't help but know her only other living relative was her sister across the country. No one could have shipped her off within hours of Samuel's death. She couldn't have left before the funeral of her grandson.

'What the absolute Hell?' he asked the barren waves of dirt.

His mobile phone's vibration sang out a sharp *brrvvvt* from his pocket. The street remained quiet enough, still enough, to hear the tiny oscillating motor jiggling out its supposedly "silent" notice. Lewis fished the device out of his jeans and thumbed the answer button without looking at the screen.

'Hello?'

'Hey man,' said the kid's voice, the very same bright greeting which Lewis reminisced over in the car. 'Remember me?'

'S-Samuel?'

'Yeah. So, are you listening? I have a favour to ask.'

West Berlin—1977

THE STRANGER MOANED in Elsa's ear as he came, so close his throaty rasp drowned out the rattle of distant gunfire.

He rolled off of her and stood by the dingy mattress. A wet pop and the shriveled condom dropped next to her head. The smell reminded Elsa of a bike inner tube, dipped in water to find a leak.

Next he tossed some coins, which slid down the divot formed by the weight of her body, with a few crumpled balls of currency.

Hopefully not fucking rubles.

The man dressed and walked out without waiting for her to count it. Gunshots echoed in the city outskirts, sporadic like the leftover fireworks at the end of a celebration. Elsa, naked and sticky below the waist, locked the deadbolt and chain behind him.

In the moldy bathroom, she stood in the rust-stained, claw foot tub and filled it to her ankles. The smell was like a stuffed animal forgotten for days in the rain. With a sponge, she scoured away the funk and sweat between her legs until the skin was raw and stinging.

She told herself other mothers were doing worse to survive, but wasn't sure if she bought it.

Back in her room, she listened to the sounds of unrest that carried over Berlin's late night repose. The distant gunfire popped, refusing to give up battle. Flickering streetlights filtered through the dirty window and gave her bare legs the pallor of a corpse from an Auschwitz newsreel.

Elsa put her pants on and wiped her eyes.

She tugged a beaded chain overhead. A single bulb lit the small bedroom with a harsh light the color of piss. Milk crates stuffed with clothes lined one wall. A cracked, full-length mirror hung lopsided on another. A few black and white pictures were tacked to the nicotine-stained walls.

Elsa picked up the crumpled bills. The paper depicted bald, mustached Communist heroes in red ink. She cursed, balled them up tighter, and tossed them aside.

"Alex!"

Her son would usually climb onto the dirty, threadbare mattress with Elsa once her customers retreated back into the bleak neighborhood streets. Alex sought her out at night more, lately, with the clashes and rioting that flared up in past weeks. His sleepy embrace served as her anchor while the tumultuous seas of chaotic West Berlin tossed around them.

Elsa called again, but knew he wouldn't hear her.

She walked back out into the hall and listened to the faint music that drifted from his bedroom.

The classical tune floated through the flat like a ghost—distant and ethereal, yet pervading every square meter of the scant living space. Instead of string and woodwind instruments, each note of the rhapsody had the tinny articulation of a small, hand-crank music box. It reminded Elsa of the ice cream truck that prowled through her town as a child.

"Alex!" She entered his bedroom, knowing it didn't matter how much louder she called.

Alex's closet door stood a finger's width ajar. A roach ran across the sliver of pale light that lay across the cement floor. She pulled the light chain and more of the brown, armored pests scattered. His room stood as empty and temporary as Elsa's.

A plastic record player sat unattended in one corner, meant to distract him while Elsa entertained strangers in her bedroom. The pile included some Rolling Stones and Beach Boys she found in a back alley shop, along with some children's folk tunes.

But over the past few weeks, Alex had found something else to occupy himself.

Through the battered closet door, the rhapsody's repeating bars buzzed along her spine like Limburger had run over a grater. She pulled the door open and peeked in.

The shortwave radio was kept in a hidden room built into the back of the closet. The faux-wood panel that concealed the shortwave was set aside and Alex sat on a stool in front of the radio. Black knobs and gauges with fluttering red needles filled most of the gray, dented radio's facade. Wires from the back of the radio trailed up into a hole drilled in the top corner of the secret room. A battered microphone stand was pushed aside, not necessary for Alex's nightly task.

Elsa's son sat bent over a composition notebook. He gripped a pen tight over the paper, ready to write. His head was cocked toward the radio, waiting for the most chilling part of the broadcast. He reminded her of a dog listening to some supersonic sound that humans weren't privy to.

After the same three bars of the tune repeated, the music stopped and the voice of a young girl cut in with a message over the ghostly silence:

Achtung!

Alex leaned closer and pressed the tip of the pen onto the paper. Intent on the broadcast, he didn't notice Elsa behind him. He never did.

The girl's voice recited a string of numbers, slow, as if she knew someone sat on the other end, jotting down her transmission.

Eins, Zwei, Sieben, Sieben, Sieben, Zwei, Acht, Sechs, Sieben, Sieben, Zwei, Eins, Zwei, Nuen, Nuen, Neun, Zwei, Acht, Sechs, Sieben

Alex wrote each number in his notebook, starting where he left off from the previous sequence. Page after page of numbers.

Then, the music would play again in the same pattern—three bars of the rhapsody, followed by twenty digits recited by the girl's voice. Each string of numerals was slightly different than the last, never the same.

Music, and numbers. Over, and over.

Every night, when Elsa's johns slipped through the front door and out into the night, she would find him here.

Notebooks filled front to back with the random numbers were

stacked against the side of the radio. Loose pages, filled with numbers from top to bottom, lay scattered across the floor of the closet and bedroom like they'd been deposited through the window by a gust of wind.

"Alex." Her tone was cautious, quiet, as if he were a quivering stack of fine china. "Come to bed now."

"Just one more round of numbers," he said, each monotone syllable barely above a whisper.

"No." She stepped into the hidden room, her arms crossed to brace herself. "You must get sleep. Come."

Alex slammed his fist onto the desk. Although a slight boy, the radio jumped and a stack of loose-leaf papers drifted onto the floor. Tiny, handwritten numbers filled each page—hundreds of them, maybe thousands. "No! It could be a code from Papa!" He turned in the stool and faced her, his eyes narrowed in disgust. "What if I could find him? You're being a bitch."

She heard the same thing, night after night, but it was still a fresh knife to the gut each time. But, Alex figured the nonsense numbers were some kind of secret communiqué from a man who had been missing so long Alex probably didn't even remember what he looked like.

Elsa fought back the urge to yank him from the chair and shake the look of loathing off of his face. Instead, she reached over him and flipped the radio's toggle switch off. The lilting, metallic notes halted and the closet was left in silence.

She bit back the need to scream that his father was never coming back, was probably dead. After a deep, cleansing breath, her frustration drained into a whisper. "Come, son. Sleep now."

Upon being silenced, the music had released its hold on Alex. His eyes widened out of their apathetic daze. He stood, his thin brown hair falling over his forehead and eyes. "I didn't mean that, Mama."

She stroked his hair. "It's not you, son. Things have been hard. Why haven't you been playing with Willi?"

Alex shrugged. "He's been acting strange lately, pretty mean. Also, he's been going out with his brother a lot, wherever the fighting is happening."

Elsa sighed. With the violence in Berlin streets, there was nowhere healthy for him to just be a normal boy. The whole city burned with Molotov cocktails.

The shortwave, with its knobs like wide, coal-black eyes, seemed to glare at her.

"I don't know why I let Sepp keep that radio here," she said.

"Yes, you do. It's because he's your brother. And for the things he brings us."

"I'll have him take it away. Find somewhere else to hide it."

Alex was already walking away when he answered, "We both know you won't do that."

Before she followed him to bed, she moved the fake wall back in place to hide the radio.

Even after she left his room, she could still feel the radio's brooding, voltaic presence, waiting for another chance to have Alex to itself.

An explosion of shattered glass woke Elsa.

She started up into a sitting position and brushed her hands over her sweaty face and neck, but there were no shards. The noise must have been right outside, so close it sounded like it was her bedroom window.

Alex had slept through the noise. He lay next to her on his side, one hand under his cheek.

The distant pops of gunfire had gotten louder. Two, three blocks away? Larger automatic weapons, not just pistols—they formed longer bursts instead of the sporadic shots she'd heard earlier. Their drumming chatter was like the relentless thud of an air wrench.

Another chorus of broken glass echoed from the adjacent alley, pinging the asphalt like a storm of icepicks. Alex moaned in response and turned over, his arm around Elsa's waist.

Even with the unrest outside her windows, she almost felt comfort in Alex's presence and his firm hold. Almost.

She lifted Alex's arm off and got up to peek through the window, only exposing her head enough to see down into the street from the second floor. White-hot licks of fire roared across the roof of a car parked in the street. She had to squint and cover her eyes.

Another flaming cocktail arced out of a flat window and shattered in a trash bin. As the garbage hissed and smoked, the agitators shouted their leftist slogans. "Down with the West! Remember Viet Nam! Gaza! Hiroshima!"

A few young men in leather jackets ran down the street toward the gunfire. With their crowbars and baseball bats, they resembled a lynch mob of villagers chasing a monster.

The steady stream of protesters and ruffians became a river, rushing down the Stockumer Strasse. Innocents fought the tide in the opposite direction—but the tide of armed youths was overwhelming.

The high-low warble of sirens cut through the night in the lull between gunshots.

Alex tugged on her nightshirt. “What’s happening, Mama?”

She hadn’t heard him get up. “We just need to stay put.” Elsa craned her neck to take in more of the view from the street.

An old man—Mister Albrecht from the first floor—stood on the sidewalk in his bathrobe. Several street thugs knocked him to the ground as they ran past. He lay on the sidewalk, the front of his robe hiked up to reveal his scrawny legs and sagging underwear.

The mob thickened and the old man disappeared under thundering feet.

“My God.” Her horrified voice seemed miles away from her heart thudding in her ears.

Blood seeped into the dirty gutter water where she last saw Mister Albrecht. Through a part in the storming crowd, she could see his head—collapsed into bloody mush where he had been stomped by combat boots.

Elsa covered her mouth and turned away.

“What is it?” Alex tried to push her out of the way, but she pulled him back to the mattress.

“No, away from the window.”

“Why are they doing this? Why hurt these people like this?”

Elsa searched for some kind of response, but it was outside her understanding. She may as well have tried to explain how to split an atom.

Neo-Nazis. Left-wingers. Factions with red battle flags. Angry remnants of the Baader-Meinhoff Gang. Fascists. Communists. Capitalists.

Just an excuse to beat and loot.

“Do you think Sepp is out there?” Alex sat down on the mattress.

Elsa crossed her arms and bit down on a thumbnail, already down to the raw skin with nothing left to chew. “I’m sure he is.” She backed up and sat next to Alex.

A black and white photo, corners curled with age, hung tacked to the wall next to her bed.

The man in the picture wore a gray Wehrmacht uniform bedecked with medals. A handsome man, close-cropped blonde hair and a square jaw that accommodated his full smile. He cradled a wide-eyed baby Elsa tight to his chest and beamed down at her as if he'd just come across the Holy Grail.

The photo was taken as the soldier prepared to embark the troop trains for the Stalingrad front. All that returned was a condolence letter from his commanding officer.

A boy stood next to the soldier's leg, an arm wrapped around his knee—the only thing keeping the teetering toddler upright. Their mother flanked young Sepp, her arm hooked through the soldier's. She died a decade later trying to find bread for her children during the Berlin riots of 1953.

If something happened to Sepp because of his revolutionary compulsions, running the streets with his gang of agitators, she and Alex would be utterly alone in that crumbling city.

"I hope Uncle Sepp is all right."

"I'm sure he is fine." Elsa brought the boy in tight to her side.

A beer bottle bounced off the window and ricocheted back out to the street. Elsa and Alex flinched, and then huddled tighter. The leftover spray of amber and foam dripped down the dirty glass.

A fist pounded on the flat door, frantic. "Elsa! It's Sepp!"

The cool rush of relief flooded Elsa's body. She ran to the knocking, Alex close behind. She unchained and opened the front door, just enough for him to rush in.

"Hi, Elsa!" Sepp leaned in and kissed her on the cheek. He wore a worn leather jacket and a cardboard box was tucked under his arm.

He ruffled Alex's hair, like every other time he visited. "How are you, young man? Huh? How's my young revolutionary?"

Alex forced a smile and his cheeks blushed.

Elsa peeked into the hallway. Empty, running footfalls and slamming doors echoed throughout the building. She shut the door and chained it.

Sepp set the box down on a rickety card table in the kitchen. "Sorry, I'm in a hurry." His usually fair-skinned cheeks were flushed and he spoke in quick spurts, excited. "Tonight, we'll finally disrupt the imperialistic agenda of the United States."

The scripted lines of rhetoric drained Elsa. It was like listening to the same record over and over. Was it possible that only seconds earlier she wanted nothing more than for him to be there, safe and secure in her flat?

"I'm sorry it's been a while since I've been by." He stepped forward and held his arms out to her, but Elsa turned to the table and sat next to the cardboard box.

"What are you into now?" She lit a cigarette and lifted out the first item, a can of evaporated milk.

"It's tonight, Elsa. Finally!"

Elsa pulled out a carton of eggs and a loaf of bread wrapped in butcher paper and tied with a red string. "No Marlboros?"

"No, none today. Only some cheap Czech smokes."

Elsa set the carton of knock-off cigarettes aside and sighed. When the little things in her life were left unfulfilled, it left a gaping hole inside her. There had to be *something* to look forward to. "What were you saying? It's late."

Sepp sat next to her and scooted in close. "Tonight we will help deal a crippling blow to the oppressive West German Fascist regime and the American hold over it."

Elsa rolled her eyes. Sepp's propaganda speeches were a fitting conclusion to another day of no American cigarettes.

"Baader and Meinhoff might be in jail, but tonight we," he slammed his fist on the table, "the Red Army Faction, will strike a historic blow." Sepp stuck his chest out. It reminded Elsa of an old newsreel of Hitler screaming from behind the podium.

He stood and paced, eyes distant, and continued his ramble. "Never before has there been such an assembly of free thought and action, right here, in our own city." He ran his hand through his limp, sweaty hair. "The Red Army Faction, the 17 November Organization, PLO fighters, even Spanish guerillas, have come to help make West Berlin ground zero in a world-wide phenomenon of liberty."

Elsa crushed her cigarette butt into a saucer blackened with circles of ash. "You know I have no idea what you're talking about. Just keep bringing food until I can get a better job."

"I'm talking about the fighters that will be freeing you from this . . ." he made a wide, sweeping gesture around the flat, ". . . poverty. This slavery."

"They will, huh? With all that shooting? And the poor man I just saw . . . trampled? That was necessary?"

Sepp stopped next to her. "The tree of liberty must be watered with—"

Elsa shot up from the chair. "That's an American slave owner you're quoting!" She took a deep breath and let her irritation abate.

"Sepp, do what you came here for and go play freedom fighter elsewhere."

They both looked at Alex. He sat on the torn, threadbare couch, watching.

Sepp gave the boy a sad smile, and turned back to Elsa. "I won't waste any more of your time. We are attacking the police station. Precinct 31. I need to send a message on the radio to coordinate my group."

Elsa grabbed his arms and shook him. "*The police station?* Are you *mad?* You'll be killed."

"Just as our imprisoned brothers of the Red Army Faction will be if we don't help. Those are three of our brothers that they have in their cells. The rest of the city is in chaos. The police are spread thin. We'll be fine. We have a plan." He tapped his temple and narrowed his eyes, the same look she'd always known meant he'd made up his mind. That nothing could beat him.

Sepp walked over the Alex and dropped to his knee. "Can you go open up the closet and turn on the radio for me?"

"It's dangerous out there," said Alex. "Can't you just stay here, this once?"

His uncle patted him on the knee. "Go on, be a good boy."

Alex stood and sighed, with a glance to his mother.

Elsa shrugged, and the boy walked away. An immediate pang of regret coursed through her. She didn't have to shrug. She could put her foot down, make Sepp choose between his blood family and his street family.

But the thought of what his answer might be made her feel like a balloon with a slow leak. After riding along for months—years—on Sepp's express ride to self-destruction, she was ready to get off.

She dropped down into the plastic chair and lit another cigarette. "What will I tell Alex? He's had enough people disappear from his life."

Sepp knelt next to her and covered her hand with his. "You tell him I fought to rid our country of the Nazi pigs still in positions of power. Doesn't it infuriate you to see Hitler's cronies in such lofty heights? Chiefs of police. Minister of Finance. Minister of the Interior." He raised his hands in exasperation. "It would take me all night to list them." He stood and turned to Alex's room. "But I'll get out of your hair as soon as I can."

He stood and walked to Alex's bedroom.

Elsa pushed the ashes around in the cracked saucer with the butt of her last smoke.

Radio static purred from the back room, followed by Sepp's voice as he spoke his codes in a slow monotone.

She'd let Sepp finish his nonsense and leave. To further question and debate his beliefs, to offer his cause any more attention, would only result in more inflamed oratory. She couldn't help but think back to the teenage Sepp she remembered, the wise, protective, older brother and de facto father. Where did he go?

The same place the other boys went, like Alex's friend Willi—into the fires of revolution. Pawns pushed across the chessboard to die.

She'd rather die than watch Alex take to the streets, too.

Oiled *clicks* and *snicks*—metal on metal— came from Alex's room.

Elsa's heart dropped. She jumped up and burst into the bedroom, hoping to be mistaken.

Sepp lifted a battered sub-machine gun out of a hole in the closet floor under the radio. A small arsenal lay on Alex's mattress: an automatic pistol, a pile of bullets, and a few pineapple-type grenades. The bullets were pitted and corroded, the guns grimy and dusty.

"Sepp?" Elsa stood behind her brother, peering down at him as he closed up the hole. "I said I'd hold your radio. But I said no guns."

Alex cast worried glances at them, but then sat down at the radio and fiddled with the dials.

Sepp replaced the block of concrete in the hole and pushed past Elsa. "I've got to be there in fifteen minutes."

"Don't fucking ignore me!" Elsa grabbed his arm and turned him around.

Outside, the pistol shots—no longer distant—popped in the street right outside the flat's window. Converging sirens blared over the angry rally's shouts and cheers. Farther down the street, someone shouted commands in a bullhorn.

She pushed Sepp in the back. "Damn you."

"Fine, I'm leaving." Sepp slammed a magazine into the submachine gun. "I'm leaving."

Elsa sat down on the bed, her back to him, and buried her face in her hands. Sepp filled his pockets with clips and grenades. He shoved the pistol into his waistband and looped the machine gun sling around his shoulder and under his jacket.

In the closet, Alex turned the radio back. He adjusted the dials to cycle through the squawks and buzzes of dead air.

And then the strange rhapsody played.

Each metallic note rubbed like sandpaper over the lobes of her brain.

"Alex, not now." Elsa looked up at him. "Please, turn it off."

He sat over a notebook, hunched down with his pen, waiting for the music to end.

In the hallway outside the flat's front door, screams broke out. Authoritative shouts commanded people to get out of the way. A stampede of footsteps shook the floor.

Achtung!

"Alex, go in my room and get back in bed."

He set the tip of the pen to the paper.

Eins, Zwei, Nuen, Sieben, Sieben, Zwei, Acht, Sechs, Sieben, Sieben, Zwei, Eins, Zwei, Nuen, Nuen, Neun, Zwei, Acht, Sechs, Acht

Instead of writing the numbers, he sat up, rigid, eyes wide. He dropped the pen. It rolled over the pages and onto the floor.

"Alex?"

The footsteps and shouts grew louder in the hall.

"What's wrong?"

Alex stood and the stool plunked backward. His skin drained into the pale-yellow of cheesecloth.

"Police, open up!" A heavy fist pounded on the flat's front door.

"Fuck." Sepp racked the bolt to the rear on the submachine gun. "What the fuck?"

Alex walked to the bedroom window. His gait was automated, a robot dressed as her son.

The doorway crashed open with a solid kick that snapped the chain and tore the deadbolts from the frame. The door flopped onto the couch, completely separated from the jamb. "Hands up! Police!"

"Fuck you, pig motherfuckers!" Sepp yelled.

"No!" Elsa reached toward him, but it was too late.

He leaned into the hall and sprayed several rounds into the living room.

The firing pounded Elsa's eardrums, so loud she was sure her skull was splitting up the sides. She crouched with her hands over her ears. Too late, a distant ringing filled her head in stereo.

"Alex! Get down!" Her voice was distant and muffled, like she was screaming inside a box.

The boy didn't look back at her. He fiddled with the corroded window latch.

Elsa lunged toward him.

Drywall exploded along the bedroom wall over her head. She dropped to the floor and was showered with white powder. The room looked like a bag of flour had exploded. A ragged line of holes peppered the wall where she stood seconds earlier, each the size of American silver dollars.

Sepp fired the machine pistol around the corner and into the living room. A brass plume of spent casings bounced off the wall and *tinked* to the floor like a handful of coins.

Alex lifted the window and ducked through the opening and onto the fire escape beyond. Elsa, frantic, almost forgot about the gunfire.

Sepp let the weapon drop to his waist, suspended by the sling, and pulled a grenade from his jacket pocket.

"What are you doing, Sepp? Stop!"

He looked back at her, grenade clutched tight and a finger through the ring. "Just go! Get Alex and get out of here!" He flinched from another burst of gunfire that strafed the bedroom wall.

Elsa crawled toward the open window on hands and knees and peeked out.

Through the fire escape grating she could see Alex descending the ladder.

"Alex!"

Alex dropped the last few feet to the sidewalk without looking up at her. He pushed through the crowded street with a purpose, blending in with the writhing mass of protesters.

Fires, beatings, screams—the street and sidewalks were packed. The police stood outnumbered, unable to push forward through the angry throng.

"Go!" Sepp pulled the pistol from his waistband and tossed it to her across the mattress.

Elsa picked it up and pulled the slide back to chamber the first round before she climbed onto the fire escape. As she flew down the ladder, hand-over-hand on rusty rungs, she lost sight of Alex as he walked toward the alley across the street. He moved in a rigid, deliberate manner—a dowsing rod pulled firmly toward water.

She dropped to the sidewalk and pushed through the protestors toward the alley. People yelled, fists raised. Rocks and bottles arced over the crowd. None took notice of the armed woman who pushed through them.

Elsa elbowed and shouldered her way onto the opposite side of the road.

Halfway across the street, she looked at her flat one last time, hoping to see Sepp follow her down the ladder. But, the rapid gunfire continued—a staccato chatter that strobed in the window like a flickering flashlight. A deafening blast blew shards of Alex's bedroom window out onto the crowd. Dust and loose sheets of paper followed the glass into the street like leaves dropping in autumn.

Her heart dropped in her chest. The gun almost slipped from her grasp as she stared at the ravaged flat.

Sepp.

He couldn't have survived that.

An errant elbow thrown by a protester knocked hard into her kidney and jostled her.

Get Alex. She could hear his voice in her head despite the chaos.

Elsa turned and continued through the packed crowd.

An armored car followed the ranks of police. The steel vehicle was topped with a water cannon. A helmeted police officer blasted a group of protestors that slipped through the cordon with high-powered bursts of water.

The alleyway stood cloaked in darkness. Steam hissed from a distant pipe, which added a dream-like haze farther down the path where her son disappeared. Deep in the gloom, thuds and grunts echoed from behind a dumpster.

Elsa's palm was sweaty against the pistol grip, and the waffled handgrip dug into her skin. The alley, a path she had walked down countless times in daylight, stood unrecognizable in the darkness.

A stygian portal into nothingness.

Alex was only getting farther away, so she bit back her fear and jogged into the alleyway.

The hot steam burned her nostrils and sweat poured down her face, but she passed through the cloud in a few strides. Behind the dumpster, a group of boys surrounded a homeless man lying on the ground.

The boys, all Alex's age, took turns kicking the vagrant. Each one delivered a swift kick to the man's head or ribs. He lay on the wet concrete, sprawled like a discarded rag doll—oblivious, by then, to the onslaught.

Elsa paused, wanting to pull the boys away from them.

A gust of hot wind blew past carrying rubbish deeper into the alley, as well as one of Alex's numbered sheets that had blown out the flat window in the explosion. She picked back up to a jog around the boys, who were oblivious to everything but the infliction of pain.

As she passed them, she did a double take and then a quick halt. One of the boys, a skinny kid with a head full of curly, blond hair, stood with his back to Elsa.

"Willi?"

The boy turned to her. His freckled face was slack, and his narrowed eyes were like tiny, burning coals. Willi was no longer the smiling boy who offered a "Tag, Frau Dietrich," whenever he saw her.

Elsa backed away, deeper into the alley, as the other boys turned to face her.

They advanced in slow, automated steps.

She turned and ran into the shadows.

The boys stood shoulder-to-shoulder and watched her, then turned back to the unconscious man. Beyond the steamy backdrop near the head of the alley, the gunshots and yells of the protest had faded.

Pale orange lights high up on both sides of the alley lit Elsa's way. She ran around the garbage and potholes that littered the asphalt. Political posters lined the chipped brick walls—Communists, Fascists, Nazis, all represented on curled broadsides that featured rifles, sickles, swastikas, and promises of better futures.

The main alley ended at a fenced-off loading dock. Two smaller spurs continued left and right—too narrow for vehicles and almost completely devoid of light. Cardboard boxes, trashcans, and other nebulous shapes lined both sides.

"Alex!" Her cry echoed.

A clang of steel and the harsh meow of a street cat. The mangy animal scurried into the light of the main alley as it tore past Elsa.

"Alex!"

A burnt-orange halogen lamp ticked overhead.

"No," she whispered. The crushing loneliness was something she'd dreaded for years. "Alex!"

She waited, listening to only her frantic heart beating a tattoo in her ears.

To the left spur, footsteps crunched over gravel and glass.

"Alex?"

A black form appeared in the gloom, the same height and thin build of her son. She took a few tentative steps toward the approaching figure. Her heart sped up, hope hammering at her sternum.

Her shoulders slumped when the outline coalesced into that of a girl. A ponytail swung behind her as she walked purposely down the alley toward Elsa.

Elsa moved toward her. "Did you pass a boy back there?"

The girl slowed. She looked at Elsa as if the question were a challenge. Her eyes held the same robotic contempt as Willi's.

Elsa backed away. "Hello? Did you see anyone else?"

Behind her, gunshots echoed down the steamy path. The fighting had carried into the alleyways.

The girl's head jerked in the direction of the battle, a predator who sniffed more worthy prey. She trotted down the main street, leaving Elsa forgotten and alone at the T-intersection.

Elsa headed in the direction where the girl emerged.

Graffiti decorated the dank, dripping walls. A swastika headlined with TOTET DIE JUDEN, the rushed spray-painted text dried in mid-drip. A Kilroy nose over a fence. Farther on, a skull and crossbones with the caption FM'LATGH GOF'NN—only the skull was bulbous and alien.

The strange block letters of the last display caused her to slow as she examined them. She had a working knowledge of most languages spoken in West Berlin, but those words were unlike any she'd ever seen.

She felt countless unseen eyes probing and observing as if she were laid out on a morgue slab for all the universe to flay and dissect. Her flesh raised in pale bumps up her arms and shoulders.

She spun in a circle, gun raised, but was alone in the steamy alley.

Farther down, a gravelly voice punctuated the night.

Elsa lowered her gun and continued.

The access road led to another intersecting alley—a right turn to another major road, and a straight shot deeper into the darkness. A sign was posted on the corner over a few overflowing dumpsters and garbage cans.

POLIZEI

It was the service entrance and back doors of the police station Sepp and his friends had planned to attack.

A homeless man stood in the shadows, hunched over a large section of grating at the base of the building, some kind of basement or maintenance hatch. The man held the grating open—swung up against the building—while someone climbed out of the opening.

One child, a boy. Followed by another.

The two children walked down the alley toward her.

Elsa gave them a wide berth. Their empty eyes and slack faces gave her the same creeping dread she'd felt while reading the strange language. They walked by with barely a glance.

She ran up to the homeless man, gun aimed at him.

The old man—in baggy, dirty clothes and bare feet—watched her approach with no alarm at the brandished firearm. He still held the grating up against the building. A stone stairwell faded into the darkness after three steps.

"What are they doing down there?" Elsa motioned with the gun at the stairs. "Did a boy come through here a few minutes ago?"

The vagrant's hollow eyes looked as if they'd been pushed deep into black clay. Sun-worn crevasses lined his jowls, the corner of his mouth, and his dirty forehead. "Many boys and girls pass through here." He smiled, dried lips like slugs pulled across his face.

A roach crawled over the threadbare shoulder of his jacket and up his neck to his thin-lipped mouth. A thin, ribbon-like tongue pulled the armored pest into his mouth. The bug crunched as his jaw worked it around.

Elsa's stomach turned and the gun wavered.

The bum lunged forward and the grating crashed down. He grabbed at the gun, but she fired off an errant shot into his thigh. The gunshot hammered through the narrow alley like the opening salvo of Armageddon.

Without a cry or grunt, the man dropped to the ground.

The ragged bullet hole in the thigh of the man's trousers did not bleed. A gurgling chuckle escape from his throat, as if forcing its way out of a backed-up commode.

Through his growling laugh, he continued. "Go home and go to sleep. Azathoth, on his black throne, will—"

"Where's my fucking son!" Elsa cut him off with a second shot between his muddy, sunken eyes.

His head snapped back and bounced off the concrete with a hollow thump. His lips parted, drooling black ropes from the corner of his mouth.

Elsa peeked around the corner, toward the front end of the police station, far at the end of the alleyway. The gunshot appeared to have gone unnoticed among the other sounds of violence that filled the city. Policemen ran to and fro, preparing their sortie into the city.

Elsa picked the grating back up. She had to squat and then lift the heavy gate as if it were a barbell. Rusty rebar dug into her palms and tore her skin. With the grating pushed open against the wall, she walked down to the first step and peered into the gloom.

After seven steps, a bare passageway led straight under the police station.

She lowered the grating over her. It clanged shut, flush with the concrete. The seven steps terminated at a platform lit by burnt, flickering bulbs. The hallway continued under the police station's foundation. Along the stone wall, more light fixtures lined the hall, their plastic covers burnt and stained the brown-yellow of a baby's shit.

The rough-hewn stone wall resembled a castle bulwark. It sweated a slick coating and an incessant dripping echoed from somewhere along the hall. Her fingertips came back black and greasy after running her hand along the wall.

The air was wet and musty, like wet books in a forgotten basement.

The interval between each fixture was about six paces. Elsa hurried down the hall and after four fixtures, came to another set of stone stairs that descended deeper into the mantle of West Berlin.

As she stepped into that deeper level, faint music floated through the corridor.

Although so quiet it sounded like a melodic whisper, she knew the tune. It was the rhapsody she last heard in Alex's closet. The one he'd spent so many hours huddled over while she sold herself nightly for the price of a loaf of bread.

The music grew louder, more distinct, as she continued, and it played with the clarity not available when heard through speakers.

It was clear enough to be the source of the broadcast.

Ahead, after she passed another eight fixtures, the hall ended.

Before her, lit in the ghostly orange light, stood a plain office door with a frosted glass window. Probably a thousand like them in West Berlin. Ten thousand. She tried to find comfort in the familiarity.

A brass plaque was tacked over the door.

'SWEDISH RHAPSODY NO. 1' STATION

The rhapsody played behind the door, along with a smattering of mumbles and whispers.

The girl's voice picked up next—just feet away from where Elsa stood. The same voice Alex had transcribed into countless notebooks and sheaves of paper.

Achtung!

Eins, Zwei, Sieben, Sieben, Sieben . . .

A shadow appeared behind the frosted glass.

The doorknob twisted.

Elsa threw herself against the wall. She sucked in hard to flatten herself against the stones like she was standing on a tenth-floor ledge.

The door opened outward, shielding her Elsa, and then closed.

A girl had walked out. Slim, blonde, with dusty jeans and a t-shirt—fresh off of any school playground. The girl shut the door behind her and walked down the hall. Her footfalls echoed over the dipping pipe, even after she disappeared up the first set of stairs that led to the street.

After the girl's footsteps faded, Elsa adjusted her sweaty grip on the gun.

No use in waiting.

Elsa turned the knob. The door glided open on mercifully silent hinges.

She peeked in first, hand tight on the knob.

The room was as big as her flat bedroom, with the same stone walls and electric lights as the hall.

A desk-style console filled with lights, levers and buttons lined the wall opposite the door. The console was divided into different work stations, each possessing the same configuration of dials and levers and marked with different designations—FM, AM, SHORTWAVE, SATTELITE, PLASMA LASER, and a few others written in the strange language Elsa saw on the poster in the alley. The stations were crammed with switches and toggles, each like the cockpit of a jetliner. There were small monitors built into each console with foreign characters that scrolled across a flickering screen.

Someone sat in an office chair at the SHORTWAVE station, the high back blocking Elsa's view of the occupant. Next to the chair, a conventional microphone jutted from one of the control panels. The person in the chair held a hand-crank music box up to the microphone with small, gray hands and turned the small crank to play the rhapsody over the airwaves.

On the other side, a ball of avocado-green light about the size of a peach floated in the air. Other dials and electrodes emitted the same sickly green hue, which made Elsa's eyes flutter and her stomach queasy.

The gun—the useless hunk of steel and brass—almost slipped from her sweat-slicked hand.

The only other person in the room was a man in a crisp, khaki uniform who sat on a stool next to the high-backed chair. He wore striped, black and yellow shoulder boards and his uniform hat was ringed in crimson and gold—a Soviet officer. Elsa had seen them before at the checkpoints into East Germany. He sat facing the other chair, absorbed in jotting on a clipboard with a pencil, and hadn't noticed her walk in.

After the last bar of the rhapsody, the person in the chair leaned forward and spoke into the microphone—twenty German numbers in the same little girl voice that emitted from Sepp's shortwave radio.

After she recited the string of numbers, the office chair squeaked as it turned slightly toward the floating green ball. The person spoke into the green ball as if it were also a microphone of some cosmic design. But what she spoke wasn't German—instead, it was a nonsense string of consonants that sounded impossible for a human mouth to enunciate.

The Soviet officer made a notation on his clipboard, then gazed off with a bored look on his face.

Finally, the girl (was it a girl? Elsa had yet to see her face) held the music box up to the microphone and began again.

The consoles were interrupted immediately opposite Elsa by an entryway that opened into a room filled with children. They stood in a line that led toward a steel door. Like the door of a bank vault, it had a crank wheel like a sailor's steering column and gleaming silver dials.

There was no way to see what lay beyond the steel vault door. A halo of the same pea-green light radiated from within the portal.

As one child emerged out of the green aura and the vault, another walked in to take their place. Alex stood in the line, a few children back from the vault—motionless, his arms slack and shoulders slumped.

The last boy to exit the vault walked past Elsa, out the office door, and into the hall, with the same focused intent as the others and no interest in Elsa or anyone else in the room.

"What are you doing to them?"

The officer flinched and jumped up from the stool. His clipboard clattered to the floor.

"I want my son back." She pointed the pistol at the officer. "Alex!" she screamed at the line of children. "Get out of there!"

The officer spoke in rapid, nervous Russian. A question, but Elsa couldn't piece it together, even with her life spent in the diverse city.

He looked toward the open entryway and shouted.

A tall Soviet guard in a steel helmet stepped into the control room. He brandished a submachine gun, slung across his chest. His wide shoulders stretched the buttons of the khaki uniform coat and his small eyes were like a snake, unblinking.

“Come with me, fraulein.” The words came out of him with greasy finesse like the buzzing of a housefly. “Come.” He beckoned to her like she was a lost child.

“Fuck you. I want my son.” She turned the pistol from the officer to the guard and aimed at the bridge of his nose.

The girl in the high-backed chair spoke her alien tongue into the levitating green sphere. The officer had cringed as far back as he could against the console. His wide eyes, topped with bushy eyebrows, bounced between Elsa and the guard.

“Come with me, Fraulein. I will take you to him.” The guard’s voice vibrated and quivered, taking on even more of an insectile sibilation. The words shuddered, as if something were wriggling free of his body. He bared his teeth and his head quivered.

Alex stood in line, almost up to walk into the greenish light.

Elsa stepped forward and gripped the pistol with both hands. “Give him to me!”

The soldier’s whole body tremored.

His shoulders bulged and contorted, ripping through the uniform coat.

The skin split down the front of his forehead and over his nose, revealing a greasy, black membrane underneath.

The jacket tore at the seams under his arms. Segmented, spindly legs—like that of a crab or spider—poked through the sides of his ribcage. Quivering tentacles punched through the chest and waved around in desperate, reaching motions. The soldier’s Russian-accented German was replaced with gibbering, nonsensical consonants punctuated with slobbering screeches.

A tentacle reached out and looped around the gun’s barrel. Elsa fired with panicked jerks of the trigger into the soldier-monster’s face.

The gunshots pounded her eardrums.

The officer turned away and crouched, hands over his ears.

The tentacled soldier staggered backward. The human skin had sloughed off of its head and hung like a jacket hood. Its head was an oily black appendage, marked by the same colorful compound eyes of a common housefly. Ragged, unbleeding bullet holes had punched between its eyes.

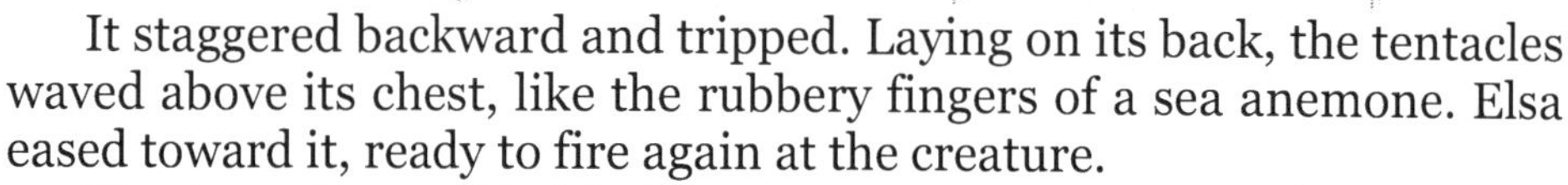

It staggered backward and tripped. Laying on its back, the tentacles waved above its chest, like the rubbery fingers of a sea anemone. Elsa eased toward it, ready to fire again at the creature.

The door slammed behind her.

The officer had fled. Running footsteps echoed down the hall.

The soldier-thing's spider-legs grabbed at the concrete floor, tips scratching stone as it clawed frantically in its death throes. Its black head imploded in a gassy hiss, and all that remained was a shriveled, dripping husk.

The high-backed chair swiveled to reveal its occupant. It was a girl, just as Elsa had pictured her. Her feet hung, not yet long enough to touch the ground. She wore pigtails in her blond hair and a plaid dress suitable for a first day of kindergarten.

"Hello," she said in the cheery voice.

The girl's face was decayed, strips of flesh teeming with maggots. Marbled, blue-veined skin. Teeth the color of rotten fruit flashed through a wide, practiced smile.

"What are you doing here?" A scrap of the girl's cheek hung loose, exposing the glistening, enamel-white cheekbone.

Elsa looked into the adjoining room.

The latest occupant of the vault walked passed them and out the office door. Alex stepped closer, next in line to disappear into the verdant mist.

Elsa screamed his name.

"I know. Let's play hide and seek." The girl stifled a giggle. She pressed a button on the control panel. The dim lights blinked off, leaving them in darkness. The only thing that kept the total absence of light at bay was the pale green glow that emitted from the vault and the console. The girl was just a shadowy outline in front of Elsa. "Want to play with me?"

The chair creaked and footsteps shuffled over concrete.

Elsa took a running step toward Alex and the adjacent room, but something grabbed her ankles. As she fell, she watched Alex step into the vault's green haze.

She landed on the dead guard. Greasy tentacles smudged her cheeks and lips. The rest of his insectile body crunched and caved under her weight like papier-mâché.

Elsa rolled off the body and pulled herself toward the next room on her elbows.

Something grasped her leg. Teeth bit deep into her calf.

Elsa screamed and kicked.

The girl pulled herself up Elsa's leg. Tiny fingernails tore through the denim and dug into her thighs.

Alex walked out of the vault. The next girl in line took his place.

Elsa thrashed and kicked while Alex walked toward her.

"Alex! Help!" She reached to him as he approached, the other hand still tight around the pistol. Her fingers brushed against his leg, just out of reach.

Her son looked down at her as if she were a cockroach underfoot, stepped over her, and walked through the outer door into the hall.

She screamed his name again, but the door shut behind him.

Elsa flattened against the floor. The look Alex gave her sucked the fight from her.

The girl's fingers cut into her shoulder blades and the nape of Elsa's neck as she worked her way up Elsa's back. The low, wet rumble from the girl's throat was almost next to her ear.

No, I can still catch him, Elsa thought. He's still there, somewhere.

Elsa flailed, flipping like a dying fish. The girl tumbled into the darkness.

The girl's skittering footsteps echoed within the gloom, just like the soldier's spidery legs scratching the floor.

A heavy weight hit Elsa as she tried to regain her feet. She landed on her back, the girl clutching at her chest. Thin fingers grasped Elsa's neck. The girl uttered a raspy chortle as she squeezed Elsa's windpipe and stared into her eyes. Elsa grabbed a handful of the girl's hair and pulled back. The girl's chin, decayed through to the bone, pointed at the ceiling. Her chortle rumbled into a growl.

With the barrel jammed against the exposed flesh under the girl's chin, she pulled the trigger.

The girl's head snapped back and the hair came loose from the scalp in Elsa's hand. The dead fingers fell from Elsa's neck.

Elsa tossed the body off and got to her feet. She threw open the outer door and fled into the hall. Alex's feet disappeared up the first flight of steps. She ran after him and bounded up the stairs. The steel grating slammed shut ahead of her. Gunshots and shouts echoed from the alley. She reached the steps up to the steel grate. With her shoulder planted against the cage, she pushed the grating up and bolted back into the alley. The steel crashed against the brick wall of the station then slammed back down in place.

Instead of just the dead bum who Elsa had shot, the alley was littered with dead protestors. A dissipating cloud of smoke rolled over the prostrate bodies. Injured men struggled with one another while sporadic gunshots were fired from behind dumpsters and out of windows.

The attack against the police station that Sepp was supposed to join had started.

Elsa crouched against the police station's brick wall.

Alex walked through the bodies, looking over the corpses.

From the alleyway spur that led to the front of the police station, shouts and commands—along with shrill whistle blasts—rang out from an approaching squad of policemen.

Alex knelt next to a dead fighter and rummaged through the corpse's pockets and ammo pouches.

"Alex! Get down!" Elsa walked toward him in a half crouch until she reached the alley intersection.

Her son pulled a submachine gun from the dead fighter and checked the magazine and bolt as if he were a seasoned soldier. Gunshots blasted the dirt and dead around him. Rounds ricocheted off the asphalt where Elsa crouched, forcing her back behind the corner. Alex took cover behind a battered trashcan and aimed down the alley toward the policemen. The bursts from his gun were white stars at the end of the barrel and each round battered Elsa's already buzzing ears.

Elsa sprinted across to the far wall, nearer to Alex. From there, she had a view of the policemen who made their way down the alley toward her son.

"Alex! Look at me!" A bullet smacked into the wall over her head. Splinters and brick dust coated her shoulders.

The boy fired off another burst, and then looked over at her.

His eyes softened as recognition tried to force its way in.

More bullets kicked up garbage near her knees. She turned and fired her pistol down the alley where the nearest policeman ducked behind a dumpster. There was no thought as to who she was shooting at.

There was only Alex.

"Run! Get out of here, Alex!"

The police inched closer. A machine gun chattered and knocked over the steel can Alex crouched behind. His eyes hardened again and he fired a burst down the alley.

A policeman fell back onto the asphalt.

"No! Stop shooting at them, Alex!"

Alex turned toward her.

She held her hands up, pistol pointed at the dark sky. “Alex, it’s me.”

Another sliver of the old Alex glinted in his eyes.

“Your mother.”

His face contorted, at battle within himself. He pointed the weapon at her.

She kept her eyes open. His face, despite the drawn look of apathy that masked it, would be the last thing she ever saw.

A sharp blow hit her thigh, another in her calf, and she dropped to her good knee. She screamed, felt as if her leg had been dipped in molten steel.

Alex hadn’t shot. He sprinted away from Elsa and the encroaching policemen, farther away into the dark alley.

Her vision clouded and shimmered as she tried to stay focused. Blood poured down her jeans and formed a black circle on the dingy asphalt. She dropped her gun, raised her arms in surrender, and screamed her son’s name over and over.

The boy disappeared into the gloom.

Her yells were silenced by the stock of a policeman’s rifle across her forehead. Elsa’s face slammed down onto the garbage-strewn alley. She tried to keep her eyes open, to make out Alex’s silhouette one more time, but the alley did somersaults and then faded into an oily, black abyss.

CIA MEMO #33-1992
DATE: August 12, 1992
FROM: Berlin Station Chief
TO: Office of Russian and European Analysis
SUBJECT: Elsa Dietrich/Hostel Riots/Precinct 31 Bombing

In August, 1977, Elsa Dietrich (“the subject”), a West Berlin prostitute, was arrested and charged with multiple crimes during the Berlin riots known as the “German Autumn.” The subject was associated, through her brother (Josip “Sepp” Dietrich), with the left-wing terrorist group 'Red Army Faction.' She was charged with assault with deadly intent on police officers, possession of illegal weapons, and conspiracy to free suspected terrorists held in Berlin's Police Precinct 31.

During the height of the rioting, a firefight erupted in the subject's flat, culminating with the deaths of three policemen and the subject's brother, a known terrorist. A short wave radio and assorted arms and explosives were found in the flat.

The subject was observed with her 13-year-old son, Alex Dietrich, attacking police officers in an alleyway adjacent the precinct. The subjects fired on the policemen, killing one more. The subject was detained, sustaining non-life threatening injuries. Her son escaped and has not been heard from since. The subject was found guilty and sentenced to twenty years of imprisonment in Stammheim Prison.

As a result of a general clemency upon the reunification of Germany (as well as good conduct on the subject's part), the subject was released early in 1991.

Upon her release, this office attempted to conduct surveillance on the subject, based on the fact that the subject befriended several suspected foreign terrorists while in prison, including Libyans and Palestinians. However, the subject immediately disappeared from Berlin upon release. It was rumored that she was training with either Basque separatists or a German cell of PLO operatives, although neither was confirmed.

On August 6, 1992, the subject was spotted near the north Berlin hostel riots, which were sparked by Neo-Nazis and involved arson and assaults against Vietnamese, Roma, and Israeli emigrants looking for work. It was suspected that she would pick up where she left off and assist in the attacks against foreigners. The subject was being followed, but she managed to shake surveillance while moving through Berlin . . .

Berlin—1992

Elsa's imminent task hung as heavy on her heart as the explosive vest under her jacket.

The Bernauerstrausse's black, rain-drenched asphalt shone like glass under the heels of the riot police as they stormed north toward the distant gunshots. She stopped at the alley that cut between Berlin's Police Section 31 and a high-rise apartment covered in puffy gray graffiti lettering.

Uniformed police crowded the front of the station. Plain-clothes supervisors shouted out assignments to the riot police being deployed to the Lichtenberg Roma tenements. Although it was noon on a Monday, the rest of the street lay quiet as if only inhabited by the dead. Two polizei cars screamed by, their high-low sirens reaching ear-piercing volume as they passed. An old lady peeked out of the window of a bratwurst shop across the road. An old man pulled her away from the window and the curtain fall back across the shop's dark windows.

Elsa turned and continued down the alley, her sweaty hand clasped over the detonator in her jacket pocket.

She had no one else in the world. Her shaky fingers and slamming heartbeat weren't for the fear of death, but for fear of whether or not she could do what she came to do, once she entered the inhuman lair buried under the Berlin streets. It was something she'd thought about every day of her fourteen years in prison. All contacts she made and favors she curried were for this moment.

The stomping footfalls and shouts drifted behind her as she made her way down the garbage-strewn alley. A cold wave of déjà vu poured over her with the approach of the last place she ever saw Alex.

She turned behind the police station.

The steel grating still remained at the foot of the building, along with its attendant vagrant. This time, the guardian was a woman in an oversized army coat and dingy hair that hung in ropes from under a threadbare beanie.

The woman lay on a flattened cardboard box. She rolled over and faced Elsa as she walked up to her.

The bum's eyes narrowed in recognition. "You," she said, flashing blackened teeth. "You!"

Elsa pulled out a small automatic pistol and aimed at the woman's head before she could get to her feet. The gunshot echoed through the alley just as it did fourteen years before—a dull crack that bounced off the dingy brick walls.

The woman's head snapped to the side. Her wide eyes stared upward while the small hole in her temple leaked a viscous, black fluid onto the cardboard.

A rusty squeal emitted from the steel grating.

A girl stood on the steps below the tunnel's entrance, her hands gripping the bars like she was in a jail cell. Empty brown eyes peered up at Elsa.

Elsa looked at the gun in her hand.

She'd thought about this moment hundreds of times while in jail.

After emerging from the underground hallway, the girl would go join her brethren and wage war on others. Elsa could put her down right now—she was already lost, anyway.

Or she could snuff out the source, and maybe break the cosmic curse that infected so many.

Elsa looked around the corner of the alley toward the front of the precinct. Nothing to indicate that her gunshot had been heard. She pocketed the pistol and lifted the cage.

The girl climbed out. She looked down at the bum, back up at Elsa. Her lips curled back in a sneer.

Still holding the heavy grating up, Elsa reached in her pocket for the pistol.

The girl walked away, her eyes fixed on Elsa. Eventually, she ran off down the sub-alley, heading toward more fruitful prey.

Elsa stepped down into the entryway and lowered the grating over her. She breathed in the damp air. The same stone walls dripped with green dew. And the same burnt orange lights that lined the hall every six paces.

Elsa curled her fingers around the detonator and walked down the hall.

After four light fixtures, she arrived at the next steps.

She made her way down each one, hesitant, and then the music met her as she descended lower.

The same tinny rhapsody that she'd last heard under this same building.

The same song that played through her head every day for fourteen years in her small, cinderblock cell.

Before her, lit in the ghostly orange light, stood the plain office door with a frosted glass window. The brass plaque tacked over the door:

'SWEDISH RHAPSODY NO. 1' STATION

A voice picked up through the door—clear, just feet away, vice broadcast over a speaker.

Achtung!

A cold wash of dread spilled down Elsa's neck and arms.

Eins, Zwei, Sieben, Sieben, Sieben . . .

The numbers were recited in cool, robotic precision, but not the same voice that Elsa remembered.

Elsa flung the door open. It banged against stone as she lunged into the room with the detonator in one hand and the pistol in the other.

The first person to react was a man with a shaved head. He shot up from the stool—the same the Soviet officer had occupied fifteen years earlier. He wore a leather jacket and dirty jeans and he fumbled for a pistol in his waistband.

"No!" Elsa pointed the pistol at him. "I've got a bomb." She held the detonator out in her locked arm.

At the back of the room, the open doorway revealed a line of children in front of the vault.

The man froze and looked at the hidden speaker in the chair. The child finished speaking his guttural, alien syllables into the floating green orb and the music stopped. The office chair squealed as it turned toward Elsa.

Staring up at her with a gray, emaciated face—withered and rotten with the strange, decelerated decomposition—was Alex.

A whimper escaped her grief-choked throat. She realized she'd fallen to her knees when he stood from the chair and approached her.

The bald guard stepped away from them, his back against the

concrete wall. He slipped a pistol from his belt, but Elsa didn't care. The only thing that mattered was that she was face-to-face with her son, probably for the last time.

Another child exited the vault, passed them, and entered the hallway. He stared straight ahead, the same vacant, slack gaze as the rest.

"You can't stop it." Alex's voice was gravelly, neutral. "Chop one head off, two more sprout." He approached her, arms open for a wide embrace. One eye—his blue eyes Elsa so adored when he was a baby—was red with burst veins and his skin hung as if about to slough to the ground. His lips were raw tatters and his breath smelled like road kill left to cook on asphalt. "It's no use. Just come with me, Mother."

Hot tears flowed down her cheeks and she tried to think of him before he disappeared. Always with a smile.

"Come with us." He put his arms around her and the smell of his skin—like sweet, musty soil—filled her nose.

But she still wanted to go with him and she leaned into his shoulder, nothing but bones and parchment-thin skin under the soiled clothes he'd worn the day she last saw him.

He wrapped his arms around her, but the embrace was empty. It was hard and forceful, like the police apprehending a dangerous criminal.

The realization plunked like a stone into a pond. It was not the tender gesture of a boy who held his mother during the gunfire of the German Autumn.

She pressed the detonator button.

All the darkness and despair within her ignited in a flash of cordite and fire.

Elsa had already stepped one foot in oblivion fifteen years before. Better late than never.

New York, September 30 CP FLASH
Ambassador Holliwell died here today. The end came suddenly as the ambassador was alone in his study . . .

THERE IS SOMETHING ungodly about these night wire jobs. You sit up here on the top floor of a skyscraper and listen in to the whispers of a civilization. New York, London, Calcutta, Bombay, Singapore—they're your next-door neighbors after the streetlights go dim and the world has gone to sleep.

Alone in the quiet hours between two and four, the receiving operators doze over their sounders and the news comes in. Fires and disasters and suicides. Murders, crowds, catastrophes. Sometimes an earthquake with a casualty list as long as your arm. The night wire man takes it down almost in his sleep, picking it off on his typewriter with one finger.

Once in a long time you prick up your ears and listen. You've heard of some one you knew in Singapore, Halifax or Paris, long ago. Maybe they've been promoted, but more probably they've been murdered or drowned. Perhaps they just decided to quit and took some bizarre way out. Made it interesting enough to get in the news.

But that doesn't happen often. Most of the time you sit and doze and tap, tap on your typewriter and wish you were home in bed.

Sometimes, though, queer things happen. One did the other night, and I haven't got over it yet. I wish I could.

You see, I handle the night manager's desk in a western seaport town; what the name is, doesn't matter.

There is, or rather was, only one night operator on my staff, a fellow named John Morgan, about forty years of age, I should say, and a sober, hard-working sort.

He was one of the best operators I ever knew, what is known as a "double" man. That means he could handle two instruments at once and type the stories on different typewriters at the same time. He was one of the three men I ever knew who could do it consistently, hour after hour, and never make a mistake.

Generally, we used only one wire at night, but sometimes, when it was late and the news was coming fast, the Chicago and Denver stations would open a second wire, and then Morgan would do his stuff. He was a wizard, a mechanical automatic wizard which functioned marvelously but was without imagination.

On the night of the sixteenth he complained of feeling tired. It was the first and last time I had ever heard him say a word about himself, and I had known him for three years.

It was just three o'clock and we were running only one wire. I was nodding over the reports at my desk and not paying much attention to him, when he spoke.

"Jim," he said, "does it feel close in here to you?"

"Why, no, John," I answered, "but I'll open a window if you like."

"Never mind," he said. "I reckon I'm just a little tired."

That was all that was said, and I went on working. Every ten minutes or so I would walk over and take a pile of copy that had stacked up neatly beside the typewriter as the messages were printed out in triplicate.

It must have been twenty minutes after he spoke that I noticed he had opened up the other wire and was using both typewriters. I thought it was a little unusual, as there was nothing very "hot" coming in. On my next trip I picked up the copy from both machines and took it back to my desk to sort out the duplicates.

The first wire was running out the usual sort of stuff and I just looked over it hurriedly. Then I turned to the second pile of copy. I remembered it particularly because the story was from a town I had never heard of: "Xebico." Here is the dispatch. I saved a duplicate of it from our files:

Xebico, Sept 16 CP BULLETIN

The heaviest mist in the history of the city settled over the town at 4 o'clock yesterday afternoon. All traffic has stopped and the mist hangs like a pall over everything. Lights of ordinary intensity fail to pierce the fog, which is constantly growing heavier.

Scientists here are unable to agree as to the cause, and the local weather bureau states that the like has never occurred before in the history of the city.

At 7 P.M. last night the municipal authorities . . . (more)

That was all there was. Nothing out of the ordinary at a bureau headquarters, but, as I say, I noticed the story because of the name of the town.

It must have been fifteen minutes later that I went over for another batch of copy. Morgan was slumped down in his chair and had switched his green electric light shade so that the gleam missed his eyes and hit only the top of the two typewriters.

Only the usual stuff was in the righthand pile, but the lefthand batch carried another story from Xebico. All press dispatches come in "takes," meaning that parts of many different stories are strung along together, perhaps with but a few paragraphs of each coming through at a time. This second story was marked "add fog." Here is the copy:

At 7 P.M. the fog had increased noticeably. All lights were now invisible and the town was shrouded in pitch darkness.

As a peculiarity of the phenomenon, the fog is accompanied by a sickly odor, comparable to nothing yet experienced here.

Below that in customary press fashion was the hour, 3:27, and the initials of the operator, JM.

There was only one other story in the pile from the second wire. Here it is:

2nd add Xebico Fog.

Accounts as to the origin of the mist differ greatly. Among the most unusual is that of the sexton of the local church, who groped his way to headquarters in a hysterical condition and declared that the fog originated in the village churchyard.

'It was first visible as a soft gray blanket clinging to the earth above the graves,' he stated. 'Then it began to rise, higher and higher. A subterranean breeze seemed to blow it in billows, which split up and then joined together again.

'Fog phantoms, writhing in anguish, twisted the mist into queer forms and figures. And then, in the very thick midst of the mass, something moved.

'I turned and ran from the accursed spot. Behind me I heard screams coming from the houses bordering on the graveyard.'

Although the sexton's story is generally discredited, a party has left to investigate. Immediately after telling his story, the sexton collapsed and is now in a local hospital, unconscious.

Queer story, wasn't it. Not that we aren't used to it, for a lot of unusual stories come in over the wire. But for some reason or other, perhaps because it was so quiet that night, the report of the fog made a great impression on me.

It was almost with dread that I went over to the waiting piles of copy. Morgan did not move, and the only sound in the room was the tap-tap of the sounders. It was ominous, nerve-racking.

There was another story from Xebico in the pile of copy. I seized on it anxiously.

New Lead Xebico Fog CP

The rescue party which went out at 11 P.M. to investigate a weird story of the origin of a fog which, since late yesterday, has shrouded the city in darkness has failed to return. Another and larger party has been dispatched.

Meanwhile, the fog has, if possible, grown heavier. It seeps through the cracks in the doors and fills the atmosphere with a depressing odor of decay. It is oppressive, terrifying, bearing with it a subtle impression of things long dead.

Residents of the city have left their homes and gathered in the local church, where the priests are holding services of prayer. The scene is beyond description. Grown folk and children are alike terrified and many are almost beside themselves with fear.

Amid the whisps of vapor which partly veil the church auditorium, an old priest is praying for the welfare of his flock. They alternately wail and cross themselves.

From the outskirts of the city may be heard cries of unknown voices. They echo through the fog in queer uncadenced minor keys. The sounds resemble nothing so much as wind whistling through a gigantic tunnel. But the night is calm and there is no wind. The second rescue party . . . (more)

I am a calm man and never in a dozen years spent with the wires, have I been known to become excited, but despite myself I rose from my chair and walked to the window.

Could I be mistaken, or far down in the canyons of the city beneath me did I see a faint trace of fog? Pshaw! It was all imagination.

In the pressroom the click of the sounders seemed to have raised the tempo of their tune. Morgan alone had not stirred from his chair. His head sunk between his shoulders, he tapped the dispatches out on the typewriters with one finger of each hand.

He looked asleep, but no; endlessly, efficiently, the two machines rattled off line after line, as relentlessly and effortlessly as death itself. There was something about the monotonous movement of the typewriter keys that fascinated me. I walked over and stood behind his chair, reading over his shoulder the type as it came into being, word by word.

Ah, here was another:

Flash Xebico CP

There will be no more bulletins from this office. The impossible has happened. No messages have come into this room for twenty minutes. We are cut off from the outside and even the streets below us.

I will stay with the wire until the end.

It is the end, indeed. Since 4 P.M. yesterday the fog has hung over the city. Following reports from the sexton of the local church, two rescue parties were sent out to investigate conditions on the outskirts of the city. Neither party has ever returned nor was any word received from them. It is quite certain now that they will never return.

From my instrument I can gaze down on the city beneath me. From the position of this room on the thirteenth floor, nearly the entire city can be seen. Now I can see only a thick blanket of blackness where customarily are lights and life.

I fear greatly that the wailing cries heard constantly from the outskirts of the city are the death cries of the inhabitants. They are constantly increasing in volume and are approaching the center of the city.

The fog yet hangs over everything. If possible, it is even heavier than before, but the conditions have changed. Instead of an opaque, impenetrable wall of odorous vapor, there now swirls and writhes a shapeless mass in contortions of almost human agony. Now and again the mass parts and I catch a brief glimpse of the streets below.

People are running to and fro, screaming in despair. A vast bedlam of sound flies up to my window, and above all is the immense whistling of unseen and unfelt winds.

The fog has again swept over the city and the whistling is coming closer and closer.

It is now directly beneath me.

God! An instant ago the mist opened and I caught a glimpse of the streets below.

The fog is not simply vapor—it lives! By the side of each moaning and weeping human is a companion figure, an aura of strange and vari-colored hues. How the shapes cling! Each to a living thing!

The men and women are down. Flat on their faces. The fog figures caress them lovingly. They are kneeling beside them. They are—but I dare not tell it.

The prone and writhing bodies have been stripped of their clothing. They are being consumed—piecemeal.

A merciful wall of hot, steaming vapor has swept over the whole scene. I can see no more.

Beneath me the wall of vapor is changing colors. It seems to be lighted by internal fires. No, it isn't. I have made a mistake. The colors are from above, reflections from the sky.

Look up! Look up! The whole sky is in flames. Colors as yet unseen by man or demon. The flames are moving; they have started to intermix; the colors are rearranging themselves. They are so brilliant that my eyes burn, they are a long way off.

Now they have begun to swirl, to circle in and out, twisting in intricate designs and patterns. The lights are racing each with each, a kaleidoscope of unearthly brilliance.

I have made a discovery. There is nothing harmful in the lights. They radiate force and friendliness, almost cheeriness. But by their very strength, they hurt.

As I look, they are swinging closer and closer, a million miles at each jump. Millions of miles with the speed of light. Aye, it is light of quintessence of all light. Beneath it the fog melts into a jeweled mist radiant, rainbow-colored of a thousand varied spectra.

I can see the streets. Why, they are filled with people! The lights are coming closer. They are all around me. I am enveloped. I . . .

The message stopped abruptly. The wire to Xebico was dead. Beneath my eyes in the narrow circle of light from under the green lamp-shade, the black printing no longer spun itself, letter by letter, across the page.

The room seemed filled with a solemn quiet, a silence vaguely impressive, powerful.

I looked down at Morgan. His hands had dropped nervelessly at his sides, while his body had hunched over peculiarly. I turned the lamp-shade back, throwing light squarely in his face. His eyes were staring, fixed.

Filled with a sudden foreboding, I stepped beside him and called Chicago on the wire. After a second the sounder clicked its answer.

Why? But there was something wrong. Chicago was reporting that Wire Two had not been used throughout the evening.

"Morgan!" I shouted. "Morgan! Wake up, it isn't true. Some one has been hoaxing us. Why . . . " In my eagerness I grasped him by the shoulder.

His body was quite cold. Morgan had been dead for hours. Could it be that his sensitized brain and automatic fingers had continued to record impressions even after the end?

I shall never know, for I shall never again handle the night shift. Search in a world atlas discloses no town of Xebico. Whatever it was that killed John Morgan will forever remain a mystery.

armageddon baby

JOHN C. FOSTER

YOU LIKE TO listen to other people's business, Mick? Of course you do, it's your fuckin' job. You like to know things. But you, you Irish prick, you don't know shit. You don't know what they say about listening at keyholes. About what happens to guys like you."

"Two minutes!" The bus driver pushed through the milling passengers and banged out the doors, letting in a rush of frigid air. It looked like townsfolk escaping a rising river or something from an old newsreel about European refugees.

All because there would be no dawn tomorrow.

But I could feel the approach of night in my marrow even as I saw it in the wide eyes around me. Already the light outside was the orange of glowing embers.

I closed the accordion doors of the phone booth to block out the chaos, people buffeting the glass in their passage. *Vera, answer the damned phone.*

Ringing in an empty apartment three thousand miles away. How many rings meant *I care*? At what point did that become *I panic*? At nineteen rings I replaced the receiver in the cradle, resting my head against the cold metal of the payphone as it regurgitated my silver. The splinted fingers on my left hand made gathering the coins awkward, but I managed.

A palm slapped against the glass and I looked into wet eyes glaring from an explosion of whiskers and wild hair. The man waved at me to follow and walked away without waiting.

I fought down an urge to try one more call and crossed the station floor, avoiding the eyes of those who remained. Big men with sloped shoulders and narrow eyes. Razors did not play much of a role in this place.

"All aboard," an announcement crackled over the antiquated public address system.

The bus belched a black cloud and took its people south.

I went north.

The maddening light of a plummeting sun. Snow fields transformed into molten seas of blood, the trees into black ink etchings. Alien. Not Chicago. Not even the planet Earth.

I kept waiting for a comment on my black eye or the purple bruise on my jaw but my driver didn't seem to notice. He pulled in at a log house calling itself a saloon and led me to a waiting Jeep with threadbare tires. A map of Alaska was unfolded on the hood and he rested a boot on the running board, showering the ground below with flakes of rust.

"You push towards Wainright." His words came in a series of grunts and I wondered how often he spoke to other people. A fingernail twice the thickness of a nickel traced the road until it reached a river. "You want this turnoff before Kuik and you'll get a guide in, they're expecting you. Give them this."

I took a wrapped, rectangular package. Cash. He gave me a grin as brief thoughts of flight crossed my mind.

"I wouldn't," he said.

I worked my bruised jaw and ignored the implication.

"You miss it, you hit Wainright. You miss Wainright, you hit the sea."

"I won't miss," I said and he grunted again, plonking a rag-wrapped bundle on top of the map. I unwrapped the checked flannel and found a greasy .38 revolver, Smith & Wesson stamped into the metal of the barrel. A box double the size of a deck of cards was filled with bullets and held an envelope in place against the rising wind. Fuck, I hated guns. Never carried one in all my years as a private dick. My camera and a tape recorder did enough damage.

I was in a new line of work these days.

My contact showed brown teeth when I asked about a phone and gestured around the side of the building. Salt and ice held the glass door of the booth shut and I had to hit it with my shoulder to get inside. More ringing. I dry-swallowed a couple of painkillers while I waited for the voice that didn't come.

The saloon was dark and windowless, smoke from a fireplace hanging below the ceiling and a woman's voice crooning in French from hidden speakers. The only live female in the place was running drinks to the scattered tables of hard men, her eyes marked by fatigue and fists. I shucked off my parka and drew stares in my wrinkled gray suit, so I slipped the coat back on. Mutters. Sidelong glances. The men here were of a piece, those who remained behind when humanity fled.

My broken fingers were still screaming so I said, "Bourbon, neat," and slit the envelope with a thumbnail. Some scrawled details on my meet-up in Kuik and then a chilling sign off. *With your shield or on it*. Goombah prick liked to play the scholar, quote Socrates while your bones snapped.

"No one does it like Edith Piaf," a man's voice crackled from the speakers and I heard my own Chicago streets in his accent. "According to the almanac, we have about three minutes of daylight left. It's gonna be a long night, people," and here the DJ paused for an uncomfortable laugh. "A real long night. Funny things happen. We start to forget about daytime, about brotherhood. The wolves will howl and we will huddle. And when you get down to the bottom and you're choosing between the taste of a bottle or a gun barrel, think about this song and make it through one more minute, all right?" He cackled again, the least reassuring radio voice I'd ever heard. "This is radio KZXX, music at the edge of the world with, 'Here Comes the Sun'."

"That fucker," the bartender said as the song filtered through the smoke and heads dropped a little lower.

"Why do you have him on?"

"All there is," the bartender said, smearing the bar with a greasy rag.

I pulled a pack of Marlboros from an inside pocket and lipped a cigarette free, lighting it with my Zippo and then putting flame to paper. The bartender glared but gave me my drink without a word.

The door bumped open and a man entered, stamping snow off his fur-topped boots. "It's here," he said quietly and conversation stopped. In ones and twos people rose and went outside. I followed the bargirl through the door.

It was dark.

"Everdark," someone whispered and a ripple of agreement passed through the men, these dangerous men, who huddled closer together beneath the cloud of their breath. Some wit aimed a bright arc of urine at the building in a gesture of defiance and drew empty chuckles.

"With your shield or on it," I said.

"Huh?" the bargirl said, but I ignored her.

Sodium lights around the building kicked in with a snap and pushed the darkness back. Big lights, humming yellow bulbs beneath metal half domes, but they weren't nearly enough. The night was enormous overhead and all around us, far larger than the great expanse of land we stood on. Alaska is said to make a man small. It reduced me to a speck.

I held up my hands, studying the details of knuckles and fingernails, the tape and splint. Making sure I was still here.

Back inside a fight erupted and no one tried to stop it. I left without finishing my drink and was a half hour north before I realized I hadn't tried to call Vera again.

There wouldn't be another chance until I killed the man on the radio.

The Jeep's heater produced more noise than warmth and my knuckles were numb on the wheel. I thought about that guinea fuck laughing while his boys broke three fingers on my left hand, nice and slow so Vera could watch me beg.

A Square John in a long coat had studied me like a bug on a slide. With his matching Fedora and briefcase he looked like a centerfold from the London fog catalogue, whatever G-Men were jerking off to these days. I knew a Fed when I saw one.

"You don't mix business and pleasure, Mick, and you don't eat another man's pie," he said as an Italian the size of a bank vault took hold of my ring finger. Vera was trying not to watch but the boss grabbed her jaw and made her witness my humiliation. "You done both."

To see her was to fall for her up on that stage under those lights. Backstage in her dressing room she said she was married and I didn't care. She told me which monster she was married to and I told her, "I can set you free."

All the times I worked divorce cases, tailed cheating wives, philandering husbands, you'd think I would have become jaded. Maybe I was until Vera cut through my defenses like a searchlight through fog.

You should have seen her.

"Why you choose this lowlife?" he asked Vera and laughed when she shook her head, disowning me. "I mean, what did you think you were gonna find listenin' in on my business, somethin' gonna make me give up my wife?"

The big man worked on my ribs until I puked in my lap. Vera was gone when the boss threw the water in my face.

"You wanna live?"

"Yes, yes."

"You gonna eat my pie any more?"

"No more, Sally," I said, hiccupping for air. "I won't eat nothin' ever again."

He leaned back and pulled a gold cigarette case from inside his jacket. That slick guinea suit cost more than six months rent on my apartment. "You gotta understand your station in life, Mick." He flicked his Bic and inhaled a lungful. "You're shit under my shoe. Girl like Vera? Maybe she wanted to walk in the wild side for a moment but she needs someone who can keep her in style." He snapped his gold cigarette case closed to make the point, the subtle fuck.

"I understand, Sally," I said, hating myself but groveling for all I was worth. "I don't know what I was thinking."

"Well, you're lucky because I might be in the mood to do a favor. You deserve a favor?"

"No I don't but you're a generous guy, everyone says so."

"That's right, I'm so generous I agreed to do this thing for this guy, but I got no one wants to go." He blew a smoke ring and screwed it up. "It's cold and outta town. Way outta town."

"I don't mind the cold."

He leaned over and sniffed me. “You didn’t piss yourself, mostly guys piss themselves when Baby Vincenzo goes to work. You stupid but maybe not a complete *vigliacco*. Maybe you can do this thing.” Sally glanced at the Square John who gave a barely perceptible nod.

I took my chance. “Anything, Sally, anything you say—”

He rocked my head with a slap.

“Gonna send you to the asshole of the world, Micky.”

The Square John approached Sally and handed over the briefcase. He left without ever saying a word.

“Who was that—” I started to say when Baby Vincenzo hit me with a ham sized fist.

I woke up on a plane to Alaska.

I crossed a bridge over the great void with nothing on either side.

Night. You don’t know what the word means when you live in a city. Even in the suburbs there are streetlights, the distant glow of town. But once the sun goes down in the nowhere, your world is reduced to the cone of light from your headlights. It’s insignificant, that light. As inadequate as all of your preparations.

“That was ‘Ode to Joy’ by,” the DJ sucked in a lungful of smoke, voice strained, “by Beethoven man, dig it. Nothin’ to do in the dark except listen, that’s what I’m doing and I’m glad you are, too.”

He took shape in my mind as I drove, growing long and lizard like in his studio, attached at the mouth to the serpentine hose of a Moroccan hookah. He’d be filthy. Uncombed hair the color of ashes and bad skin that never saw a bar of soap.

“And now we’re gonna let our hair down with m’man Clapton and ‘Sunshine of Your Love’.”

“Are you kidding me?” I said to the radio and he cackled back as if he’d heard.

Rock, classical and then some tribal stuff with drums. In between he rambled and ranted about anything that came to mind. Religion. Communism. A marriage, presumably his, failing. This guy was higher than a kite and the only radio station on the air. How did he get such range?

“They don’t know, they don’t know, man, lemme tell you, *they know*.

Your new HD-TV with voice control? It's always listening, even when you turn it off. Think about that, man. You like to jerk off to Internet porn? Man I hope you cover that camera with some tape because they can see you. Yeah, yeah. They say they don't know how many people cops kill every year? Of course they know, they don't want you to know but they know. They know everything and they like it." He took a breath to cough and I could hear the static-laden suck of a pipe. "Know what they don't like? I know what they know. I can hear them in their little bunkers and they hate it."

He was crazier than a shit-house rat.

"This is gonna be a humanitarian gesture," I said and Johnny Cash answered by singing he once shot a guy in Reno. I was getting squirrelly. Popping too many painkillers and doing everything I could not to think about the phone ringing with no one to answer. After two years of playing postman with Vera, I had enough dough stuffed in my mattress to get us down to Mexico where the dollar went far and the tequila flowed like liquid gold. I wanted dirt on Sally so he'd leave us alone but he found the bug I installed on his phone. Then he found me backstage with Vera.

I was picturing her in the dressing room when the fire blazed up on my right and I flashed right past it, unaware until I hit the brakes that I was doing eighty miles an hour. I fishtailed to a screeching stop and threw the Jeep into reverse, backing up with a high whine of the engine into the crimson glow of taillights. I jerked to a stop in front of a collection of low structures surrounding a bonfire.

The domelight came on when I shoved open the door, the loneliest nightlight on the planet. Squinting helped me make out shapes moving around the fire, wide and lumbering things leaking a high-pitched chant. Dogs were howling.

"Hello," I called out, reluctant to abandon the delicate spill of illumination.

"Shit." I headed in amongst the buildings—low slung things, wooden frames with hide walls that shimmered and flapped in a weird approximation of life. Some kind of Indian shit. I stepped close to one and touched it, wincing at the grease and stink. I thought I heard a rhythmic grunting from within when a hand slapped against the hide from the inside and I stumbled away, panting.

"The fuck?" I wiped slick fingers against my coat.

The smell of charred meat was strong on the air and the chant continued as I moved past the outer ring and into the central circle where the strange silhouettes sang and swayed. A carved post rose out of the fire, the faces of unrecognizable animals bellowing silently all the way up to a winged shape at the top. Why it wasn't consumed by the blaze I couldn't tell but a bundle wrapped in chains was attached to it, shapeless and blackened, dripping fat visible as it trickled into the fire.

"Qui etes-vous?"

A bundled figure emerged from the nearest building, the hide entrance slapping closed before I could see anything but a faint glow inside. She was short and wide in a seal skin coat trimmed with fur. Her cheeks glistened with bear-fat, framed by pendulous black braids.

"What?" I said and the chanting stopped as if I'd tripped a switch. Long-haired women gathered in between me and the fire. Squat in their native winter gear, a museum display come to life. They held spears tipped with white bone.

"English? Do you speak English?" I asked, looking back and forth between the crowd and my questioner. A woman detached herself from the group and said something full of liquid clicks before approaching me.

"Why are you here?" Her words strangely accented. She was a full head shorter than me, eyes narrow in a round face.

"I'm Shaw," I said. "I'm supposed to meet my guide, take me to KZXX. The radio station."

That eerie liquid tongue spilled from a dozen mouths and the English speaker turned to them, shouting and slashing the air with her hand. She turned back as the group quieted and said, "Not good there, not good for men."

"I don't understand."

"Dark." She waved overhead to encompass the starry sky. "Sound." She opened her mouth to keen in that disconcerting way. The women behind her took up the chant and spread out to circle the fire again. "Sick." She stepped close enough for me to smell the onions on her breath as she tapped my temple with a blunt finger.

I thought of the people who had stayed behind to the south of me, almost all men. The sense of despair. The fight at the bar.

"Go home," the woman said.

"Can't."

She snorted and shook her head, the beads at the end of her braids clacking. She held out her hand and I pulled the thick bundle of money from my pocket, placing it in her palm. She jerked her head in a "follow me" gesture and set off around the dancers.

The chanting took on a grating quality as I drew closer, the sound of an invisible ant scratching and probing inside my ears until I chanced to look up at the cooking bundle on the pole.

Christ.

"Come," my guide barked and I shook myself into motion. I crunched through the snow after her, slip-sliding in my smooth-soled shoes as we hurried past a row of tied-up dogs that snarled and snapped at my passage.

"Dog sled?" I said and she snorted in disdain before pulling the tarp from a snow mobile with an incongruously yellow fuselage. She straddled the long seat and waved impatiently for me to climb on behind her, forced to press myself into the feral stink of her clothing. She gunned the machine to roaring life and twisted the throttle several times, blotting out the awful chanting with the mechanical roar.

Damn me but even as the machine lurched forward and my toes dragged in the snow, I couldn't resist a last look at the charred shape broiling over the bonfire, struck by the shocking whiteness of the man's staring eyes.

We rattled and buzzed recklessly through an evergreen tunnel with the looming trees on either side and branches interlocking overhead. Sight was minimal, the narrow cone of brilliance thrown by the snowmobile's single headlight an invitation to disaster. The sound was a deafening pressure against my ears, my eyes watered and my cheeks burned from the frozen dagger of the wind. Every muscle in my body screamed protest as I hung on for dear life, whipped from side to side and slammed down with teeth-rattling force.

Never stopping. Never slowing.

Our light flashed off metal in the trees but we were past before I could make it out. Ground opened to the right and a vast, circular shadow rose against the starry sky. My guide shifted and weaved the machine as we passed domes of concrete. Three great obelisks. It was a haunted high-tech landscape of metal and ice that had no place in the Alaskan wilderness.

I doubted my sanity. My consciousness. I saw the white of a burned man's eyes and felt the awful heaviness of a month-long night. In my ears the liquid singing keened against the murmuring voice of a madman riding a cannabis high and over it all the buzzing of the mechanical steed that carried me ever north—

I slammed my broken fingers against my thigh and the wind snatched away my cry of pain before I could hear it. Reality reasserted itself.

We slid to a stop and she switched off the machine. The silence pounded in my ears and beneath the inner thunder I heard a murmuring voice that was not my own. In the last flicker of the headlamp I saw a large bundle hanging from a tree, its lower edges sprouting crimson icicles.

"Oh God," I said. Me, who hadn't been inside a church since my balls dropped.

The dark settled around us like a giant's hand and I fought the urge to crouch. The ticking of the engine was loud and unnatural against the susurrus of breeze and branch, the crunch of snow as my guide moved purposely about the snowmobile removing items from saddlebags. When I moved to get out of her way the murmuring grew louder and I realized a voice spoke on the night wind.

"What is that?" I asked, but she gave no answer.

What I thought were wind-blown flakes turned out to be the outriders of a storm and I wondered if I would get snowed-in after I did this thing.

"Hey," I said, staggering as she shoved a cloth-wrapped bundle against my belly. I caught it by instinct. "What is this?"

"Give to him," she said and unlimbered a rifle from a tube that ran along the length of the machine. She slung it over her shoulder with easy familiarity. "Follow."

"I can't see anything."

"No light. Follow."

I glanced back at an eerie yip-yip-yip drifting through the trees from the direction of the cement towers. The sound wasn't repeated and I turned back to find my guide nearly vanished in the forest ahead.

The wind and snowfall picked up as she led me through the trees towards a glowing red light. The voice defined itself, clarified into the rambling cadence of the DJ riding a hundred speakers hung throughout the trees. It was a maddening sound, the voices slightly out of synch due to distance so that some words continued long past their allotted time and others were chewed and dragged under by the chorus. Close to understanding. Some words ringing clear but the larger meaning obscured just enough to lure a listener forward.

A snow-covered hump up ahead turned out to be a squat building made of equal parts cement and native logs, as if it had been expanded ad hoc since its original construction. A giant metal radio tower rose beside it but other than that, details were hard to make out.

The red light was a sign over the front door, the familiar words out of place in this remote wilderness:

ON AIR.

Twice I lifted my hand to knock on the metal door but hesitated, as well trained as any dog not to make noise while the ON AIR light was on overhead. I turned around to say something to the woman, but the woods were empty save for the echoing voices.

"This is stupid," I said and knocked on the door, three sharp raps that hurt my knuckles. It was solid as hell, like striking a fifty-five gallon drum full of ice. I wondered if the man inside heard me over the din of horns that filled the forest, Wagner maybe.

I was lifting my hand to knock again when the door opened to bathe me in orange light and I felt a warm puff of air. A little man with a wild beard, Hawaiian shirt and cargo shorts grinned up at me.

"Hey Mick, I'm Don," he said in that familiar voice. "Nice to meetcha." I caught the odor of marijuana and buttered popcorn riding on the tropical air currents. "Come in and warm—"

I pulled the pistol from my coat pocket, thumbed back the hammer and shot him in the chest.

It made a flat bang. A horrible sound. It seemed as if the music should stop but it didn't, continuing to wail and thrash as he sat down hard and his teeth clacked. He winced as if that hurt, the teeth, then flopped onto his back, mouth working like a suffocating fish.

The hole in his chest was a low pressure faucet pumping thick syrup. I stepped inside that comforting miasma of weed and popcorn (a black and white movie was playing on a TV in the corner) and jabbed the .38 down at his contorting face before pulling the trigger. His forehead collapsed as if slapped with a hammer and a spray of blood-veined oatmeal spilled across the floor. A wet fan of all that he had ever thought and been and I fired again, the bullet taking him through the gawping mouth, .38 caliber fellatio and I shot him again and would have shot him until the sun burned cold and the earth was finally consumed by the everdark but the gun was empty, the cylinder rotating dutifully with each pull of the trigger, the hammer uttering its oily snap, snap, snap.

A rushing wind swept through my mind as I dropped the gun, turning and tottering out into the rosy glow of the ON AIR light, not fleeing so much as stumbling from the scene of the crime. The murder. I turned back to pick up the revolver when flames reached from the tree line and invisible fingers plucked at my coat. Thunder rumbled as splinters threw themselves from the log walls. Sparks illustrated the meteoric impact of bullet against door as I looked over my shoulder, not comprehending the moving shadows and muzzle flashes. Low shapes trailing snarls as they flew across the snow, dogs with dripping fangs charging with predatory speed.

I lurched inside, tripping over my victim as fully automatic fire blasted all around the door and sent flaming metal wasps darting over my head. I thought, *They have a machine gun!* even as I kicked the door shut and scuttled backwards to land in the moist smear of Don's offended skull.

Breathing hard as the wet seeped through my pants, I read the warning spray-painted on the inside of the door.

BEWARE DEAD AIR

The operatic music quieted and in the silence I heard no more gunshots, was instead absurdly concerned at the thought of dead air and turned, the seat of my pants sliding in gore. I looked around the endless shelves of record albums covering every wall and heard the old fashioned clicking of a record player as a ghost hand lifted the needle to one side.

A tiny green LED lit up on an engineer's panel of dials and switches and a cassette engaged. "Hey now," the disc jockey's voice filled the room. "I can't think of a better way to end the show than 'Ride of the Valkyries', can you? And what an ending of the show this is, cats and kittens. The *end* end. The Big D. That long awaited day has come and it's time for me to go off the air. But don't worry! I'm leaving you in the care of a man who will treat you right, come all the way from Chicago to make magic on the airwaves—I'm talking to you, baby, start with turntable two."

I looked past an elaborate record press to the turntables lined up like a weird devolutionary display from the Museum of Broadcasting History, starting from a high-tech digital job and going all the way back to an old Victrola with a giant brass speaker horn.

"Everybody give it up for Micky Shaw!"

Applause drowned out the DJ's voice until silence filled the room when the tape clicked off. I crossed the studio in three great strides and turned the power knob on the second turntable until it popped and I heard a feedback *thumpf* over the speakers. The slightly warped record began to spin and I lifted the needle, lowering it into the outer groove.

"JEREMIAH!" The shout filled the room and I ducked as the speakers continued bellowing, eyes raking across the annotated index cards taped hither and yon across the control panel. I saw one marked *In-Studio Volume*. I spun the dial and braced my hands on the console as the singing dropped to a dull roar.

"What the fuck?" I was a broken record, repeating it over and over. "What the fuck?"

A black chair on wheels was turned to face me and a Memorex cassette tape sat on the cushion with an index card on it. Cheerfully round loops of magic marker spelled out: ***MICKY, PLAY ME.***

How did he know my name? I turned the plastic cassette over and over in my hands and was still doing so as "Joy to the World" faded from the speakers.

Dead air again.

"Shit."

I snapped off the power knob and grabbed a boom mic dangling at the end of a telescoping arm, tore off the index card commanding ***TALK INTO ME*** and flipped a switch at the base from OFF to ON.

"This is Micky Shaw," I said. *Micky?* "Coming to you from the great white north. It's been a strange day, my friends, one strange f—" I caught the curse before it escaped on air, "—darned day, really weird, but there's dead air and everyone knows we can't have dead air so here it is—" A flailing hand picked up an album and I shook it from the sleeve, whipping *Three Dog Night* off of the turntable and dropping the new record in its place. "'I Wanna Be Your Dog' from the one and only, Iggy Pop."

Fuzzy guitars filled the air as I picked up the cassette with my name on it and stuck it into a tape player. Checked to make sure it was only an area speaker and hit play.

"Hey Mick, I know you've got a million questions, not the least of which is how I know your name . . ."

"No shit," I told the control panel.

". . . but you gotta listen to me now, right fucking now." The hippy tones were gone and he sounded intense, even scared. "First thing is, never let the dead air last. The music keeps everything calm down below. Second, by now you've figured out those Eskimo bitches won't let you leave. They think you're infected. Get it through your head, amigo, you're *never* gonna leave. Ever."

"Says you."

"And last, but definitely not fucking least: drag my body down into the cellar. Keep going down through the subbasements as far as you can go until you find the well, understand? Throw my body in the well. Your life depends on it."

I looked at the corpse resting in a gummy pool of blood.

"Oh, Mick, if I say anything down there—don't answer."

"You don't have much time," Don's voice crackled over the old, Walkman headphones. "And there's a lot you need to know."

A bare bulb swung back and forth on a cord overhead and my shadow danced wildly while I dragged the body down the steps, wincing at each cruel thud of the head on wood. The staircase rocked beneath me and descended towards a weird, blue glow. I was sweating from more than just the cloying humidity and I paused to take off my jacket, draping it over the railing. I untangled my tie from the headphones' cord and tossed it over one shoulder.

Thud . . . thud . . . thud.

"You're gonna get a call soon, whoever they're holding over you," the DJ continued. "Probably Vera, right?" A wave of cold washed through me when the dead man said her name. "They're gonna hurt her, make her scream, man. But they won't kill her yet because they want something from you, something only you can give them."

Me?

Dark stains were soaking through the blanket in which I'd wrapped the body and I felt squeamish as drops of my sweat dripped on the awful burden. I was relieved when my shoes scraped on the gritty cement of the floor.

"I left instructions for you upstairs." Feedback squealed on the tape and I reached for the Walkman on my belt. A blue spark of static electricity stung my hand. ". . . tell you how to listen with the dishes, where to listen to give them what they want. I'll say it again, with this place, you can eavesdrop on just about any electronic conversation in the world, man, dig it? That's what they want. The mob. The G-Men, but here's the thing, I tried to tell them but they don't care . . ."

He paused and I stopped still, listening.

"It only lets you listen to poison, something that means bad news for someone. It doesn't just *want* ugliness, it needs it. Sucks it down through those big dishes and radio arrays like a junkie."

I turned and saw row upon row of leafy marijuana plants arrayed beneath sapphire-tinged grow lights. "You're kidding me."

The madness began to make some kind of sense.

Don spoke through a smoker's cough. "Now, quick, find the next cassette and do what I say." The tape ended and the PLAY button on the Walkman popped up.

I wanted to sit down and laugh until I cried, to pull off a couple leaves from old Mary Jane and chew them until I drifted away. This was too strange and getting more so by the minute. But he'd scared me, this DJ who knew my name. Scared me enough that I was following a dead man's voice down into the frozen bowels of the earth.

You don't have much time. Right.

The perfume of the plants was thick in my nostrils as I moved through the blue light between towering bushes, stepping over a coil of hose before I found what I was looking for.

I pushed aside shovels and other long-handled tools to reveal a heavy steel door set into the sweating wall. Some kind of disabled security card reader was mounted beside it.

UNAUTHORIZED ENTRY FORBIDDEN BEYOND THIS POINT was a faded stencil on metal.

I leaned a shoulder into the door and pushed because there was no way to pull. It was only by accident that I discovered the door was designed to slide to one side. After a moment of effort it did so and I jerked away from the rain of rust.

A plastic clatter caught my attention and I picked up another cassette and fed it into the Walkman, tossing the other tape into the basement jungle.

The audio whirred to life as I trotted back through the plants. Static. Sounds of movement. I stood over Don's body, trying to figure out when a dead hand had slipped free from the blanket cocoon, struggling with the bizarre idea that I was acting in the present while listening to a voice recorded only a matter of hours earlier. Time was splitting.

His voice kicked in: "Stop fucking around, man. Get my body through the door and down to the well, now!"

A shout, panic in his voice. "Do you know that guy who picked you up at the bus station? He called Salvatore to let him know you were on the way. Right now while I'm talking into a microphone you're driving north to kill me. Far out." A choking sound and I imagined tears.

"Look, man, I don't blame you. I knew this would happen when I threatened to play the record. Maybe I wanted it to happen, I'm so damned lonely up here." He laughed through his tears. "I mean, if I really wanted to end the world I would have just played the fucking record, right?"

"What record?" I asked the ghost.

"Enough messing around, get my body, man, do it. You really have to move."

I grabbed the feet and walked backwards, dragging the corpse through the dark opening.

The next set of overheads flickered reluctantly to life and I let out a harsh breath. Goddamned lights always took an extra few seconds before the motion sensors triggered, so that for an eternal moment I was overcome with an onslaught of nyctophobia while David Bowie sang over the tinny sounding PA system. I thought the Alaskan night had taught me about darkness. What a child. True darkness was underground where the sun didn't exist.

"Put on a stack of records and let 'em play through. Keep track of the records, of the time," the DJ had instructed. Bowie meant that I still had plenty of time. I wondered if this is how I would sleep in days to come, dependent on a stack of records.

My laugh fell flat in the bizarre tunnel with its nonsensical letters and numbers beside doors I was told to ignore. The tunnel itself was ribbed and lined with tubes whose function I could only guess at. The whole thing designed by someone who thought *The Jetsons* meant the future.

"Knock it off," I said and backed down the hall again with my grisly burden, footsteps muffled as we dragged a worm-trail through the dust. Stairs, he told me to look for stairs. Bowie sang about Andy Warhol and I tried to hum along.

"Keep going, Micky, keep walking through the fear," my old friend on the radio was saying. "I know you're freaking out, I sure as hell was. Like they built this place to give a guy the heebie jeebies, so deep with no air. And man, how the sound falls flat, right?"

Was he fucking with me?

"But you gotta get me down to that well, so find those stairs and ignore everything but my voice from this point on, no matter how weird things get."

Mounted on the wall I saw fire extinguishers. Axes. Coiled hoses. Something marked a DECON STATION. Everything rusty. My broken fingers were throbbing and my nose ran from the clouds of dust I kicked up.

The body rasped along the floor as I pulled it into another inky spill of shadow and hesitated, awaiting the delicate touch of a bony hand on my shoulder . . .

The light overhead buzzed into radiance but never found its stride and flickered madly as I hurried beneath it. My ears filled with the sound of my own ragged breath and I wondered where my guide—

"I know you're freaking out, hold it together." I heard him inhaling deeply. "Let me tell you about this place, this damned place that was never used after millions of dollars and seven people—*seven*—died during construction." I heard him blowing, imagined the cloud of smoke until he resumed with a crackle. "It was the Cold War, man, and the military wasn't going to listen to anyone, especially not a bunch of fucking Eskimos with their fucking legends about a bad place. A hungry place. *Perlertok tonrar*."

I stood up straight as a sound rolled down the corridor. Someone giggling.

"Hungry Devil is what they called this place, a place that makes men sick. But the military dug and dug and woke it up, gave it the tools to amplify its reach. Boost the devil's signal, man, can you dig that?"

I bent back to my burden when he screamed in my ears and I jumped. "THEY MADE IT STRONGER! IT CAN REACH AROUND THE WORLD AND TWIST THINGS, TURN THINGS AND MAKE PEOPLE DIE."

I pulled forward now with my uninjured hand while the sweat poured down my face in rivers and my hair became a salty swamp. A laugh bounced off the walls from somewhere behind me as one by one, the lights back there went dark.

"Hey Micky, Micky?"

The voices were dopplering and I realized that Don wasn't speaking to me through the headphones. I lifted a padded earpiece free and cocked an ear at the nearest PA speaker, but the voice wasn't coming from there.

"Don't throw me down the well, it's so cold down there."

Every muscle in my body went rigid as I stared at the blanket-shrouded body.

"Let's go back up and smoke awhile," the voice wheedled from beneath the blanket.

"Oh shit," I said and if I hadn't found the door marked STAIRS just then, I would have dropped the body and run. But there it was and I ripped it open. Dragged the corpse through until the heavy metal door swung closed on the head and we were stuck. I pulled viciously until it squeezed through with a wet crunch.

It was like stepping from a steam room into a meat locker and I fell against the door, shivering as a yellow lamp on the wall buzzed to life. The metal burned with cold and I pulled away, breath clouding. I felt an eerie constriction on my temples as short hairs froze.

Black veins of ice lined the walls and I slipped on a slick stair, jarring the breath from my lungs when I fell. The body tobogganed downward until it crashed at the landing and spilled free from the blankets. The impact was so great and the icy cement so slippery that the corpse rebounded around the corner and teetered on the edge of the next flight downward. "No . . ." I moaned before it was sucked down and out of sight.

Rubbing at my abused back, I stood and picked my way down the stairs, fingers growing numb on the metal railing while the voice in my ear spouted delusions and kept me company.

" . . . part of the Distant Early Warning Line, get it? Code named White Bear. Things went wrong before they put the system online, all those construction deaths, but once they cranked up those dishes everyone with a pair of headphones got sick." I touched my own headphones involuntarily and looked down the next flight as the weak overhead lamps lit themselves. The blanket lay in a heap on the landing below me but the body had continued its careening slide and vanished around the right-angled turn for the next set of descending stairs.

"When the month-long night came, they went crazy. Started seeing Russian bombers every time the wind changed direction. Pushed us to

Defcon Two half a dozen times before Washington figured out there was a problem with the site. Then the operators up here started killing each other and, well, can you imagine that meeting at the Pentagon?" He wheezed in my ears and I realized he was laughing. "Sorry, General, looks like we should have listened to the natives. White Bear is haunted."

I followed an organic smear down flight after flight beneath the inadequate lights until I was uncertain how deep beneath the earth's surface I had traveled. I blocked out my companion's voice, worry increasing as the precise, government stenciling on the walls grew looping and stick-like. At first the symbols were recognizable as letters and numbers but the shapes grew more distorted the further down I went, until I couldn't identify them at all.

There, the body was piled bonelessly against the door to the next subbasement only one more flight below.

The PA system went silent as I reached the dead man and I waited, teeth chattering violently, listening anxiously to the whir and click of another record dropping into place over the PA system. A liquid clicking crackled from the speakers and then a horrible keening filled the air. It was a song sung by fleshless mouths, mandibles and teeth clicking together beneath a strange, warbling chant. The same as that sung by Inuit women while they circled a fire in which a man was cooked alive.

I cast about wildly as if the strangely marked walls would offer some explanation, tell me how those murderous hags had replaced the next album. Were they above me right now, waiting with guns and dogs? Where they trying to frighten me onward to this lowest and final subbasement where an ancient well held a devil?

"No way."

I made it to the first step when a cold hand gripped my ankle.

I squeezed the sponge in both hands and pink, frothy water cascaded back into the bucket. A smoldering joint dangled from my lips and I blinked against the rising curl of smoke as I resumed scrubbing at the mess inside the door. My broken fingers barely hurt at all.

I heard a voice, not the radio, and I looked fearfully at the old brown door that opened on an unsteady flight of wooden stairs down to the basement.

"Shut up, you can't talk any more." I eyed the bloody fire axe leaning against the door. Three great whacks at the joint of neck and shoulder and Don's head had bounced free, still gibbering. His blind body stumbled after me and I ran, trapping him in the subbasement. Sounded as if old Don had crawled up to the cellar.

Never did throw the body in the well.

Outside the wind howled and Don's collection of homemade, shiny steel records rattled on the walls. As if in echo, the cellar door shook and I looked away, trying to block it out.

The phone rang and I wiped my soapy hands on my pants before turning down the volume on Sondheim's *Pacific Overtures*. A blue spark jumped from my finger to the control panel and I hissed. The place was thrumming with a static charge.

I answered the phone. "KZXX request line."

"Oh Mick, Mick!" Vera said and it went the way Don told me it would. She cried and Sally threatened and I begged in spite of myself. I loved her, the real thing, promised Sally I'd do whatever he needed.

She sounded scared, you should have heard her.

He told me and I sat down in the chair, following the instructions Don had written out on lined notebook paper. The ground vibrated beneath my feet and I could hear the shriek of tortured metal outside as great concave dishes rotated. The devil reached out across the miles and I recorded a senator and his mistress exchanging sweet nothings.

Don's record press looked complex but wasn't hard to operate once I played around with it. His notes said something about magnetic fields from the special recordings wiping tapes after only a few minutes. Had to lay those tracks down on an album if I wanted the recording to last.

I used the press the way Don instructed, fed in a blank steel disc and listened to the scritch-scratch as the recording was transferred. In another life I would have thought it was pretty cool.

I thought about Sally's words, about what happened to guys like me. About listening at keyholes. I felt sick in the pit of my stomach but I made some adjustments at the control panel and entered a phone number on the keypad.

" . . . some place warm, Sally. It's so cold this time of year, I need to feel the sun."

Vera's voice filled the studio and I pushed back in the chair. Held my Zippo to the joint and inhaled deeply, my heart and the tip smoldering in tandem while I listened to Vera planning a romantic getaway. Sally wanted to go to Italy because he was a fucking cliché. Vera wanted Aruba. The way she wheedled, I thought she'd get her way.

I disconnected and cried a little bit, smoked a bit and thought about how little Sally knew about guys like me. About what we're capable of when you take everything away.

I started looking at all those homemade records Don hung on the walls.

The record that got Don killed was titled *Doomsday* and the track listing was filled out by hand. Ten tracks, most of them foreign names. World leader types I recognized from the news. I thought about what the devil would let Don record and I don't think any of the guys back in Chicago would have recognized my smile.

I lit another joint and put the gleaming metal record on turntable number two. My vision shimmered as I played with the power knobs on the console, turned everything up to ten. The fillings in my back teeth buzzed painfully and static electricity lifted the short hairs on my forearms. I thought we'd reach Russia easily. Canada, the main body of the United States. Further.

I heard the devil laugh.

I grabbed the boom mic and leaned in. "To the folks at home and all the ships at sea, it's Micky Shaw coming at you from the top of the world. I want to play something special, a last gasp from DJ Don." I pushed off from the console and the chair rolled over to the turntables. I lifted the needle into place and rolled back to the mic. "This one's dedicated to a real happening couple in the Windy City."

The pop and hiss of a bad recording filled the air and I pressed my hands over my ears. God it was loud. Shouting in Chinese. Whatever he was saying was sure to upset somebody.

I grinned and tasted blood when my nose sprung a leak. "Fuck you, Vera." A red spray left my mouth with the curse.

I staggered towards the door and stepped out into the deafening cacophony of a hundred speakers in the trees. Snow flakes danced like agitated electrons and pine boughs shed their white mantles with the muffled *whumpf* of distant explosions.

The wind plucked the joint from my mouth and I held onto the doorframe. I hoped I wouldn't get shot before the last track played.

Track ten: "The President of the United States".

Armageddon baby, can you dig it?

WHEN I WAS a younger man, I preferred to work the graveyard shift because I slept easier during the day. But in my current line of work, graveyard's not an option. My shift starts around noon, when I wake up, turn on my modem and log in with the web host. I make sure the camera is centered on my backdrop—a poster of a snowy mountaintop—and get into costume. Minutes later, I hear a ping and the image of a cherub-faced boy, maybe three years old, fills my computer screen.

I clear my throat and say, "Ho, ho, ho." In an instant, the boy is beaming and clapping his hands. The children always recognize the beard. What's scary is that they trust the person wearing it, and that fills the Lurking Man with dark notions. This is why SantaCam.com is so popular. A kid can talk to St. Nick without having to sit on his lap. Can you believe that people used to take their kids to the mall to do this?

"Who's this little boy?" I say, and the kid squeaks something that sounds like "Greg." My left hand is hidden inside a pocket. The children only see my right hand. The left one would scare them off. "What would you like for Christmas, Greg?"

He just smiles, unable to talk, so I say, "Would you like a pony?"

A man's voice comes from off-screen. "Go on, tell Santa what you want," but the kid just stares like I'm a celebrity, which, in a way, I guess I am.

"How about an Xbox?" I say to Greg.

The father coughs. "Or how about a new toy truck?"

I count the syllables in that question. *Or how about a new toy truck?* Eight. Round numbers are nice. But eight is not as nice as ten. Odd numbers are out of the question. Odd numbers make me feel as if the Earth is listing to one side. "How about a flatscreen TV?" I say.

The child claps his hands over his head. He says, "flatscreen," except it sounds like "flap skween."

The father's fat, balding head appears on my computer. He's sitting too close to the webcam. "Greg, Santa doesn't make televisions. He makes toys. Why don't you tell him what *toys* you want?"

Twenty-two syllables. Not bad. Twenty-two times five is a hundred-ten, which feels nice. It loosens the knot in my gut a little. "Technically, Greg," I say, "Santa doesn't make *any* toys. The elves build everything."

The child laughs.

"That's a good one," the father says. "Santa's a real comedian."

Twelve syllables. Twelve times twelve is a hundred-forty-four. Not divisible by ten, but still interesting. "In Santa's workshop, we can make anything. Even a flatscreen."

"Flap skween," Greg says with a laugh. "Flap skween. Flap skween."

The father says, "What were those toys we talked about before?"

Finally, a ten, and I feel less anxious.

"Ho, ho, ho," I say. "Santa will bring you a flatscreen Christmas Eve."

"Maybe," the father says. "All right, tell Santa bye-bye."

"Flap skween."

"Ho, ho, ho. Merry Christmas."

The screen goes blank as the webcam disconnects.

After a few hours, I need a cigarette so bad I'm shaking. I step outside, and my neighbor Dave is there, sucking an American Spirit down to the nub. "Busy day?"

"Like a salt mine," I say. "You got a light?"

Dave takes out a Zippo and lights my cigarette. He looks me over and throws up a smirk. "You're looking a little scruffy today. Lose your razor?"

"What?" I ask, and then remember that I'm still wearing the fake white Santa beard. I pull it down beneath my chin.

"You do a lot of drugs as a kid?" Dave asks.

"A little. Why?"

"No reason," he says with a laugh.

I hold the cigarette with my left hand. The burning stick is wedged between the first and second fingers—the only ones left besides the thumb, the doctors couldn't save the other two. I take a deep drag and hold it in until my lungs burn. I tell Dave about the first time I did acid, but don't tell him about the Lurking Man. How do you talk about the parasite that hijacks your thoughts? The man who says the most vile things, who shows me videos of things that haven't happened, of me doing horrible things. Instead, I ramble on about other things.

"If you ask me," I say, my cigarette crackling down to the filter. "Your head's screwed on right so long as you can tell the difference between sight and perception. No matter how many chemicals you put in your body. Don't you think?"

Dave doesn't respond. I continue, "Sometimes I perceive things that aren't really there. And that's OK, because I know they're not really there."

Then I realize that Dave has gone back inside his apartment. How long have I been out here talking to myself?

Dave once asked me if I ever sleep. He's seen the blue glow of the television flickering in my window in the small hours of night. I tell him, yeah, the TV's on, but only for background noise. It's nice to have voices in the room other than my own. I can't sleep through the night, and often wake to the pitch-black of solitude. The mind can go to bad places in the time it takes to reach the remote.

"That would drive me crazy," Dave told me, "all that racket."

What troubles me is the silence.

Funny thing about the Lurking Man: He's loudest in the dark. Throw on the light and he's reduced to a whisper. Even the dimmest light is better than none. That, neighbor, is why I sleep with the TV on at night.

"What is your name?" I ask the girl sitting on her mother's lap.

She's a tiny thing, like her mother, who can't be more than twenty. Two butterfly clips contain her hair behind her ear, the velvety black of it coiled around her copper neck. I'm describing the mom. She is smiling, even more than her child, like it's *her* first time talking to Santa. Eventually, the kid will go gaga for St. Nick, but at this age, it's all for the parents.

"Her name's Aiko."

"What a beautiful name. Ho, ho, ho."

The webcam is a knothole into other people's lives. This is my way to live in the world without leaving my apartment. Aiko's house is cozy and warm. There is a red-brick fireplace, a wine glass on a wooden countertop and a dog bed in the corner.

"Is this your first Christmas?" I ask.

"Her second," says the mom.

I add up the photographs nailed to the living room wall and it's a perfect ten. The house is an unbearable white. A cream-tile kitchen is in the background, with a stove, an oven, a dishwasher. I imagine myself there, making eggs Florentine for breakfast on a lazy Sunday. The computer monitor catches the glint of the mother's wedding ring, and I imagine how the matching band would feel on my finger.

Except the ring finger on my left hand is gone. I cut it off.

The mother bounces the kid on her knee. "Can you say hello to Santa?"

Instead, Aiko starts screaming. I should be focusing on the kid, but can't take my eyes off the mom. She is so happy. It's a look I can't replicate. She is wearing a yellow top, and she's soft and smooth around the edges.

"What's *your* name?" I ask the mother, but I don't think she hears me.

"Aiko, can you say bear?" she says, and I start growling to impress the mom. I stand and wave my arms like a bear, but this only disturbs the child. I realize my left hand is showing, and I quickly pull it down and stuff it into a pocket.

"Ho, ho, ho."

"Maybe we'll try again later," the woman says as she slips a pacifier into Aiko's mouth. The child spits it out. She won't stop crying.

"Don't go. Just tell Santa what you want. Merry Christmas. What's your name, Mom? Aiko, what's Mommy's name?"

The connection is cut, and I decide that's enough work for today.

When I told my neighbor Dave how the TV thing works, he asked me what shows I liked to watch. Sitcoms, cartoons, I told him, but *always* reruns. He asked why, and I told him it's the certainty that I like. A rerun can only end one way, and that's the way it's always ended. People can only say the things they've always said. There are no variables, no risks. In a world of chaos, reruns are safe harbors where we are in control of our universe. We know everything before it happens, and we laugh not because we're surprised, but because we knew it all along.

I'm shaken up by my session with Aiko, a name that I've transferred from the child to the mother. Aiko. My beloved. A beauty like her deserves a name, and if she wouldn't share it with me, it's mine to create. I think of her ivory house. I think of her pearl-white life. And then I think of mine.

I shut down my computer and take off the beard and scratch my itchy face. That beard is a killer. I work for SantaCam four weeks in December, and by the end of it my neck is as red as the Santa suit. I look at the poster behind me. It's a mountaintop, probably in Colorado or Canada, places I've never been, but it's good enough, I suppose. I've checked out the other SantaCam actors, and some go all out: actual Christmas trees for backdrops, plastic reindeer. One guy turned his den into a wonderland, and another put felt antlers on his Boston terrier. Me, I put up a poster, but it's better than nothing. If not for that, the kids would see an efficiency apartment long overdue for a cleaning.

What do kids know of loneliness? Enough. They may not understand it, but they recognize it when they see it. Maybe the poster itself is a giveaway—or maybe just the fact that a forty-year-old man would dress up in a costume and talk to children over the Internet for money. No wonder that kid was crying. Nobody wants to meet a sad Santa.

I realize after I take off the Santa suit that I have no clean clothes to change into. Washday passed without notice, and every piece of clothing I own is smelling up the linen basket. It's got to be ten below outside, and all I've got for clean clothes is a pair of Hawaiian shorts and an undershirt. How am I going to walk to the laundromat dressed like that? I realize the Santa suit is the warmest, cleanest thing I own. I put it back on, except for the beard, of course, and carry my linen basket outside. I pass Dave on my way out of the apartment.

"Don't forget to check your list twice," he says.

Asshole.

During the two-block walk to the laundromat I imagine what I could have said to Dave. Or better yet, what I should have done. I should have dropped the basket and kicked him in the side of the knee. Right at the joint. The fucker would drop in the snow, howling in pain, and I'd calmly pick up my basket and walk away.

When you have anxiety, the whole world is a weapon. Chain-link, loose rocks, subway platforms. Everywhere, I see the thousand ways I could be the victim of a killing or mutilation—or worse, the ways in which I could be the perpetrator. At the laundromat, I imagine shoving an elderly man into the dryer and loading it up with quarters. A small child could easily fit inside the turbo washer. Maybe two. The violence that could be wrought with laundry detergent and wire clothes hangers is particularly gruesome, and in a pinch, you could just fill the slop sink with water and hold someone's face under.

These are the movies the Lurking Man shows me that I don't want to see. The worst thing is that once seen, I can't forget them. They keep replaying, and all I can do is watch. Imagine the worst thing you can think of—pounding a hammer against your own forearm, or gutting a loved one—and now imagine thinking about that all day. Maybe then you'd understand.

It's officially evening when I get back from the laundromat. I check the mail: two overdue credit card bills and a check from Anomie Inc., the company that runs SantaCam.com. They pay me fifteen cents a minute, which works out to nine bucks an hour. Except, I don't get paid for every minute I'm logged into the Web host—only the times I'm actually connected with a customer. Some days I'll be logged in for eight hours, but only get paid for two.

The check is for seventy-six dollars—a week's work.

If I have the energy, I'll cash it tomorrow.

I make macaroni and cheese for dinner. I don't have an oven or a stovetop, like my customers do, just a one-basin sink, a microwave and a hot plate. I eat dinner straight from the pot with ketchup for spice. I can't stop thinking about Aiko. I wonder if she's back online, trying to get her baby a bear. I log into SantaCam.com in case she's there. There are only two other Santas on the clock right now. We don't get many hits at ten at night. I sit around for a few minutes, and then I get a ping. I click on the button to go live, but instead of a child, the stupid, grinning heads of two teenaged boys fill the screen.

"Check out this one," the dark-haired one says. "Check out this fat fuck."

There are five syllables in the phrase, *Check out this fat fuck.*

The other one—a skinny punk with acne so bad the right side of his face looks like a blister—points at me with a laugh so twisted it looks like he's melting. "What is that, a ski poster? Where's your tree, Santa?"

I think about that for a moment, but don't answer. I smile and say, "Ho, ho, ho," and this only makes them laugh harder. This happens sometimes, especially in the later hours. I complained to the web host, and he or she (I don't know because everything is done by e-mail) said it happens to all the Santas. I think it only happens to me.

The dark-haired one has full, pink lips, and though he's got that misshapen look most teenagers have, I bet he does better with the ladies than his pizza-faced friend. He slides his tongue across his lips. "You ass-fuck any elves tonight, Santa?"

That question has ten syllables. It's perfect, and I let out an easy breath. Our SantaCam training manual says to play it straight. Never break character. "Santa's married," I say. "To Mrs. Claus."

The red-cheeked kid is howling now, and the good-looking one falls to the floor holding his gut. I go with it. "What would you boys like for Christmas?"

They're laughing so hard they squeak like rodents. The acne kid stands up. He's got on gray sweatpants. "I know what you want, Santa,"

"Ho, ho, ho," I say, because tacked on to what the kid just said it adds up to ten.

The kid loosens the drawstrings and lowers his pants. His tiny, uncircumcised cock fills the monitor. He shakes his hips so that it swings back and forth like the clapper of a church bell. Behind him, the other kid starts singing a Christmas carol badly off-key.

"Ho, ho, ho," I say. "Merry Christmas."

You might wonder, neighbor, why I put up with this, why I log in to SantaCam at a time when only cruel, shallow people are online. I'll explain that the same day you can explain why I fantasize about cutting the webbing of my toes with a razorblade.

Around eleven-thirty, I turn off the computer and turn on the TV. I lie down and flip through the channels looking for sitcoms and cartoons. I'll even watch infomercials. My favorites are for food gadgets. If someone's found a faster way to cook a turkey, I'm glued to the screen, even if I've never made a turkey. There is comfort in watching other people chop vegetables, knowing they won't suddenly start carving up their co-host.

Soon, it's past midnight, and we're entering the small hours. The ones, the twos, the threes—we're a long way from ten. The Lurking Man can show up any time of day, of course. But the small hours—this is where he lives. We're in his home now, passing through in darkness like the moon crossing the ecliptic plane.

I try to call up a new movie, one set in Aiko's kitchen. In this film I wake up each day and actually look forward to what's ahead. I wrap an arm around her narrow waist and don't even mind her morning breath. I make coffee without fear of throwing it in anyone's face. I run the blender, and there is only juice inside. No blood, no bones. I hold my left hand in front of my face and wiggle my fingers. They're all there. They're all there. My eye catches the glint of the gold band on my ring finger.

And here's where the movie falls apart. There is no ring. There is no finger. Aiko's world is illusion, and I can only glimpse it through my webcam. But if I watch the screen just right, my reflection is transposed onto the houses on the other end. This is how I inhabit their lives. On my computer screen. It's like watching myself in a rerun. I am there in Aiko's kitchen. In a place she can't see.

hush

REGINA SOLOMOND

THE DOG-EARED NOTEBOOK sits on my bedside table, numbers claustrophobically crowded between blue lines. Placing my finger in the phone dial, I gently scroll to the first number. The dial clicks along as I spin to the remaining six digits. I press the phone to my ear, shivers traveling down my spine like rain drops trailing down a window.

There's the familiar click as someone answers the phone, followed immediately by a "Hello?" The voice is definitely female, and a bit raspy. Probably belonging to an elder, or maybe just someone who smokes a pack of menthols a day. "Hello?" she repeats. "Harpers' residence."

I close my eyes and breathe in deeply. The Harpers' residence. The voice on the phone must be Mrs. Harper. Her hair is probably pulled back in a mousy brown bun, graying wisps framing her face. Crows feet mark the corners of her hazel eyes, and her thin lips are usually pressed together as if she's trying to forget a bitter taste. She works in a grocery store seven days a week, even though her husband promised he would work enough to support them both. After work she smokes cigarettes, waiting for Mr. Harper to return home from the factory. Some days she smokes two or three cigarettes. Some days she finishes the pack.

"Hell-oooo?" she says again, a hint of annoyance creeping into her voice. There's a large exhale from across the line, a click, then the beeping of a lost connection. I will most likely never hear the voice of Mrs. Harper again, but I've still managed to become a tiny blip on the radio wave of her life. Our paths, for however briefly, have intertwined.

When I return home from working the evening shift at St. Anthony's Senior Care Center, it is usually after ten. My back aches, my feet are sore, and everything smells of disinfectant. With my key in the lock, I often imagine what it would be like to have a family awaiting my return on the other side of the door. I would burst into the room with a "Honey, I'm home!" like a retro sitcom, and my wife would kiss me hello, a sleeping baby in her arms. I twist the key and am greeted by my apartment with its peeling floral wallpaper and wet-sock smell. The lights flicker on, and something with too many legs scuttles for safety beneath the couch. *Honey, I'm home.*

With no other company, I turn to my phone. I dial a number, writing it down in my notebook so I can look back on it later like a diary entry, a reminder of a life I've touched. Goosebumps spread as the rings reverberate. Who will pick up on the other line? It could be the president of Australia, a whitened-teeth celebrity, or a blue-haired grandmother. The pope, my high school math teacher, or a drug lord. Maybe it's a single mother balancing three jobs, or maybe it's a teenager who's already wrecked their third car. The possibilities are endless. It's like pushing two quarters into a slot machine, turning the handle, and holding your breath as your prize clinks to the bottom of the chute.

But I never speak. I have nothing to say.

Most people think my call is just a bad connection or spam. There's a "Hello? . . . Hello? . . . " a click, and they're gone. Others stay with me for a bit longer. Some girls listen to the silence for a moment before bidding me farewell with a "fuck off, pervert." Some people think I'm their ex, still pining over them. "Shelley, look, I know it's you. You have to stop calling, baby. Move on. I have . . . Shelley?" Some think I'm a ghost. "Joshua, is that you? What's it like up there? I miss you." In the silence, people hear what they expect to hear.

My phone is my conduit, my medium, reaching through space to connect with disembodied voices. She is a beautiful mahogany rotary phone with gold detail, smooth to the touch and refreshingly cool as I press her metal handset against my ear. I do have a cellphone that I take to work, some flimsy thing that doesn't even have real buttons—just a touch-screen. Cellphones take away the intimacy of a phone call. With my rotary phone I feel connected, as if the wire connecting the phone base to the handset also connects me to the ones I call. An umbilical cord nourishing us with the same life force.

Growing up at the city's edge, my mother worked three jobs to support our two-person family. The dark bags under her eyes and callused hands proved she loved me. But with Mother at work all the time, I was a bit lonely. None of the kids at school wanted to be my friend. When I try to talk, my tongue swells up, and the words in my brain trip over each other as they scramble out of my mouth. That's how I earned the nickname Stuttering Thomas—a clever parody of the biblical Doubting Thomas, or maybe just an unclever insult, since my name is Thomas and I do, in fact, stutter. The name stuck from elementary school to high school graduation. I laughed along with the kids. God, I just wanted a friend. Someone to share stories with, someone to care for, someone to sit in comfortable silence with. Someone to simply exist with.

I was ten when I made my first phone call. My mother had an olive-green rotary phone on the table near the couch, but forbade me from ever using it, except for emergencies. The only numbers I knew were the numbers of the bars and the factory where she worked, and 911. But Mother was working an overnight shift, and I was lonely. I picked up the plastic phone, and dialed a series of random numbers.

My heart pounded against my chest with each ring.

"Hello, you've reached the Millers."

My words stuck in my throat. I was trembling from head to foot in my threadbare superhero pajamas, a hand-me-down from a nice mother at church.

"Hello, is anybody there?" the voice asked. I was thrilled. It sounded like a boy my age! I wanted so desperately to say hello, to ask him how his day was, maybe see if he needed a friend—but my tongue had swelled like an overripe tomato. I knew that if I opened my mouth, he would hear my stutter and laugh. So I only listened as he repeated "hello" a couple more times, and eventually hung up. I made several more phone calls that night, and on other nights when Mother was at work. With voices speaking into my ear, I didn't feel so lonely.

When Mother got the phone bill at the end of the month, her face whitened and her hands crinkled the corners of the page in her tight grip. "Timmy, have you been using the phone?" When I confessed that I had been calling my friends, she yelled. We couldn't afford to talk on the phone whenever we pleased. I should've known better.

After that, I only made calls from phone booths, when I was lucky enough to find spare change on the ground. Sometimes, I even skipped lunch so I could use the lunch money Mother had given me. Hearing new voices was all the nourishment I needed.

As a nurse, I get to be around people all the time. People depend on me—maybe even look forward to seeing me every day as I administer their pain killers and see to their needs. They might even consider me their friend.

I make several more calls that night after calling Mrs. Harper, and each new voice is as sweet and refreshing as the first bite of an apple.

"Hey, what's up?"

"Dígame."

"Hello, you have reached Comfy Cups, home of the original knitted potholders . . . "

"Mm'yellow?"

So many different greetings, different voices, different people.

The watch on my wrist, my grandfather's old leather-strapped ticker, reads eleven twenty-five. My eyelids have tossed down their anchors, my body aches, and the mattress where I sit calls me to lie down. This will be my last phone call tonight. I twirl my finger along the rotary circle seven times, then wait as the ringing sings into my ear.

The phone clicks as someone answers. I wait with bated breath for them to say some form of "Hello," to reveal some part of themselves to me.

Silence.

Silent as a January snowfall.

Silent as a film from the early 1900s.

Silent as a spring blossom unfurling its petals.

Silence.

I slowly exhale. Leaning back against the headboard of my bed, I cradle the phone against my ear. I don't say a word, and neither do they. Why tarnish the silence with our guttural vowels and biting constants? The sweet hush is beautiful. It envelops me, and I surrender to it. I close my eyes, and can see the dark space before the dawn of creation, before sound existed. Just darkness and our presences. We are all there is.

I wake up to rain drumming against my windows, and the steady humming of a lost connection. I gently pick the phone handset off the pillow where it lies next to me, and place it back on its rest. I check my notebook to find the number of the last person I called, and use my pen to carve it into my bedside table.

As weeks pass, the silent phone call becomes the sun I revolve around. I find myself constantly checking my wristwatch at work, waiting for my shift to end. It must look like I have a nervous tic, the way my eyes keep jerking to my wrist. The number is everywhere. It's in the margins of the papers containing patients' orders, it's scrawled across the back of the "Get Better Soon!" cards I deliver. The numbers are sharp and jagged, the ink pressed deep. It's only when I catch myself engraving the numbers into the wooden door of a bathroom stall that I realize the one writing them is me. By the end of the day, my shirt is soaked in sweat and I jump at the slightest sound.

"Calm down!" A patient scolds me as I measure out his medicine with trembling, sweaty hands. "You're making me nervous!" I wince at the abrasiveness of his gravelly voice. Everything sounds much louder now. The squeak of my shoes on the linoleum floor makes me want to tear my ears off. The clattering of the plates on the trays I serve the patients sounds like armored knights wrestling. The constant hum of the fluorescent lights is as torturous as having my fingernails peeled back one by one.

When I finally make it back home, I retreat to my bedroom, where my phone awaits on the bedside table. Sitting on the edge of my bed, facing my window looking out upon the city lights, I call the number. There is usually two or three sweet rings of anticipation, a click, then silence.

And, just like that first night, we stay like that for hours, phones pressed to our ears without saying a word. And the silence is so, so much sweeter than it would be if I, say, locked myself in my closet with a pair of earplugs. Because this silence is communal. I stare at the darkening navy blue sky, barely breathing, and somewhere else they are also staring at their own view, sharing the same silence. And while I know nothing about the other—not their age, their sex, their race, their religion, their past, their dreams—I feel like I know everything about them. Everything that matters, for we are familiar souls.

One day, they don't answer. The phone rings and rings. Each ring seems more shrill, more panicked. Then a calm, automated voice asks me to leave a message. I hang up.

They don't answer the next day either. Or the next.

I am a mess. I am a bundle of frayed nerves. I don't sleep at night, and I see fear in the eyes of the patients at the home. I return to calling other numbers, but their voices have lost their magic. Their "hello"s sound crude, desecrating the silence.

I call the number carved into my table, pulling out my hair by the fistful. The rings sound like screams, making my ears bleed. I need to find the silence. I need to find the silence. So I call the number again and again and again and . . .

"Hello?"

My breath is stuck in my chest.

"Hello?" repeats the voice. It sounds like it belongs to a woman, between her twenties and forties.

I know it is not their voice. I have shared their silence for months, and I know what their voice is not.

"W-who is this?" I ask, my words cutting my throat.

"Were you looking for Rosalyn?" she says.

Rosalyn.

"Yes," I say. "I'm t-trying to find Rosalyn."

"This is her daughter," she says. She takes in a gulp of air. "Rosalyn passed away last week."

I don't say anything.

"Were you one of her friends?"

I nod my head. "Yes, w-we were f-f-friends."

"That makes me really happy to hear. I thought Mom always seemed so lonely. I kept telling her to get out more, maybe join some church activities to meet more people, but she never wanted to." She sighs. "Mom always hated small talk. Why break the silence with meaningless prattle, she would say."

I'm surprised at the warm, salty water running down my cheeks in rivulets. "Th-th-thank you for t-telling me." I place the handset back on the phone base and curl up on my sheets in the fetal position. I press my pillow over my ears and muffle the world. In the quiet darkness, I return to the womb. I am safe, and Rosalyn's silence washes over me. Our souls are entwined, like twins formed from the same embryo. I don't want to leave this warm cocoon; can't bear the thought of facing the world with its incessant ticks and clacks and murmurs and yells. I want to stay a part of the silence. I want to be with Rosalyn.

I wake up hours later to the waxen moon peering through my window, filling the room with its soft light. The phone rests on the bedside table, but I still hear a ringing. It stays with me through the night and into the morning. It follows me even when I leave my apartment, drive to work, talk to patients. As constant as my heartbeat. Like a lover's voice, it is the last thing I hear at night and the first thing I hear each morning. The ringing is coming from between my ears, from inside my being. It calls for Rosalyn. It sings of a lost connection.

It calls for Rosalyn, and will not hush until she answers.

feedback loop

JOSHUA CHAPLINSKY

THIS IS KDK 12 calling KDK 1."

Brian took his thumb off the talk button and waited for a response. He rubbed the grill of the hand mic against the peach fuzz on his upper lip. The sound it made inside his head echoed the leaves rustling outside the tree house, like the static of dead air.

"This is KDK 12 calling KDK 1. Come in."

"What the hell are you even saying?" Dylan reclined on a military-style folding cot, playing with his iPhone. The lower half of his body disappeared into the soft mouth of an orange sleeping bag.

"Just something my dad taught me. He says anyone who knows the right response is okay to talk to."

"So it's like some secret code for screening perverts."

"Don't be a jerk." Brian zipped up his jacket and fiddled with the tuning dial. Snippets of different conversations faded in and out as he searched for an open channel.

. . . Peace. Shalom. Bonjour tout le monde. Witajcie, istoty z zaświatów. Ni strebas vivi en paco kun . . . up 2.3 percent from last quarter, an increase deemed unacceptable to shareholders . . . that was

Vivaldi's Concerto No. 4 in F minor performed by the English Chamber Orchestra . . . results which the community greeted with considerable skepticism. Despite winning the Nobel Prize for his work linking HIV and AIDS, Montagnier's observations . . . 女子中学生が太るのは自然です . . .

Dylan held his phone at arm's length and swung it in a slow arc above his head.

"Cell reception sucks out here."

"Nearest tower isn't for miles," Brian said. "We barely get a signal at the house."

"Must be boring as shit. How do you live?"

Brian sighed. Sometimes he wondered why he bothered hanging out with Dylan. For an 8th grader, he could be pretty immature.

"This is KDK 12 calling KDK 1."

"Can't we just go back in the house and go online?" Dylan said.

"The computer's in my dad's room."

"That's lame. Even my little sister has her own laptop."

Dylan scanned the tree house. It contained two cots, a table and chair, and a HAM radio, all illuminated by a single bare bulb hanging from the ceiling.

"You ever bring any girls up here?" Dylan said.

"No."

"You could touch a lot of boobs in a place like this. You'd probably pass Ronnie Shapiro as the top boob-toucher in class."

Brian didn't respond.

"I touched Jessica Fletcher's boob once," Dylan said.

"When?"

"In line during lunch. She bumped into me."

"Sounds more like her boob touched you."

"Whatever, man. It's more action than you ever get."

"This is KDK 12 calling KDK 1." Brian released the button and listened, hoping Dylan would take the hint. He basked in ten seconds of precious silence, and then the radio crackled to life.

This is KDK 1. We're receiving you. Over.

It was a man's voice, garbled and faint.

Brian's face lit up. He turned to see if Dylan shared in the excitement, but he'd already turned his attention back to his phone.

"Sounds like your dad," Dylan said. He emphasized the word *dad* with derision.

KDK 1 to KDK 12, how are you getting on over there? Over.

Brian thumbed the talk button. "Doing just fine—"

"But our cell reception's for shit!" Dylan yelled across the tree house.

Brian shot Dylan a death stare. He continued to eyeball his friend as he brought the mic back to his mouth, rubbing it against his upper lip. When he felt confident Dylan wouldn't try to embarrass him further, he pressed the talk button.

An enormous squawk of feedback tore through the tree house. Brian recoiled, falling backward in his chair. Dylan's sleeping bag writhed like a salted slug. As the concentrated burst of sound reached its shrill peak, the overhead light bulb popped.

"Jesus!" Dylan dropped his phone in his lap, the touchscreen now their sole source of light. Brian opened and closed his mouth, finger pressed against his ear. The afterimage of the light bulb's glowing filament danced across his vision.

"You all right, man?" Brian got up and brushed himself off. He looked out the window towards the house. Despite the distance he could still see the porch light through the trees. At least he hadn't blown a fuse.

He turned to see his friend transfixed by the pale glow of the phone.

"Sorry about that," Brian said. "I don't know what happened."

Dylan continued to stare. A hairline fracture appeared in the corner of the screen. It snaked its way across the phone as they watched, the glass popping like ice in a warm drink. As it reached the other end, an energy-saving feature kicked in and the screen began to dim. Darkness filled the tree house.

Brian held his breath while he waited for his eyes to adjust. He felt unstuck in time. The familiar rustle of the wind through the trees sounded like the white noise of empty airwaves. Even though no power fed the unit, Brian flipped the OFF switch on the radio, just in case. It snapped like a broken bone. Dylan jumped, involuntarily. Brian walked over to his friend, tiny glass shards crunching underneath his feet.

"Dylan?"

Dylan didn't take his eyes off the inert phone. "I think we should go inside."

"Since when are you afraid of the dark?" Brian tried to sound casual.

"Please."

Something about the way Dylan said the word gave Brian the chills. Meekness did not suit his friend.

"Sure, man. C'mon, let's get out of here."

Brian opened the tree house door in a daze. He stepped out onto the surrounding platform and climbed down the ladder. He'd gotten halfway to the house before he realized Dylan hadn't followed. He looked back towards the tree house. He had never been afraid of the woods, but part of him was reluctant to retrace his steps. Another part worried that if he didn't go back for his friend, there'd be no friend to go back to.

He suppressed the thought and jogged back through the trees. He climbed the ladder and paused as he reached the door, which hung slightly ajar. Exhaling slowly, he put his hand against the wood and pushed. It creaked as it swung open.

Dylan hunched over his phone, eyes fixated on the dark screen.

"You coming or what?" Brian couldn't bring himself to cross the threshold.

"I think we should go inside," Dylan said in an almost whisper.

"Yeah, you said that already." Brian's fear manifested as impatience. "Let's go."

But Dylan wouldn't budge. Brian willed his own legs into motion and stepped inside the tree house. He snatched the cell phone from his friend's lap and broke the spell.

Even after Dylan came back to reality, Brian had to lead him by the hand through the trees. Dylan would have made fun of him for holding a guy's hand—no matter what the reason—so Brian dropped it as soon as they cleared the woods. His father stood in the kitchen making coffee when they entered the house.

"How's it going, Hamsters? Make any contact?"

"We had a problem with feedback," Brian said. "Dylan's phone cracked."

Brian Sr. frowned. "That's odd. Let me take a look."

Brian handed him the phone. Brian Sr. shook his head.

"Bet you wish you'd gotten yourself a DynaTAC, huh?" He handed the phone back to Brian, who handed it over to Dylan. "I can't imagine how that happened, but the repairs are on me."

"Thanks." Dylan slipped the phone into his pocket, stared at his feet.

"You all right there, son?" Brian Sr. said.

"I guess."

"You're awful docile. That must have been some feedback."

Dylan looked up at the man. "I feel like it's still inside me."

Brian Sr. cocked his head. He put a hand on Dylan's forehead and peered into the boy's dilated pupils.

"My bones are singing," Dylan said.

Brian Sr. stepped back and sized him up.

"You weren't electrocuted, were you?"

"I don't think so."

"No, of course not." Brian Sr. put an arm around the child. "Believe me, if you were electrocuted, you'd know it. It does NOT tickle." He led Dylan to a chair and got him a glass of water. "Drink this. You'll feel better."

Dylan took the tiniest of sips and retched, emptying his stomach onto the floor. A droplet of spittle clung to his lower lip.

"I think I'd like to go home now," he said. The droplet fell.

"Of course. Brian, get my keys. I'll give Dylan a ride home."

Dylan wasn't in school the following day. When Brian got home that afternoon, he tried calling his house. No one answered. Dylan's dad worked late, but his mother rarely went out. A fist formed in Brian's stomach as he hung up the phone.

Dylan was absent the next day as well. After school, Brian helped his father replace the light bulb in the tree house and test out the gear. Everything seemed to work fine.

"KDK 12 to KDK 1," Brian Sr. said into the mic. The words made the fist in Brian's stomach clench and unclench.

By the time dinner rolled around, anxiety had shot Brian's appetite to shit. He stared past his dad, out the window and across the backyard. The tree house, normally obscured by the woods, stood out like a movie set, lit up from within.

He jumped as the jangle of the phone interrupted his reverie. Like most of the technology in the house, it skewed analog. His father owned an electronics shop downtown and never bought anything new.

"Hello?" his father said into the receiver. Brian hadn't seen him get up. He could tell by his father's demeanor that whatever the news, it wasn't good.

"Uh huh. Uh huh. Sure. We'll be there right away."

He hung up the phone and looked at his son. Brian's throat went dry.

"Dylan's in the hospital. They want you to go down and get checked out."

They left without clearing the table. Dinner's awkward silence took the ride with them to the hospital. Brian didn't even bother turning on the radio. He didn't want to fill the airspace with unnecessary noise. A million questions already bounced around in his head. Questions he knew his father didn't have the answers to.

After three hours of testing they still didn't have any answers. Brian had been poked, prodded, stuck, bled and scanned, but no one told him why. When he tried to ask the nurse, she told him the doctor would explain everything. When he asked if he'd be able to see Dylan, she made a face like a thief caught in the act and beat a hasty retreat. The whole time his father sat there and held his hand, just as nervous as Brian. Their frustration peaked by the time the doctor finally showed up.

"And how are we this evening?" the doctor said, oblivious to the flippancy of the question.

"You tell us." Brian Sr. said.

"Right." The doctor looked down at his chart. "Everything checks out. You're free to go."

Brian got up to leave, but his father held him back.

"Just like that?"

"Better than the alternative, wouldn't you agree?" It sounded like a taunt.

"What about Brian's friend?"

"Yeah, what about Dylan?" Brian chimed in.

"I'm sorry, but I won't be able to discuss your friend's case with you. Doctor patient confidentiality and all."

"Can I see him?"

"I'm afraid that won't be possible."

Brian hung his head in defeat, but his father didn't give up so easily.

"Now wait just a minute. I was told the kid had some kind of infection. Obviously you thought my son might have the same thing, so I think we're well within our rights to ask."

The doctor mulled it over.

"All I can say is your friend seems to have come in contact with a mild pathogenic bacteria. Chances are, this occurred before your little slumber party."

"It wasn't a slumber party," Brian said, more to himself than anyone.

"So then why all the secrecy?" Brian Sr. said.

"We didn't want to cause a panic."

Brian's dad opened his mouth to speak, but nothing came out.

"Luckily the effects of the bacteria seem to be benign," the doctor said.

"Seem to be?" Brian Sr.'s voice rose in pitch.

"Absolutely." The doctor tousled Brian's hair. "The boy's fine. We'll just need to see him for a follow-up next week. Make sure he hasn't sprouted any extra limbs."

Brian Sr. shook his head.

"So why can't I see Dylan?" Brian asked.

"Dylan's not here," the doctor said, already on his way out the door. "He's been transferred to another facility."

Brian kept waiting for Dylan to return to school, but he never did. The phone company had disconnected his phone and someone had hung a "For Sale" sign in front of his house. Small town rumors ran amuck, but in reality no one knew what happened. It made Brian feel guilty for ever having questioned their friendship.

His guilt blossomed into a full-on stumbling block, inhibiting his ability to make close friends. He dropped out of high school and enrolled in an out-of-state telecommunications program. After that he spent eight years in the military as a COMSEC Repairer. It wasn't until after his father got sick that he finally returned home.

"I missed you so much, I went and got cancer," his father would joke. Brian smiled through gritted teeth whenever he said it. His father went through a slow, steady decline, and it took its toll on both of them. By the time the man passed, Brian figured he might as well finish out his life where it began. He thought of it as a closed circuit.

The funeral was a low-key affair. Not a lot of people turned out, but they didn't live in a huge town. Mostly regular customers from his father's shop—the kind who used the excuse of a twenty-cent part to hang around and shoot the shit. Brian was surveying their faces for the umpteenth time when he noticed someone familiar in the back row. He looked bigger and balder than when he'd seen him last, but Brian recognized Dylan right away. His old friend gave a slight nod, as if to confirm his identity.

"Sure was sad to see your old man go like that." A wrinkled face popped into Brian's line of sight, blocking his view. Brian tried to look past the old-timer, but the man possessed ninja-level eye contact skills. He locked on like a heat-seeking missile.

"Thanks, Raymond. I appreciate it."

Raymond just stood there smiling like an idiot. Brian pulled him in for an impromptu hug so he could see past him. The back row was empty.

Other than that, the evening passed uneventfully. After the priest said a prayer and the stragglers finished straggling, Brian found himself standing by his car in the parking lot. He stared up at the sky as the last of the taillights receded into the night.

"It sure is something, isn't it?"

Brian didn't have to look to put a face to the voice.

"I thought I'd seen a ghost."

"Who says I'm not?"

Brian could hear the grin behind the words. He turned in their direction. Dylan stood a good twenty feet away. Brian resumed his stargazing. He couldn't bring himself to devote more than one sense to the possible apparition at a time.

"Those stars are the real ghosts," he said. "Their light traveled millions of years just to let us know they existed."

The two men lapsed into silence.

"I guess I owe you an explanation," Dylan finally said.

"I don't know if it even matters at this point."

"Fair enough. How about a drink?"

"Everyone's headed over to the Hat Rack."

Dylan pushed some gravel around with his foot. "It'd be better if no one knows I'm in town."

Brian looked at his friend—*really* looked at him. His face was haggard, unshaven. He wore loose fitting clothes with worn elbows and patched knees. A weariness framed his eyes. He resembled a hungry dog, looking for a handout, willing to bite if necessary.

"You need a place to stay?" Brian motioned towards the car. "You can crash at my place."

Dylan didn't move.

"If it's okay with you, I think I'd rather walk."

Brian studied him some more, but couldn't glean anything further from his appearance.

"Suit yourself. I've waited this long . . . "

Brian unlocked the car and got in. He watched Dylan in the rearview as he pulled away. Dylan didn't start walking until after Brian had turned out of the parking lot onto the road.

He didn't expect Dylan to show up, but he left the porch light on anyway. After pouring himself a cold cup of coffee he went into his dad's room and booted up the old computer. The dial-up modem roared like a prehistoric beast. When it finally connected to the ISP, he did a simple Google search. Even at 56 Kbps, it didn't take long to find the info he wanted. He fell asleep in his chair waiting for the police report to load.

He tried not to think about Dylan in the days that followed. He distracted himself by attending to his father's affairs, minding the shop and cleaning up the house. The garage alone housed floor to ceiling broken equipment and spare parts. He hesitated to use the "H" word, but his father had never been one for throwing things away. Sorting through the detritus helped him feel more connected to his father, which in turn made it harder to get rid of anything.

A few nights later he found himself staring out the kitchen window, drinking a bottle of beer. The trees behind the house had crept closer over the years, encroaching on the backyard like Birnam Wood. Their shadow obscured the old tree house. *When was the last time anyone had been out there?* He grabbed the rest of his six-pack and went to investigate.

As he approached he saw the dilapidated condition of the place. Its angles had warped like a funhouse as the tree grew, causing half the roof to cave in. Luckily the ladder remained intact. He assumed he'd have to lay into the door, but it took only a gentle push for it to swing open. Brian stood at the threshold and looked back in time. The place looked as though it had been hermetically sealed. He flipped the light switch and the bulb surprised him with light. The ancient radio equipment looked like it had seen regular use.

"I cleaned the place up a bit."

"Jesus, fuck!" Brian whirled around, dropping the beer. Glass cracked and brown liquid spread across the platform like sea foam.

"Didn't mean to scare you," Dylan said from the ground. He looked somewhat better than the last time Brian saw him. He had recently shaved, and wore layers of weather-appropriate clothing. Adrenaline flooded Brian's senses as Dylan climbed up the ladder.

"What are you doing out here?"

Dylan bent to inspect the mess. He came back up with two unmolested bottles. He held one out to Brian.

"We were gonna have a drink, remember?"

"Right." Brian said it slow, willing calm into his voice. He extended a timid hand and accepted the beer. He popped the cap on an exposed nailhead and went inside the tree house to sit. Dylan did the same.

Brian gulped down half his beer. Dylan took a patient pull on his own. The wind through the trees provided ambient noise. An owl hooted its call sign.

"So . . . " Brian picked at the label on his bottle.

"I thought you said it didn't matter?"

"I guess I changed my mind."

Dylan exhaled slow, as if the weight of his confession had been preemptively lifted.

"Where to begin? Did you know I'm allergic to radio waves?"

Brian blinked. "Like those people who're afraid of cell phones and wear tin-foil hats?" Even before the words left his mouth, he wanted to cram them back in. Dylan took it in stride.

"Ironic, isn't it?"

"I'm sorry," Brian said. "I didn't mean anything by it."

"That's okay, I'm used to it. But the fact of the matter is, electromagnetic hypersensitivity is a real disorder that affects thousands of people every day. Some of us can't use cell phones or listen to the radio. Others have to live completely off the grid."

Brian connected the dots. "That's why you wouldn't get in the car with me."

Dylan nodded.

"You know, you could have just asked me to turn the radio off."

"I didn't want to risk it. A few residual waves is all it takes to make me violently ill. Disorientation, nausea . . . sound familiar?"

"Are you saying that's why you got sick that night?"

Dylan took another slug of beer, shrugged his shoulders. "I wound up in the hospital with a hundred and three fever."

"Was that the hospital's diagnosis?"

"No." Dylan shook his head. "EHS hasn't been formally recognized by the mainstream medical community. They said I contracted a bacterial infection. But guess what? Bacteria transmit their own electromagnetic signals."

"I . . . wasn't aware of that."

"On a lower frequency than radio, but yeah, they do. Their DNA acts as an antenna. It's like wireless internet."

"Oh. Well, you know me. I never had a mind for computers. I still use Dad's old dial-up."

"I remember that machine." Dylan smiled. "We'd wait forever just to see one measly pair of tits."

Brian smiled back.

"Your dad was a good man." Dylan raised his beer.

Brian met it with his own. The two men locked eyes.

"Thanks."

And then the moment passed.

"Anyway," Dylan said, "my parents had insurance, so of course the hospital ran every test in the book. They hooked me up to an EKG and the thing went haywire. Next thing I know, I'm being air-lifted to a military hospital three states over."

"They told us you weren't contagious."

"CDC regs speak louder than words. The bacteria I came in contact with turned out to be a complete unknown. They used that as an excuse to hold me hostage. Over a year of constant tests and they never found anything wrong with me."

Brian took a swig of phantom beer from his empty bottle.

"So why didn't you come back to town sooner?" He tried to make the question as innocuous as possible.

Dylan hesitated.

"I . . . laid low for a while. Worked through some personal stuff. As you can imagine, I had problems trusting people after that."

"Sure."

"But things got better. I found this group. Like-minded people, who understood what I'd been through."

"Like a twelve-step thing."

"Sort of. They helped me come to terms with who I am."

"An electrosensitive?"

"An antenna."

A thousand responses went through Brian's head.

"I'm sorry, what?"

"I'm an antenna. I send and receive electromagnetic information."

"Oh." Brian kept his voice neutral. "That's what I thought you said."

"All lifeforms emit electromagnetic waves. Some of those waves contain biological information. They're like seeds—when they find suitable ground, they flourish. That information interacts with the DNA of the recipient, changing it in subtle ways. The DNA acts as an antenna and sends the modified signal back out, to look for a new recipient with which to repeat the process. Combine a whole bunch of these small antennae and you wind up with an even bigger one. Hence—me."

"I can see how coming to terms with something like that might be difficult."

"You're making fun."

Brian threw up his hands. "I'm just trying to understand. Basically, what you're telling me is the radio got you pregnant and you're incubating alien life."

"I'm participating in evolution." Dylan delivered the words with emphatic force.

"I just—wow. That's why you came back?"

"I always planned on coming back, eventually. When I heard about your father, I figured the time was right."

"Somehow I sense there's more to it than that."

"You're right, there is. I need to boost the signal."

Brian looked over at the HAM radio.

"Have you . . . "

"No. I wanted to wait for you."

"And you don't expect me to try and stop you?"

"I don't even expect you to believe me."

Brian nodded, putting down the empty bottle.

"Good point. I also don't want you to bash my head in like that security guard."

Dylan looked down at his shoes.

"You know about that, huh?"

"Google. I know about a lot of things. I know you've been in and out of institutions for the last ten years. I know the police are looking for you."

Dylan looked back up, eyes glassy. "I would never do anything to hurt you. We're friends."

Brian went quiet. He mentally calculated the distance between himself and the door, weighing his odds of escape. He got to his feet. Dylan watched him expectantly.

"I guess that settles it," Brian said.

He flipped the radio's ON switch. There was a click and a hum as the ancient tubes started to warm. Dylan backed up as far as he could within the tiny tree house. "It still works." He said it with reverence.

"It's these old tubes," Brian said. "They were made to survive the end of the world." He fiddled with the tuning dial. Snippets of different conversations faded in and out.

. . . Taiyyātunā lil-'adiqā' fil-nujūm. Yā laytā yajma `unā al-zamān. Paz e felicidade a todos . . . that's a negatory, good buddy. Traffic's jacked up for at least a good . . . it's not pseudo science, these phenomena are naturally occurring and require further investigation from . . . KDK 12 calling KDK 1 . . . the only station in the Four County area playing the rarest 78s . . .

Dylan jumped out of his seat, almost out of his skin.

"Holy shit! Go back."

Brian fine-tuned the dial. They listened.

. . . This is KDK 12 calling KDK 1. Come in . . .

It was a kid, garbled and faint.

"That's your voice," Dylan said.

"Come on, man, it's just a coincidence. Hammers have been using that line since my dad's day."

"You're telling me that doesn't sound like you?"

. . . This is KDK 12 calling KDK 1 . . .

"It could be an old broadcast bouncing around the atmosphere," Brian said.

"What are the odds?"

"It's not *im*possible."

Dylan motioned to the radio. "Only one way to find out."

Brian picked up the hand mic and brought it to his mouth. He felt the familiar touch of the grill against the hair on his lip. The sea of static inside his head.

"This is KDK 1. We're receiving you. Over." He looked at Dylan as he said it.

No response.

After a few moments of silence Brian held up his hands as if to say, *You see?*

"Try again," Dylan said.

"KDK 1 to KDK 12, how are you getting on over there? Over."

Still nothing. The seconds stretched thin. Minutes to hours, hours to years. Both men leaned closer. And then . . .

. . . Doing just fine—

—But our cell reception's for shit!

A second voice interrupted the first, calling from across the room, from across the years.

“Holy shit!” Dylan jumped back up.

Brian stared at the radio, dumbfounded.

“How can that be?”

Dylan stuck his hand out, greedy with excitement.

“Let me talk.”

“It’s not possible.”

“Gimme the mic.”

But Brian couldn’t hear him, his mind somewhere else. So Dylan grabbed the hand mic and pressed the talk button.

The tree house filled with sound like a balloon about to pop. The shriek of it wrenched Brian from his stupor. Dylan dropped the mic and fell to his knees, hands over his ears. He cowered, incapacitated by the immensity of it. In that moment it was neverending.

Then, with a tremendous squelch, the feedback ceased.

It took a minute of silence before they realized they could move again. They unfurled from their fetal positions in slow motion, testing newborn limbs. Dylan held his palms out in front of himself, grinning. He turned to his friend.

“I think it worked.”

Brian saw Dylan’s mouth move, but didn’t hear the words.

“Huh?”

“I SAID I THINK IT WORKED.”

Brian nodded his head. “That’s great. I think I’m deaf.”

“WHAT?”

“Never mind.”

Dylan opened the door of the tree house and stepped out into the night.

“WHERE THE HELL ARE YOU GOING?” Brian yelled to make sure his friend heard him. Dylan looked back.

“To celebrate.”

“HUH?”

“I did what I came to do. I’m going to turn myself in.”

Brian wasn’t sure if he’d heard right and he didn’t care. His skin tingled and his head ached. He gave his friend a confused smile and laid down on the floor. Dylan climbed down the ladder and ran off through the trees.

"This is KDK 12 calling KDK 1."

Brian took his thumb off the talk button and waited. Somewhere out there a response rode the waves, like the resolution to a hanging chord. He could feel it.

"Can't we just go back in the house and go online?" Dylan asked.

"The computer's in my dad's room."

"Yeah, I know. You say that every time I ask."

"This is KDK 12 calling KDK 1." Brian used the words to block out his friend. He basked in ten seconds of precious silence before the radio crackled to life.

This is KDK 1. We're receiving you. Over.

It was a man's voice, garbled and faint. Brian lit up.

"Sounds like your dad," Dylan said.

KDK 1 to KDK 12, how are you getting on over there? Over.

Brian jabbed the talk button with his thumb. "Doing just fine—"

"But our cell reception's for shit!" Dylan yelled across the tree house.

Brian shot Dylan a death stare. He knew numbnuts was going to say something stupid like that. He continued to eyeball his friend as he brought the mic back to his mouth, rubbing it against his upper lip. He felt confident Dylan wouldn't try to embarrass him further, so he pressed the talk button.

An enormous squawk of feedback tore through the tree house. Brian recoiled, falling backward in his chair. Dylan writhed like a salted slug. As the concentrated burst of sound reached its shrill peak, the overhead light bulb popped and the screen on Dylan's iPhone cracked.

"Jesus!" Dylan dropped his phone in his lap, the touchscreen now their sole source of light. Brian opened and closed his mouth, finger pressed against his ear.

"You all right, man?" Brian got up and brushed himself off. He turned to see his friend transfixed by the phone's pale glow. "Sorry about your phone. I don't know what happened."

Dylan continued to stare. An energy saving feature kicked in and the screen began to dim. Darkness filled the tree house.

Brian walked over to his friend, tiny glass shards crunching underneath his feet. A thin trickle of blood dripped from Dylan's ear.

"Dylan?"

"I think we should go inside," Dylan said, his voice flecked with distortion.

"Do you feel okay? You sound weird."

"Please."

. . . *Pleasepleasepleasepleaseplease* . . .

The word ghosted from the radio, awash in static, despite the lack of power. It gave Brian the chills.

"C'mon, let's get out of here."

He'd made it halfway to the house before he realized Dylan hadn't followed. He looked back towards the tree house. Part of him was reluctant to retrace his steps. Another part worried that if he didn't go back for his friend, there'd be no friend to go back to. *Maybe that wouldn't be such a bad thing,* he thought, then immediately felt bad.

He suppressed the idea and jogged back through the trees. He climbed the ladder and paused. The door hung slightly ajar. Brian pictured Dylan still hunched over his phone, eyes fixated on the dark screen. He exhaled slowly, put his hand against the door, and pushed.

Dylan wasn't hunched over his phone. He sat on the chair in front of the radio.

"Jesus, dude. What are you doing?" Brian couldn't bring himself to cross the threshold.

"I think we should go inside," Dylan said in an almost whisper.

. . . *goinsidegoinsidegoinsidegoinside* . . .

"Yeah, you said that already." Brian's voice was weak. "Let's go."

But Dylan refused to move. Brian willed his own legs into motion and stepped inside the tree house. It took three more deliberate steps for him to come within arms reach of his friend. The blood from Dylan's ear dripped down his neck in a thin, red line. Brian reached out to touch Dylan's shoulder.

Brian cried out as a tiny spark lit up the tree house, sending him stumbling backward. Dylan still hadn't moved. The radio crackled and hissed.

. . . *idon'tfeelsogoodfeelsogoodfeelsogoodfeelsogood* . . .

The words hadn't come out of Dylan's mouth. They came straight from the radio. Brian started to cry.

"What's happening?"

The only response he got came from the radio. A conversation across time on an infinite loop, growing louder and stronger with each completion of the circuit.

. . . *this is KDK 12 calling KDK 1 calling KDK 12 calling KDK 1 calling KDK 12 calling KDK 1 calling KDK 12 calling KDK 1 calling KDK 12 calling KDK 1 calling KDK 12 calling KDK 1 calling KDK 12 calling KDK 1 calling KDK 12 calling KDK 1 calling KDK 12 . . .*

The echo of the words bled into one another, overlapping and morphing into a seamless, percussive rhythm. Brian felt their vibration in his bones. His skin resonated with invisible friction. He opened his mouth to speak and then the words were coming out of him.

Everything went black.

He awoke to the same rhythm, strapped to a gurney ensconced in clear plastic. He could only move his eyes, his peripheral vision confined to a narrow strip. A man in a spacesuit sat to his right, belted to the wall. To his left, a mirror image. His twin, a doppelganger, strapped to his own gurney in his own plastic tent.

Dylan.

The helicopter blades whirred hypnotic. He felt their vibration down to his cells, lulling him back into unconsciousness. The last thing he saw before he woke up in the hospital was the spaceman, giving him the thumbs up. The gesture offered little comfort.

little girl blue, come cry your way home

DAMIEN ANGELICA WALTERS

JACKSON HEARS BRIANNA crying before he even opens the front door. The baby may only be three weeks old, but the cry isn't anything he's heard before and panic oil-slicks his tongue. It takes him three tries to fit the key in the lock and two hard yanks to get it back out again once the door opens. He drops the packages of diapers and wipes, takes the stairs two at a time, and runs into the nursery, heart thumping a painful tattoo. Tess is holding Brianna close, whispering, "I'm sorry, baby. I'm so sorry."

"What is it? What's wrong?" he says.

Tess turns toward him, eyes as wide and wild as a snake-startled horse. "I don't know. She started crying and now she won't stop. I fed her, I changed her diaper, and I don't know what's wrong."

"Want me to try?"

Tess nods. He puts Brianna against his chest and paces back and forth in the room, rubbing her back. "Hey, babygirl. It's okay. Everything is okay now."

Tess picks up something from the floor—the baby monitor, the small device that usually sits on her nightstand. Her face creases into a strange expression. "I brought it in with me and dropped it," she says, the words flat.

The minutes tick by and Brianna's cries don't let up. "Why don't you call the doctor?" he asks.

"Do you think we should? What if it's just gas?"

"Better to call and find out it's nothing, right? She's never cried like this before, has she?"

Tess shakes her head. "Okay. Okay then."

Several hours later, they're home with a diagnosis of colic and assurances it will go away on its own by the time Brianna is three or four months old. Jackson watches Tess rock their still-crying baby, his chest tightening. Is this their fault? Did their genetic blending gift Brianna with this? He scrubs his face with his hands. Dumb-ass, he thinks. The doctor said there was no known cause. Lots of babies had it; it wasn't their fault, just bad luck.

Brianna's cries begin to hitch and soften. He and Tess exchange a hopeful look. Slowly the baby's eyelids flutter shut and the tension in Jackson's shoulders bleeds away. Tess carries her upstairs, and when she doesn't come back down, he heads up to find Brianna in her crib and Tess in their bed, fully clothed and sound asleep, the baby monitor gripped loosely in one hand.

He tries to fall asleep, but instead, stares wide-awake at the shadows on the ceiling while the minutes drag by. The monitor crackles with static and he jumps. Brianna's cries fill the room and Tess is out of bed and near the door before he can kick off the sheets.

"Do her eyes look different to you?" Jackson asks.

"What?"

From his end of the sofa, where he's sitting with Brianna on her back, stretched out along his upper thighs, he fixes Tess with a look. She's busy fiddling with the baby monitor, turning it over and over, her face pensive. Thankfully, she has the volume turned low. This time of night, Brianna is wearing out, her cries not quite as ear-splitting.

"Her eyes. Do they look different to you?"

"What? No, of course not."

"You didn't even look."

"Trust me, I see them all day long."

"Right, but you can see them here in the light and they look different." They look lighter, but that isn't all. There's something else, something he can't put his finger on.

Tess scoots over, peeks at Brianna, and says, "They look the same to me," before moving back to her end of the sofa.

"You know you can put that thing upstairs." He nods toward the monitor. "She's right here with us."

"I know that. I can hear her." She gets up, clips the monitor to her waistband, and extends her arms. "I want to feed her, then put her to bed."

"It's a little early, isn't it? And didn't she just eat?"

Tess barks a laugh. "My boobs say it's time."

He hands over the baby with a wry grin. "Who am I to argue with your boobs. Feed away."

At the end of the day, Jackson's boss stops by his cubicle, leaning against the half-wall with the air of a man unable to stand on his own. An act, Jackson knows, never mind the deep grooves in Charles's face and the sagging skin beneath shrewd eyes. The man ran several miles each day with a near-religious fervor. "How's fatherhood treating you?"

"Colic is another word for hell."

"You look like hell yourself." Charles laughs to soften the words. "With kids, it's always something. Just wait until she's a teenager. These days will seem like cake."

Jackson groans and after Charles leaves, he inputs numbers into a spreadsheet until they blur into nonsense. His co-workers file out, and he texts Tess to say he has to work late, but he closes the spreadsheet and rests his head on folded forearms. Brianna was up most of the night and although Tess did her best, he didn't get much sleep.

He wakes to a stiff neck, a small puddle of drool, and the sound of a vacuum cleaner. "Shit, shit, shit," he mutters. It's just shy of eight o'clock and the half-dozen messages from Tess range from *Coming home soon?* to *Your dinner's in the fridge* to *Hello???* He texts a hasty *Sorry. Charles pulled us into an emergency mtg. Left my phone at my desk* to which she responds *Fine*. The lie mixes with guilt on his tongue, but Charles *is* known for spur of the moment, end of the day meetings and sometimes, they run for several hours.

Still, he drives well over the speed limit, giving cursory checks for cops, and races through yellow lights that turn red before he's through the intersections. Tess is in the living room, the shadows beneath her eyes a dusky purple and her eyes filled with silent accusation. Through the baby monitor, Brianna's cries are low and plaintive.

An hour later, Jackson turns in for the night, but the nap works against him. From the way she's breathing, he can tell Tess isn't asleep either, but she's on her side, facing away. Definitely still angry. The monitor crackles, the sound stretching out longer than it seems it should, long enough for him to wonder if it's broken, then Brianna cries, and Tess stumbles from the room like an extra in a zombie movie.

He wakes in the middle of the night in an empty bed, the sheets on Tess's side cool to the touch. He hears a low, rhythmic creak coming from the baby monitor, and it takes a few seconds for him to identify the sound: the rocking chair in Brianna's room. Tess is whispering, soft and low.

"I'm sorry, sweetheart. Everything will be okay. I won't do it again."

He frowns in the dark and rolls over as Tess hums a lullaby.

"I feel so helpless." He stands in the hallway outside Brianna's room. Her arpeggio cries are sometimes softer, sometimes louder, but always insistent. While taking out the trash, he mentioned to his elderly neighbor that the baby had colic, and she suggested a bit of whiskey.

"For the baby or for us?"

She grins. "Both."

"I tried to balance the checkbook today," Tess says. "And it was impossible, I couldn't concentrate, so I put her in the stroller and took her around the block." She cups her elbows in her palms.

"And?"

"What do *you* think?"

"In a few months, it'll be better."

Tess half-laughs, half-sobs. Runs her fingers over the baby monitor clipped to the waistband of her pants.

"You don't have to carry that around all the time," he says, gentling his words.

She shrugs. Doesn't meet his eyes. Finally, she says, "I know."

"Do you think the static's normal?"

"What?"

"The static from the monitor. Right before it picks up her cries, there's static and it sounds weird."

She blinks rapidly, her fingers drifting to the monitor again. "No, it works fine. That's just interference or something."

"All right, if you think so. Hey, what did you mean last night, you wouldn't do it again?"

"What are you talking about?"

"I heard you through the monitor when you were feeding Brianna. You told her you were sorry and you wouldn't do it again."

She waves one hand. "Oh, that. It was nothing. I moved and my nipple popped out of her mouth." She smiles, but it doesn't reach her eyes and the shape is off. It's too small and too tight. He lets it go, not wanting to provoke an argument. They're both way too tired for that.

He scoops a crying Brianna from her crib, angling her so the light strikes her face. Her eyes *are* different, no doubt about it. The blue isn't nearly as deep, but it's not just that. She looks . . . afraid. His cheeks burn and even though Tess is still downstairs, he glances over both shoulders. Of course the baby's scared. He's holding her with outstretched arms, her legs dangling in empty space. In a few years, she'll probably love it, but babies like to be wrapped up tight. He tucks her into the crook of his arm and whispers, "It's okay, babygirl. Daddy's got you. It's okay."

Tess, dressed in jeans and tennis shoes, is waiting in the kitchen, jingling her keys in one hand, and after a quick peck on the check, she grabs her purse. "We need diapers."

"I would've picked them up on my way home."

"I know, but I need to get out of the house. I won't be gone long, and I just fed her so she'll be fine for a little while."

"Was today a bad one?"

"You can hear her, can't you? And she isn't nearly as loud now as she was earlier." Her face creases and she blinks away the glitter of tears.

He nods. He's pretty sure the neighbors can hear her, too. Whiskey might not be such a terrible idea, he thinks. For all three of them.

Another peck on the cheek and she's out the door. It's only when the car pulls away that he realizes he can't hear the telltale echo of Brianna's cries and the baby monitor is nowhere in sight. As ridiculous as it seems, he suspects Tess took it with her. Truth be told, he's glad. He'd turn it off anyway.

Upstairs, he lifts Brianna to his shoulder and bounces her gently, whispering, "Come on sweetface, give Daddy a little break. There's no reason to cry. Everything is okay." She continues to cry. He tries singing to her, rocking back and forth the way Tess does, dancing around, making silly faces, blowing raspberries, all with the same result. Finally, an ache firmly nestled in his temple, he places her back in her crib, shutting her bedroom door behind him. It helps, a little.

Charles calls him into the office for an after-hours meeting, and he sends Tess a message, but she doesn't respond. Fortunately, the meeting doesn't run very long.

Tess is asleep on the sofa and Brianna must be as well because the house is quiet. He breathes a sigh of relief. Maybe it's only a momentary peace, but he'll take it.

He brushes a stray lock of hair away from Tess's cheek and her eyelids twitch. "Hi, honey. I'm going to change, but I promise, I'll be quiet."

She murmurs something indistinct.

In jeans and a t-shirt, he peeks in Brianna's room, but he can't see the baby and his fingers tighten on the doorframe. Brianna's too small to wriggle around much and—

"Jackson," Tess calls out from behind, her voice thin and bird-chirp high, and as he turns to look, Brianna lets loose with a sudden, keening wail.

He rushes over to the crib. "It's okay, babygirl," he whispers into her hair.

Tess runs into the room, the monitor in hand.

"Is she—"

"She's fine. A wet diaper, that's all. Can you shut that off? Hearing her cry is bad enough. We don't need to hear her in stereo, too."

Tess comes downstairs in her pajamas, her freshly washed hair wrapped in a towel, Brianna's cries echoing from the monitor in her hand.

"You took that in the bathroom with you? I was with her. I told you I was putting her down."

"I know. I just like having it near. It makes me feel better, hearing her. And *I* told *you* that before."

He lets loose with a bitter laugh. "We can hear her fine without it, all the neighbors can hear her, and hell, *she* can probably hear it, too."

"So I'll turn it down. Will *that* make you feel better?"

"Just turn it off. Jesus, Tess, you carry it everywhere. You don't need it."

He goes to grab the monitor and she whirls away with a snarl.

"I said I'd turn it down," she snaps.

"What the hell, Tess?"

She fixes him with a blank stare and doesn't answer.

"Fine. Leave the fucking thing on if you want." He stomps into the kitchen, the echo of Brianna's wails following him in.

At a small café halfway between his office and his sister's, Jackson slides into a booth and waits for her to arrive. She's a few minutes late, as always, and the first thing she says is, "You look like hell."

"I love you too."

"I assume the screaming mimi is still screaming?"

"Like nobody's business."

"It'll pass, I promise. Just like a kidney stone."

He groans. "That's not even funny."

After they've ordered, she traces her finger in the condensation from her water glass. "Everything else okay?"

He shrugs.

"Come on. Fess up. I can tell something's bothering you."

"It's Tess."

"And? You have to give me a little more than that to work with here."

"She carries the baby monitor around all the time. I mean all the time, even when Brianna's in the same room."

"Uh-huh."

"Don't you think that's weird?"

"Did you ask her why?"

He drops his chin and peers up through his lashes. "Of course I did. She said she feels better keeping it close."

"And don't you believe her?"

"No. Yes. Hell, I don't know. It's just weird. It's like a kid with a security blanket. And every time it turns on, right before it picks up Brianna's cries, this weird static thing goes on. It's making me crazy."

"Well, there you go."

"What? The static?"

"Okay, we'll blame this on a serious lack of sleep, but never mind the static, you just explained the whole monitor thing to yourself. Brianna cries all the time, right?"

"Pretty much."

"So instead of a precious newborn to cuddle, you have a little crymonster. I mean, it can't be easy to cuddle with her when she's crying."

"No, but . . ."

"So, maybe Tess is transferring that wish to the monitor."

"That has to be the dumbest thing I've ever heard."

"Really? It makes perfect sense to me. I bet once the colic is gone, Tess'll be fine. I bet you both will, or, at the very least, you'll manage to get more sleep. Let her carry the damn thing if it makes her feel better."

"Yeah, yeah, I guess you're right. It's a ridiculous thing to even worry about."

"I agree, it is. But you're a first time parent. Everything is something to worry about."

The pediatrician, a middle-aged woman with a kind face, frowns as she measures Brianna and it deepens after she puts the baby on the scale. "She's eating well?"

"Yes, very much so," Tess says.

The doctor nods and re-measures Brianna's head. "Yes, yes, we can hear you, little one. Just a few minutes longer." She bends close to the baby's face and shines a light in her eyes.

Jackson's gut clenches, but when the doctor finishes, the frown is gone. "Okay, she's a little smaller than I'd like, but she's healthy," she adds. "Let's try supplementing her daily feedings with eight ounces of formula. Four sometime in the morning, and four again at night."

"Okay," Jackson says.

Tess is chewing her lower lip.

"Not to worry, Mom," the doctor says. "You're not doing anything wrong and I'm not overly concerned. She might just be a slow grower, but we'll see what happens with the formula. And you—" she turns back to Brianna "—I'll see you back in a month. Maybe we'll get lucky and your colic will be gone. That will make everyone happier, won't it?"

He wakes up in the middle of the night alone again. This time, the monitor is gone too. He tiptoes down the hall and sees Tess standing beside the crib, her head bowed, rocking slowly from side to side even though Brianna's not in her arms. She's whispering, but whatever she's saying, it's too low for him to hear, and he creeps back into their room before she notices him there.

On Saturday afternoon, with Brianna's cries reaching every corner of the house, Jackson takes Tess gently by the shoulders. "Why don't you go out for a little while? Go to the coffee shop or the bookstore. Just get out of the house and give yourself a break? You just fed her so she'll be okay for a while, and if she isn't I'll just give her some formula."

Her face shifts with indecision, but finally, she says, "I haven't been to the bookstore in ages."

"I know you haven't."

"If you're sure?"

"I'm positive."

"Okay, maybe I will. It'll be nice to get out of the house and be a grownup for a change instead of just a mom."

He watches as she gathers her keys and purse, saying nothing as she slips the monitor into the latter, but after she goes into the powder room, he pulls the monitor out and rearranges things so hopefully its absence won't be immediately noticeable. Her face wreathed in relief, she heads out the door, and once the car is out of sight, he sinks down on the sofa.

The monitor is about the size of a walkie-talkie. Plastic, with two switches on top. One to turn it off and on, the other to adjust the volume. He exhales through his nose. His hands are shaking and he doesn't know why. A hunk of plastic is nothing to be afraid of, but still, unease settles into his chest as he turns it off. The house falls silent. Instantly. As though Brianna's cries were severed with a knife.

He turns it back on. There's the too-long crackle of static before Brianna begins to cry again, but it doesn't sound like a fresh cry. It sounds as though she paused mid-cry to take a breath and the monitor picked it up right in the middle. If that were the case, he still should've heard her; the door to the nursery room is open.

He flips the switch again. Silence. Is it possible something in the monitor itself is making her cry? There are people who can feel electric wires hum in the amalgam fillings of their teeth; maybe it's using a frequency that hurts her ears. He puts his ear near the monitor and turns it back on. Listens to the hiss of static and hears something else faintly in the background, something he can't define, can't explain, but then Brianna cries and the static is gone. His arms go all over goosebumps.

He turns the monitor off again and takes the steps two at a time. Something's not right. That cry, that cut-off cry. He's heard it before. And what he heard behind the static . . . He walks into Brianna's room and his mouth goes dry. Her crib is empty.

Tess comes home with a bag full of new books. Jackson has Brianna in his arms and the monitor, with the volume turned down, in the middle of the coffee table.

"How long have you known?"

The bag drops from her hands. Her mouth works.

"But the more important question is, how many times have you done it?" He presses a kiss to Brianna's forehead and places her gently on the sofa. Stares at Tess while he closes the distance between them with long, lazy steps. He curls his hands into fists, but what he really wants to do is grab her by the shoulders and shake her. The only thing that keeps him from doing so is the fear that if he starts, he won't stop. Won't *want* to stop.

She drops her gaze. "I only did it a few times, I swear," she says in a rush. "You have no idea what it's like to be with her all day, every day. You have no idea how awful I felt that I couldn't make her feel better. So I, I—"

"You shut her off. You sent her away."

Tess wrings her hands. "Jackson, I swear, I didn't mean to—"

"How could you, Tess? How the hell could you do that to our daughter? You have no idea what it's doing to her, let alone where she goes when she's not here. Maybe this is why she's crying all the time. Maybe she's terrified we'll send her back. Did you even think about that? Did you even fucking think?"

"No, I didn't. I didn't think. You get to go to the office all day so you don't hear it. I can't think, I can't sleep, I can't read, I can't even take her for a goddamn walk!"

Brianna's wails grow even louder.

"And she's fine. She isn't hurt. She comes back perfectly fine."

"She's fine? Do you remember what the doctor said about her being too small? And her eyes? Do they really look fine to you? Because let me tell you, they don't. They look scared. Wherever she goes, wherever it sends her, it isn't a nice place. And tell me this, were you ever going to tell me, or was it your little secret?"

"I don't know, okay? I don't know."

"Well, no matter. It's over now. I'm going to put an end to it."

With Brianna back in his arms, he races up the stairs, Tess at his heels. "What are you going to do, Jackson? What are you going to do? Please, don't do anything. Please. We can figure something out, okay? We can . . ."

He shuts the door to Brianna's room in her face and locks it.

"Jackson, no, please. Let me in. Let's talk about this some more. Please."

The monitor's child unit is plugged in the outlet behind Brianna's bureau. Ignoring Tess, Jackson pulls the furniture away from the wall. "Don't worry, babygirl, everything is going to be okay now." With one quick move, he pulls the cord free, and Brianna stops crying. Tess falls silent as well.

He rubs Brianna's back. "See? You're all better now. Daddy fixed it."

He unlocks the door . . . steps out into the hallway. Tess's face is streaked with tears and her mouth opens, but all that emerges is a steady hiss of static.

all that you leave behind
PAUL MICHAEL ANDERSON

For sale: baby shoes. Never worn.
—Author Unknown

Week 21, Third Trimester

CARRIE CAME HOME to a house with a heartbeat, walls throbbing and windows rattling.

She stopped in the entryway, counting Mississippis, the floor vibrating beneath her feet. The *th-thump-th-thump* reverberated down the stairwell, opening up into the entryway and the living room beyond.

At twenty-one Mississippis, the heartbeat transformed into a baffled *sshhhh-pop*, and then resumed.

She hung her keys on the hook beside the door and dropped her shoulder-bag, heavy with material for an article. The recording upstairs didn't stop.

She walked into the kitchen, not trying to soften her footsteps across the hardwood. She flicked on the overhead kitchen light and searched loudly through the cabinets. In the refrigerator, a Tupperware container of meatloaf on the top shelf looked the least moldy. She pulled it out and slammed the door hard enough for it to open again.

Now the recording upstairs paused. Carrie waited in the center of the kitchen, Tupperware in one hand, plate in the other.

She thought she heard the desk chair creak.

She waited some more.

When Danny didn't call down, she fixed herself food she didn't want and sat down at the kitchen table. Mail was strewn across the surface. Not indicative that Danny had gone to work today, but at least he'd left the house.

She ate mechanically, riffling through the circulars, the bills. She didn't look down the hall, where the kitchen light would hit the corners of the closest boxes marked BABY CLOTHES or BABY BEDDING in her spiky shorthand. A list of everything was already in the tax folder upstairs, also written in her shorthand. Danny had never gotten around to it.

At the twenty-first week, the fetus has eyebrows and nails.

When she finished, feeling more bloated than sated, she dropped the dishes into the sink, briefly ran the faucet, and dumped the meatloaf, container and all, into the garbage can beneath.

Another chair-creak upstairs, but no floor creaks. At the twenty-first week, the fetus is more active; the movements you *thought* you felt during the previous month become apparent. You already know this, but the realization that something is alive inside you becomes more pronounced.

She started up the stairs. Guest bathroom at the top, door closed, hallway to the left. At the sixteenth week, the fetus's bowels begin collecting meconium, a tarry kind of proto-poop. That had been Danny's term for it. Hysterical at the time.

Door on the left was the guest bedroom-slash-office, painted a gender-neutral green during the twelfth week. A fetus's gender doesn't form until around the twenty-fourth week. Evelyn if it'd been a girl. Ethan if it'd been a boy.

Danny sat at the small desk, head buried in his crossed arms on the desktop, turned away from her, tincan headphones on his head. On the computer, Windows Media Player was up, playing the forty-five-second-long file. The pieces of the crib that Danny hadn't taken out of the room yet leaned against the opposite wall. The single bed that had used to be in here was still in the basement.

At the twenty-first week, the fetus is a half-foot long, weighs nearly a pound.

The crib was for later, after the basinet.

Danny's shoulders shook, minute twitches, and Carrie raised her hand, as if to touch him. But she stood in the doorway, almost ten feet away, and she wouldn't enter this room. Not unless she absolutely had to.

She continued to the master bedroom.

Television on the dresser tuned to CNN and Anderson Cooper's strangely symmetrical face, work clothes shoved in the hamper. The basinet was already gone, removed three weeks ago. She'd been the one to remove it.

She couldn't avoid looking at herself in the shower, even when she had the water set to scalding and the bathroom fogged. The stretchmarks along her hips seemed even more pronounced then, like accusatory slashes on her body. She scrubbed these areas raw.

At least her nipples had finally lightened back to roughly their natural color. The vertical line on her lower belly had faded away.

Her hands pressed against it. Carrie had only felt movement once, early one morning during the sixteenth week. She'd rolled to wake Danny up, but it had stopped before she could touch her husband.

Her face grew momentarily hot. She took a deep breath and went back to scrubbing.

Much, much later, she was still awake, turned away and facing where the basinet would've been, when Danny finally shuffled through the dark. The mattress settled and shifted as Danny laid down. Before, he would rub the spot between her shoulder blades, a silent good night whenever he came to bed late and thought she was asleep.

Now, she waited, but his breathing slowed and lengthened far on his side of the bed.

She didn't roll to him.

She listened to him breathe, and, eyes wide, stared at the empty space in the dark.

Week 25, Third Trimester

Before becoming pregnant, the alarm on her smartphone was enough to wake her up. During the pregnancy, continual morning sickness was her internal clock. Commonly, sickness lasts between the sixth and fourteenth week, though in rare cases it goes longer.

She was sick the entire length of her pregnancy.

Now, consciousness came slowly, grudgingly, like it was something dragged from the embedded silt of a murky riverbed. All three of the alarms on her phone weren't enough to wake her up. Danny often had to shake her.

This morning, it was sunlight from the bedroom window that brought her around.

During the twenty-fourth week, the fetus is on a regular sleep schedule.

"Danny?" she croaked. Christ, it sounded like she hadn't spoken in weeks.

Squinting, she rolled over, towards her husband's side of the bed, guided more by feel than sight. Rumpled blankets. The bedsheet was cool.

She cracked one open eye wider. "Danny?"

No answer. That hum in your ear when emptiness and silence were your only company.

She flopped onto her back. Danny wasn't home. Right. It was Saturday and he had . . . a thing.

Carrie rubbed her face, as if that would make the answer come.

Nothing.

"Pregnancy brain", or "Mommy brain", are common symptoms in women. Increased levels of estrogen and progesterone are noted within the brain, heightening the sense of forgetfulness that comes with body-stress and lack of sleep.

"I'm not pregnant," she said.

She shook herself and sat up in bed, looking around. The bedroom had two windows, plenty of natural light, and it was like she'd never seen it before. The past few weeks, everything had seemed so goddamned gray.

Her hands cradled her still-flat stomach, fingers splayed.

"*Goddammit!*" She launched from the bed, nearly falling when the sheets tangled around her ankles. She kicked and spat at them until she was free, then stood beside the bed, heart thrumming.

She swallowed. "This," she said, then closed her mouth.

Deep breath. "This is getting ridiculous."

For a moment, her face crumpled like paper, her eyes hot stones in their sockets. She ground her teeth together and her face smoothed.

Her husband was gone for the day. He had told her where—she *knew* this—but couldn't remember and, further, couldn't even remember the fucking conversation where it had been mentioned. She couldn't remember the last time her and Danny had exchanged just a few words. More than a month since the

(miscarriage)

and she still had goddamned pregnancy-brain.

Her fists unclenched, moved to grip her belly and she forced them back to her sides.

"I can't do this, anymore."

Her eyes fell on the space where the basinet, a hand-me-down from Danny's sister, had sat for those few weeks. They had accumulated slowly, tentatively as the calendar moved from first trimester to second. It wasn't until afterwards that they—*Carrie*, really—had realized how much shit they'd gotten.

The basinet here. The crib there. The boxes of clothes and bedding. The laundry basket of toys probably still in the back of Danny's Jeep. Dishware. Books.

So far, the basinet had been the only thing removed. By her; Danny, if he was in the house, refused to leave the guest bedroom and the ultrasound recording.

Burning in her chest and she grimaced. "Goddammit. *I* carried her. *I* felt her going. That was *my* blood."

Heat gathered in her face again and she pressed her fists into her eyes. She counted Mississippis, ragged breath after ragged breath, until she cooled.

"Okay." She moved her hands to the line no longer on her stomach and looked at the spot where the basinet had been. "Okay."

Carrie collapsed onto the single mattress in the guest bedroom and laid there until her heart stopping whamming her breastbone quite so hard. Her head throbbed, a cloud of heat surrounding the crown. She hadn't moved this much since before the pregnancy.

The crib was gone, shoved into the back of her Subaru along with all the boxes and containers. She'd hauled the pieces to the single bed up from the basement and now they leaned where the crib had. Danny still had baby things in the back of his Jeep, she presumed, but she could get those out when he came home tonight.

She shoved herself off the mattress, tottered, and went to the little desk, where a glass of water sweated into the scattered paper crap and fiberboard. She drank half the glass at a glut, and when she said *"Ahhhh"*, it wasn't an affectation.

She set the glass down, then froze, her hand still holding the glass.

"What?"

She moved her hand, knocking the glass over onto the carpet and not even noticing, and brushed aside random papers. A thin, clear CD case lay beneath.

"What?"

She fell into the chair; if it hadn't been there, she would've fallen onto the ground. Her legs were a million miles away.

She picked up the case with shaking hands. MY BABY'S DVD, the green DVD label read. Beneath, in smaller print, "This DVD is provided to you and your family as a personal record of an important family experience."

Her other hand covered her mouth, although there were no words, no sounds. Her chest was a solid thing, incapable of beating blood or taking air.

"I threw this away," she said through her fingers.

It'd been in her purse for weeks; she'd actually forgotten about it. Another attack of pregnancy-brain. The sonogram appointment had been at eight in the morning and as the ultrasound tech had handed her the DVD, Carrie, as she came down from the rush of watching the fetus

(evelyn)

move and its

(her)

heart beat and counting its

(her)

toes and organs, had been craving more coffee and-or a nap. After seeing the picture in real time, the DVD had been an afterthought.

During the fourteenth week, very fine hair called lanugo covers the baby's head. The baby's bones begin to firm. The liver and pancreas begin secreting.

When Carrie had found the DVD at the bottom of her purse during what would've been the eighteenth week, she'd thrown it away, buried it in the kitchen garbage before she could stop and think. She hadn't even told Danny.

Danny.

He must've seen it in the trash.

She gripped the case until a silver crack shot across the front. "Danny." It came out as a hiss.

She dropped the case back onto the desk and, when the inevitable urge to put the DVD into the computer surfaced, she swept the entire desktop off to the side and into the garbage can.

(I carried her. I felt her going. That was my *blood.)*

Her eyes burned, her face crumpling like tissue paper, and she turned her gaze to the computer and its geometric screen-saver.

She swatted the mouse and, of course, the download folder was open with only one file in it.

"Ultrasound—Week 8."

The file was exactly forty-five seconds long.

Eyes wet, she right-clicked on the icon and selected DELETE. Are you sure, the computer asked.

She clicked Yes only because she couldn't punch a hole through the screen itself.

Her husband was a bastard, but now the download folder was empty.

She hugged her stomach, which was also and of course empty, as she had when the first whamming cramps had come during the seventeenth week. No cramps now, though. Nothing.

She rested her head against the edge of the desk and squeezed her wet and burning eyes closed.

"What?" Danny said, louder than she'd heard him speak in weeks.

She roused herself, rolling over on her bed. She had no memory of coming in here. The windows were dark. Danny's nightstand clock read seven-thirty.

"What?" Danny said again. He was in the other room. The hardwood creaked heavily under his feet.

She sat up, shook the cotton from her brain, and stood. The room swayed around her and she had to throw a hand to the wall to steady herself. She made her way to the guest bedroom, fingers trailing the wall, her movements stiff, her muscles.

She found Danny sprawled in the little chair, almost falling off it, and staring at the empty download folder on the computer. His shoulders shook. Behind him, the single bed was reassembled and remade, complete with the pillow and comforter she'd pulled from the closet.

He turned to her and his eyes were red and wet and irritated, his face slack.

The fetus doesn't begin to open and close its eyes until the thirty-second week.

They stared at each other, and the memories rebuilt themselves in Carrie's head.

Danny's mouth worked. "You deleted it."

There were many words that could be said, but what came out was, "And I threw away the DVD of the sonogram. Again."

He blinked at her. "What?"

Her muscles tightened. It wasn't due to overwork. "I can't do this alone, Dan."

He gaped at her and her fist wanted to go through that expression the way it had wanted to go through the computer screen. "What?"

"*You're not the only one who lost!*" she yelled and the wet, shrill sound of her voice just made her stiffer. "You're not the only one who can't sleep! Can't eat! Can't fucking *focus*! I *carried* her! Do you *get* that? *Do* you?"

He flinched at the last word and it took all her will to tamp down the scream that wanted to explode.

"I *felt* her, Dan. *I* felt her go, and *I* felt the *pain* of her going. *Me*. *Not* you. You've done *nothing* but listen to that . . . that . . . that fucking *track* for weeks on end!" She squeezed her eyes closed, willing the tears back. "*We both lost something and I'm the only one paying for it!*"

She opened her eyes again and Danny's face had lost its slackness, was tightening and darkening. A brief, bitter surge of animal triumph swept her like heat rush. *Now* he felt something other than his dopey fucking stupid sadness. *Good*.

She lowered her voice. "Where were you? Where were *you*? In here, wishing things hadn't turned out the way they had? *Well, so do I!* But I don't have the luxury of pining the fuck away like *you* do! I've had to carry this whole goddamn thing! You listen to that track, you kept that fucking DVD when you *knew* it was in the garbage for a reason, and have you once—have you *once*—come to me? Talked to me? *Been* with *me*? You skulk around here in your own bullshit, *completely* forgetting *I'm the one who felt our fucking child die!*"

His face was completely dark, his eyes hard. "Wait a fucking minute—"

"No." She sliced the air in front of her with the side of her hand. "No, I've been waiting long enough, thanks." She'd started hunching over and she made herself straighten. "You wanna be alone, then *be* alone. What's the difference *now*, right?"

She turned away, but not before she saw the hardness wink out of Danny's eyes, and there was a true moment of emotional divide in her head. She felt that heat-rush of going-for-the-kill triumph, bitter and green and ripe . . . but she felt her heart open at the same time.

"We *are* alone," she said and went back to the bedroom, slamming the door hard enough to rattle the nightstand lamps.

She jumped onto the bed and screamed into her pillow until her throat, red and raw and shredded, gave out on her.

Later, on the line between awake and dreaming, she heard Danny, still in the guest bedroom, say in a thick voice, "I *have* been wishing. Wishing we were whole and fine and a family. Wishing that we weren't alone. That's all I *ever* wanted."

She crossed the line into sleep and didn't know if she'd imagined the episode or not.

Week 32, Third Trimester

An extra picture-frame sat on her desk.

She stopped in her office doorway, holding a box of red pens. She had Pandora up on her computer—"These Days" by Foo Fighters played—and it was the only sound in the long, low building. Her office was the only source of light besides the red EXIT signs at either end of the main hall. The next day's issue of the *Register-Mail* had been put to bed, sent to the printers. Not even cleaning people remained.

And there was an extra picture-frame on her desk—turned away from her, of course, so that the photo would be visible when she sat down. She'd worked for the newspaper for six years, had been in this office for four, and there had always been two photos on her desk—one of her and Danny on their honeymoon, in New York; the other showing Danny teaching at Knox College. She'd looked at those photos so often she no longer saw them; they'd assimilated into the general *look* of her desk.

And now there was a third frame. An *extra* frame. A wasn't-there-when-shc-got-up-to-go-to-the-supply-closet frame.

"Hello?" she called, her eyes locked on the frame, and then winced. What a dumb fucking horror movie move.

But she heard a *creak*, weight on the floor, and adrenaline dumped into her system by the gallons, and the spit in her mouth turned acidic, and she stiffened, and the creak came again, and she realized—Jesus fucking Christ—it was herself making the floor creak. She couldn't stand still.

Carrie took a breath, whistled it out, took another. But she didn't move from the doorway. The sweat of her palms softened the cardboard box.

She should be home right now. Danny would be home. She should be home and Danny should be home and they should be talking. She shouldn't be here, copy-editing every article the copy-editors had left behind because she couldn't bear to *go* home, couldn't bear to be in the quiet house, couldn't bear to be surrounded by the ghost heartbeats of what wasn't to come.

She shouldn't be standing in the doorway, staring at the back of the picture-frame that shouldn't be on her desk.

"Oh, fuck this," she said and walked in. The air seemed thicker, less yielding, as if trying to push her out.

She walked around the desk, slamming the red pens down, and looked at the picture in the suddenly-new frame.

And froze again.

"Oh, fuck this," she repeated, and her voice was a sigh.

It was a sonogram photo, showing the fetus in a sliver-moon pose.

During the thirty-second week, the fetus loses the lanugo and begins to develop real hair. It blinks, practices breathing. With the right assistance, the fetus would survive premature birth.

The *thump-thump* of a heartbeat came to her; not hers, but the memory of that damned forty-five-second recording.

She reached for the photo, then pulled her hand back, fingers curling in, as if it might burn her. She tried again, and this time touched it. It did not disappear in smoke, or crumble, or become intangible. She felt glass. Plastic.

She picked it up, ran her fingertips over it. The way the picture was set, the border cut off the date at the top of the photo. This could be some anonymous photo, something printed from a Google Image Search put here to fuck with her,

(by who? when?)

but it wasn't. This was hers.

This was what she carried. Evelyn.

The *thump-thump* increased in sound, until it twinned with her own pulse.

Carrie's vision blurred and she blinked. "Oh, fuck," she breathed and her voice was wet.

Her stomach clenched suddenly, viciously. She dropped the frame onto the desk and dashed back into the hall, hand covering her mouth as her throat filled, barely making it to the restroom in time before her lunch jumped up and out. Her throat worked, her stomach pushed, and her face burned.

(like morning sickness all over again)

That earned another clench and she vomited again. Finally, she flushed, then laid her head on the seat, eyes closed against the restroom fluorescents, breathing heavily through her mouth.

(who would do this? when?)

Her mind instantly said, *Danny,* but it wouldn't hold. They hadn't spoken more than one or two words since the fight, passing each other like wary tomcats. But did it really seem like Danny? Danny, moping around? Danny, lost in his own pain? Danny, who had absolutely collapsed when she'd laid into him?

(you wanna be alone then be alone)

"Shit," she whispered.

(we are *alone)*

She tightened her closed eyes, but tears escaped, anyway. "Shit, shit, shit."

She grabbed a wad of toilet paper, wiped her mouth, then flushed again. She staggered to her feet, using the sides of the stall for support, and walked out, pausing briefly to check the mirror. She used minimal makeup, but she looked like a raccoon, anyway.

After the brightness of the restroom, the hallway was pitch-black. She shuffled back to her office doorway.

And, upon returning, the picture frame was gone.

"The fuck?" she said and rushed to the desk, looked under it, moved around papers. She looked at where the frame had been sitting and only now noticed that, when the picture had appeared, the other two photos, as well as her little paperclip cup, had been arranged to accommodate it. Picking up the frame had left a hole in the arrangement.

Now the set-up was as it had been before.

The third picture had never been there.

She sat down and looked at her hands. She *remembered* the feel of the glass, of the plastic backing.

It took a moment to notice that the *thump-thump* of the heartbeat was gone, as well.

"The fuck? The fuck *is* this?"

Hallucination popped immediately into her head, as well as *nervous breakdown*. That got her moving, switching her to automatic before any thoughts could really unspool, turning off her computer without shutting it down—killing the Rolling Stones in the middle of "19th Nervous Breakdown", *oh* how *apropos*—grabbing her bag, and getting the hell out of there.

Week 35, Third Trimester—Day 1

She came home to an empty house and Dutch Master daffodils on the kitchen table.

She stopped in the kitchen archway, the day's mail still in her hand. The flowers had been set in the center, arranged in a clear vase, tied with a fat pink ribbon. A folded cardboard note hung from the ribbon.

She and Danny still weren't speaking. Moreover, the things that they should be saying were piling up, filling the house more quickly than baby detritus had. Soon it would push one of them out, although Carrie hadn't gotten that far in her thinking, mainly because she couldn't bear to.

(you wanna be alone then be *alone)*

She touched one of the daffodils. It was cool against her fingertips, slightly moist.

When would Danny have done this? He left before she did. He wouldn't have allowed some random florist into their house.

She pulled a flower out, smelled it. Outside, winter was only grudgingly giving way to spring, but the wet-earth smell of the daffodil made it like spring had already arrived.

"Danny," she said and it didn't come out as a hiss.

She set the flower back in the vase, then opened the note.

Only a month away!,

it read in Danny's scratchy handwriting.

And everything in Carrie turned down. The memory of the recording—*thump-thump-shush-thump-thump*—filled her head, pushed other thoughts out. Her eyes traced the words again and

(only)

couldn't quite
(a month)
believe what they amounted to.
(away!)

"What in the holy *fuck*?" she said, loud in the empty kitchen, trying to overpower the sound of the ghost heartbeat, and dropped the note, jarring the vase with the back of her hand so that some water sloshed out the side. She backed away, the muscles of her face flexing between confusion and rage.

She didn't need to put together what was a month away.

"What," she said and couldn't immediately find more air. "What the *fuck* . . . ?"

She fumbled for her smartphone, then went into the hall. She pulled Danny's cell from her Recent Calls list—the back of her mind noting how far down the list it was—and hit SEND.

It rang into his voicemail: "Hi, this is Dan Finney. Sorry I missed you; leave a message and I'll try to correct that."

She stabbed the END button, then thumbed through contacts for his office line. The air in the house grew moist, as if the daffodils had brought the greenhouse with it. She slammed open the front door and onto the front porch.

Danny picked up on the third ring. "Professor Fin—"

"What the fuck is wrong with you?"

"Carrie? *Carrie*? What—"

"*What the fuck is wrong with you*? You think this is *funny*? That I would *laugh*? Are you out of your fucking *mind*?"

Danny didn't answer for a long time. Carrie breathed through her clenched teeth.

"I . . . " The resignation in his voice was the cold clear admission of guilt she needed. She opened her mouth, and then Danny said, "I have no idea what you're talking about, Carrie."

She straightened. "What?"

"I said, I have no idea what you're talking about, Carrie."

She screwed the phone hard into her ear, tried to pick up the telltale clues in his voice. She'd known Danny for almost two decades, and he lied very rarely, but she was a good journalist.

"You *didn't* leave flowers on our kitchen table." It should've been a question, but her voice refused to leave a low rumble. "And you *didn't* leave a note telling me we were only a month away."

A sigh from his end. "Why the hell would I do that?"

"*Because I just saw them on the goddamn kitchen table*! Fresh! Still cool! *Still fucking wet!* You're telling me *you* didn't put them there?"

Another sigh. She could've cheerfully reached through the screen and squeezed his neck until her fingers tore into his throat.

"Carrie," he said, then stopped for a beat. "Carrie, I haven't been home all day. You *know* this is my late day. Three classes and two advisor times? Plus mentoring? My schedule's been the same for five years, hon."

She blinked. The phone casing creaked a little more. "Then. What. Did. I. See. *Danny*."

He said nothing. It was answer enough.

"*Goddammit*!" She yanked the screen door open and stomped back into the house. "Stop fucking around, Danny. It's *your* handwriting on the goddam note and—"

She entered the kitchen and, for the first time consciously, the there-then-gone frame at work popped into her head.

The daffodils were gone. No water spillage on the table from when she'd jostled the vase. Just the mail she'd dropped.

"And? And what, Carrie? It is *physically* impossible for me to have done what you said. Shall I produce witnesses? Security video?" A pause. "Or is it *you* who's fucking around?" His voice dropped. "*Are* you? Because, don't. Let's not do this like this, Carrie. Not like this. You and I—"

"Shut up, Danny." Her voice was a whisper. Her eyes were locked on where the daffodils weren't.

"What? I couldn't hear—"

"Come home," she said, louder this time. "Come home right now."

"I'm gone," he said, and the line was dead.

She let her arm fall, then slumped against the archway, staring.

When *hallucination* and *nervous breakdown* entered her head this time, she didn't shake them off.

And the sound of the heartbeat was gone again.

They sat at opposite sides of the kitchen table, the center open and bare and dry—of course—between them. Outside the window, night had fallen.

"You need to talk to someone," Danny said.

Carrie rubbed her face with her hands. "That's ironic."

"I'm serious." He ducked his head so he could meet her eyes. "I don't like any of this."

"And I'm having the time of my life?" She closed her eyes, took a breath. "I'm sorry. I feel like I'm losing my mind." She dropped a hand to the spot where the vase had been. "I *held* that note, Dan. I *held* that frame. I could *feel* them. There was water right *here*—"

"But there wasn't," Danny reached out and took her hand, held on when her knee-jerk reaction was to pull away. "I have *not* been helpful. Neither of us have been. The past months have been the worst in my life, and yours." He squeezed her hand. "But, y'know, maybe this is good. The right scare to get us back on track."

She pulled away, slumped in her chair. "I don't know. Who would I even speak to about this?"

Danny aped her movements, then crossed his arms. "I can speak to some people; frame it as research for a paper, or something. Some won't buy that, but enough will."

"It's just . . . " She shook her head. "They were right *there*, y'know? The flowers, the frame . . . " She stopped, looked at Danny. "The DVD?"

He blinked at her. "The DVD?"

"'Baby's First DVD'. Remember?"

Slowly, his eyes lightened. "Holy shit, I *do*. We got it after the sonogram appointment . . . " He trailed off, forehead scrunching. "Was that what you were talking about . . . " He gestured vaguely. " . . . before?"

"You didn't pull it out of the trash?"

"I didn't even remember it until just now. Too much had happened." His face darkened. "You threw it away?"

"When I first found it in my purse, after the miscarriage. Then I found it under papers on the desk." She let out a deep breath. "What the fuck, Danny." She studied him. "And nothing's off with you?"

"Beyond cataclysmic depression?" He shook his head. "Nothing like what you've experienced." Danny leaned forward. "Listen, I'm going to talk to some people. Get some good names. I'll take care of it, okay?"

She nodded. "Okay, Danny. Okay."

This time, when he took her hand, she didn't pull away.

Week 35, Third Trimester—Day 3

Carrie's phone dinged with a text as she came out of the shower.

Two weeks, Danny wrote. *Afternoon appt. Dr Morley. Ok?*

During the thirty-seventh week, the fetus is considered "full-term" and will begin to turn, dropping lower in the womb in preparation of birth. Body fat has increased to the point that the movements are more noticeable because the space is more confining. All the organs are ready to function on their own.

Her fingers hesitated over the screen keyboard. It *was* okay, but . . .

The DVD.

The photo.

The flowers.

She'd *held* those things. *Studied* them. Heard the heartbeat of the daughter that never would be while they were in her hands.

(but they weren't there)

Go for it, she typed. *Thank you. Love you.*

The reply was immediate: *Love you too.*

The sudden feeling of relief was as real as the things she'd imagined holding.

"We'll get through this," she muttered, setting the phone down and resuming drying. "We're not alone."

Later, she passed the guest bedroom on the way to the stairs and, for just an instant out of the corner of her eye, saw the crib instead of the single bed, all set up.

Her head whipped around.

Just the guest bedroom. Bed, small dresser, fiberboard desk and computer.

She left the doorway slowly, as if turning away would make the crib appear.

"This is so stupid," she said, and continued on towards the stairs.

Week 36, Third Trimester—Day 6

Simon, the news editor, slouched against the receptionist's desk, talking over the partition while Julia sorted through the overnight e-mails. He looked up when Carrie came in. "What are you doing here? You pop already?"

Carrie stopped in the doorway, the pneumatic arm bringing the door back to bump her in the ass, sloshing coffee onto her wrist. She didn't immediately feel the burn. "What?"

Now both Julia and Simon were looking at her. "It can't be *that* boring at home." His eyes dropped to her stomach. "I mean, you *did* pop, right? Last I saw you were as big as goddamn *house*." Julia reached up and smacked his arm. "Why didn't you alert us? We would've sent something."

Something in her head ground to a halt. "What?"

Julia stood up behind the desk and Simon straightened. Their gaze was sharper, their mouths mutually turning down into *moue*s of concern. "Are you all right?" Julia asked, coming around.

The reception area of the *Register-Mail* was small, and Julia would be next to her in an instant.

(don't touch me don't touch me don't touch me)

As if thinking it would help, the nerves on her wrist became aware of the fact that scalding Starbucks coated it. She jerked, splashing more coffee from the lid's opening.

But it was enough to get Julia to stop, although her and Simon's *moue*s were deeper now.

(get me outta here get me outta here get me)

"Excuse me," she said, heading directly to the hall. She didn't run, but it was close.

Although the ladies restroom was enough for two people, she bolted the door, then threw her Starbucks cup into the sink, where the lid came off and it splashed all over. She went to the first stall and sat down on the toilet.

She held up her hands and watched them shake. Her heart thwacked, making her breath shallow.

"This is not happening. This is *not* happening."

She held her head in her hands because she couldn't stand to watch them shake any longer. She focused on breathing. She focused on the darkness behind her lids.

(simon and julia are not a frame a flower a DVD)

(then what are they?)

And the soundtrack to it all was the damned memory of Evelyn's heartbeat, forty-five seconds long, endlessly repeating.

She squeezed her eyes closed tighter, until neon lights burst behind the lids.

During the thirty-sixth week, the vernix—the soft proto-skin that allows real skin to develop—is thicker.

Her skin didn't feel very thick at all.

(julia's going to come knocking i looked like a psychopath out there)

She tensed, waiting, counting the seconds until the inevitable knock-and-knob-shake occurred.

It didn't.

(we are alone)

After a while, it felt vaguely absurd to be in here. The sound of the heartbeat faded, like losing a radio signal. Slowly, she stood, as if *that* would start Julia's inevitable knocking.

It didn't.

She picked up her shoulder bag and moved to the door. Unlocked it.

The hallway was empty. Open offices up and down let out a steady incomprehensible stream of conversations and keyboard clickings and printer hummings.

She moved down the hall, waiting for someone to jump out and ask if she was all right. No one did, of course.

Simon and Julia were still in the reception area, in the same positions they'd been when Carrie had entered the building.

Simon looked up. "Hey! When did you get in?" Julia glanced up from her computer screen, offered a quick smile.

Carrie's mouth was shot full of Novocaine. "Um . . . "

Simon straightened and, goddamn, the *moue* was back. "You okay? You look a little flushed." This time Julia looked up for a little longer and, yes, she had a *moue*, too.

(you guys could be fucking twins)

She put her hands to her stomach, which felt like the undulating waves of a choppy sea. "Yeah, no, I think I'm gonna work from home. Stomach bug's giving me some issues."

Simon winced at the word *stomach*

(get me the hell outta here)

but recovered quickly with a full-on frown. "Yeah, okay. You do that. You look like hell, kiddo."

Carrie ran out, thinking, *This isn't an object this isn't an object those were people those were* people.

She didn't tell Danny what happened.

Week 37, Third Trimester—Day 1

Hon, Danny said. *Honey. She's kicking the hell outta my back.*

What? she said, sounding like she did when she was more than halfway asleep, although her lips weren't moving.

(this is a dream)

The voices weren't in her head.

The creak of bedsprings as Danny turned over. A phantom touch against her stomach and the *weight* there. She remembered that weight. She remembered it well.

The little bug's an insomniac, he said.

Don't remind me, she replied. *I was just about to drop off.*

Only a few more weeks, he said. *Just shine it on a little longer.*

Then we both *won't be able to sleep?*

The phantom touch left and Danny chuckled. It sounded like windchimes.

Drowsing, she put her own hands to her stomach and it was full and heavy and good. She felt, faintly, the tiny heartbeat. She felt Evelyn move, adjusting for a better position. She'd gained weight all around during the second trimester, but it had moved to the kiddo during the end and now—

—Carrie shot up in bed, hands on her smooth stomach, Evelyn's heartbeat still in her head, but now with the *sssssh-pop* of the ultrasound sensor moving, a reminder that it was just a memory.

(not live, just Memorex)

She bit her lip to stifle the scream.

Danny turned over slowly in bed, blearily looking at her. "Hon? You okay?"

Carrie ignored him. The room didn't have enough air and all she could do was pant. Morning was beginning to break through the window, turning their bedroom into shades of gray.

Danny sat up, put a hand on her arm. "Carrie? What is it?"

She drew her knees up under the sheet and rested her forehead, still holding her stomach. She closed her eyes.

And I laid back down, feeling Evelyn get comfortable, and I was exhausted and I knew I wasn't going to sleep deeply, but that was okay because Evelyn was there and safe and sound—

"Bad dream," she said and her voice was thick. "A bad dream."

Week 37, 3rd Trimester—Day 2

Carrie passed by the guest bedroom and the crib was back.

She stopped, knowing it was a hallucination, knowing that all this would be gone by tomorrow night after talking with Dr. Morley, but knowing she couldn't *not* turn and look.

And it was still there when she did.

Her shoulder bag dropped to the floor with a bang she didn't hear. It was early afternoon. Staff meeting day, and she had no overnight assignments. Danny was still at work.

"Holy shit," she said, and approached the door.

The gender-neutral green paint seemed more vibrant, making the white crib gleam. Canvas squares of cartoon animals—lion, giraffe—were nailed, step-like, to the wall. In the corner was the changing table, with bags and bags of boxes and diapers spread out like the givings of some bizarre Christmas tree.

(the gifts from the shower Danny still hasn't put away)

She closed her eyes. There hadn't been a shower. There wasn't any of this.

But the hope was there, oh yes. Beneath the confusion and the sorrow and the rage, but hope was there. Hope that *this* life was the hallucination, a stress-induced bad dream as she neared the end of her pregnancy.

(i have been wishing . . . that's all i ever wanted)

Wasn't that what Danny had said?

Why couldn't it be true for her?

"But it isn't," she said and popped her eyes open, like a kid playing red-light-green-light.

And Evelyn's room was still set up. Carrie's mouth dropped open.

(don't believe this don't believe this the frame dvd flowers felt real too)

But that voice sounded a million miles away.

She felt Evelyn's heartbeat within the tremors of her own skin.

Carrie reached the doorway, hand on the frame, and the room immediately shimmered, like an old movie seguing into a flashback, and she reached into the room, as if she could grab the air itself and make it stop, and that only made the change faster, until she was just reaching through the doorway of the guest bedroom, with nice but definitely-not-baby green walls and the Danny-version of a made single bed.

Carrie's arm dropped and she just looked for a moment.

(look upon my works ye mighty and despair who said that danny would know)

She couldn't even find the energy to cry, although her eyes felt sandy and red. She hung her head and started to turn away when a flicker of movement caught the corner of her eye. She raised her head, feeling stupid for the upsurge of hope in her gut, and saw it was just the computer's geometric screensaver.

She started to turn away again when it occurred to her that the computer had been *off* the last she saw. Since she'd deleted the audio file, Danny was rarely on the desktop, and she had her own laptop plugged into the wifi. She used the desktop for banking. Rarely.

Brow furrowed, she walked into the guest bedroom—the first step hesitant because Evelyn's room might come back and she called herself stupid for the thought. She batted the mouse and the triangles disappeared, revealing the download folder, which had four files in it.

"The hell?" she whispered, sitting down and wheeling the chair close.

She recognized the top file immediately: "Ultrasound—Week 8".

Evelyn's heartbeat.

Carrie's breath caught in her throat, but only long enough to see the other file names.

The next was another mp4 file, with a date falling during the nineteenth week. The size was larger than the first.

The next was an mpeg file, entitled "Sonogram 1—Week 16".

The final file, also an mpeg: "Evie's face!".

It had been saved last week.

Carrie forced herself to breathe, but the air was too thick, impossible to take in. Her eyes fell to the scattered papers on the desktop, and saw a note in Danny's handwriting: *Can play the audio with the second sonogram—show Carrie.*

She squeezed her eyes, counted to ten.

(not there not there this isn't happening and tomorrow i'll be able to stop it oh god please let me stop it)

She opened her eyes, cautiously this time. The files were still there.

Her hand reached for the mouse, hesitated, then rested lightly. She paused the cursor over the top one.

(might not be the same it won't be the same)

(oh please)

She clicked on it and Windows Media Player opened and there was Evelyn's heartbeat, in all of its ghost-like glory. The steady *thump-thump*, the *sssshhh-POP* as the sensor had moved and the recording had reached its end.

"Oh shit."

(i just deleted it i never emptied out the recycling bin danny could've)

(???BUT WHAT ABOUT THE OTHERS???)

She X'ed out of the Player and moved to the second file. Clicked it.

Media Player again, another heartbeat, but it sounded . . . stronger. More regular. Like something that's had a chance to get some practice in and really had the whole thing down.

Evelyn's heartbeat. *More* of her heartbeat.

(none of this is real none real NONE REAL)

(why couldn't it?)

But that was a thought Carrie didn't want to pursue, not out of an avoidance towards hope—hope that this *was* the hallucination, that she really *was* still pregnant—but out of the possibility, the *probability*, that she was tilting further and further into mental places no one, not even the lauded but-still-unknown Dr. Morley, could pull her from.

She X'ed out of the second file and opened the third file: "Sonogram—Week 16".

The Media Player dutifully opened once more, but instead of the music-note icon, the screen was black with details sketched in with strikes of white. Like one of those Magic Eye pictures, it took a moment for the vision to come together, but when it did, the bean-shaped outline of a fetus was clear.

Evelyn.

The file was silent, but the fetus moved, adjusting its proto-legs, stretching its forearms.

Carrie stretched a hand towards the screen, laid her fingertips against the fetus's head.

During the sixteenth week, the fetus will begin to move and stretch. It has transparent skin, which you wouldn't notice on a sonogram, anyway.

This was the video from the DVD. The video Carrie had thrown out. Twice.

"I'm sorry," she told the screen. Tears spilled down her cheeks. "I'm sorry."

The video was a hair under three minutes, but it went by quickly, fading to black before looping back to start.

She watched it twice more before X-ing out of the Player.

One more file—"Evie's face!"—recorded one week ago.

During the thirty-sixth week, the fetus has been breathing for a month. It's bigger, close to what its birthweight will be. The womb is cramped with its fullness.

Carrie hesitated again.

(last chance to get out of this madness)

"Oh, it's too late for *that*," she said, her voice breaking, and clicked open the last file.

The final file was shorter, only a moment, but recorded as a 4D ultrasound, which allowed an almost-three-dimensional image of Evelyn's face.

Carrie stopped breathing.

The child's eyes were closed, but one could see the way she practiced breathing, mouth slightly open, nostrils

(she got danny's nose of course she did)

(SHE'S GONE STOP THIS STOP THIS RIGHT NOW)

flaring. The curve of her forehead. The roundness of her cheeks. The cleft in her chin—Danny's. The stem of her neck.

Carrie shook, hugged herself, shook some more. Her stomach had never been more empty.

(this was mine this was mine this was mine)

(but it's GONE it's GONE and all you're doing is TORTURING)

(SHE WAS SUPPOSED TO BE MY DAUGHTER)

Carrie shoved away from the desk. The computer tower beneath the desktop came into view, the white glowing power button shining, and she lunged for it, stabbing it over and over until her finger bent back painfully. The computer cut out.

She slouched on the floor, shivering, rubbing her shoulders as if cold. All thoughts, even the contradictory voices, had ceased. But Evelyn's heartbeat was still *thump-thump*ing away in there, oh yes.

Finally, she reached out and turned the computer on.

"You'll be gone now," she said. "Everything will be back to whatever the fuck passes for normal now."

The screen fuzzed on, went through its logo-rific start up, then opened to the desktop screen. Reaching up, Carrie moved the mouse to the file folder icon on the Systray and clicked it open, then—pausing for the briefest of moments—clicked on the Download folder.

There were four files inside.

Carrie fell back against the side of the bed, staring up at the screen.

(none of this is real none of this is real why is it here?)

(that's all i ever wanted)

"We are *alone,*" she said to the download folder. She wiped her nose with the side of her hand, felt the wetness of tears on her cheek. In her head, Evelyn's recorded heartbeat played on and on. "*Alone.*"

"You ready for tomorrow, hon?" Danny asked, pulling back the blankets on his side of the bed.

Carrie had been staring at the same page of the Gillian Flynn novel. She blinked. "What? Yeah, I think so."

Danny paused as he climbed in. "You okay?"

She offered the best possible smile she could, which wasn't much. "As okay as the circumstances are allowing."

He slid into bed, pulled the covers to his waist. "You see anything else?"

She looked away, turning down the page of the paperback and closing it. "No. You ready for bed?"

"Christ, yes." Danny slid farther under the covers and clicked off his lamp.

Carrie aped him and, in the dark, felt his hand on her shoulder, light and warm

(like touching my full stomach)

against her skin.

She closed her eyes, and listened to Evelyn's heartbeat, counting Mississippis.

Week 37, Third Trimester—Day 3

Evelyn's heart continued to beat as Carrie crossed the parking lot to the Bennell Building. There was no *shhh-POP* now. The ghost of her child was close and getting closer.

Her head throbbed with the sound, how it muffled the clack of her low heels across the asphalt, stunted the glare of the sun. The traffic of Galesburg Boulevard was a distant hum. Even the recognition that the building reminded Carrie of the Dakota building in New York was a faded, faraway thing.

It followed her through the lobby, to the bank of elevators on the right. It grew louder, blocking out the sound of the lobby clock as it tolled the hour—eleven o'clock. Carrie couldn't even hear the Muzak piped in from the elevator speakers.

The elevator opened up onto a gallery with a glass railing, overlooking the lobby three storeys below. Carrie took a step out of the elevator—

—and stomped her foot in the footwell of Danny's Jeep.

Carrie jerked, head spinning around. She sat in the passenger seat of Danny's old Jeep Wrangler, parked in its spot behind the Old Main Building at Knox College.

She heard birds call outside the crossover. She smelled the remnants of Danny's morning coffee.

"What?" she asked and had a moment to notice that she couldn't hear Evelyn's heartbeat anymore when the *thud* hit her lower stomach, reverberating through the rest of her nerve-endings. She squawked and coughed, hands going to her stomach, when the second *thud* hit her, pushing at her crotch, sending another crackling wave of pain through her body.

She screamed, doubling over and hugging her stomach, head resting on the dash.

(not like this the cramps weren't like this)

Time them! she yelled, but her mouth wasn't moving. *Goddammit, Danny, I keep losing track! Jesus, this hurts!*

And then, insanely, she heard Danny's high-strung laugh. *Holy shit, she's not waiting any longer! Holy shit! Holy* shit*!*

*Stop laughing and fucking COU—*And then another *thud* slammed into her vagina. Carrie screamed again, eyes squeezed closed, hugging her flat stomach, but her *fingers* felt nothing flat, felt only the fullness of pregnancy and Evelyn was coming—early, yes, but Evelyn was finally *coming—*

Danny's voice, still half-laughing, *We're gonna make it, we're gonna make it, you two hold on because we're gonna* make it—

Thud and it was the worst yet and Carrie screamed as the pain rocketed through her, frying her nerves, making her limbs seem distant—

Someone knocked on the glass.

And there was no pain. Not even a tingle. Not a hint.

Carrie opened her eyes and stared down at her shoes, spread to each side of the footwell. She felt her silk blouse and her flat—*flat*—stomach. Her muscles quivered, confused and jerky with ghost-adrenaline.

And then Danny's voice, muffled by the glass, "Jesus Christ, Carrie, what—"

And she heard the lock disengage and the passenger door was opened and Danny's hands encircled her, pulled at her, and Carrie resisted for the briefest of instants—

(i was in labor*)*

—before going limp in his arms.

Danny's voice, over and over, "Carrie, Carrie, Jesus, Carrie—"

He pulled her out of the car, and she put a foot on the runner to keep from spilling the two of them onto the asphalt. She got her arms free and grabbed at the side of the Jeep's doorframe.

"I got it," she said and her voice was a croak. "I got it."

Danny's hands left her reluctantly and she stepped out of the car, watching her feet. She heard a rustle of people around her.

(well this is fucking great)

"What the hell, hon?" Danny asked.

She couldn't stand there, watching her feet like a kid in trouble, but it was harder to raise her head than she would've thought.

Danny stood a few feet away, hands ready to catch her. He was dressed for class, but his blazer was gone, his tie askew around his neck.

And, yes, people surrounded Danny's Jeep—a dozen or so students, with a couple of faculty members Carrie remembered from Christmas parties thrown in.

(jesus christ)

She pulled her phone from her pants pocket and didn't know whether to be surprised or not to see it was just now eleven-oh-two.

"One minute in the elevator," she muttered, "the next here."

"*What*?" Danny asked.

She raised her head and looked only at him. The crowd of people rustled again.

"Take me home, Danny. Actually, take me back to my car."

He blinked at her.

"It's still in the parking lot at the Bennell Building," she said.

Danny spluttered, and a faculty member said, "Go ahead, Dan. I'll post your classes." This earned a third rustle from the people.

(christ they're like birds)

Danny and Carrie stared at each other, his gaze wide and uncomprehending and frantic, hers tired and resigned.

And then she turned and climbed back into the Jeep, shutting the door.

Danny stood there for a moment, looking completely unplugged, then walked around the Jeep. As he got into the Jeep, Carrie realized she could hear Evelyn's heartbeat again, but it sounded softer than before.

(that's because she's being born)

(somewhere else, anyway)

Carrie leaned her against the passenger window and, with the crowd of people still watching as Danny fired up the Jeep's engine, closed her eyes.

Danny matched her step-for-step up the stairs, arms bent, as if he might grab her.

She led him to the guest bedroom and the air shimmered, like a ripple across pond water, showing Evelyn's room—crib, changing table, animal prints. The presents from the shower had been put away. She didn't stop, but she sensed Danny hang back for the briefest of instants, enough that he wasn't walking on the backs of her shoes.

(you DO see this)

(see i'm not crazy)

She sat down in front of their desktop and nudged the mouse. The geometric screen saver disappeared and the Download file was open. She had a moment when

(what if it's gone and the files are back in my world)

but the four files were right there, exactly as she last saw them.

"Do you see this?" she said, without looking around.

He stood close behind her, but didn't touch her.

"This is the one we had originally." She moved the cursor to each file. "And these are the new ones. Look at the dates."

Still nothing from Danny.

She riffled through the scraps of paper on the desk and held up the one with his handwriting—*Can play the audio with the second sonogram—show Carrie.* "This look familiar?"

He took the paper. She didn't look up at him.

(right now somewhere else my daughter is being born)

A tingle swept through her lower stomach.

Finally, Danny said, "None of this makes sense."

"The photo on my desk," Carrie said, "the flowers. These files. Somehow going from my therapist to your car all the way across town instantaneously. I went into work last week and the receptionist and the news editor acted like I should be on maternity leave. I rushed into the bathroom and, when I came back out, they asked how I'd snuck past them, like they hadn't just seen me come in."

Now she looked at Danny. His face was as tight as a drumhead, his eyes darting from the computer to the paper, to her, and then back again.

"This is all happening," she said. "You saw it when you came in—how the bedroom would've looked if Evelyn had been born."

He winced at the mention of her name and, Carrie realized, it had always been *the pregnancy* or, at its most painful, *the baby* to Danny. Never a name.

She turned and clicked the first file. "I erased this, and it's back. And there are more. Videos, too."

The sound of Evelyn's heartbeat filled the room. She watched Danny's face. Muscles rippled like snakes under the skin and his eyes took on an unnatural shine.

"And how could I get to your car all the way across town? When I don't have a key? And you know how rush hour is?"

They both heard the *shhh-POP* and then the recording looped.

"Do you want to see the other files?" she asked.

Danny's Adam's apple worked and he shook his head. "I . . . I don't understand, any of this."

"Neither do I." She bit her lip. "I've heard voices, too."

He blinked and the air suddenly cooled between them.

(wrong step)

The sound of Evelyn's heartbeat didn't seem so loud now.

"Conversations between you and I," she said, speeding up, "but ones we're *not* having. Like, they're conversations we *would* have if I hadn't lost Evelyn. I woke up one night and we were feeling Evelyn kick. This morning, I was yelling at you to time the contractions because Evelyn's coming early. And I *felt* the pain. You were laughing, delighted, and it was *agony*—"

Danny straightened. "Stop." The last consonant came out like a soft thud. He swallowed, looked at her, then at the slip of paper still in his hand.

Then, quite deliberately, he balled the paper up. Dropped it in the trash.

He looked at the computer screen, watched the little geltab timer on Windows Media Player. "I have to go, now."

And, with that, he turned and walked out of the guest bedroom.

Carrie sat for a moment longer, then vaulted out. "*Danny*?"

He was rummaging around in the bedroom and she came in to find him shoving socks, underwear, and shirts into his overnight bag.

"What are you doing?"

He shook his head. "Nope. I can't. I can't deal with this right now."

"*What*?"

He stopped, hands buried in his bag. When he turned to her, his face was tight again, and he wouldn't meet her eyes. "I can't explain how you got into my Jeep, that's true, but the file you pulled from the trash folder."

"*What*?"

He started moving again, going to their closet, yanking two button-shirts, and bringing them back to the bed to roll up. "You could've gotten the other files online, easy."

Carrie was rooted to the spot. "Do you hear yourself?"

Danny stomped into the bathroom and she heard him rummaging around in there; the slam of the medicine cabinet door opening and hitting the wall, the rough, hollow-metallic scrap of him shoving objects around on the shelves. Something plastic thunked into the sink. When he came out, hands hugging assorted toiletries to his stomach, he said, "Do you *hear yourself*, Carrie? Phantom labor pains? Ghost photos and flowers? Fucking *voices*? How do you think you sound, hon? Really. How?"

Danny was vibrating—no, she was shaking so much her vision trembled.

"*That's why I told you, you son of a bitch!*"

"No, you didn't," he said, unloading the toiletries into the bag. "You're telling me *now*, Carrie. You didn't say *any* of this before. But today, when you're supposed to be talking with a professional, what happens? Oddly enough."

She couldn't make her legs move and that was good. Good because her fists were at her sides, hard rocks she wanted to send into his face over and over and over again. "You motherfucker!"

He zipped up the bag. "I can't deal right now. I'm sorry, I wish I was a bigger man, a better man, but I can't. I need to sort what this means out."

"*It means I need help, you bastard!*"

He looked at her and it was there in his eyes—he didn't believe what he was saying. He didn't know *what* to believe, but the look in his eyes was that of a panicked animal, caught within fight or flight. "You *do*, but not the way you *think*, Carrie."

He moved towards her, but stopped when she didn't move from the doorway.

"Do you want to hit me?" His body was off-center, as if the overnight bag weighed him down. "I can't blame you, but it doesn't change any of this. I need to think. I need to think *away* from this. I need to think of how I can actually *help* you."

Danny moved around her, into the hall, and she followed. Her teeth ground together. A scream was building, center of her chest, gaining pressure and momentum, working its way up her throat. She had hated a lot of things in her life, passionately, but nothing in that moment as much as she hated her husband Dan Finney.

And then he stopped, froze, in the doorway of the guest bedroom.

It had become Evelyn's room. The computer was gone. It was seeing it missing to realize that, although Carrie had never hit stop on the recording, Evelyn's heartbeat had stopped playing.

Danny's mouth worked. The muscles of his face were on the move again.

"Is that the help I need, Dan?" she said, softly. "Do you need some, too?"

Danny's mouth snapped shut with a click of his teeth. "You weren't the only one who lost the child."

And he turned, walked down the stairs, and out the door. It clicked shut behind him.

"*THEN WHY AM I THE ONLY ONE SUFFERING FROM IT, YOU FUCKING BASTARD!*" She slumped against the wall beside the doorway of Evelyn's room, the heels of her fists to her eyes.

When the immediate storm passed, she looked through the doorway.

It was their guest bedroom again, though the computer was shut down.

Not that it mattered, she thought.

Day 1, Post-Birth

Drowsing in the murky line between wakefulness and sleep, the hospital bed is comfier than she had ever thought possible. Her lower body is numb—the epidural—but she senses the throb within her lower belly and vagina, biding its time, like a banked fire that just needs a little fuel. Her legs feel odd.

(like how stretch armstrong would feel if toys could feel)

But what she really feels is an emptiness. *Not a hollowness, like something was taken, but like something has* separated.

(evelyn evie she's here)

She hears her child cry to her right, lusty bursts from new lungs. She tries turning, but the sheet over her is too heavy and she is so, so tired. The dim throb in her lower belly stirs.

Shhh, *she hears Danny say.* I got it, hon. Rest. Lemme check the little princess.

Hungry, she wants to tell Danny, but her jaw is too heavy. Better to lie on the bed, better to feel the sheet. Everything is good. Everything is right. *They'd had a scare, early in the pregnancy, but that was a nightmare, brief and as easily dispersed upon waking.*

Carrie moves her arm, feels the cool sheet—

—and realized she was feeling Danny's cold side of the bed.

Carrie opened her eyes and the gray light of dawn was beginning to seep into the bedroom. She sat up, the throb fading as Evelyn's cries dwindled from her head. Her hand went to her stomach, felt the flatness there, felt the firmness that had returned as her body had purged the unnecessary weight.

(in the other world my stomach's flat, but not firm. i am not *stretch armstrong.)*

She fell back onto the bed. She couldn't hear Evelyn's heartbeat, anymore. Of course she couldn't. Evelyn, somewhere else, was born.

Carrie rubbed her flat stomach.

The alarm on her smartphone went off an hour later, but she was already awake.

Evelyn's room was set up when she passed it three hours later.

Carrie stood in the doorway, hand on the frame. She didn't walk in. Looking at the room, deep in shadow because the sun was on the other side of the house, was like looking at a museum display. What would this one be titled? Baby Culture of the Early 21st?

(life for the new parent)

(i'm not a part of this world)

The air shimmered, slowly, and the guest room slowly resolved before her.

Danny called, but she missed it; she was at a staff meeting and had left her smartphone in the bag. He didn't leave a message.

She called back without thinking, but when the line clicked over to voicemail, she hung up.

She didn't try again until after lunch, and the same thing occurred. As if knowing what would happen, she went to the restroom and when she returned saw a missed call—Danny.

I can't talk to you, these calls said. But I want to.

I just can't yet.

(somewhere, danny and i are getting used to the idea of being parents and, somewhere, evelyn is getting used to being alive.)

Carrie opened the door and Danny was screaming, *bellowing*, upstairs, while the house itself shook with the amplified cries of an infant.

"*My CHILD!*" Danny shrieked and Carrie jumped. "*THIS IS MY CHILD, GODDAMMIT! She's here, she's BORN, and you either make time or you DON'T! This isn't something to be DEBATED!*"

"*Danny?*" Carrie yelled, but she couldn't even hear herself. She glanced back at the driveway—only her Subaru. "*DANNY! WHAT ARE YOU DOING?*"

"*YOU THINK THIS IS A FUCKING OVERREACTION?*" Danny screamed. Meanwhile the recording of the crying infant—*Evelyn*, she'd know that girl anywhere—kept going on and on. "*ARE YOU OUT OF YOUR FUCKING MIND?*"

"*DANNY!*" Carrie dropped her bag and vaulted up the stairs two at a time.

And the sound of Evelyn and Danny faded. As she ran up the stairs, it was as if she was running away from it. She reached the top, used the newel post to swing her around, and vaulted for her bedroom, passing Evelyn's room without a glance.

But Danny and the recording were gone.

She stopped in the doorway, panting, her nerves singing with adrenaline. The bedroom had been rearranged. The computer desk sat where the low bookcase next to her bed had been.

She walked around the bed and saw that a fifth file had been added to the open Download file: "Evelyn's hunger cry."

Carrie swallowed hard.

The computer desk began to fade, becoming translucent, as the bookcase returned. She blinked and she was back in her own world.

She sat down on the bed, and stared at the bookcase.

Tomorrow, she thought, without even wondering what she meant. *Tomorrow we come home.*

She shook her head and pulled her smartphone out of her jacket pocket. Danny had called again, but she didn't have the energy to play the game.

Tomorrow, she thought again, and stared at where, in the other world, the home computer sat, complete with its recordings of her daughter.

Day 2, Post-Birth

Thursdays were reserved for meetings, first amongst general staff, then amongst the various sections, then one-on-one with the editors and photographers, if needed. Contacts were exchanged. Background info was dug through. It was a day where lunches were ordered in and Carrie watched the steady rain through her office window, periodically checking her phone.

Danny called her three times, no messages.

She called the same amount, with the same result.

Today, she would think, out-of-context with whatever else might be going on.

When she left that evening, her car was gone.

She stood on the curb of the parking lot and looked where it should've been—as if, by staring, the car would fade back into the world.

It didn't.

The sound of traffic on S. Prairie Street, heavy with the weight of rush hour faded as she stepped off the sidewalk and crossed to her spot.

No cubes of broken window glass on the asphalt. No tire tracks.

"Shit," she muttered, and reached into her jacket for her phone.

Which wasn't there.

She held her hand in her pocket a moment longer, open, as if the phone, too, would materialize.

The rain, which had become a light drizzle, gained force. Slowly, like a hunter stalking skittish prey, her other hand wandered to her other pocket, where she kept her keys.

That pocket was also empty.

(of course it is)

She straightened, and looked back at the *Register-Mail*'s building. Most of the windows were dark. A few copy-editors and layout people were still present, but far in the back. Her passkey was on her missing ring. She'd have to scale a fence to get to their windows.

(i'm unmoored and i can't even call anyone)

"We *are* alone," she said and thought of Danny saying he had just been wishing to be whole again, to be a family like they were meant to be, and how, holy shit, that so hadn't happened.

If Danny tried calling, would she pick up? And would he realize it's not the Carrie he'd walked out on, the Carrie who didn't share this history with him?

She started for the street. Her first step didn't immediately put her in another part of town.

She took a second step, and the same non-thing happened.

Third step and still present and accounted for.

She picked up her pace, even as the rain came down harder.

Galesburg wasn't that large, and home wasn't that far away.

Even if it wasn't her home, anymore.

Danny waited in the mouth of the driveway, as soaked as she was, staring bemusedly at their Jeep and Subaru. With the rain had come an early evening, and the streetlights at the far corner were already powering on.

"Hey," he said. He continued to stare at their vehicles.

"Hey."

He took a deep breath. "I would've called—again—but my phone was gone."

"Mine, too."

He looked at her with one eye, head slightly canted, like he was examining her. Fat droplets fell from his hair. "It's where I think it is, isn't it?"

She crossed her arms, cupped her elbows. "Where do you think it is?"

He nodded, as if he'd expected that answer. "I'm sorry, Carrie."

She didn't respond.

He turned back to the cars. "None of this makes sense."

"We're not in our world, anymore."

He glanced at her.

"I mean," she said, looking down the street, at the streetlamp growing brighter, "it's our world, but where I didn't miscarry. We're just in the world next door."

He rubbed his face with his hands. "Fuck, I'm not good at this. I teach post-modern lit, for Chrissakes." He dropped his hands. "Why? Do you know that?"

She shook her head. "Not a clue. Maybe you wished it. Maybe we both did."

A light came on in their house, the downstairs living room, its soft yellow glow falling across the darkening lawn and highlighting half of Danny's face, showing how tired and worn he was. He'd aged ten years in the past ten weeks.

They moved across the lawn without speaking, not going to the door, but to the window itself. Carrie saw herself, slumped on the couch, in a baggy shirt she'd never owned. She was dozing, but trying not to, her head cocked as if she were listening to someone talking.

"Jesus Christ," Danny whispered.

Carrie had read about doubles and doppelgangers in fiction, but she felt no strange vertigo; it was like looking into a warped mirror, where what you saw wasn't how you perceived yourself. This was a version of Carrie who had given birth, who had gone on maternity leave.

(that isn't standing outside the window with her shoes slowly sinking into the soft cold mud)

Carrie took in her other's skin, the way the hair needed washing, the soft brown bags under her eyes, the way how, in spite of all that, she exuded that aura others called a *glow*.

She's content, Carrie thought.

"Holy shit, hon," Danny whispered, taking her hand. "Look."

He pointed and his double came into the room, holding Evelyn, wrapped in the receiving blanket from the hospital.

"Oh, holy shit," Danny repeated, and his voice was thick. "Holy shit, holy shit." He squeezed, and she squeezed back, hard.

The other Danny sat down next to Carrie, still talking, and Carrie turned so she could view the child. From the window, Evelyn was mostly turned away, but Carrie saw a plump cheek, the infant version of Danny's nose.

Carrie's eyes burned, and tears mixed with the rainfall.

They watched their doubles talk to the child and each other, both exhausted, both glowing, both ignorant of their childless, other versions watching.

Danny raised a hand to touch the glass and she said, "Don't."

He stopped and looked at her.

She tried to smile. "That's not us, hon."

He stared. His eyes were wide and glassy and wet. His Adam's apple bobbed frantically.

"This isn't ours. It's theirs. Okay? It's theirs."

His face crumpled. "Why not us? Why couldn't we have had that?"

She sniffed, wiped her nose with the back of her hand, began to cry even harder. "I don't know, Danny. But we couldn't."

He pulled her in and she cried into his shoulder and he cried into hers as, through the window, the other Danny and other Carrie cooed to their daughter.

"I'm sorry, Carrie," he said into her neck. "I'm so sorry."

She hugged him tight.

Slowly, the fierceness of their grips lessened and they looked first at each other, then through the window.

The family was gone, but Carrie caught flickers of movement through the archway leading to the kitchen. She bit her lip. Did she breastfeed? Formula?

Holding his hand, she turned away and led the way back down the lawn. "Let's go. Let's let them live their lives. We have ours to fix."

"How?" Danny asked as they were reached the street.

She shrugged. "I haven't a goddamn clue. We have our own version to live." A glance at the house, with its warm lights and center. "It just isn't *that*."

Danny followed her gaze and his face rippled. "At least we got to see how it would've turned out."

"*Did* turn out. For them. Not us. Those are ghosts, Danny. Ghosts of What Might've Been."

"*We're* the ghosts."

She looked down at the streetlamp on the corner, its bright cone of white light on the wet pavement. "They got their happy ending."

"What about us?"

"Let's start with a walk, figure it out from there. Shit, it's not like we can go into the house, anyway."

He surprised her by laughing and squeezed her hand.

They started walking, heading for the corner. To anyone who looked, they would've appeared glowing. Then the watcher would blink, realize he or she could see *through* Carrie and Danny, see the bright flare of the corner streetlight.

They faded, faded, and, by the time they reached the corner, they were gone.

[CREDITS]

Max Booth III (editor) is the editor-in-chief of Perpetual Motion Machine Publishing and the managing editor of *Dark Moon Digest*. He's the author of several novels, including *How to Successfully Kidnap Strangers* and the forthcoming *No Sleep 'Til Dying*. A columnist for LitReactor, Slush Pile Heroes, and Gamut, Max resides in a small town outside San Antonio, TX. Follow him on Twitter @GiveMeYourTeeth.

Lori Michelle (editor) is the CFO and layout specialist at Perpetual Motion Machine and the editor-in-chief at *Dark Moon Digest*. Lori is also the author of the novel, *Dual Harvest*, and has several stories appearing in anthologies such as the Bram Stoker® nominated *Qualia Nous* and *Slices of Flesh*. She spends her time working as a graphic artist for a trophy shop, teaching dance for a baton twirling group her daughter belongs to and telling her son to quit playing iPad. You can find Lori on Facebook.

Matthew Revert (cover design) is the author of *Basal Ganglia* (Lazy Fascist Press), *How to Avoid Sex* (Copeland Valley/Dark Coast Press), *The Tumours Made Me Interesting* (LegumeMan Books) and *A Million Versions of Right* (LegumeMan Books). Revert has had work published in *Le Zaporogue, The Best Bizarro Fiction of the Decade, In Heaven Everything Is Fine: Fiction Inspired by David Lynch, The New Flesh, The Bizarro Starter Kit (Purple)* and *Gone Lawn Journal* among others.

Luke Spooner (interior illustrations) currently lives and works in the South of England. Having graduated from the University of Portsmouth with a first class degree he is now a full time illustrator working under two aliases; 'Carrion House' for his darker work and 'Hoodwink House' for his work aimed at a younger audience. He believes that the job of putting someone else's words into a visual form, to accompany and support their text, is a massive responsibility as well as being something he truly treasures.

Scott Nicolay (introduction) writes Weird Fiction. One of this stories won an award. He also hosts the Weird Fiction podcast *The Outer Dark*. *The Outer Dark* won an award too. His second collection, *And at My Back I Always Hear*, will appear in 2017.

Matthew M. Bartlett ("If He Summons His Herd" & "Where Night Covers") is the author of *Gateways to Abomination*, *Anne Gare's Rare Book and Ephemera Catalogue*, *Rangel*, *Creeping Waves*, and the illustrated chapbook *The Witch-Cult in Western Massachusetts*. His short stories have appeared in *Xnyobis #1*, *Resonator: New Lovecraftian Tales From Beyond*, *Faed*, and *High Strange Horror*. He lives in Northampton, Massachusetts with his wife Katie and an unknown number of cats.

T.E. Grau ("Transmission") is an author of horror, crime, and dark fiction whose work has been featured in dozens of anthologies, magazines, literary journals, and audio platforms. His debut book of short stories, *The Nameless Dark: A Collection* (Lethe Press) was nominated for a 2015 Shirley Jackson Award for Single-Author Collection, and ranked as the bestselling book published by Lethe Press in 2015. A novella, *They Don't Come Home Anymore*, will be published in late 2016 through This Is Horror. Grau lives in Los Angeles with his wife and daughter, and is currently working on his second collection and his first novel.

Josh Malerman ("The Givens Sensor Board") is the author of *Bird Box* and the singer/songwriter for the band The High Strung.

Joseph Bouthiette Jr. ("From: Item L51610RDE, 'The Dangsturm Interruption'") is co-editor of Carrion Blue 555 and an avid board gamer. He put more work into this bio than he did his contribution to this anthology.

David James Keaton's ("Sharks With Thumbs") fiction has appeared in over 50 publications. His first collection, *FISH BITES COP!* (Comet Press), was named the 2013 Short Story Collection of the Year by *This Is Horror*. His second collection, *Stealing Propeller Hats from the Dead* (PMMP), received a Starred Review from *Publishers Weekly*, who said, "Decay, both existential and physical, has never looked so good." He lives in California.

Tony Burgess ("Bad Lieutenant") lives in Stayner, Ontario, with his wife Rachel and their two children. He is the author of The *Hellmouths of Bewdley, Pontypool Changes Everything, Caesarea, Fiction for Lovers* and *Idaho Winter. Pontypool* was made into a film by Bruce McDonald.

Michael Paul Gonzalez ("How the Light Gets In") is the author of the novels *Angel Falls* and *Miss Massacre's Guide to Murder and Vengeance.* A member of the Horror Writers Association, his short stories have appeared in print and online, including *Gothic Fantasy: Chilling Horror Stories, 18 Wheels of Horror, the Booked. Podcast Anthology*, HeavyMetal.com, and the *Appalachian Undead* anthology. He resides in Los Angeles, a place full of wonders and monsters far stranger than any that live in the imagination. You can visit him online at MichaelPaulGonzalez.com.

George Cotronis ("Darkhorse Actual") lives in the wilderness of Northern Sweden. His stories have appeared in *XIII, Years Best Hardcore Horror* and forthcoming in *Futuristica Vol 2.*

Betty Rocksteady ("The Desert of Wounded Frequencies") is an eclectic author and illustrator from Canada. Her early exposure to Stephen King, *The Weekly World News*, and EC horror comics shaped her into the woman she is today. With art and fiction, she explores personal fears and resonances. Her debut novella, *Arachnophile,* is part of Eraserhead Press' 2015 New Bizarro Author Series. Her short fiction has been published by Halloween Forevermore, Grievous Angel, and Nothing's Sacred. Learn more, and check out her macabre pen and ink art at www.bettyrocksteady.com. Keep in touch and keep up to date at www.facebook.com/bettyrocksteadyart.

Christopher Slatsky ("Eternity Lie in its Radius") is the author of *Alectryomancer and Other Weird Tales*. His stories have appeared in the *Lovecraft eZine, Innsmouth Magazine, Dunhams Manor Press*, and others slated to appear in the *Year's Best Weird Fiction v. 3, Strange Aeons, Nightscript v. 2*, and elsewhere. He currently resides in the Los Angeles area.

Amanda Hard ("Rosabelle, Believe") is a former journalist and magazine editor currently pursuing an MFA in Creative Writing (Fiction) at Murray State University. A 2015 finalist for Glimmer Train's "New

Writer Award," her horror fiction has appeared in (or is forthcoming from) *Ruthless Peoples Magazine,* several flash fiction anthologies from the *Daily Nightmare,* two volumes of the *State of Horror* series from Charon Coin Press, and the anthology *Idolators of Cthulhu* from Alban Lake Press. She is a member of the Horror Writers Association and lives in the cornfields of southern Indiana.

Gabino Iglesias ("The Last Scream") was born somewhere, but then moved to a different place. He has worked as dog whisperer, witty communications professor, and ballerina assassin. Now he hides near a dumpster in Austin, Texas, where he works as a freelance journalist and impersonates a PhD student. His nonfiction has appeared in places like *The New York Times, Z Magazine, El Nuevo Día*, and others. The stuff that's made up has been published in places like *Red Fez, Flash Fiction Offensive, Drunk Monkeys, Bizarro Central, Paragraph Line, Divergent Magazine, Cease, Cows*, and a few horror, surrealist, and bizarro anthologies. He is the author of *Zero Saints.*

Dyer Wilk ("The Man in Room 603") is a bit of a writer. Often he's known to pull an all-nighter. Dedicated he is to weirdstuff and words. Known some to dabble in things quite absurd. But bios are not his strong suit, he'll warn ya. He lives and he writes in North California.

Ashlee Scheuerman ("The Sound of Yesterday"), author of *The Damning Moths* and its looming sequel, has also written short apocalyptica which can be found nestled within the award-winning anthologies of horror, *Surviving the End* and *Qualia Nous.* Hidden in Western Australia with her collection of pine cones, Ashlee renders speculative fiction, takes too many photos of pigeons, toadstools, and moss, and probably has enough pets—for now.

Matt Andrew ("Children of a German Autumn") is a retired US Marine officer who lives and works near Dallas, Texas. His fiction has appeared in *Thuglit, Blight Digest*, and *Pantheon Magazine*, among others.

H.F. Arnold ("The Night Wire") is another "lost" author from the days of the pulps, something that is quite surprising since "The Night Wire" was considered the most popular story ever published in *Weird Tales.* What few sources give any information about his life say that he was born in 1901, worked as an author and journalist and died in 1963, but even these sketchy details (and his actual name, for that matter) may, or may, not, be true. All that is known as fact about Arnold, is that his fictional output, at least in the fields of science fiction and horror, consisted of only 3 works: "The Night Wire", appearing in *Weird Tales* in 1926; "The City of Iron Cubes," serialized in the March and April issues of *Weird Tales* and a two-part serial "When Atlantis Was," that appeared in the October and December 1937 issues of *Amazing Stories*. Outside of that, Arnold remains an enigma.

John C. Foster ("Armageddon Baby") was born in Sleepy Hollow, NY, and has been afraid of the dark for as long as he can remember. A writer of thrillers and dark fiction, Foster lives in New York City with the actress Linda Jones and their dog, Coraline. Dead Men was released by Perpetual Motion Machine Publishing on July 22, 2015 and Mister White by Grey Matter Press on April 5, 2016. Mister White the Short Story was included in the anthology Dark Visions Vol. 2 in 2013, also by Grey Matter Press. For more information, please visit johnfosterfiction.com.

Vince Darcangelo ("The Small Hours") is the author of *The Red Tags*, published by Comet Press. He is also an award-winning journalist, author and photographer.

Regina Solomond ("Hush") is a technical writer by day and fiction writer by night. Besides literature, her other loves are good sandwiches, bad pop songs, and her hamster, Chad. Her short stories and poems have been published by Eunoia Review, Every Day Fiction, and Eye Contact.

Joshua Chaplinsky ("Feedback Loop") is the Managing Editor of LitReactor.com. He has also written for the popular film site TwitchFilm and for ChuckPalahniuk.net, the official website of *Fight Club* author Chuck Palahniuk. He is the author of *Kanye West—Reanimator*. His short fiction has appeared in Zetetic, Motherboard, Vol. 1 Brooklyn, Thuglit, Dark Moon Digest, Cracked Eye, Pantheon Magazine, and more. More info at joshuachaplinsky.com.

Damien Angelica Walters ("Little Girl Blue, Come Cry Your Way Home") is the author of *Paper Tigers* and *Sing Me Your Scars*. Her short fiction has been nominated twice for a Bram Stoker Award, reprinted in *The Year's Best Dark Fantasy & Horror* and *The Year's Best Weird Fiction*, and published in various anthologies and magazines, including *Nightscript*, *Cemetery Dance Online*, *Nightmare Magazine*, and *Black*

Static. She lives in Maryland with her husband and two rescued pit bulls. Find her on Twitter @DamienAWalters or on the web at www.damienangelicawalters.com.

Paul Michael Anderson ("All That You Leave Behind") is the author of *Bones Are Meant to Be Broken* and he's from Virginia.

James Newman ("SOMETHINGINTHECODE") is the author of *Odd Man Out*, *Animosity*, *Ugly As Sin*, and [redacted] He lives in [redacted] with his wife, G[redacted] and their two sons. He hopes he hasn't placed readers in danger with his contribution to *Lost Signals*, but suggests [redacted] [redacted] [redacted] or visiting www.james-newman.com for immediate assistance.

IF YOU ENJOY3D

LOST SIGNALS,

DON'T PASS UP ON THESE

OT7ER TITLES FROM

PERPETUAL MO9ION MACHIN3 . . .

TRUTH OR DARE?

EDITED BY MAX BOOTH III

ISBN: 978-0-9860594-5-2
Page count: 240
$14.95

Halloween night. The freaks are out and having the time of their lives. The kids of Greene Point High School have organized a massive bonfire out in the woods. One drunken teen suggests **playing** a game, a g9me called Truth or Dare. That's always a fun game. Always good for a laugh. By the en8 of this night, nobody will be laughing. Alcohol, sex, deadly secrets, and oceans of BLOOD await them. ***DO YOU DARE TO PLAY?***

Truth or Dare is a **SHA**red-world horror anthology featuring the mor**bi**d writings of many prominent AUthors in *THE* field today, as well as quite a few new kids on the block you're gonna want to keep an eye on.

PLEASE STAND BY

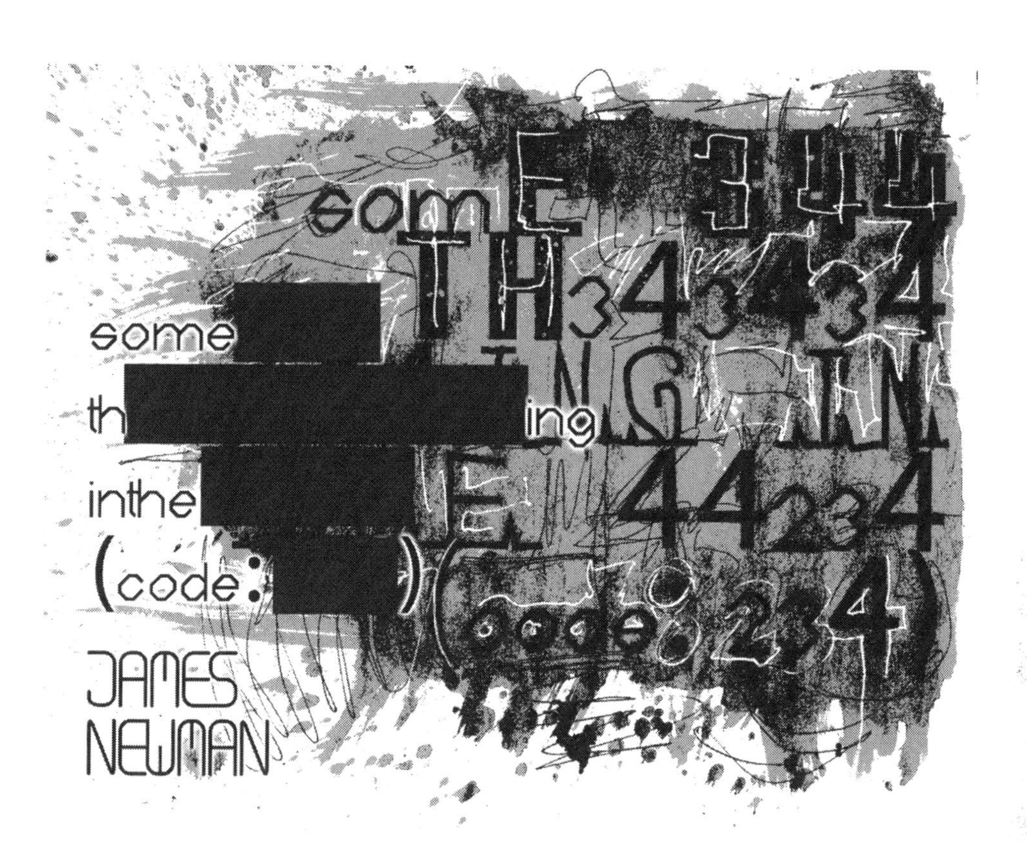

THE EARTH IS UNDER ATTACK, AND ONLY YOU CAN SAVE IT!

ALIEN INVADERS from the planet Hellstarr have traveled through TIME AND SPACE, ravaging galaxies wherever they go. Their most recent goal: to enslave the human race!

The war has waged for 1,000 YEARS. MANKIND WILL FALL.

But now, using newly-developed time travel technology, Earth's forces have stolen ADVANCED WEAPONRY from the invaders themselves. A glimmer of hope can be seen through the clouds of smoke and ash, a silhouette wielding a BIG GUN and a desire for REVENGE . . .

Enlist now, for YOU are humanity's LAST HOPE!!!

—*unused selling copy for* Galactic Recon
(©1993, UltimaTech Entertainment)

From *Gamers Gonna Game!* (Internet podcast), Episode #209:

EDDIE SPAGHETTI: Speaking of worst games ever, how about that *E.T.* game from the '80s?

PIXEL PETE: Dude! That thing was so freakin' lame Atari literally *buried it in the middle of the desert* where no one would ever find it.

EDDIE SPAGHETTI: Like a dead hooker. So the story goes.

PIXEL PETE: I heard they hauled, like, a million cartridges down to Mexico, left 'em to rot in some landfill.

EDDIE SPAGHETTI: Kinda reminds me of what happened with *Galactic Recon,* if you believe the rumors. Except the only thing *E.T.* was guilty of was sucking goat balls. At least it never—

From *Paranoid Punks* (Internet podcast), Episode #113:

CYNICAL STEVE: —killed a bunch of kids, right.

MISS RAVEN: Happened in the mid-'90s, in a place called Jakesboro, North Carolina. Our listeners shouldn't be too surprised if this is the first time they're hearing about it. The government swooped in, made the whole mess go away, then stole the tech for their own nefarious purposes.

CYNICAL STEVE: Of course they did. Meanwhile, the sheep don't have a clue what's going on right under their noses.

MISS RAVEN: It's why this show exists. To keep shining the light on Uncle Sam's bullshit.

CYNICAL STEVE: At least until he cuts the power!

MISS RAVEN: We need to talk about this some more. But first, how about some mood music? Here's the Clash, with "Clampdown" . . . .

From *Carolina Profiles: Business Edition*—Spring, 1990:

Ask a hundred people the first thing that comes to mind when you mention North Carolina, and chances are most of them will say "tobacco" or "college basketball".

Before long, though, you might find a few who look to the Tar Heel State as a leader in the *video game* industry.

Located in the foothills of the Blue Ridge Mountains is a town called Jakesboro. Its population: just under six thousand. *Economics Today* recently referred to Jakesboro as "the little Silicon Valley of the South," and if business continues to thrive for UltimaTech Entertainment, the company at the heart of its growth, the town's nickname is well deserved.

UltimaTech's titles have won numerous awards for their innovative graphics, and since the company's inception in 1979 they have consistently outsold those of its competitors two-to-one. UltimaTech's main site of operations in Jakesboro handles not only the design and programming of its merchandise, but all manufacturing, packaging, and distribution as well. At press time, nearly seventy percent of the town's adult population is employed by the growing enterprise.

UltimaTech C.E.O. Edmund W. Stern jokes, "The secret of my success? Free (product testing). I have a lot of employees. My employees have children. And children love video games. Especially games they get to play before the rest of the world!"

From the *WNCW Channel 12 6:00 News*—September 12, 1994:

ANCHOR: Residents of one local mountain town are concerned about the escalating suicide rate among children between the ages of five and seventeen. In fact, some are calling what is happening here a disturbing "epidemic".

For Jakesboro, North Carolina, the trouble started this past spring. During February and March, a dozen children took their own lives. By early June, a total of thirty-four youths had committed suicide, some of them barely old enough to attend kindergarten. Most recently, the tragedies at Lake Ramsey—in which nineteen high-school seniors drowned themselves in a bizarre mass suicide—and Maples Farm—in which a group of over forty middle-school students gathered inside a barn and doused it in gasoline, before setting the building on fire—have left this community desperately searching for answers.

Earlier today, a visibly shaken Jakesboro Police Chief Raymond White had this to say . . .

CHIEF WHITE: We're trying to find some connection, but . . . these were all good kids, ya know? Kids from happy homes, never been in any kind of trouble. I spoke to one mother who lost her twin sons to the thing at Maples Farm, she told me she never had to fuss at her boys about anything except for staying up all night playing videogames. I'm sorry . . . that's all I've got . . . "

From *Game On: Your Home Entertainment Newsletter*—October, 1994:

Tragic news for gaming fans: UltimaTech Entertainment's lead programmer and "rock star" game designer Darren McKay—author of such best-selling titles as *Werewolf Wars, Secrets of the Ninja,* and the *HeroQuest* trilogy—was found dead last week in his Asheville, NC condominium. The cause of death was a self-inflicted gunshot wound.

UltimaTech recently cancelled the release of its much-anticipated title *Galactic Recon* (for reasons unknown at press time), which the thirty-year-old McKay called his "dream project" in interviews conducted during the game's development over the last two years.

McKay is survived by his mother and one sister.

UltimaTech Entertainment
INTERNAL MEMORANDUM
Re: existing copies of "Galactic Recon" (Job# UT-477644/0)

ATTN: ALL EMPLOYEES

Note that pre-production of the UltimaTech property "Galactic Recon" has ceased, and the project has been cancelled. All existing (prototype) copies of the game should be DESTROYED immediately. This includes copies approved for home use, product testing, etc—NO EXCEPTIONS.

Please see your immediate supervisor or the Human Resources Department with questions or concerns.

From an abbreviated *Fox News* interview with UltimaTech Entertainment C.E.O. Edmund W. Stern—January 5, 1995:

STERN: Darren McKay suffered from severe depression, and any speculation that he took his own life because of his work on a *videogame* is not only ridiculous, it is offensive to my friend's legacy as one of this industry's most brilliant programmers. Now, I am not a vengeful man. But you all should know that UltimaTech will seek swift legal action against those who choose to libel the company's good name with talk of

. . . ahem, I can barely say it with a straight face . . . a *game that kills anyone who plays it?* Asinine.

(STERN'S ATTORNEY): No further questions. Let us pass. Ladies and gentlemen, no further questions!

The boss wants to make this all go away. But even if by some miracle Stern is able to save his company what ~~we've~~ I'VE done will never go away.

~~People~~ Innocent CHILDREN are dying.

Don't know why it only affects the kids. All I know is, it's MY fault.

It's something in the CODE. Something that causes a glitch in their brains. Some kind of "fatal error" that shuts down the will to live after playing the game for more than a few hours.

I've tried to find my mistake. But I'm not as good as everyone said I was. The wunderkind is a fraud. I am a MURDERER.

Please God forgive me. I wish I never created that fucking game.

—note found in a spiral notebook in Darren McKay's condo the day after his suicide

BILL OF LADING

DATE: 11/29/94

SHIPPED FROM: UltimaTech Entertainment
212 Bonham Avenue
Jakesboro, NC 28778

SHIPPED TO: Polk County Solid Waste Disposal &
Recycling Center
884 Stone Mountain Rd.
Midnight, NC 28782

DESCRIPTION OF CARGO: game cartridges
QUANTITY: approx. 2,000,000 (two million)

COMMENTS: destroy upon receipt

From *the Asheville Citizen-Times*—February 3, 1995:

Authorities reported that an as-yet-unidentified shooter killed six people and wounded four others late yesterday at the offices of UltimaTech Entertainment in Jakesboro.

Early reports suggest that the suspect was a disgruntled employee, and that the victims were all members of upper management. One of the deceased, it has been confirmed, was the company's Chief Executive Officer, Edmund W. Stern.

REVISED BILL OF LADING

DATE: 12/01/94

SHIPPED FROM: Stahl Transportation—Western NC Hub
442 Warren Avenue
Hendersonville, NC 28791

SHIPPED TO: U.S. Department of Defense
Washington, DC

DESCRIPTION OF CARGO: game cartridges
QUANTITY: approx. 2,000,000 (two million)

COMMENTS: contents are now property of U.S. government

From *U.S. Business Daily*–May 1, 1995:

It was announced last week that UltimaTech Entertainment will cease operations at the end of this month. No official statement regarding reasons for the sudden closure was available at press time.

From *Paranoid Punks* (Internet podcast), Episode #113:

CYNICAL STEVE: By this time, Uncle Sam's sporting a boner the size of the Washington Monument over *Galactic Recon*. Can't wait to get his hands on it. What this programmer guy inadvertently created, it's too valuable to end up in some landfill somewhere.

MISS RAVEN: Brings to mind the MKUltra experiments from the '60s that we talked about in Episode #100. Thirty years later Sam finally strikes gold, thanks to a *glitch in a videogame*.

CYNICAL STEVE: Fast forward a few months. People who used to work for UltimaTech—the ones who might have some clue what really went down? They start dropping like flies. Some of them pull a Jimmy Hoffa and disappear altogether. Eventually, the only ones talking about *Galactic Recon* and what it did to the kids in that town were the loonies in the tinfoil hats. The conspiracy freaks.

MISS RAVEN: The paranoid punks.

CYNICAL STEVE: You know it.

From *Faded Dreams, Forgotten Places: Exploring the Ghost Towns of America* by James L. Heatherly:

Unlike similar communities that once flourished but were eventually left to the mercy of the elements, a walk through the desolate streets of Jakesboro, North Carolina gives one the impression that its citizens left suddenly. As I explored each residence, I was reminded of the Lost Colony of Roanoke: I saw dusty tables set for supper, bathtubs drawn before bedtime now filled with stagnant green water, and children's playthings rotting in weed-choked backyards. I stumbled upon one home where a dog had been chained to a tree then cruelly abandoned; a small pile of bones lay at the edge of a cracked driveway as if Fido still waits for a family that will never return for him.

Jakesboro's fate is one associated with bizarre urban legends and conspiracy theories. Such rumors and speculation will not be repeated here. Most likely, it was the demise of a once thriving software company that killed Jakesboro in the mid-1990s. Seventy percent of the town's population was employed by said company; seemingly overnight, several thousand residents lost their jobs and were forced to move elsewhere.

Today, the empty buildings that were once the company's headquarters overlook the dead town like a weary parent doomed to gaze forever upon the repercussions of his past sins.

FROM: U.S. DEPT OF JUSTICE, in conjunction w/the N.S.A.

OFFICIAL NOTICE
Re: existing copies of *LOST SIGNALS*

TO WHOM IT MAY CONCERN:

By order of the U.S. Government, all existing copies of the Perpetual Motion Machine anthology *LOST SIGNALS* (edited by Max Booth III and Lori Michelle) must be immediately forfeited for destruction.

Further review, use, disclosure, production, and/or distribution of this publication—particularly of the segment titled "*SOME ███ TH█████ ████ING IN THE █████ (CODE: ███)" by James Newman, which contains confidential information previously seized by the N.S.A.—is prohibited.

Non-compliance with this order will result in legal action by the federal government, with maximum penalties allowed by the law (up to and including treason, an offense punishable by death).

NO
SIGNAL
FOUND

Printed in Great Britain
by Amazon

67428272R00225